Apricot Kisses

Jun 2017

Apricot Kisses

Claudia Winter

Translated by Maria Poglitsch Bauer

amazon crossing

This is a work of fiction. Names, characters, organizations, places, events, and incidents are either products of the author's imagination or are used fictitiously.

Text copyright © 2014 Claudia Winter

Translation copyright © 2015 Maria Poglitsch Bauer

All rights reserved.

No part of this book may be reproduced, or stored in a retrieval system, or transmitted in any form or by any means, electronic, mechanical, photocopying, recording, or otherwise, without express written permission of the publisher.

Previously published as *Aprikosenküsse* by the author via the Kindle Direct Publishing Platform in Germany in 2014. Translated from German by Maria Poglitsch Bauer. First published in English by AmazonCrossing in 2015.

Published by AmazonCrossing, Seattle

www.apub.com

Amazon, the Amazon logo, and AmazonCrossing are trademarks of Amazon.com, Inc., or its affiliates.

ISBN-13: 9781503947542

ISBN-10: 1503947548

Cover design by Shasti O'Leary-Soudant

Printed in the United States of America

All characters and events in this novel are the product of the author's imagination, and your map search for the Tuscan village Montesimo will be in vain. The fictitious community serves as a substitute for all small Italian villages in which we hope to find what we long for. Any resemblances to real people, businesses, or events is purely coincidental.

Prologue
Fabrizio

Floor wax, apricots, a thick bean soup. Some aromas are as closely associated with my childhood as the scar on my wrist—a tiny white worm tattooed there by a bike accident when I was six. While memories of the pain and the rage I felt from making a fool of myself in front of my friends have faded, I clearly remember the smell and sticky smudge my grandmother's lipstick kisses left behind.

I surreptitiously wipe my cheek, even though now I'm so tall that Nonna can barely reach my face. Still, I'm always on the lookout, because she grabs every opportunity to kiss me whenever I am anywhere near her red mouth. Unfortunately, Dr. Buhlfort's waiting room has plenty of chairs, leaving no excuse for me to stand.

"Sit down, Fabrizio," Nonna says and pushes me into a chair. Squinting, I wait for the inevitable: Nonna's pinch—as if she planned to tear the skin from my cheek with her bony index and middle fingers—followed by the smacking of her lips.

When nothing happens, I sneak a glance in her direction. Nonna, leafing through a magazine, seems to have forgotten me. I suppress a grin—she's studying the pages as if she understood every word. She is mumbling every now and then and moving her head from side to side as if it were attached to a pendulum.

"Verrrry interesting, this magazine," she whispers when she notices me watching. She points to the magazine rack, which covers an entire wall of the waiting room. "This professor must be an excellent doctor. He reads quite a bit."

I nod instead of pointing out what Nonna doesn't want to hear anyway. She has been convinced that Buhlfort is the best heart specialist on the planet ever since I Googled him.

For generations, the Camini family has had an unexplained affinity for everything German. German cars, German soccer, German doctors. The last is why we're wasting this afternoon in a crammed Berlin waiting room. Nonna Giuseppa Camini is perfectly healthy, but it's always the same with her: whatever she sets her mind on eventually happens. I look at her out of the corner of my eye.

Nonna is sitting bolt upright in her chair ("Sit up straight, Fabrizio, otherwise you'll turn into a hunchback") with her knees touching and both feet on the floor. She's wearing pumps, of course. ("Remember, a true Italian is buried in heels!") Like all women in my family, she is slender, despite her age. When I once asked her why she always buys dresses two sizes too large, she advised me, with raised index finger, "You never know if you'll put on weight as you age. Tell me, then what would I do with my good clothes?"

The cover of Nonna's magazine, *Genusto Gourmet*, catches my eye. It shows a crate of apricots. The cursive German text is difficult to decipher, so I lean against Nonna's shoulder to read. "Delicious recipes with sun-ripened apricots . . ." Nonna turns the page, and the image of apricots disappears.

"Fabrizio, there's something about us!"

"About us?"

Since I don't seem to get it, she pokes me in the ribs. I automatically straighten up, just like I do when she punches my back to correct my slouch over a plate of pasta. Nonna continues to rustle the pages.

"Fabrizio!"

"Nonna?" I like keeping her in suspense. She impatiently taps the magazine, which now rests on her knees, open to the page of the article. She's right. The picture of a stone building on a cypress-covered hill looks familiar. Butterflies dance in my stomach: the Tre Camini house in a German gourmet magazine. I've never even dared to dream about such a thing.

"Are you deaf, kiddo? Somebody wrote about our *ristorante*."

"I heard." I want to tear the magazine out of her hands, but instead I just grin at her excitement. The elderly couple sitting across from us sizes us up disapprovingly—typical Germans. "Is everything all right?" I ask them in their language, with a smile. That keeps them quiet—also typically German. Nonna tugs on my sleeve. The V of wrinkles on her forehead has reached a dangerously steep angle. "Why don't you give it to me, so I can read it to you," I say.

Even though it's been years since I've read anything long in German, my brain takes to the task and I translate fluently. But I understand what I'm reading only after the second paragraph, and then I hear a sound next to me that I cannot immediately classify.

Then I look up, and within a few seconds everything has changed.

82-Year-Old Woman Dies during Routine Examination

On Wednesday, June 11, an 82-year-old Italian woman suffered a heart attack during a routine visit at Charité University Hospital in Berlin. Despite immediate resuscitation efforts, the woman died in the waiting room of cardiologist

Professor Buhlfort's office. An investigation found no fault with either the specialist or his clinic. The woman's cardiac weakness had apparently not been previously diagnosed. The woman's remains will be brought to Italy by a relative after her cremation.

Chapter One

Hanna

Berlin is probably the only German city that delivers what its tourism brochures promise. The city is huge, colorful, and confusing—you can get lost in it even if you grew up here. Long ago, I stopped trying to decide whether I love it or hate it, and I made up my mind to tolerate its otherness. But I know that, underneath its ugly asphalt skin, the city is more alive than all other German cities combined.

I notice a tuft of grass that has fought its way through a crack in the cobblestones and step to the side with a smile. A pit bull's jaw has been spray-painted around it. Weeds always win out over pavement around here, especially in the areas where kids let loose with their graffiti. In avoiding the weed, I step into a puddle, and muddy brown water sloshes into my pumps—shoot!

It's less than five minutes from the subway to the editorial offices of *Genusto* magazine on Zimmerstrasse, but when I finally arrive, I'm drenched, even with my umbrella. If time were measured in sheets of rain, the walk would be an eternity. I hurry through the revolving door, but before I can step onto the carpet of the foyer, something yellow rams into me at what feels like fifty miles an hour. Something else falls to the floor, and I hear a noise that sounds like an exploding water balloon. My ankle twists, and I stagger into the reception area, but my umbrella catches in the revolving door.

"What the—! Sorry!" The canary-yellow somebody, a woman in a raincoat, crouches down by a brownish puddle and gathers up Styrofoam cups and plastic lids. The enticing aroma of coffee fills the foyer. My eyelid twitches.

"Good morning, Sasha." I inspect the woman's crocheted beanie and the fine blonde hair that curls along the back of her childlike neck. Something about my intern has irritated me from the start, and it's not just her questionable way of dressing. The girl's a total nutcase—and clumsy on top of that. No day passes without her getting grease spots on important papers, spilling drinks, or breaking china. The revolving door grinds to a halt behind me.

"That's the end of the umbrella for sure," Sasha giggles. Rolling my eyes, I turn to the elevator while she fishes a soaked chocolate brownie out of the pool of coffee. She straightens up and looks at the sopping-wet paper bag in her hand. "Darn. Fifteen euros down the drain."

The elevator display shows it's stuck on the third floor—probably the janitor blocking the door with his cart again. I check my watch nervously. Colliding with Sasha has cost me five minutes of valuable working time and also left a coffee stain the size of a saucer on my light-gray suit. Shoot!

"Hanna?" Sasha, now at the reception counter, calls over to me. At least she's organized a trash can and mop from the janitor's office. "Do you have a moment? I need to talk with you about something important."

Should I use the staircase? I can take only short steps in my tight pencil skirt. No way can I climb stairs. I bang on the elevator button. There's a whirring sound, the second-floor indicator lights up, and then the first floor—finally!

"Wait, I'm almost done," Sasha screeches. I hear clattering and rumbling but don't look back. The elevator goes *pling* as the doors slide open, and I jump inside. In my mind, I'm already going over the phone calls I've planned for this morning. One of them will be with a colleague from the *Michelin Guide* who hates nothing more than people who are late. Unfortunately, just as the doors start to close, a spanking-green ankle boot pushes itself between them. Sasha squeezes past me and drops her handbag with a relieved sigh.

"You seem mad at me. Did you get hurt when I ran into you?" Sasha's violet-blue eyes meet mine in the elevator's mirror panels. Now I notice how she's dressed for this middle-of-June day—pink tights that somehow harmonize with her rubber-ducky-yellow raincoat and green ankle boots.

"You're late!" I answer with icicles in my voice. I push the fourth-floor button.

"I got here just two seconds after you." Sasha grins.

I focus on the floor-number display above the door. "Did you want to discuss your working hours with me?"

My intern actually blushes. "No . . . of course not." She bends down and rummages in her messenger bag. "Where is it? I swear it's in here—this bag's a freaking Bermuda Triangle—ah! Here it is." With an air of importance, she hands me a tattered piece of paper. I anticipate trouble—and not just because of the curled corners.

"I had a cool idea last night," she says, "and wrote it all down."

"Hm." I keep studying the floor numbers. Second floor. This thing is as slow as if we were hauling ourselves up with a pulley. What if I pretend not to understand what she wants? Maybe she'll lose her nerve and give up. But I know that's wishful thinking. Sasha has already imagined a movie—starring herself—about her winning a Pulitzer Prize.

"So I obviously got up right away," Sasha goes on. "Writers like us have to put our ideas on paper immediately, or—poof—they're gone in the morning." She pats me on the shoulder as if we played in the same league. I step away.

"Sasha, you do realize that you're not employed to write articles."

"Urban vegetable gardening!" she shrieks, making me jump. "I bet it's a hot topic!" She's beaming as if she'd just invented the light bulb.

"Vegetable gardening?"

She nods. "In pots on balconies—carrots, for example. Grow your own herbs without chemicals and stuff like that."

"You want our readers to grow vegetables on their balconies? That's . . . interesting." Third floor. Can this thing not move any faster?

"Will you read my article? I worked on it half of last night, and maybe—well, only if you like it . . ."

"Of course. Put it into my yellow box, and I'll look at it later."

Sasha exhales. "You mean the tray where my other articles are gathering dust? The one you haven't checked for the past two months?"

Fourth floor. I try not to appear stressed. The doors glide open. Sasha, looking like a chastised little dog, doesn't move. Now I really feel like a bad person, so I sigh and take the paper out of her limp hand.

"I'll look at it. Promise," I say. "But first, do what you're supposed to do: make coffee, dust the shelves, and file papers. Keep your eyes and ears open and learn—just like any other intern. Next week I'll recommend you for the mail room. There you'll realize what order and accuracy really mean."

Sasha's eyes open wide. "Hannaaa."

"I have your best interests in mind, sweetie."

Sasha pouts. Now she looks like a Berlin street waif, with a few damp strands of hair plastered to her forehead, the soaked Coffee Fellows bag in one hand, and the other hand clenched into a fist. I head toward our open-plan office and focus on the etched "Food and Lifestyle" on the glass door.

"Order is completely overrated," I hear her say from behind, but I'm already pushing down the door handle.

Fabrizio

Nonna had insisted that her hotel room face east, toward the sunrise. She didn't care that the red-brick facade of Coffee Fellows fills the view out the window, so you have to tilt your neck to see just a little bit of sky. Forget about seeing the sunrise. All you get is street noise and exhaust fumes, and not even a balcony.

I turn my attention to the task waiting for me in the middle of the room: four suitcases, not counting mine, and bags from practically every boutique in Berlin's city center. I sit down on the edge of the bed. The blanket is neatly folded and the pillow fluffed up, as if nobody ever slept here. The room seemed small to me before. Now it's tiny. Can rooms shrink?

"How the hell am I going to carry all that stuff to the airport, Nonna? Do I really have to transport a dead woman's clothes all over the place, clothes nobody'll wear anymore?"

I imagine her reply, *"Of course you have to, Fabrizio. Such good quality."*

The porcelain urn could be mistaken for a vase. The undertakers had been friendly and professional. Very German. They hadn't flinched a bit when I selected the ugly red-and-blue-striped one. It was the only damn vessel with a little bit of color. Nonna loves—used to love—colorful things.

I cautiously fish something blue out of a shopping bag—on closer look, a square-cut dress. The next dress is red, the same style, with a narrow belt and a scarf, the fluttering kind. More dresses in the next bag—some with flowers, others with stripes, a yellow one, a red one. They all look the same to me.

"Who will ever understand women?" I sheepishly mumble in Nonna's direction. She replies promptly in my head, *"You don't know what you are talking about."*

I have no idea who could use the stuff. Lucia is heavier than Nonna, Alba is too young, and let's not even talk about Rosa-Maria's dimensions. Giving away Nonna's things to strangers is out of the question. So I'm back at square one. The dresses fall to the floor in a pile of yellow, blue, and red. I avoid the shopping bag of underwear. Even the dead have a right to some privacy.

You really thought of everything, didn't you, Nonna? You disappear and make your grandson the butt of jokes for the entire town with all this luggage. After hesitating for a moment, I reach for her well-worn leather handbag. Ever since I was little, I've been dying to find out what Nonna lugs—lugged—around in it. Exploring its magic depths just got me whacks from her beringed fingers. Marco and I would goof off by asking Nonna for the craziest things imaginable, and she would oblige by fishing scissors, pastry scrapers, sweets, or toothpicks out of this leather monstrosity. Once she even pulled out a real pistol—but that's another story.

I don't have to be afraid of a slap on my wrist anymore, but my heart nevertheless races when I zip open Nonna's bag and spill the contents onto the bed.

I am disappointed. The items could be from almost any woman's handbag: handkerchiefs, a tube of lipstick, creams, a powder compact, a nail file, a wallet, boutique ads, a shoe-store coupon, tape, a pen, and Nonna's day planner. I leaf through it—more because I don't know what else to do than because I'm curious—and swallow when I see her familiar, proper handwriting. Daily entries, some marked with stars. Birthdays. I open it to the twenty-fourth calendar week. My left temple throbs, announcing a migraine, as I stare at the date and what Nonna wrote. It says: *twelve o'clock, Dr. Buhlfort's office.*

I suddenly hear my father's voice in my head: *"You can go on bawling as long as you want, son. It won't bring back your mamma. Now wipe your nose and take care of your little brother."*

Defiantly, I wipe my face with the back of my hand. I almost missed the penciled entry below it: *four o'clock, Isabella Colei!* It's underlined and ends with an exclamation mark. Who the hell is Isabella Colei?

Nonna's address book gives me a preliminary answer: the entry for Signora Colei lists a Berlin phone number. I could just close the booklet and forget about the entry, but something makes me pick up the phone. Nonna always stressed the importance of keeping appointments. And maybe I do it out of more than a sense of duty—I haven't talked with anyone in two days, other than the lawyer who's going to investigate that article. I don't like the guy, but he seems to know what he's doing. I decide to let the phone ring three times—just three times—and if nobody answers, I'll hang up.

"Hello?" A woman's voice, hurried but friendly.

"Please excuse my calling so early. Is this Signora Colei?" I speak so fast that the sentences blur into one word.

"Yes. Speaking."

"My name is Fabrizio Camini and I . . ." Breathe, Fabrizio. Breathe! "Hello? Are you still there?"

The woman on the other end immediately switches to Italian. "What can I do for you, Signor Camini?" But her voice is suddenly ten degrees colder.

"I think you had an appointment with my grandmother, Giuseppa Camini, four days ago. I'm sorry that I'm calling so late, but I need to inform you . . ." What am I doing, telling a stranger that Nonna is dead? "My grandmother asked me to tell you that she's unfortunately unable to meet with you right now."

Silence.

"Signora, are you still there?"

"I've never heard of your grandmother. I am sorry."

"But she listed an appointment with you in her daily planner—for Wednesday, the eleventh."

"Probably a mistake."

"But . . ."

"Have a good day, Signor Camini."

The woman hangs up. I'm still staring at the receiver when someone knocks on the door. "Not now," I mumble.

"Housekeeping," I hear faintly.

"No, thank you," I say, louder, but someone is already opening the door. *Che merda!* "I said no, thank you!" I scream at the shocked maid, and a sharp pain cuts across my forehead. She turns as white as her apron and stumbles a few steps back. She points to the sign on the door handle that says "Please Make Up the Room," but I can't apologize. Instead I wave her away impatiently, and she shuts the door. I swear that Nonna's room has shrunk even more, and I feel like I'm suffocating.

My stomach rumbles. My last meal was a sandwich at noon yesterday that tasted like a mixture of cardboard and Styrofoam. No wonder I'm behaving like a jerk. I hang up the receiver to stop its beeping and stare at the urn. Oh, Nonna, I'm sure you imagined a different trip home.

Determined, I get up from the bed. Unpleasant things don't get better by being postponed. I'll grab some food at the airport. I leave twenty euros and all the coins from Nonna's purse on the pillow for the maid. It doesn't make me feel any better.

Hanna

Claire looks at me, aghast, and leans on my desk. "You're not serious! Sasha in the mail room? *Mon dieu*, that won't end well. You know how fussy they are down there."

"Whatever." Unmoved, I open my mail folder. It's almost bursting: letters from readers, comments about my most recent article, and inquiries from restaurants wanting to be reviewed. I can't believe what has stacked up during my two-week absence. In the future, I should forget about vacations and all the sentimental reasons why I flew to Italy, of all places. I look up, since my forehead is starting to tingle. My colleague is gnawing on one stem of her eyeglasses and scrutinizing me. Claire Durant is one of the few people who can manage to criticize you without saying a word.

"What is it?" I mumble.

"You don't exactly look recuperated."

"Don't I?"

Her eyes narrow. Claire, my French colleague, is less than five feet tall and as slender as a deer, yet she completely unnerves me.

"It doesn't have anything to do with the circles under your eyes, does it?" She waves a magazine at me, which I guess is the newest issue, with apricots on the cover. It gets me going. Just thinking about that horrible trattoria makes me livid. How long do you have to cook vegetables to make them gray like that? I needed a whole glass of wine to rid my mouth of the taste of MSG in the ribollita. Claire sets the magazine on the table with raised eyebrows. The headline jumps out at me: "Tre Camini Spoils *la Dolce Vita*!"

"Believe me," I say, "it was high time someone spoke openly. I know what good Italian food is supposed to taste like. And at that place"—I stab at the red-shingle roof in the photo—"they definitely don't serve good food. The chef should count himself lucky he only had to deal with me. My mother would have skinned him alive."

But Claire isn't listening. Her pine-green eyes drilling into me, she lowers her voice. "*Bon sang.* Give me a break. You were in Italy! The country of gorgeous art and *savoir vivre*, the country that also happens to be your birthplace. You're supposed to come back tanned and happy with at least four more pounds on your tushy. Instead, you wrote five articles, e-mailed every three hours, and wrote thirty letters to the editor. And your behind is as skinny as it has always been."

"I happen to love my job," I say. "Italy might be your dream destination, but my only connection to it is my mother's last name. Besides, it's not *savoir vivre*. It's *la dolce vita*."

"I see. Still, I'd like to know why you can't live without your laptop for a couple of days."

"Stop bugging me, Claire," I say. "It was a bummer of a vacation. It rained ten days out of fourteen, I wasn't relaxed for a second, and I definitely had no nostalgic feelings for the place. I combed through village after village, surrounded by stupid Italians who drove like they all won their driver's licenses in a lottery—not to mention chefs who should have been delivering newspapers instead. Of course I work during vacation." I shrug. Claire wouldn't understand anyway—being a food journalist is all that has survived of my dream of being a serious writer. I worked night and day, typing till my fingers were raw, all just to get a column of my own. And my column, and the influence it gives me in the food world, means everything to me. Even if it isn't always pleasant.

Claire's expression softens. "How bad was it really?" she asks. I rummage in my purse and come up with an ashtray, two dessert spoons, a soap dish, and a sugar shaker. Claire sighs. "Do you have the addresses so I can send these back?"

"Of course I have the addresses." I fish in my handbag some more. On each restaurant's brochure, I meticulously marked down what I swiped from the place. Embarrassed, I add a tampon case to the loot—souvenirs of six gastronomic bombs within two weeks. Greetings from *la dolce vita*.

"Wow, what a cute sugar shaker!" Sasha sneaks in, and a few brown drops fall on my papers.

"My god! Look at you." Claire adjusts her glasses and assesses Sasha's raincoat. "Why are you wearing a kid's coat? And such an awful hat. Did you crochet it yourself?"

"I just like this coat. And I like my hat, too." Sasha shrugs and leans against my desk. "Why do we always have to return the trophies you take from the places you tear to pieces in print? Why don't you keep the stuff? It's not worth anything anyway."

"But that would be theft." I shake my head.

"It would be . . . Hanna, I think you've lost your mind."

"Shut up, Sasha. That's not true." Claire points to the clock on the wall. "And you were late today."

"Hanna was late, too," Sasha says, her revenge for our conversation in the elevator. I gasp, but Claire is faster than I am.

"Just as a reminder, *mademoiselle*," she says to Sasha. "We are the journalists and you're the intern. We might not be sticklers for hierarchy in this office, but the rule still applies: you're the one who makes the coffee. That means your workday begins before ours, so you can turn on the machine. Understood?"

"So I'm late because I stood in line for you at the coffee stand. Well, that makes my day." Sasha rolls her eyes.

"I knew you were smart. Now get lost and bring me a *café au lait, s'il te plait.* And after that, you'll send Hanna's mementos to their owners without mouthing off anymore. The way it's always done."

"Coming up! *Immediat . . . amente.*" Sasha salutes, then ducks when Claire tosses a pen at her.

"Get lost?" I grin. "Claire, you're a sweetheart."

"I'm not sweet at all—stop kissing up. Hellwig wants to see you. Today. At the airport. And it didn't sound like an invite for a chat."

Absentmindedly, I pick up Claire's ballpoint pen from the carpet. "I thought the boss was in Helsinki."

"He fit in a layover in Berlin before flying to Vienna. The Austrian office—oh, don't even ask."

I don't need to ask to know what Claire means. Our Viennese office manages to win the internal award for most boring edition every single month. It drives our editor in chief crazy.

"Do you know what he wants to talk to me about?" It can't be a good sign that Hellwig is summoning me to meet him at the airport. I hope he isn't considering transferring me to Vienna. Although, come to think of it, Viennese coffee and those delicious buttery confections might sway me.

"Well . . ." Claire purses her red lips.

"Don't make me pull each word out of your nose."

"You want to pull words out of my nose? You Germans are seriously crazy."

"Claire!"

"Honestly, I have no idea what he wants. All I know is that you have exactly an hour and a half to arrive at the airport on time. So chop chop."

Fabrizio

I don't know what I expected. An empty restaurant at noon? Respectful silence, as hurrying people learn, from one look at my face, that I can't tolerate being jostled?

With my carryall on my shoulder and Nonna's urn under my arm, I wind my way through the crammed airport restaurant. I'm lucky: there's an empty table in the back of the place, right by the window. I navigate around a baby stroller, climb over pieces of luggage, and nod to a woman who graciously pulls her suitcase out of my way. I drop into the chair and push away the last person's tray—an abandoned plate of spaghetti that the gourmet splattered with ketchup. A waitress shows up out of nowhere, her order pad at the ready. Her smile reveals an impressive row of white teeth.

"What can I bring you?" she asks.

"Your dentist's phone number."

Her smile widens. "You're Italian."

"That so? Thanks for reminding me." I have no choice: I smile back, even though she's wearing too much makeup and I'm not in the mood to flirt. "I haven't looked at the menu yet. What would you recommend?" I try not to stare at her full chest.

She giggles. "We're not a starred restaurant, you know."

"You aren't?"

"The daily special is pork roast with mashed potatoes. It's only six euros."

"Who could resist that." I grin and set Nonna on the upholstered chair next to me. She's not very stable. Changing my mind, I plop the urn on the table. "All right, I'll take the special and some water."

"Are you in the food-service industry?"

"What makes you say that?"

"You scrunched your nose when I told you our daily special."

I glance at the red-and-blue monstrosity. It doesn't seem right to put one's grandmother next to instant mashed potatoes. And Nonna didn't like pork.

"You should study psychology," I say. "Your powers of observation are amazing." Maybe I should put Nonna on the windowsill. That way she'd have a view of the runway.

"Actually, psychology is one of my minors," she says. There's a pause. "All right. I'll go and get your order."

"Sorry?" When I glance up, all I see is her round, disappearing backside. Very pretty.

I turn away and watch a Lufthansa plane dock at a gate. A man in a yellow security vest drives a cart toward it. As another worker opens the cargo door, my briefcase starts to vibrate. Well, my phone, which I've been successfully ignoring for two days. It's probably Lucia, or maybe Rosa-Maria. If I'm unlucky, it's Marco. They'll kill me even before I touch down on Italian soil. I can't blame them after the stammered message I left on the trattoria's answering machine: *Nonna died. I'll arrive Friday.* That's all I said.

I bend down to my briefcase with a sigh. I can't find the phone right away; instead my fingers touch something stashed in a side pocket that I'd rather forget: the magazine from the waiting room. I automatically flip to the article, which I've read at least twenty times, and wish for the hundredth time I hadn't translated its harmless-looking sentences for Nonna.

Tre Camini Spoils *la Dolce Vita*!

How lovely it could have been, sublime, really, if this magazine handed out stars for the most beautiful location. Because Tre Camini is definitely pretty, especially for adventuresome guests who dare to leave the Strada Provinciale 88 shortly after the little village of Montesimo and follow the unmarked gravel road. Their reward? A picture-perfect vista of Tuscany, the kind that tourists love to send home on postcards: a grand manor house crowning a hill that is covered with wildflowers, a hill that is as perfectly round as the puff-pastry bonnet on Paul Bocuse's famous truffle soup.

The ocher-yellow stone building seems to lean a little, but not enough to cause uneasiness when you enter. You're the only patron at 8:00

p.m., but even this doesn't arouse suspicion at first. After all, you've been told in the village that the kitchen "up there" is the best, far and wide. But if you believed it at first, disillusionment sets in quickly. The friendly young server is overtaxed when asked for a wine recommendation, and then brings a glass of red wine instead of the requested pinot grigio. It's the house wine, she says. The nameless wine is light and fruity with a velvety aftertaste, so you are inclined to forgive her ignorance.

Unfortunately, this is the overture to a culinary tragedy beyond compare—and that in a country celebrated worldwide for its cuisine. Half an hour later, the guest sits without a spoon in front of the trattoria's specialty, ribollita. The famous Tuscan soup turns out to be made with store-bought broth and some frozen vegetables that bob up and down like corpses. It is served with stale bread.

The second course tempts you to a game of pick-up sticks with the undercooked noodles hidden under a mountain of mysterious green sauce. The cook makes a valiant attempt to increase your revulsion with the main course: lamb, the consistency of a leather sole. No trace of a side of vegetables or a salad, just two tough, meaty rags accompanied by a dab of mustard from a jar. By now the guest knows better than to order a dessert—

"Really, our roast doesn't look *that* bad."

Startled, I fold the wrinkled magazine and glance at the indifferent assortment of meat, mashed potatoes, and grayish-brown gravy that's appeared in front of me. Then I look up. The waitress returned in record time.

"Forgive me. My thoughts were elsewhere."

A frozen smile, the one she probably uses for hundreds of customers, replaces the woman's earlier flirty one. "That's all right. Enjoy."

I put the magazine back into the bag and grab my fork before the waitress says anything else. I'm relieved when she stalks away with swaying hips. Women.

Hanna

Airports always impress me. They are gigantic, colorful, and noisy. Loudspeakers blare the airlines' broken promises, while the beginnings of a thousand possibilities are detailed on the Arrivals and Departures boards. The Arrival terminals are my very favorite. I already watched some hellos when I arrived at Berlin-Tegel this morning, but still, I'm bummed I don't have time to savor a few rounds of reunions, which, like the last few minutes of *Love Actually*, always send me reaching for a package of tissues. But I have no time to indulge today, so I race through the terminal, a challenge in high heels.

As I expected, the airport restaurant is crammed. I squeeze through a group of green-capped seniors that has commandeered the bar area and look around. Knowing Hellwig, he's probably reserved a table, probably somewhere in the back. And, indeed, I spot his familiar profile at a table near the window. I catch myself before I can raise my hand to wave. Hellwig hates to be the center of attention and loathes whoever puts him there.

I force myself to approach him slowly on my stilettos. Unfortunately, it's obvious from my panting that I don't go to the gym regularly. I feel like a pupil summoned to the principal without knowing what she has done wrong.

It's always like that when I meet with Hellwig. There's something about this athletic, good-looking man and his pale eyes that intimidates me. Claire suspects that something else is responsible for my jitters—total nonsense, of course. Who'd be stupid enough to start something with the boss? Then a suitcase on the floor ruins my dignified approach. I stumble.

"Ouch! Damn." Pain pierces my shin, my boss shoots me an irritated look, and for a millisecond my eyes tangle with another startled pair—espresso-colored ones.

"Scusi, signora.*"* The stranger at the neighboring table picks up his briefcase. I force a smile and then ignore him, even though he has espresso-colored eyes.

"Hello, boss! Sorry for being late." I congratulate myself on my recovery—I'm a little out of breath, but otherwise it's as if the last three seconds didn't happen.

"Frau Philipp. A grand entrance—as usual." Hellwig's expression remains neutral. I sink down into the empty chair, hold back the urge to rub my shin, and reach for the menu.

"Are you hungry?" he asks.

"Honestly, just nervous."

Hellwig scrutinizes me silently and then laughs—he doesn't sound amused. "You, nervous? Never."

"All right, you win. I'm curious. It's not every day I'm summoned to the airport."

"Then I won't hold you in suspense any longer." He looks at his watch. "There is actually a problem."

"And the problem involves me?" I ask as casually as I can.

"We're being sued because of your last article."

"Again?"

Although he doesn't usually take hot-and-bothered restaurateurs seriously, Hellwig doesn't return my grin. His recurring sermon: if you investigate thoroughly, stick to the facts, and don't insult anybody, you can attack anyone—even top chefs, for all he cares. Research, facts, respect. I've always followed these rules—strictly.

"So you think it's funny?" Hellwig stirs his empty teacup. The scrape of metal on porcelain makes my hair stand on end.

"Of course not!" An alarm shrills in my head. This is not going the way I thought it would.

"Good—since this situation is *not* amusing." Hellwig leans over the table, and the subtle aroma of peppermint drifts to my nose. The boss is a health freak. He never drinks coffee, and it's rare to see him in a suit and properly tied tie, like today. Usually he wears jeans and polo shirts.

"The plaintiff—a Signor Camini—wants a five-digit sum."

"Five digits!" I clench my fists in my lap. Hellwig looks at his napkin's flower pattern. "And he demands your head."

My voice deserts me.

"For some reason, Signor Camini's lawyer thinks that your article killed his client's grandmother."

"But that's ridiculous," I manage to say, though it sounds pathetic.

"I don't think so at all. I can imagine how an old lady who suffers from a heart condition would come across your sharp pen . . ." Hellwig pauses and slowly shakes his head. "Of course, nobody can force a magazine to fire its writers. I mean, where would we be if we allowed that? But Donnermuth's law office is pretty good at making offers that are hard to refuse."

I can't laugh about the butchered *Godfather* quote. Pressure plays an accordion in my chest. My article killed an old lady.

I killed an old lady.

I didn't mean to.

I didn't. Really.

"Donnermuth has good media contacts and is not shy about using them. You can imagine how it could play out, how everyone you've insulted in the course of your career will react to the story of the sweet Italian granny whose restaurant has been in her family for generations. They'll tear you apart. Frau Philipp, I love the magazine, and I do believe that journalists are replaceable."

"But everything I wrote about Tre Camini is true," I say. "The food is a catastrophe; the soup alone . . . the pasta was . . . and the service—"

Hellwig interrupts me with an indignant gesture. "I'm not discussing with you whether or not your review was justified. Obviously the article is not responsible for the old woman's death. Herr Camini, however, views the whole matter more emotionally, and so we have to control the damage."

"But if we aren't wrong, then why should we relent? Why should we sugarcoat an article that informs our readers? This is an attack on the freedom of the press."

"Maybe because you're smart and you like your job?" Hellwig says. Am I mistaken, or does his face show some pity? Everything is clear to me now, and it sweeps away every ounce of security in my life. Hellwig gave up on me long ago.

"You can't be serious."

"I am completely serious. You're a brilliant writer, but you've become somewhat expensive lately. Our lawyers pull in their heads whenever your name comes up, and after the Rothfeld matter . . ." He looks troubled, but his eyes remain cold as steel.

My mouth feels stuffed full of cotton balls. "Rothfeld is a con man. The report from the Institute of Food Technology *proved* that he was selling trout as arctic char."

"Here we go again." Hellwig sighs. "Just tell me, what restaurant critic would send a piece of fish to a lab? You're losing your sense of scale, Frau Philipp. We aren't the Office of Criminal Investigation. You aren't solving ritual murder cases, but writing an entertaining column in a food magazine that sells for three euros and eighty cents. It's as unrelated to *Guide Michelin* as my laptop is to the Voyager program."

"I know that," I whisper, but the boss isn't done.

"It's not that I don't admire your courage," he says. "You're a career woman with backbone, and you don't mince words. But you are going too far. Sometimes you don't have any sense of moderation or tact. You'd probably have been burned at the stake if you'd lived during the Middle Ages."

"Does that mean I'm fired?" The palms of my hands are dripping wet; I feel blood rushing to my head. I'm losing control of myself. I scan the table for something that will put an end to this feeling. Other than Hellwig's teacup, the table is empty. What's with this restaurant? If it's too much to offer a vase with some pathetic artificial flowers, couldn't they at least put out salt shakers? I mean, I can't swipe the spoon from my boss's saucer.

I start to tremble. My eyes fall to the windowsill, which has two huge planters—and a striped porcelain vase.

"So this is what you'll do, Frau Philipp. You'll publish a friendly retraction of your article in the July issue. You will apologize for your error. And then you will make Signor Camini drop this absurd suit, even if you have to kneel in front of his stable door to do it. I know it's humiliating, repenting publicly and eating humble pie, so I'll put in a good word for you with the board of directors." As Hellwig turns away to grab his jacket, I act with lightning speed.

The vase is not only ugly, but heavy to boot. Fortunately it fits into my handbag. My trembling stills at once and I exhale in relief. The accordion in my chest relaxes. Hellwig leafs through his money clip and then gives me a noncommittal smile. "I've got to go. I am sure you'll find a solution that satisfies everyone." He hands me twenty euros. "Please pay for my tea—and order a piece of cake for yourself. I hear that carbohydrates do wonders for stress."

I take the money, smile thinly, and stop myself from saying anything snarky. "Have fun in Vienna," I say instead, without meaning it. To my surprise, Hellwig winks at me, taps his forehead, and turns away without a word. He navigates through the throng of people and finally disappears.

The chubby server doesn't look at me while telling what I owe and handing me my change. Instead she stares at the man at the neighboring table. I completely forgot about him, since Hellwig had blocked my view.

The Italian is sitting there with his eyes closed, facing the window. Earphones wrap around his head. He's good looking, I notice absentmindedly. He has dark, wavy hair run through with copper brown, and distinct features. His lashes are so long that they throw shadows under his eyes. I don't know if it's because he's tapping his feet to the beat under the table or because he's smiling—which makes dimples in his unshaven face—but the man moves me. Mostly I'm just envious that he seems so relaxed. In his sound cocoon, there's probably nothing that could upset him.

I straighten and pick up my handbag, which is much heavier than before. Passing a mirrored wall on my way out, I automatically glance at myself. I was definitely taller when I came in.

Fabrizio

My mood has improved by the time I get to airport security. Zucchero's boozy voice gave me half an hour of escape from my worries and that waitress, and I can think clearly again.

As I expected, the metal detector peeps when I walk through. Compared to Italy's, German airport security is top-notch. That's what I get for not removing my cross necklace. The security official points to the bench for sinners behind a folding screen. I'm rolling my eyes.

"Shoes," the uniformed guard tells me.

Yes, I do have some.

"Take off your shoes!"

I give him a confused look. I've loved driving German guardians of the law up the wall since my student days. The official points to my wingtips. I bend down to fumble with the shoelaces. *"Make two knots, child,"* Nonna always told me. *"That way you'll never end up running around with untied laces."* The first shoe clatters to the floor. Nonna really had the right advice for every situation.

Suddenly I freeze.

I stare at my hands, the untied second shoelace, and then the official's legs. He jiggles his foot impatiently. My gaze drops back to my feet. My left sock has a hole in the big toe.

Holy shit!

I see that my briefcase has already gone through the baggage scanner. Another uniformed officer approaches me with some official-looking papers in his hands.

"Herr Camini? You're transporting some special luggage?"

Nonna! I jump up and push my shoes into the surprised officer's hands. "I'll be right back."

With that, I race past passport control in my socks and, followed by astonished looks and giggles, whiz out of the security area.

Chapter Two

Hanna

For the first time since I joined the magazine two years ago, I take the staircase. When I get to the top, I realize why I've always preferred the elevator. There are one hundred and twelve steps. Panting, I'm standing in front of my department's door, unable to even push down the handle. Then Sasha hops up to the top of the stairs behind me with a pile of magazines under her arm, whistling and showing no sign of being out of breath. I try to remember how many years ago I, too, could do that.

"You all right, boss?"

Actually, if I'm being honest, I can't remember ever hopping up such a huge flight of stairs—and certainly not whistling.

"Take my bag!" I gasp and lean against the wall. "Give me a moment."

Sasha takes my bag and opens the glass door with her elbow. "Was the meeting with the boss that exhausting?"

I straighten up and suck in a wheezing breath. "Absolutely not." I ignore Sasha's mocking look and stalk by her with my head held high.

In the office kitchen, I catch Claire red-handed with my jar of Nutella in her lap. "That makes you fat, Madame Durant."

"Mostly it makes you feel good." She unrepentantly puts the spoon into her doll-like mouth and screws the lid back on. "You look like you could also use one or two spoonfuls."

"We have a problem." I drop into the only chair that is not covered with jackets and bags. I have no idea who's made the cozy employee lounge into a closet. Lately there are even shoe boxes under the corner bench. Our intern is probably not entirely innocent.

"Do *we* have a problem or is it you?" Sasha pushes past Claire and sets my handbag on the table, which is strewn with empty Thai takeout boxes. "What in the world are you hauling around? This weighs at least ten pounds."

"Please return the ugly vase to the airport restaurant." I sigh and turn to Claire, who looks at me expectantly. My eyes are burning. "I think I really bungled things badly this time."

Claire frowns. "What's a bungle?"

"She means that she made a mess of things." Sasha steps closer, interested. I open my mouth, but the sentence sticks in my throat. Claire sits down next to me and takes my hand.

"What happened?"

"The article about Tre Camini . . . Do you think it's mean?"

As I wait anxiously for their reaction, Claire and Sasha exchange a glance.

"Well, I wouldn't call it nice," Claire begins. "But your articles rarely are, *n'est-ce pas*?"

"That bad?" I say.

"I thought it was funny," Sasha says. "Especially the part about the frozen vegetable corpses in the instant soup. And the spinach mush on raw spaghetti." Sasha grins, but she shrinks back when Claire gives her a critical look.

"Are we dealing with a letter from some lawyer again?" Claire sounds matter-of-fact, and I'm grateful.

"The owner of the trattoria believes that my article was the cause of his grandmother's heart attack." The pain in my chest comes back.

"Ouch, that's new!" Sasha says. Claire raises her finger and Sasha responds by busying herself with my handbag. I keep talking—fast, so I don't start crying. I can't remember ever losing my cool like this—and in the office, of all places.

"Now this Camini wants me fired."

"That's not nice," Sasha says.

"And I couldn't meet his damages claim in ten years, if ever. I'm done for." In utter disgust, I open the jar of Nutella. Forget about the stairs; what I need is sugar. Lots of it.

"We'll find a solution." Claire glances toward our intern, who is setting the striped vase on the table.

"I doubt it," I say.

"Hanna . . ." Sasha has turned very pale. How nice that she's worried about me even though I'm sometimes a horrible boss. I sniff the Nutella jar.

"Could you hand me the spoon?" I ask Claire. Why should today be the day I start getting in shape?

"Hanna!"

"What?" I say to Sasha. "If Claire can stay thin even though she eats Nutella by the pound, I should be allowed a little spoonful."

"This thing here—that's no vase." Sasha's voice trembles.

"What are you talking about?" Mmm, the Nutella tastes amazing.

"I don't think you'll like the answer." Sasha looks as if she's about to throw up. And she's the one who usually takes everything in stride. Is something gross stuck to the vase? Claire is about to touch it, but then she shrinks back with wide-open eyes.

"Mon dieu," she whispers.

"Girls, what's the matter with you? It's just—"

"An urn," Sasha mumbles with a sepulchral voice. "My gramps got one. But it wasn't so colorful."

It is suddenly deadly quiet. I'm not in the mood for chocolate anymore.

We stand around the table and stare at the porcelain container as if it were a poisonous striped puffer fish.

"Are you sure?" I whisper.

"Be my guest and check it out," Sasha whispers back. "I'm definitely not looking inside."

"How would an urn end up in an airport restaurant? It's ridiculous. And why are we whispering?"

"Out of reverence," Claire says softly and cleans her glasses. At least she's talking again. The shock isn't too much for her. It is for me. I stole a corpse. Oh my god!

"Reverence, sure," Sasha says. Claire's nostrils flare, a clear sign that she's smelling a story.

"Maybe someone forgot it in the airport restaurant."

I reach for the urn. "I just don't believe it."

"Nooo!" they both scream, and I recoil.

"But I have to see if you're right," I say.

Finally, Claire musters the courage to carefully lift the urn. She examines the container from every side, checks the cork seal, and turns the urn upside down. "There's a plaque."

"Is something written on it?" Sasha peers at the bottom, but stays a safe distance away.

"Yesss."

This time Sasha and I speak in unison. "What?"

For some strange reason, Claire seems about to either laugh or cry. "*Quelque chose ne tourne pas rond*—something is definitely wrong," she mumbles in French and adds a phrase I don't understand.

"What do you mean?"

Claire carefully puts the urn back on the table and looks at me with part pity and part amusement. "I'm afraid that this time you won't be able to return your souvenir by just mailing it. Look at it yourself."

I've never touched a dead person. Sure, it's not actually a corpse, just ashes, and inside a porcelain container, but . . .

"She's not going to bite you." Claire's upturned nose twitches.

So it's a woman. Breathe, Hanna. Breathe! The urn doesn't feel like an urn. It's smooth and cool and could be a milk jug. I read the engraving once, then a second time: *Giuseppa Camini, 1932–2014, Tre Camini, Toscana.* It takes a few seconds before everything clicks in my head.

"What's the probability that this isn't what I think it is?" I ask calmly.

Claire lifts her hand. The space between her thumb and index finger is barely big enough for a pencil. I nod slowly.

"So I not only killed an Italian *nonna* with my article, but stole her urn on top of it."

"In France we call that destiny."

Fabrizio

"What in heaven's name did you think you were doing, Carlo?"

For the past half hour, I've been furiously pacing the kitchen while Rosa-Maria has kneaded the dough as if her life depended on it. To be honest, rage is the only feeling I've been able to muster since I arrived. Rosa's freshly baked panini won't change that. Carlo nibbles on a toothpick, unruffled.

"Eh, Fabrizio! Sit down and have a glass of wine. Your bad mood is hard to stomach." My friend shakes his head. His grin, revealing gaps between his teeth, drives me crazy.

"How could you allow this jerk to cook in my kitchen, Rosa-Maria?" I point at Carlo's stained T-shirt, which displays the logo of our national team, Gli Azzurri. Rosa-Maria slouches, which makes her look even more square-shaped. Her face turns tomato red, and the dough bubbles feebly in the bowl when she pushes it down. Under normal circumstances I would feel bad—Rosa-Maria is like a mother to me. But nothing has been normal these past few days.

I can still hear Lucia's desperate sobbing when I told her what happened in Berlin. I had expected Marco's disapproving expression, but he'd been wise enough not to make a stupid remark. Alberto has been missing since yesterday. He's probably sharing his sorrow with his chickens.

"Carlo said he had your permission." Rosa-Maria shoots a livid look in Carlo's direction.

"In my opinion we shouldn't discuss this in front of an employee," Carlo says arrogantly. "You know that as the arm of the law I have to uphold *la bella figura* in front of all residents."

"I don't give a rat's ass whether or not you look good," I say. "And Rosa-Maria isn't an employee; she's part of the family. So why was the trattoria open when we had decided otherwise?" I again address Rosa-Maria, who has started to sneeze violently.

"It's not her fault, honestly." Carlo eyes Rosa-Maria's thyme rolls. Out of pure spite, I push the bread basket out of his reach. So he mumbles, "It was my idea." I move the basket even farther away. "Rosa-Maria was ill. She was coughing like my old Fiat that I scrapped last year. So I said to myself, 'Carlo, why don't you do your good friend Fabrizio a favor?' A closed restaurant isn't a good restaurant, eh? Nothing against your culinary skills, Rosa-Maria, but I can whip up some pasta blindfolded. There was only one guest anyway, and she tipped little Alba generously."

Rosa-Maria's skin darkens another shade. She clears her throat several times and licks her hairy upper lip, but her silent cry for help gets lost in our village policeman's sea of smugness.

"You let the maid serve?" I say. "Where the hell was Lucia? How much did Alba get?" I ask warily—around here, an overly generous tip does not mean a compliment for the kitchen. Carlo raises two fingers triumphantly.

"Twenty euros?"

"As I said, it was good."

For a few seconds, I want to beat the magazine—which I've been carrying in the inside pocket of my jacket for forty-eight hours—round Carlo's head. But the urge remains just a very satisfying image. Our house doesn't need another troublemaker. "Don't you realize that Tre Camini has a reputation to lose? We can't afford botched kitchen jobs—or the tourists won't come."

His black mustache trembles, a clear sign of uneasiness. He would never admit it, though. You can catch Carlo Fescale with his finger in the honey jar and he will still claim it wasn't him. He was born without a conscience. Maybe that's why he's such a good custodian of the law.

"I can't stand foreign tourists anyway," Carlo says. "They have no idea what *al dente* means. Could I have a thyme roll?"

"You're hopeless."

"I meant well. Now give me a panino and tell me what's really bothering you," Carlo grumbles and reaches for the bread basket.

Maybe it's the carefree attitude of his that I've known since childhood. Possibly it's the warmth emanating from the oven—or the aroma of freshly baked panini. My rage crumbles like the crumbs Carlo scatters on the table as he cuts through a roll. He smears it thickly with salted butter.

"The urn. I lost Nonna." My throat feels as if I'd swallowed a cup of flour.

Rosa-Maria's mixing bowl shatters on the terra-cotta tiles. She whimpers and crosses herself several times. Carlo scrutinizes me, chewing. It feels like an eternity, with Rosa-Maria's sobbing as the soundtrack. Then Carlo scratches the back of his head.

"Fabrizio?"

"Yes?"

"Do you have some more salted butter?"

Hanna

I've tried sleeping on it, but the night did nothing to help the way I feel. Since I didn't want to leave the urn at the office, I took it with me to my apartment in Wilmersdorf, a decision I have since regretted. After all, a dead person is not your average houseguest. I didn't sleep a wink and got up several times to move the unwelcome visitor. I couldn't find a single spot in my six-hundred-fifty-square-foot apartment that didn't offend either my or Signora Camini's sense of propriety.

Now, I sit totally bleary-eyed on a wooden bench in the Berlin zoo, my shoulders resting against the spot where I carved *H.P. + D.A.* four years ago with the key of Daniel's BMW. I flushed the same key down the toilet a few months later, just to bug him. I scratched out his initials after we broke up and haven't allowed another pair of letters into my life since then. But I held on to Sunday mornings at the zoo, even though I'm not much into animals. Birds actually scare me. On the other hand, I find meerkats cute. Daniel nastily called them "bastards."

"Hello, Hanna!"

"Morning, Helmut!" I wave to the stocky man in Wellingtons who is entering the meerkat enclosure with two buckets.

As a teenager, I used to visit the zoo almost daily—mainly to skip school, but also to secretly attach myself to Southern European extended families, people I've always found strangely attractive. I would simply trot behind a Turkish family and imagine that I was their adopted daughter. Unfortunately, it never went well for long. I usually ended up as a human found item in the lost and found at the zoo's administration offices, where my name and face became well known. Eventually I moved my adventures to the Kaufhaus des Westens department store, and that had consequences. My adolescent escapades didn't seem to particularly bother my parents, but the juvenile-court judge, who sentenced me to forty hours of community service for shoplifting, took the matter much more seriously. I will never forget how I felt in the courtroom when the intimidating, black-robed man said to me, "Child, what did you think you were doing?" while simultaneously staring down my parents. It was the first and last time I saw my father look embarrassed.

When the zookeeper empties the bucket, the meerkats rush to devour pieces of banana, eggs, and peanuts—no chicks today, to my relief.

Unfortunately, the diversion doesn't last long. As the last banana disappears into a smacking mouth, my thoughts return to my strange visitor. It feels as if I've given shelter to the actual living Giuseppa Camini. She shuffles in slippers through my apartment and shakes her head when she sees how empty it is and how I haven't unpacked all the boxes from my move, even though I've lived there for a year. She investigates cupboards and reads my mail, and she's expecting me to bring home the Sunday paper, which I won't be able to afford if I lose my job.

"Salut, ma belle!"

I look up in surprise and see a petite shape against the sun. "What are you doing here?"

"Keeping you company." Claire sits down next to me and fishes a croissant out of a paper bag. We sit silently for a while.

"It's Sunday," I say.

"Hmmm," Claire responds, chewing.

"Did you have a fight with Jan?"

"Jan doesn't know how to argue." She offers me the paper bag. "Croissant or chocolate roll?"

I suddenly have a lump in my throat. "Claire, why are you here?"

"To stand by a friend. Isn't that the phrase?"

"I'm your friend?"

"Mostly you're a silly goose." Swallowing the last bite, she grins. "So what are we going to do about the Caminis?"

"I'm going to write a heart-melting letter of apology and ask Signor Camini to drop the charges."

"You actually intend to send poor Giuseppa to Italy in the mail?"

"What else am I supposed to do?"

"You really should know the answer yourself. Why do you make yourself so complicated?"

She always says that, and I hate it. "Forget it, Claire," I mumble.

"It's too late. I already called the boss and he finds my idea *magnifique*!" She curls a lock of hair around her finger. "And before you curse and swear like a raven—"

"It's 'swear like a sailor.'"

"Whatever." She makes a dismissive gesture. "Before you get mad at me, listen first. Signor Camini is Italian and you are half-Italian, *n'est-ce pas*? So nobody is more aware that a letter does nothing to soothe the pride of a Mediterranean man. I thought carefully, Hanna. You have to go back to Italy. Talk with Signor Camini, tell him that you are sorry and that you'll make amends. You'll hand over the urn, and everything will be all right."

"You mean the stolen urn," I say.

"The found urn."

"But I can't do something like that. I suck at conflict resolution!"

"Seriously, Hanna. Life is filled with conflict. It's about time you learned how to deal with it." Claire is unrelenting. "Hellwig already gave the go-ahead on my idea for a special Tuscany issue. Your ticket is waiting for you at the airport. You'll go on a business trip, you'll wrap the

Caminis around your little finger, and you'll also write a few nice—the operative word is *nice*—articles about local restaurants."

"You covered all the angles, didn't you?"

"Most of all, I thought of you," Claire says softly. "Sometimes it is better to confront the ghosts that haunt you rather than running away from them. It can be healing."

Honestly, I don't have the slightest idea what this French girl is talking about.

Chapter Three
Hanna

"What do you mean, the car is not available?" I say. "Here's the online confirmation from your company. It clearly states medium-size car, Florence airport car rental, reserved for Monday, June twenty-third. That's today!"

I thought I was prepared for anything, but I wasn't ready for my personal Italian nightmare to start right when I arrived in Florence. First, the workers threw my luggage onto the baggage-claim conveyor belt last, as if they knew that I was in a hurry. Then, I was randomly selected for a special customs check and had to take my underwear out of my suitcase and spread it out in front of a clerk with a mustache and an Adam's apple that jumped up and down. Next, my heart sank when the customs clerk held Giuseppa indecisively in his hands for a while. But, unexpectedly, the urn slid through as a souvenir. He shrugged his shoulders and put her back in the suitcase. I guess I don't look like a drug smuggler.

Of course, by then the rental-car line reached all the way to Arrivals. When I finally got to the glassed-in counter two hours later, I was ready to board the next plane back to Berlin—regardless of my job or the urn. And now this!

The fat Italian in the bright-yellow booth looks at me nonchalantly. "No car available."

He must be joking.

"Yes, you already said that," I reply in German. "But that's not my problem, I'm afraid."

"Is not a problem, signora. Just come back tomorrow, and then a car will be here."

"Tomorrow?" I can feel the frozen smile on my face melting.

"Maybe late morning. But not too late, because then we have lunch break." He is still completely indifferent.

"You can't be serious."

"I can do nothing. Come back tomorrow. *Basta.*"

"Listen, I'm here on business and don't have time to be the victim of your lousy organizational skills," I say—in a much higher pitch than I planned.

The fat guy shakes his head and starts to roll down his blinds.

In desperation, I put both hands on the window and start screaming in Italian. "You'll get a car for me pronto, even if you have to weld it together yourself! Otherwise your little yellow box will explode. *Basta!*"

Suddenly the clerk is no longer blasé. He rushes out of his glass box. "Luigi Cartone, signora, at your service. Why didn't you say you were Italian in the first place?"

I cut him short. "So are we now solving the problem the Italian way, or should I sic my mother on you?" I ignore his outstretched, pudgy hand. Cartone looks at me approvingly. My reaction doesn't seem to astonish or offend him. I push my chest out even farther and pout, something I wouldn't do in Germany even if my life depended on it. Cartone makes a calming gesture—hands flat, paddling downwards—and scurries back into his fishbowl. He reaches for the phone, an antique with a dial, while he texts furiously on his cell phone with the thumb of his other hand.

"Giacomo, come over here, OK? And bring the key for the Spider for a pretty signora. What? I don't care if it's reserved." Ignoring the excited response on the other end, he puts down the receiver and raises a thumb. "No problem, signora"—he glances at the rental contract—"Signora Philipp. If I may give you some advice, from one countryman to another: speak Italian in Italy. That opens windows and doors for a beautiful woman—car doors, too."

Driving a car in an Italian city is a life-threatening activity, especially if you don't know the rules, which aren't posted anywhere. Basically, remember that the faster car always wins, pass in the most dangerous spot you find, and watch for motorbikes and Vespas that suddenly dash out of tiny side streets with total disregard for traffic lights. Italians also tend to tailgate, following so closely that you cannot see the grille of the car behind you in your rearview mirror.

When I instinctively take my foot off the gas pedal, a cacophony of car horns sounds around me. Despite Cartone's directions—both spoken and pantomimed—I miss the freeway going southwest and land in the middle of Florence. Sweating blood in what feels like a-hundred-plus degrees and feeling no appreciation for the beauty of the city, I drive around the roundabout on the Piazza della Stazione for five minutes, looking desperately at the exit signs. None of them, even after three rounds, points in the right direction. I'm in a spanking-new Alfa Romeo Spider, but it doesn't make me feel any better in this bumper-to-bumper chaos. Besides, now I'm sorry I was too chicken to ask for a GPS. I don't remember when I last balanced a street map on my knees while driving. Other than that, the convertible is a dream.

"Damn it!" I start when a Vespa roars by just inches from my side mirror—the driver in shorts and sandals with his cell phone wedged between his ear and helmet.

A blue Fiat—which has trailed me, honking, for the past two rounds—moves up to my side. Two young Italians in mirrored sunglasses call out to me, *"Che bella donna! Dove vai?" Beautiful woman, where are you going?* I'm at the end of my rope. So instead of swearing at them, I wave my map and shrug my shoulders.

"Where to? Where to?" they shout.

I start my fifth circle of the roundabout. The Fiat doesn't move from my side.

"South? Perugia? Montepulciano?" I scream back. It's worth a try. The boys grin, and one raises his thumb. The Fiat's engine revs, and the little car scoots into a space in front of me. The passenger gestures that I should follow them. Relieved, I follow them out of the traffic circle after a sixth round, heading in the exact opposite direction from the one I thought I should take. All I can hope now is that my new friends aren't luring me into some horrible neighborhood to pinch my purse.

Fabrizio

I tighten the muscles in my back, inhale, and raise my arms. The axe smashes down on the log and cuts it cleanly in half. Another piece of wood—my sixty-eighth—is next. I knock it out with one blow, paying no attention to the blister on my thumb. I deserve the pain.

I once read that one can gauge a person's popularity by counting how many are crying at the graveside. If that's true, my grandmother outranks soccer legend Enzo Bearzot.

The entire village came to pay last respects to Nonna this morning. The black-clad crowd—a sighing, crying colony of ants—invaded the cemetery and reached all the way to Via Capelli, where cars, tractors, motorbikes, and bicycles were lined up like pearls on a necklace. I don't know who was more desperate: Padre Lorenzo, fearing for the graves that were trampled by countless feet, or me, who had to offer the mob of mourners an empty urn.

My shirt is sticking to my back. Sweat stings my eyes; I haven't wiped them with my bandana since round fifty-seven. I wind up for the sixty-ninth blow, this one intended for the sharp-faced notary Lombardi. I couldn't keep him from going to read Nonna's last will right after the funeral—he didn't want to pay the cab fare from Pisa twice. The testament will be read in public, in the community hall, this very afternoon, the way Nonna stipulated. How crazy is that? My wooden adversary topples off the chopping block, but I don't feel triumphant.

"So whom exactly do you want to kill, son?"

I notice that Alberto is leaning against the shed, his thumbs wedged under the straps of his blue overalls. Thin smoke escapes from his nose—the result of a hasty secret cigarette, no doubt. Our estate manager is as immune to medical advice as Nonna was.

I reach for another piece of wood, pretending that Alberto has not just materialized out of thin air. I have no idea how long he's already watched me. He has almost perfected the art of creeping up on people.

"You mean since I made a good start with Nonna?" Round seventy. Whack. Next, please.

"Don't talk nonsense."

I look for an especially impressive log instead of replying. I call the log I find Titan and fight the urge to cross myself. I'm on the outs with God lately, like I'm on the outs with everything else. Titan's neck breaks in a fraction of a second. Amen.

"Your granny knew that she wasn't well."

"But I didn't know it. Otherwise I'd hardly have let her fly to Germany."

"You better believe me that no power in the world could have kept her from taking that trip, not even being tied to a tractor." It sounds as if Alberto wants to add something, but he only shakes his head and laughs, as if what happened was just Nonna playing one last macabre trick on us.

"I would have thought of something," I say. If I inherited one gene from Nonna, it's stubbornness. The next piece of wood—but my axe misses, cuts only the edge and whizzes into the chopping block. Relieved, I let go of the wooden handle.

"You couldn't have prevented the heart attack. Sooner or later—"

"I would've preferred later!" The words are hardly out of my mouth when I realize that, yes, I lost my grandmother, but Alberto lost the person he's loved his entire life. Tension tightens my chest. "Sorry. I just would have loved to . . . say good-bye. Instead, I took that possibility away from me and from all of you. I will never forgive myself. Never."

Alberto scrutinizes me for a long time before looking to the courtyard where Vittoria, my grandmother's favorite white hen, is scratching in the mud.

"Finding her ashes won't change that she's gone forever. Say good-bye here." He taps his chest. By now, our estate manager has used up more than his weekly allotment of words in this conversation, a sign that he means what he says. I look into his watery eyes, which almost disappear beneath his heavy brows. I guess I'll have to get used to feeling guilty all the time.

"You're right. Forgive me."

Alberto pats the back of my neck with his hand, a gesture I know from my childhood, when he would slap the back of my head if the situation warranted it. "Finish up, son. It smells of rain."

Hanna

I don't end up in a scary neighborhood. Right after the city limits of Florence, I say good-bye to the nice Italians by honking and screaming, *"Grazie, grazie!"* I leave the freeway at the next exit, courageously choosing the local road that runs parallel to the *strada provinciale*. Even though this will double my traveling time, I'm happy with my spontaneous decision. Within half an hour the fields and woods of the Arno valley open up in front of me.

I am not a nature lover, but it's unbelievable how the mellow landscape of this quiet side street affects me. On my right, the Arno winds its way through the hills like a serpent, copper colored in the late-afternoon sun that breaks through the clouds. The wind brushes against the back of my head, and I suddenly don't regret anymore that I entrusted my hair to an obviously mad hairdresser who dyed it a brownish black and cut it very short. Tiny villages and farmsteads—houses with faded awnings, and little gardens with laundry lines—fly by. I hum along with an Italo-pop hit playing on the radio and wave to a bicyclist I pass; I just can't resist. The air smells of meadows, lavender, and something sour that I can't quite define. I'm almost at peace—at least for ten minutes until the idyll is destroyed by a bang and billowing black smoke.

"Damn!" I step on the brake and come to a stop behind a tractor that is taking up most of the road. My car chortles violently, burps a few times, and then dies.

Of course. Did I seriously think I could reach this godforsaken place—what's it called?—without incident? I fish around the armrest for the crumpled piece of paper with the address. Montesimo. A short look at the map confirms what I thought: Montesimo is unreachably far. The next village is about two and a half miles away, and who knows whether it has a gas station, let alone a garage. The tractor has long since puttered out of sight, and an invisible mockingbird in the underbrush next to the road is having a loud laugh at my expense. My forehead drops onto the steering wheel.

I know as much about cars as a carpenter knows about crocheting. It takes me ten minutes just to locate the lever that opens the hood. Above me a rain cloud—a rather large one—rumbles ominously.

Fabrizio

Umberto Lombardi is a tall, gaunt man with a beaked nose that somehow complements his starched shirt collar perfectly. From the lectern, where bingo numbers are usually called and award ribbons attached to the overalls of chicken farmers, he's lording it over us. The community hall fills with the same black crowd that trampled down Padre Lorenzo's graves this morning. Nobody wants to miss the public reading of a last will and testament, especially not if it's the one of Giuseppa Camini.

I glance around with my head bent, trying to endure the pitying looks and at the same time to act aloof enough so nobody speaks to me. The mayor's wife, who starts to waddle toward me with a sorrowful expression, hits the brakes and instead presses Lucia and Marco to her ample bosom—making sure that everyone witnesses her expression of condolence.

The proceedings in the darkened room seem strangely staged to me, almost as if, from behind the velvet curtain, Nonna were directing her own funeral feast (a horrible expression for the mountains of spaghetti, vats of minestrone, and buckets of panini). Nonna liked best the sesame-topped panini, some of which are right now disappearing into Lucrezia Gosetti's pockets. Her son, Stefano, in shirtsleeves and bow tie, is sitting with the Bertanis. One row in front of them, Rosa-Maria sits in tears next to Alberto, who is more composed. Our foreman, Paolo stands by himself at the window, hands buried in his pants pockets and gaze directed outside as if he wished he were in the fields. I understand the feeling exactly.

Lombardi coughs quietly, condescendingly—typical of his profession. He leafs through his folder. It's obvious that he doesn't feel comfortable with this group of peasants who are so different from his rich clients in Pisa. The lawyer has been taking care of our family's affairs for two generations, but I've never understood what Nonna saw in this stuffed shirt. He can't finish a sentence without using a word from a foreign language.

Lombardi clears his throat more emphatically, but the room quiets down only when the mayor sits down and takes off his Panama hat. Chairs scrape across the floor, last morsels of food disappear into mouths, and glasses are deposited on the floor next to muddy shoes. All hundred and twenty or so curious pairs of eyes fixate on the lectern, as if someone shouted "Bingo." I can almost hear Nonna whispering from the great beyond, *"Bread and games, child. Even the old Romans knew the only effective way to get people to do what they have no intention of doing."* I almost laugh out loud. *What the hell is your plan?* I wonder.

I eye Carlo, who stands by the door with his legs apart and arms folded, making his famous *bella figura*. Then I focus on a square of sunlight on the floor.

"Ladies and gentlemen, I welcome you in the name of the deceased, whose wish it was that the testament be publicly read. This is the last will of Giuseppa Camini, born Graziano, signed on February 10, 2014." Lombardi clears his throat and rustles some papers, an eerie sound in the deep silence nobody dares disturb. "'I hereby revoke all previous testaments and declare the following to be my ultimate wish. I appoint Umberto Lombardi of Grufo & Millotti as executor of my will. My loyal estate manager, Alberto Donati, has the right to live on the estate for the rest of his life. This right shall not be affected even if the estate should be leased, rented out, or sold.'"

A tinge of excitement runs through the room like a slight cosmic disturbance. The notary looks up and adjusts his tie. I glance over at Alberto. The relationship between him and the deeply Catholic Nonna was an open secret, much gossiped about in the village. Alberto's expression gives nothing away, but the way he squeezes the cap in his lap tells me enough. I offer a silent prayer of thanks to the heavens.

"'To my dear Rosa-Maria Alberti I leave my silver rose brooch and a stipend of five hundred euros per month for the rest of her life, to be taken from my life insurance. The rest of my jewelry, including a diamond necklace by Visconti, a gold bracelet by Gioielli, and my grandmother's diamond ring, I leave to Lucia Camini, the wife of Marco Camini.'" Lombardi reaches for his bottle of water but then decides to continue without drinking. "'My grandson Marco Camini gets the oil painting in the living room, but has no other claim on the estate. He received the statutory share on October 7, 2005, as noted in the attached document.'"

A murmur runs through the room. Most people in the audience look surprised, some gloating, and others nod seriously. Marco stares straight ahead and Lucia contemplates the tips of her shoes. This fair deal is no news to them—but my brother messed it up when he ran his bookkeeping firm into the ground.

"'I designate my grandson Fabrizio as the sole heir of Tre Camini and all the tracts of land attached to it, since I know he will administer the estate the way I intended. I stipulate that he obtain possession of his inheritance as soon as he has entered the holy state of matrimony. Should Fabrizio Camini decline to accept the inheritance under this condition or not be married within a year after the reading of this testament, I designate Marco Camini as my sole heir. Until that time, my estate manager, Alberto Donati, is entrusted with the management of Tre Camini.'"

The mayor's wife lets out a satisfied guttural sound and rams her elbow into her husband's side. Mothers turn to look at their daughters. Lucia stares at Lombardi as if he just revealed that Nonna left all her possessions to the church, and Marco inspects his fingernails.

And what do I do?

I run outside, far away from the chattering mob that's pretending to be stunned by what they heard. And far away from the smile playing about Marco's lips.

Hanna

"Hello?"

"It's me. Hanna."

"Carissima!" my mother says. "How wonderful to hear your voice. What's that horrible noise in the background?"

"It's raining."

"But it's sunny outside."

"I'm not in Berlin, Mamma."

"You aren't?"

"I'm in Italy," I say, "doing research on an article. But my car got stuck somewhere in the middle of no—"

"Wait, sweetie—my cell phone is ringing. I'm on call because Isadora went to the hospital. The poor girl, her nerves have finally caught up with her. And we had to admit a Croatian woman with three little kids last night, even though we're crammed, and it's only me. Isadora? How are you, dear? Did you—"

"Mamma?"

"Just a second, *carissima*. I'll be with you in a moment. What do you mean, Isadora, they're keeping you in the hospital? For how long? Did they tell you when you can get back to work?"

I fiddle with the radio while listening to Isadora's hard-luck story, which interests me about as much as the weather in Majorca. I turn the dial all the way to the left and then all the way to the right. All I get is static that's interrupted twice by crackling voices. It's no wonder—out here the end of the world seems about to begin.

"I'm sorry, but this was really important," my mother says, finally talking to me again. "So tell me again, child, why are you standing in the rain while calling me? Please go inside."

I look up at the convertible's canvas roof in frustration and shrink deeper into the seat. I'm just glad I managed to find the button for the roof. Otherwise I'd be sitting in a motorized bathtub.

"If you'd been listening to me," I say, "you'd know that my car broke down on an Italian country road."

"Italy? Did they send you there on another business trip?" She sounds alarmed, like she always does when the topic of her home country comes up—one of the reasons I didn't tell her that I not only wrote nasty articles during my last vacation but also did some research into my background. I wasn't successful, since there are more Coleis in Tuscany than drops in the ocean. It's strange that she keeps her family such a secret; after all, it's mine as well. Unfortunately, that's not the way she looks at it.

"Forget it, Mamma. I just wanted to talk with someone. I didn't mean to keep you from anything important."

"Where exactly are you now? Oh, the phone again! These cell phones are the scourge of mankind. Isadora? What else?" My mother's warm voice, whispering words not intended for me, bubbles through the phone. I can see her in front of me, how she's probably pacing in the kitchen, her bracelets jingling, the phone jammed between chin and shoulder. Her short, brunette curls bob up and down. Every part of her is in constant motion.

My heart jumps when I hang up and throw the phone into the glove compartment. Really, I didn't expect anything else. Mamma always worries more about everything and everyone else than she does about those who are right next to her.

Fabrizio

Lombardi has a letter for me. I have no idea how he found me. After I ran in circles in the rain for a while, torn between sorrow and a hot, scary rage, I hid in the men's room of the town hall. When he pushed a crumpled piece of paper under the stall door, I just stared at it. There it is, next to the puddles of water that have formed at my feet. Lombardi leaves the room with a starched "I wish you well, Signor Camini. You know where you can find me." Only then do I pick up the envelope. I turn it in my hands, not daring to open it.

My grandmother always subscribed to the erroneous opinion that matrimony was the only lifestyle that's agreeable to God. I have no idea why she was so fixed on that idea, why she had pursued it with relentless zeal late in her life. I was fourteen when her matchmaking efforts started. The first future Signora Camini was a girl in my class—she was two heads taller than I was, preferred hopping to walking, and had braces. So everyone called her The Brace. I ran away as fast as I could, and Nonna slapped me for it, saying, "How is a girl supposed to catch you, Fabrizio, if you're always running so fast?"

I didn't want to be caught—and that didn't change when the girl in question was the baker's daughter, the baker's daughter's cousin, or the baker's daughter's cousin's friend.

I found the girl that Nonna didn't want me to find at all when I was an adult, and it took me four years to realize that my grandmother's doubts were justified. After that, there were countless women. They made me laugh and warmed my bed, and their shapely legs earned me the envy of other men. None of them touched my soul. None of them was Sofia.

I laugh without humor. How silly of me to believe Nonna would stop her scheming just because she met the Grim Reaper. I go to the sink, avoid looking into the mirror, and turn on the faucet. While the water is running, I tear open the envelope.

Montesimo, February 8, 2014

My dear Fabrizio,

It probably is unusual to start one's last words to a loved one with an apology. Since you're reading this, Signor Lombardi has just finished reading my testament and you are scared to the bone. You are furious and desperate, and I can understand how you feel. The Lord told me some time ago that my time is up, and so, with a heavy heart and deep conviction, I made the decision that might be the end of Tre Camini. Maybe you'll understand my motives better after reading this letter.

First of all, I want you to know that I am very proud of you. None of the Caminis, except your late father, has ever been as closely rooted to our estate as you are. Your love for it is palpable and present everywhere—shown in the calluses on your hands, in the way your laborers look up to you, and even in the taste of every single apricot. Our farm could be in no better hands than yours, of that I am sure. Yet, in the same way that your brother lacks attachment to our land, you lack insight into what makes a Camini a true Camini.

Tre Camini is much more than just an agricultural estate. It's a family business steeped in Christian values and traditions. In good and bad times alike, the family has guaranteed growth and a future. Without family, this country estate has no reason to exist. That's why I want you to marry and pass on the family legacy in the face of God, as your grandfather and your father did. Fill Tre Camini with the laughter of children, because that is why it exists.

You might say that this is not your way. You might think that I am old fashioned because I place so much value on these matters. But most of all, you believe that you will not find another woman you can love.

Trust a stubborn old woman's experience: love often grows where one least expects it.

It is sometimes not enough to just trust that things will grow and thrive out in the fields. You are a Camini—and in their hearts, all Caminis are husbands, wives, mothers, and fathers.

Your Nonna, who loves you very much

PS If you are not willing to try for Tre Camini, try for me. I don't want to have to turn in my grave because Marco is doing something stupid with my apricots.

Hanna

I readily admit that there are worse things.

On a scale from one to ten—with ten equaling being struck by a deadly disease; nine, giving birth to triplets; and eight, having an overdrawn credit line—a cloudburst on a deserted country road is not all that bad. True, I'm drenched, but the rain, which has lightened from shower to spray, is lukewarm. I carry the urn safely in my arms—it seemed wrong to expose the old lady to a bumpy ride in a wheeled suitcase. The cyclist from before passes me and rings his bell somewhat maliciously. I can live with that.

I don't know how long I've been walking, but the afternoon sun is low, and each step seems to take me farther and farther from civilization. I pass a soaked cardboard sign with "50" painted on it, languishing in the ditch. A similar sign with a washed-out message dangles from a fence a quarter mile later. I detect only three humans—two women and a man in a field, carrying large bundles of hay on their backs. Otherwise I meet just horses, sheep, and a herd of donkeys. The herd, ears hanging, is gathered under a leafless tree, and I wonder if they're longing, just as I am, for a dry place and a bowl of soup. Maybe not for the soup.

I only notice the truck when it stops directly next to me. It's a panel van, mottled yellow and brown, as if someone poured a bucket of dung over its ecru paint. The driver leans over and winds down the window.

"Signora! You need help?" he asks in broken German. Is it obvious at first sight where I'm from? Warily, I step closer. Paolo Conte's "Via Con Me" wafts out with the sharp smell of aftershave and sweat. I wonder if it's possible to recognize by their appearance psychopaths who sew coats out of women's skins. The man, who seems to be well groomed, is wearing a black Sunday suit. "Saw your pretty car on side of street."

I nod cautiously and glance at the faded direction sign. "Montesimo 6 km." That's almost four miles too far to be skeptical about strangers. Obeying Cartone's advice, I answer in Italian. "I'm on my way to Montesimo. Is this on your way, by chance?"

The man's face lights up, and he straightens and opens the door. "Of course! Get in. I'll bring you there. No problem."

Sometimes I actually believe there's a God, even if his angel, on this occasion, wears a toupee.

"It seems you like Italian music." The man, who introduced himself as Ernesto, smiles at me. Embarrassed, I stop tapping the beat of "Siamo Soli" on the dashboard. I can't help it—the seat is pushed forward so far that my arms don't fit in my lap. With my feet tucked up on my suitcase, which Ernesto crammed between the seat and the dash, I feel like a canned sardine.

I nod and check out the back of the truck. Envelopes and packages fill the Ford from top to bottom.

"I am the mailman of Montesimo," Ernesto says when I look at him questioningly, and pride tinges his voice. That explains a lot. I smile politely when Ernesto fishes a dark-blue cap from the side panel and points to its sewed-on logo. "It's my favorite job. I do it three times a week: Monday, Wednesday, and Saturday. I'm late today because we had a funeral this morning and then the testament was read in the community hall. Such public proclamations don't happen often." He grins as if it had been deliciously funny.

"How interesting," I lie. We rumble over a pothole and pass a direction sign that says "Montesimo 10 km." What? I start to perspire. Did Ernesto make a turn that I didn't notice? Why wasn't I paying attention?

"Trust me, signora. We are taking a shortcut." The mailman steps on the gas, and, although the van replies with a scary noise, it does accelerate obediently on the dirt road. I slump down. So I'm going to end up as a coat—or dead in a ditch.

"This way is longer, but Carlo won't take snapshots of us with his new toy. We can drive faster, so it's shorter." Ernesto pats the steering wheel as if the postal van were a Ferrari.

"Who's Carlo?" My tongue feels furry.

"Our village policeman."

"You only have one policeman?"

"Montesimo is a small place." Ernesto shrugs. "But we have lots of good pasta."

"Oh." I look at him, confused.

"Do you like pasta?"

"If it's cooked correctly . . ."

"We're in Italy, signora. The only pasta you'll taste here is good pasta or better pasta."

The conversation is telling me I still have a lot to learn about this country and its inhabitants. Ernesto seems to be an especially weird specimen.

"And what's the difference? I mean, between good pasta and better pasta?"

The mailman snorts as if I just asked the difference between a fast-food joint and a Michelin-starred restaurant. He watches the road silently for a while, pondering his answer. He comes up with, "If you like it, it's a good one. With the better one, you can't stop eating." He grins mischievously and adds, "Gotcha! Your eyes are as big as a cow's—a very pretty cow." His giggling is infectious, and I laugh out loud.

"And what was the very best pasta you've ever eaten?"

"That's easy. I eat it every Sunday at Salvi's."

Sighing, I ask, "Who is Salvi?"

"He's the village innkeeper."

"The only innkeeper, I assume."

"You learn fast. Salvi makes *pasta alla Zanolla*, like Ernesto Zanolla." Ernesto points to his chest. "That's me."

"That's nice of Salvi to name a pasta after you."

"Nice of me to share my recipe with him," he grumbles.

"So tell me—what's so special about your pasta?"

"Something unexpected." Ernesto smiles mysteriously and smacks his lips. "But you know what, signora? Why don't you find out for yourself? My invitation. You're probably staying in our beautiful Montesimo for a few days."

God, I hope not.

"That's nice of you. But actually I didn't—" I evade his curious look by staring out the window. "I just have to take care of something quick."

"And where do you have to take care of it?" he asks. "Not because I'm curious—but I have to drive you there. It's still raining, you know."

Some people are hard to contradict—I didn't expect Ernesto Zanolla to be so persistent. Besides, I'd rather hang dead from one of these fences than walk one more step in the rain. So I rummage in my purse for the address. "Do you know how to get to Via Carega, number ten?"

"I'm the mailman, signora."

Fifteen minutes later, after driving along a hair-raisingly narrow winding road, Ernesto stops in front of a low stone wall with an open iron gate. It seems vaguely familiar. The mailman cuts the engine and scrutinizes me.

"We're here?" I ask.

My new friend answers with a smile. While I'm partly relieved to be here alive, I also regret that I have to get out. I boldly plant a kiss on Ernesto's closely shaven cheek and then untangle myself from my seat.

"That's a nice vase," Ernesto says casually.

"I agree," I say. I swear that I don't for one second consider leaving the urn on the passenger seat, as a thank-you—an elegant solution if all I needed to do were to return the urn. "Thank you for everything, Ernesto. It was a thrill to meet you."

I really mean it. He hands me the bundle of mail to deliver to the trattoria. Holding the letters against my chest, I slam the truck door.

"Give my regards to Fabrizio." He winks. "And if you change your mind, my dinner invitation stands."

I wave at the dirty yellow van until it disappears, honking, behind a curve. Then I turn around slowly to face the cypress-lined driveway. An army of tiny fists drums inside my chest. I don't know what I'm more afraid of: the people at Tre Camini or returning to Berlin. What happens in between will decide everything.

Chapter Four

Fabrizio

I must have dozed off in the armchair, with the folder of balance sheets on my chest and Nonna's letter—which I've read at least a dozen times—on top of it. When I wake up, the rock inside my chest has shrunk to fist size, but I feel even more confused. I can't decide whether I should be furious, sad, or disappointed.

I hear dishes clatter downstairs and squint at the old grandfather clock. Five o'clock. I struggle to get up, and the folder drops to the floor, spilling out a few sheets of paper. Why the hell did nobody wake me up?

As I head down the stairs, I smell roasted meat, apricots, and wine, a scent I could pick out from a thousand others. The recipe is as old as the steps under me, steps that quite a few Caminis have run up and down, or staggered up, and a few have been carried down. I hear Nonna say, *"Death has been ever-present in this house, my boy, as has life."*

And you orchestrate whatever happens here even after *your death.* I swallow back my indignation and listen to the voices in the kitchen below. Rosa-Maria's grumbling mixes with Lucia's singsong, which I can hear clearly even though the kitchen, part of the main building, is separated from the annex by thick stone walls. I tiptoe down the stairs, skipping the next-to-last one with the squeaky board. The kitchen door is slightly open.

"Shouldn't we wake him? He always gets upset when we let him sleep in."

"I don't care if it makes him mad as hell. He needs his sleep."

"He looked horrible when I last saw him. Ashen."

"It's a miracle he hasn't collapsed. The worries about the farm, Nonna's death, the lost urn—and now this last will. Did you hear the mayor's wife? The village really has something to gossip about now. What in the world did Nonna think she was doing?"

"It's not just Fabrizio," Lucia says. "Marco hasn't said one word since we heard the testament, and he's been jogging around the outer apricot field for two hours."

"What can you do? They can rant and rave and run around, but she's still dead. And she left more heartache than is good for all of us."

I picture them: Rosa-Maria crossing herself and Lucia biting her lips. I shuffle my feet outside the door, clear my throat, and count to three. When I enter the kitchen, I don't wait for them to answer my hoarse "Ciao," but bend down to fetch the pasta maker from under the stove. "Is the pasta dough ready?"

Lucia, her back to me, is shredding Parmesan powerfully, putting her entire body into it. She's small but as strong as a farmworker. She needs every ounce of it—after all, the poor thing is married to my brother. Rosa-Maria doesn't look up from the rabbit-and-apricot stew.

"Of course the dough's ready." She points with her chin to the counter near the window. I bite back a smile. Ever since I can remember, the trattoria has been closed Mondays, and the extended family gathers to cook and eat together. It seems that, despite the funeral, no one is prepared to give up this tradition—a comforting thought.

I set the pasta roller next to the bowl of dough. Nobody remembers who came up with the Monday dinner menu, but it never changes.

Before the main course, there's a pasta dish, the *primo piatto*. Foes of carbohydrates—non-Italians—try to leave it out, but it's impossible to imagine or justify the meal without pasta. For us Italians, good pasta is far more than just a starchy side dish. It embodies what we mean when we talk about *home*.

I reach for an onion and a knife. Even though the kitchen is the women's realm, one of my Monday tasks is making the pasta—another custom nobody is giving up. Rosa-Maria has already put out the ground meat, carrots, tomatoes, and olive oil. A good ragù doesn't have many ingredients, but they must be fresh and top quality. Besides that, all you need is concentration, some skill, and time. Especially time. Evading Lucia's gaze, I start to cut the onion. We'll talk later, and I'm not looking forward to it.

Hanna

I want to turn on my heels and get out of here. I made it this far, but let's be serious. It's impossible to right everything that's gone wrong in my life recently. So why am I risking a bloody nose when I could get away with just a slightly blackened eye?

Best-case scenario: the magazine and Camini's lawyer settle, and all I lose is my job. Every fourteenth person in Germany goes through that. My apartment is too big for one person anyway; I don't even have to pack, since I never unpacked; and until I find another job in my field, I could work at Sabine's breakfast café. It wouldn't be the end of the world.

So instead of walking up the driveway like a humble pilgrim, I could simply drop the grandmother into the mail at the local post office, and Ernesto could deliver—

Whoa! I jump, startled.

Less than two feet away, a chicken is looking at me with murder in its eyes. "Bloodthirsty" might be an exaggeration, but I had a traumatic fowl experience as a kid. I step to the side cautiously. To my complete horror, the chicken puffs its white breast, waves its little wings, and makes a terrible sound. A screech, really.

My reaction is predictable. I let go of the mail, and letters scatter across the driveway and flutter into its puddles. The chicken hops onto the dirt road outside the gate, blocking my escape to the village. I dive to my knees to gather up the letters within reach—abandoning envelopes that landed too close to the beast's beak and claws—and then run up the cypress-lined driveway.

Soon I'm standing in front of the stately stone manor house, next to the covered parking spots. I don't have to read the plaque out front to know what it says: Trattoria Tre Camini. And I thought I'd never come back. Wrong again.

Not sure what to do, I put down my suitcase, which suffered damage on the long dash: one of the wheels broke, and the expensive exterior is full of dirt. I slide the urn into its huge side pocket, wipe my face, and look at the trattoria. Maybe it's the weather—or is it my aversion that dims my view? It looks shabbier than last time. Rain runs down its flaking plaster. There are holes in the masonry, as if someone came along and picked stones out of the wall. Puddles fill the front yard, and moss covers the planters flanking the door. The palms in them look as bedraggled as I feel. The rain has managed to soak through my clothes, and now a small brook runs down between my breasts. My shoes squeak as I step forward and then back again. Is God doing this on purpose?

"All right, I made a mess of things," I say aloud. "But does that mean I have to throw the champagne out with the cork?" As expected, there's no answer from above.

Instead I hear Claire speak from my conscience's headquarters. *"Ooh, Hanna. Why do you look like that?"*

Just be quiet, I tell her. *You're the one who got me into this mess.*

"No, no, chérie. You can thank yourself. Don't chicken out now! You can try to pretend it wouldn't be that bad to lose your job, but it would *be bad. So show some backbone!"*

My stomach flutters as if I just swallowed a little bird. I can't. I just can't.

"Coward," Claire says.

I raise my chin defiantly into the rain. It's true. *I'm a coward, and you are far away.* So I will sneak around the back and stash this ugly porcelain vase on one of the windowsills. That will show, at least partly, that I'm sorry. And then I'll write a letter of apology to this Signor Camini, and I'll write it far away from this unsightly place—somewhere with my feet in warm sand, somewhere where Italy delivers what it promises in its brochures.

Fabrizio

"I can't stand this any longer."

Lucia's Parmesan shredder clunks onto the counter. My sister-in-law leans against the sink and crosses her arms. I stir the ragù one last time and put the lid on the pot.

"Could I have a dish towel?" I ask evenly. Lucia throws the rag at my feet.

"I'm going to have a coffee in the bar," Rosa-Maria announces, taking off her apron. She smooths her skirt, and I reach for the rag with a sigh.

"Fine, Rosa-Maria," I say. *Just disappear and leave me alone with the little witch.* When the door slams shut behind Rosa-Maria's generous behind, Lucia's eyes flash licorice-colored sparks at me. Intimidating sparks. "What can't you take any more, Lucia?"

She must have expected more resistance, but her surprise lasts only seconds. She straightens her shoulders, trudges over to me in her slippers, and drills her finger into my shoulder blade.

"You aren't the only one who's mourning in this house," she says.

"I know that."

"Then why are you behaving like a rabid dog, Fabrizio?"

"Weren't you listening when the notary read Nonna's testament?"

"So that's what all this is about?" I can see in the way Lucia hugs herself—as if she would otherwise melt away, like pancake batter containing too much milk—that she's not only angry but hurt. It moves me. But not that much.

"For right now, that's all."

"We are a family," she says. "It doesn't matter at all who owns the estate, as long as we're here for each other."

"You don't understand, Lucia. And it's also none of your business."

She is silent, and I see that I hurt her again. I glance at the clock on the wall. At dinnertime, the ragù will be perfectly done. It will taste of meat and herbs, earthy and spicy, with a touch of sweetness from the tomatoes—just right.

With no warning, Lucia throws her arms around me. They are doughy, and her hair smells of almond cake and tickles my chin. She sobs into the crook of my neck, soaking my shirt collar. I clumsily stroke her back and feel awkward. It has been a while since I've been this close to a woman. Fortunately she disengages herself after a few seconds, wipes her eyes with the hem of her apron, and with one step separates her sorrow from mine.

"Paolo was looking for you earlier. He's hired the Poles for the harvest," she says, sounding halting but businesslike. Women are confusing. One minute they're blubbering and the next they're pretending the whole uproar never happened.

"I know. I was at the stables this morning chopping wood." I show her my hand. The burst blister, now a pink scar, is proof of my self-punishment. Lucia raises an eyebrow.

"You should talk to Marco."

"I should?" I'm not fast enough to follow her leaps from thought to thought.

"He finished the semiannual report."

I was afraid of that. My brother, the bean counter, finds every little flaw. He loves to rub every negative number under my nose. "I don't care what the numbers say. We are not going to sell the apricot orchards as long as I have something to say about it. Nonna didn't want that and neither do I." Well, she didn't want it before she came up with this damn testament.

"Nobody is talking about selling."

Oh, you naïve woman, I think. *Don't you see that some things don't need to be said?* Why am I the only one around here who knows exactly what that dry-as-dust bookkeeper is planning? But Lucia doesn't deserve to always be the buffer between two brothers who can't stand each other. Better change the subject.

"Have we heard from the employment agency? Are they going to send us the girl?" At the end of last year, we decided to hire a kitchen assistant since the work has become too much for Rosa-Maria. The agency has only suggested a single applicant so far, and that was weeks ago. Montesimo is not exactly a dream location. My sister-in-law gives me a suspicious look. "Well? Did they write or didn't they?" I repeat in a friendly tone.

"All right, go ahead and change the subject. You're impossible!" Lucia snorts like a stubborn donkey and turns her back to me. I'm not a smoker, but I suddenly feel like having a cigarette. Nonna's pack of Marlboros, which she hid behind a box of cereal in the cupboard, is almost full. Everyone knew that Nonna smoked, but she enjoyed her secret so much that we just nodded whenever she lectured us on how unhealthy it was.

"I'm going to get some air."

"Maybe your kitchen help is waiting for you at the back door" is Lucia's snappy reply. She picks up the cheese shredder like she's planning to kill someone. In the end, only chunks of Parmesan bite the dust.

Hanna

The L-shaped back of the manor is more to my taste. Fresh gravel covers the ground from the terrace to the edge of the pasture. Wooden tables and chairs, wet from the rain, are spread among olive trees in terra-cotta planters. The countless hanging lanterns make me imagine the sea of lights this must be at night. I remember that I also liked the inside of the restaurant. Even though this Camini doesn't know anything about good cooking, I can't deny that he has style.

The trattoria looks closed. So they either went bust (likely, but too bad, because of what they must have spent on renovating this part) or are closed on Mondays. I'd like that.

The sun is just breaking through the clouds when I spot the perfect place to put the urn. Under the eaves, where firewood is stacked all the way to the dormers, I see an opening for a window. A dry place, and pretty, too. I set my suitcase down and open the side pocket.

"I don't believe it!"

Someone steps out from the semidarkness of the porch, almost giving me a heart attack. I've been so preoccupied with the urn that I haven't checked to see if someone was home.

"Where have you been? We've been waiting for you for weeks."

Hm . . . yes. Since I can't come up with a clever retort, I just smile. The man grinds out his cigarette, disposes of it in the flowerpot on the windowsill that I'd intended for Granny, and then ambles toward me. Tall for an Italian, he moves with the ease common to confident men. I hastily close the side pocket and step back. He stops and looks me over.

"I won't bite," he says curtly, waving away a dark curl on his forehead. Something about him seems familiar. I nod cautiously, feeling like I'm fifteen years old again and have been caught shoplifting—although I haven't been a teenager for years.

Claire whispers in my head, *"Introduce yourself, hand him the urn, and apologize. How hard can that be?"*

I smile again and hand him the mail, saying nothing. Something about this guy reminds me of . . . I think frantically. An actor? Maybe a singer? The man takes the letters with a frown. "I'm Fabrizio Camini. And you are?"

Claire giggles. *"Hanna Philipp, the woman who wrote a nasty article about your restaurant and then pilfered your granny."*

"Hanna," I whisper, eyes dropping to the ground. My heart beats like crazy. So this is Fabrizio Camini.

"Ooh là là!" Claire gushes. *"He's good looking."*

Shut up, Madame Durant.

"You're sopping wet," Fabrizio says. "That's all I need, you getting sick on your first day at work."

"Did he say work*?"* Claire screeches.

"Don't look so scared. Come in. I'll show you your room." He doesn't wait for an answer but picks up my suitcase and rolls—no, drags—it into the house. I stare after him, flabbergasted, my nose itching and body twitching.

"Achoo," I manage.

"Hanna," he calls from inside. "Dinner is in an hour. If you'd like to take a shower first, you better get your ass in here."

Above me, the clouds thunder their support. Studying the door, I race through all my options. A hot shower is tempting, even if Fabrizio is mistaking me for someone else. Can't I always clear up the mistake later and then throw myself remorsefully into the mud? I take one step, then another . . . and then I'm in the dark hallway. It smells of chestnuts and lamp oil.

Fabrizio

She's odd, this kitchen helper. Not as young as I thought at first—tiny wrinkles surround her childlike eyes. She's probably in her late twenties, but I'm not good at guessing. To my pleasant surprise, she doesn't seem to notice that her room is only seventy-five square feet, just barely enough space for a bed, a wardrobe, a small desk, and a chair.

"I know it's small, but it has its own bathroom, and the kitchen is just down the stairs. Anyway, you'll only be here to sleep." I realize too late that I'm making it sound like she'll be expected to work twenty-hour shifts. "Of course, the entire house is open to you . . . in your free time, and so . . ." I'm spluttering on, waving my hand. Lucia usually handles the staff, and now I know why—she's better at it. But the woman doesn't seem to hear me. When she looks at her suitcase, her jaw twitches.

"I must speak with you about something urgent, Signor Camini." Her cool, proud voice doesn't match her appearance at all, and her accent makes me curious. She's German—that's why she wants to discuss her employment contract right now. That's how the Germans are. Without a contract and health insurance, they won't touch a dishcloth.

"It doesn't have to be right away, does it? We wouldn't want raindrops on your contract." I eye her with amusement. It's touching how desperately she's trying to appear dignified, even though she looks like a wet cat. Even the prettiest dress isn't more than a wet rag after a downpour, and hers sticks to her body—a decidedly appealing body. She looks confused.

"I don't understand—"

"You're leaking." I point to the carpet, which is spotted with wet patches. Unfortunately, she doesn't seem to get my joke.

"I'm sorry. I will pay for the cleaning, of course."

So here's another unpredictable woman. For some strange reason, I'm disappointed. I thought she'd have a sense of humor.

"Don't be silly," I say, more brusquely than I intended. "Take your time cleaning up, and we can discuss your employment later. I'll be in my office, one floor up, third door to the left."

I nod briefly and leave the room without waiting for her answer. It's best to take care of this quickly and then return to business as usual. Besides, she probably won't be with us for long. Rosa-Maria is allergic to high heels and nail polish.

Hanna

This Fabrizio Camini is an unpleasant man. Really. I have an aversion to Italian macho men anyway, the types who undress every woman with their eyes, but on top of it, Fabrizio Camini has the charm of a log. *"You're leaking."* What man says something like that to a woman he doesn't know?

Snorting, I glance into the mirror above the washbasin. It's fogged from my shower, and it hangs at midget height. Because of my size, most people assume I'm German rather than Italian. Standing up straight, I can see only cleavage, which is as red from the hot shower as my face is.

I pad from the ten-square-foot bathroom into the bedroom and almost fall over my open suitcase. It takes up the entire space between the narrow bed and the wardrobe. It's Cinderella's quarters in here. I put on some jeans and a thin sweater, and then I look at my suitcase's outside pocket. I'm proud I've come so far, but the hardest part is still ahead of me—or, rather, up the staircase.

That reminds me of the way Fabrizio turns down the corners of his mouth, of his gloomy, espresso-colored—and suddenly I remember: the Italian at the airport. How did I miss it? So that's how the urn landed on the airport-restaurant windowsill. Sasha would call it a wicked coincidence. With a sigh, I lift the striped container from the side pocket, straighten, and breathe in deeply. Fabrizio Camini has obviously not recognized me, which might give me a tiny advantage.

"We'll jog his memory, won't we," I say, pressing Giuseppa against my chest as if she were my ally. "Let's hope he's happy about your return."

Fabrizio

Nonna was nineteen when she married Eduardo Camini, a coarse, taciturn man whom, if one believes Rosa-Maria, nobody dared address by his first name.

I study a framed picture of them. It's the model for the large oil painting, now in the living room, that my grandfather commissioned shortly after their wedding. I'm sure the painting cost a bundle—proof of how much the old gent must have loved his wife, though I'm not so sure the feeling was ever mutual. What drove the educated daughter of a well-to-do Northern Italian family into the arms of a fruit farmer who wasn't even particularly nice to her? Whatever it was that tied the sensitive Giuseppa to the sullen Eduardo—until the fatal combine accident that left her alone with her only son—Nonna never allowed any doubt that she had found in Eduardo exactly what she had been looking for.

My thoughts turn to Nonna's letter again. It's hidden under the desk pad because I could no longer stand to look at her handwriting.

I consider Alberto and the all-too-obvious attraction between him and Nonna that no one in the family ever mentioned. Nonna was a strictly Catholic love expert; she took her marital vows so seriously that she didn't allow another man under her sheets even after her husband's death. Did she fool anyone else—or only herself? "You must have had a damn bad conscience, Nonna," I mumble.

"Excuse me?" a clear voice replies.

Damn! I didn't hear a knock on the door. The kitchen help gives me a confused look. Her short black hair is still damp, and her green child's eyes haven't changed, but now her face is made up and her lips painted bright red. Her mouth is too narrow to be sensual. She steps in hesitantly, but before I can take my eyes off her boyish figure, my eyes get stuck just underneath her breasts. My brain fills with air. The new kitchen help is holding Nonna in her arms.

"You . . . you have . . ." I watch helplessly as the woman comes closer, puts Nonna on my desk, and sits down in the extra chair on the other side of the desk. Her back doesn't touch the back of the chair. She pauses before opening her red mouth. All I can think is that I preferred the wet-cat look.

"Signor Camini, I think this belongs to you." When I don't react—I'm unable to—she continues. "I am sorry that I didn't contact you sooner. But I thought I should bring you your grandmother in person."

"You aren't a kitchen assistant," I say stupidly. At least I can talk.

A narrow eyebrow shoots up. "My name is Hanna Philipp. You know me indirectly. I'm a food writer. I work for a gourmet magazine in Berlin that you are familiar with." She pauses again, and her face reveals what, if her overall appearance wasn't so damn composed, one might call a sliver of anxiety. "I wrote the article about your restaurant that made you sue us."

"You did?"

"I can understand that you're not pleased."

Not pleased? *Not pleased!* Does this woman have a screw loose?

"How did you get my grandmother?"

"We were in the same restaurant at the airport," she says. "In Berlin. You might not remember—I tripped over your briefcase."

"And?" I don't let on that I remember the haughty lady in the suit, the one who brushed me off like an insect, very well.

"The urn was on the windowsill," she says, as if this explains everything.

"And that gave you the right to take it?"

Finally her face gives away something approaching a guilty conscience. "I know it was wrong. It was . . . a spur-of-the-moment . . . a rash reaction."

"Just so I understand you correctly: you stole a four-pound porcelain container from a windowsill and claim it was an accident. Do you think I'm stupid?"

While she doesn't look at me, I still see no sign of remorse or dismay. "Signor Camini, I did bring it back to you. Don't you think you should at least show some gratitude?" she says aloofly.

I'm not quite sure what's happening. Fact is, she's said the worst thing she could possibly say. And then something comes out of my mouth that I never imagined saying.

Hanna

My heart thuds in my mouth when Fabrizio Camini leans back into his chair. This conversation is a nightmare. I hate Claire with all my heart for talking me into coming here. If only I had just written a letter.

"Keep the urn."

"Excuse me?" I stare at him in surprise, but there's no humor in his eyes.

"Keep it. I don't need it anymore." He crosses his arms and rocks his chair back and forth.

"Are you crazy? What am I supposed to do with a grandma who isn't even mine?"

"Not my problem." He grabs a pencil from his desk organizer and plays with it.

"That's not . . ." My voice fails me. "Signor Camini, I understand that you're mad as hell at me. But you shouldn't let your grandmother pay for it."

"Oh, I'm not letting my grandmother pay for it. You're paying for it."

The pencil snaps in half.

"Do I need to be Italian to get that?"

"Actually, all you need is a little bit of heart."

I breathe deeply. What an arrogant twerp. I have more than enough heart. Would I be here if I didn't? "Well, since you apparently believe I have none, could you at least give me a hint?" I say coldly, and I reach for the pencil half that rolled to my side of the desk. He puckers his lips, so well shaped that a woman might envy them.

"The fact of the matter is that you, not I, owe my grandmother something. After all, Nonna's condition had something to do with your ridiculous article, so it's not good enough to just bring her ashes home."

"It wasn't a ridiculous article. Some things might have been phrased somewhat harshly, and I'm sorry about that. But the article doesn't say anything that isn't true. With all due respect, Signor Camini, the food that day was more than underwhelming—to put it mildly."

"It was an accident."

"Oh," I say. "An *accident*."

"My cook was sick that night and the trattoria was supposed to be closed."

"But it just so happened that it wasn't."

"Right. Still, your article doesn't give an honest picture of our kitchen. I don't need you to tell me that my friend Carlo is an abominable cook."

"Your friend Carlo cooked? The village policeman?"

"You know him?" Fabrizio says.

"No, I—does it matter? What does any of this have to do with your grandmother?"

"I think you're deep in debt to her, and I'm generously offering you the opportunity to pay it off. I'll only take the urn after you've seen our business in a fair light, up close."

"You want me to eat at your trattoria again?" I ask.

"I want you to work for us, in the kitchen, for one month—without pay, obviously. Free room and board."

"That's ridiculous."

"I don't think so."

"I can't just not show up at my job for a month."

"You're a journalist. You can write anywhere, and we even have Internet access."

"How impressive. What if I still say no?"

"Do you have a fireplace at home?"

"Excuse me?" I say.

"The urn will look good on your mantelpiece. By the way, my grandmother loved Berlin." A cruel smile plays on his face, showing me that in the course of this absurd conversation I've lost whatever surprise advantage I had. He's on top, and I don't like it at all.

"What kind of person are you? Inside"—I point at the urn but then pull my finger back because it's trembling—"is your flesh and blood. I always thought family meant everything to Italians."

"Oh, I have plenty of feelings for my family," Fabrizio says. "But Nonna is already gone, according to all the ceremony and stuff. So the topic is officially over. Your article, however, endangers our family business. We live off tourists—including German ones. I'm sure you can imagine that I'm more interested in clearing our name than putting my grandmother's ashes where they belong."

An ominous silence settles on the room. The bad thing is that I kind of understand Signor Camini. What's worse is the realization that I ran into a trap.

"Just to play devil's advocate," I say slowly, "if I should decide to accept this horse trade and write another article about your restaurant, what happens if your kitchen still doesn't impress me?"

"That's the way it is. My bad luck."

"And you drop the charges against my magazine?"

"First things first. The urn, and then I'll consider your second request." He makes a dismissive gesture, as if the discussion is over. My fist wraps around the pencil stub.

"That's not a fair deal."

"We are in Italy, Signora Philipp. Italian business deals are seldom fair, but they're useful. Shake on it or don't. I've got nothing to lose. But you do."

"I'll stay for one week—max."

"Two—at least. But that's enough for now. You look as if you could use some dinner."

With shaking knees but head held high, I follow Fabrizio downstairs. I'm an adult. Nobody can keep me from leaving the urn on the next chest of drawers and escaping this "Italian deal" right now. I'd lose my job, but my pride would be intact. But my hand sticks to the railing as if it belongs there—who knows why. When we pass the door to my room, I take a deep breath, slip in, set the urn on the chair, and come out again. My chance to flee is gone. We continue down the stairs. Shoot.

Claire, in my head, laughs at me. *"Two weeks of kitchen duty—so what? It won't kill you, although you might break a few fingernails."* I roll my eyes, but before I can attack her with an imaginary reply, Fabrizio stops and steps aside. I feel his hand on my back and smell tangy aftershave. Then warm smells waft toward me. I almost fall into the kitchen when my high heel catches on the high threshold.

"There she is. Come here, girl. Sit on the bench." A round, red-faced woman in an apron takes my arm and directs me to sit on the bench at the window. Even though I resent the uninvited touch as much as I resent that she uses the familiar Italian way to address me, I plop down without resistance next to a pile of dime novels. It gives me a chance to look around surreptitiously. Judging by the soot on the ceiling and the smell of fire, we are in the main building and it's at least a hundred years old. Claire would be in seventh heaven here—just looking at the mosaic tiles and coal-burning stove of this picture-book kitchen would make a style-section photographer swoon.

"She looks like a boiled crab," says the old man at the head of the table. He doesn't take his eyes from the small television set, which is competing valiantly with the radio. Embarrassed, I touch my burning cheeks. People can always tell when I'm worked up.

"What a pretty house," I say politely. I notice a basket of fruit and vegetables on the counter. Unexpected, like the herbs in flowerpots on the windowsill.

"Old and about to collapse," the fat woman mumbles. She is stirring the contents of a huge pot. Without turning away from the TV, the old man shovels sugar into his coffee. He is the epitome of an Italian grandfather: slight of build, with drooping cheeks that would make a bloodhound proud. His sparse hair sticks to his skull as if he'd just taken off a hat.

"Alberto! *Non zucchero!*" A chubby woman hurries over, scolding. All I see at first are flying curls and strong eyebrows. Standing on tiptoes to reach the cupboard, she takes out a new cup and a packet of artificial sweetener. Then she gently wrests the first cup out of the old man's gouty hands. Alberto clicks his tongue as she sets the sugar container out of his reach. Only then does the woman look up, beaming at me.

"Forgive my impoliteness," she says, "but if one isn't fast enough, people around here send themselves to early deaths. And Rosa-Maria can't have her eyes everywhere, damn it."

At the stove, Rosa-Maria hisses, shakes her head, and crosses herself. Paying no attention to her, the young woman offers me her hand, which is rough but well groomed—with a perfect French manicure, like Claire's. "I'm Lucia Camini, married to the clan." She wiggles her gold-ringed finger with a grin. "When I realized what I'd gotten myself into, it was unfortunately too late."

"My name's Hanna." I take her hand slowly—it looks like a doll's hand in mine. Lucia's smile is infectious. It's soft and airy, like a silk scarf. I like her immediately.

"Her name's Hanna Philipp, to be precise." Fabrizio Camini, leaning against the door, looks at me with half-shut eyes. My throat feels dry.

"Hanna Philipp?" Lucia frowns. "Isn't that a German name?"

"Very common in Berlin." Fabrizio studies his nails. He wants to embarrass me, the bastard.

"But I thought you were our new kitchen help—and Italian." Lucia gives me a questioning look.

"And I am," I say firmly, determined not to be intimidated. "I am both—your new kitchen help and Italian, at least part-Italian. My mother is from this area, but she's lived in Germany for almost thirty years."

"Oh, and now you want to find your roots by working in our beautiful *Toscana*. How exciting!" Lucia says. My laugh sounds a bit faked, but she accepts the explanation, and Fabrizio seems to lose interest in annoying me further. I gratefully accept a glass of wine from Lucia as Fabrizio rolls up his shirtsleeves.

"Where's Marco hiding out?" he says. He drops a clump of golden dough onto a floured countertop. I'm about to answer by asking, "Who is Marco?" when I realize that he's talking to Lucia, who's now setting the table. I get up to help her.

"Marco isn't feeling well and he doesn't want to eat anything. Don't get up, Hanna. You're our guest tonight."

Fabrizio frowns. "That's strange. I thought he had every reason to be in a good mood." His sarcasm is unmistakable, and my reporter's ear perks up. A plate slides out of Lucia's hands and crashes on the table. Alberto giggles, probably something funny in his TV show, and the moment is over so fast that I decide I just imagined the tension between Fabrizio and Lucia. They are an interesting pair.

But I don't have time to speculate about who this seemingly moody Marco might be—presumably a teenager sulking in his room. I watch Fabrizio handle the pasta machine, fascinated by the way he rolls out the dough and then slides the fresh tagliatelle into boiling water. His movements are as smooth as if he does this every day, all day. I take a sip of red wine and stop in surprise. The wine is excellent, full and velvety with a touch of . . . apricots?

Lucia, finished with the table, sits down next to me and looks at me expectantly. "Tell me about your family here in Tuscany."

For a moment I consider lying. I peek at Fabrizio, who has stopped turning the pasta machine and is looking at me as inquisitively as Lucia is. I swirl my wine to gain time, noting the oily streaks—a sign of high alcohol content—left on the glass.

But Claire always tells me that I'm a miserable liar—and she's right. My situation is tricky enough. No need to complicate it more by making up stories that would quickly give me away. On the other hand, should I share with strangers that my mother almost throws up when she hears the word "Italy"?

"To be honest, I don't really know anything about my mother's family. I was born in Berlin and grew up there."

"But then you have to find them!" Lucia looks at me like I'm the heroine in a Hollywood drama. Even Alberto peels his watery eyes away from the screen, where a sparsely clad blonde is fishing bingo numbers out of a glass bowl.

"She has a pretty nose," he says hoarsely and blows his own nose into his napkin. I'm confused. He can't be talking about my nose, which is too long for my narrow face and has an ugly bump in the middle. As a teenager I pestered my parents about getting a nose job—maybe just to hurt my mom's feelings, since I inherited it from her—but eventually made my peace with it. Alberto returns to his bingo blondie, offering no explanation. Lucia looks at me compassionately and then continues her inquisition.

"So what do you do in Berlin?"

My face heats up when I realize that my next answer will cost me the sympathy of everyone in this house, assuming all of them know about the article. I glance at Fabrizio for help, but he is pointedly busy with the noodles. Why should I expect him to help? I shoot up a brief prayer and stammer, "Well, actually I'm . . . I mean, I'm not . . ."

"Don't be sad," Rosa-Maria interrupts me. "Lady Prudence has exactly the same problem as you." She sits down on my other side and points seriously to the dime-novel installment on top of the pile. The cover shows a curly-haired vixen, her frilly blouse sliding down too far, leaning toward a hulk in a Scottish kilt. "The poor girl has been searching for her family for years, and nobody knows that she's actually the heiress of Duffleton—even though Hugh MacKay has seen the birthmark on her left buttock."

Lady who? I look from the tasteless cover to the cook's enraptured expression. Then it clicks, and I almost can't hold back an explosion of laughter. Fortunately, Fabrizio speaks up.

"Spare us your pulp-fiction heroes, Rosa-Maria." He points to the pot of pasta. Rosa-Maria blushes like a schoolgirl and pushes Lady Prudence and the lusty highlander under the seat cushion. "Call Paolo. The pasta is almost ready."

. . .

I read once that the first lie is the mother of all those that follow. There's truth in this. While Lucia bombards me with questions for the next hour, I begin to understand what it's like to be on the other end of my interviews. Three glasses of red wine make it easier to heap lie upon lie, but harder to keep them straight.

"What village does your mother come from?"

"Montetresino." I hope that such a village doesn't actually exist.

"Never heard of it. Did you try to get information from the registration office?"

"Of course. But you know how it is with Italian bureaucracy . . ."

"You could also post an ad in *La Nazione*," Lucia says.

"I did, but it didn't get me anywhere, unfortunately."

"And your mother has no pictures or other documents from before? That's strange."

It's true. I don't know how many times I turned our apartment upside down while she was away at the women's shelter playing Mother Teresa. Yet I never found a single damn photo. It was as if her life had begun with my birth—or she'd destroyed all records with a fire ritual in the sink when she'd decided to break with her past.

"Unfortunately," I continue shamelessly, "there was a fire at our apartment building. Everything was destroyed."

Lucia covers her mouth with her hands. "How awful!"

"Yes, it was horrible."

"Doesn't your mother at least remember an address in this Montetresino, or acquaintances, friends, maybe neighbors?"

I shake my head. "She has partial amnesia." Seeing Claire's stunned expression in my mind, I barely manage to suppress a grin. "Because of the fire."

Lucia shakes her head and Rosa-Maria moans. Alberto and Paolo, Rosa-Maria's husband, eyeball me silently.

"Her mother lost her memory," Lucia explains, whereupon Alberto and Paolo nod and continue chewing. There you go—Claire can't call me a bad liar anymore. Fortunately Lucia doesn't ask any more questions about my mother's amnesia. "Tell me, are you married, Hanna?"

"Good god, Lucia," Fabrizio says tersely. "Give the signora a moment to eat. She'll be here for a while—you'll have plenty of time to drill her with questions." Now I notice that he looks not only irritable but exhausted, too.

"We all know that you don't give a damn about the people around you," Lucia shoots back.

"I do care about others. But that doesn't mean I have to worm every minute detail of their lives out of them."

"So tell me, what's Rosa-Maria's favorite color?" Lucia's eyes flash and she clenches her hands into doll-size fists. "What is Paolo's favorite drink? Alba's major? My mother's first name? All you care about are your damn apricots."

Fabrizio grimaces. "If you look at it that way, then you're right. You're not a nosy goat—you're just interested in people. And I'm ignorant because I'm trying to make a living for all of us. Am I allowed to finish my dinner now?"

"In this house everyone works to make a living for all of us—without exception." Lucia snorts. She really does resemble a stubborn little she-goat. I suddenly almost feel sorry for Fabrizio.

"Don't worry. I really don't mind the questions." But my cautious attempt to arbitrate goes nowhere. Lucia mumbles something and Fabrizio lowers his head. He presses his thumbs and index fingers against his temples.

"It's high time you produced something that would keep you busy with crying and diapers," he says in a low voice. It's not low enough, and Lucia's face darkens. Her muttering stops. I stare at Fabrizio in disbelief.

"That was really mean," I blurt. Fabrizio's eyes narrow.

"It's none of your business, Signora Philipp. It's a family matter. Besides, Lucia started it."

"No, it's not just a family matter," I say. "It's a matter of attitude—your attitude toward women, Signor Camini, which should be knocked out of you with a rolling pin."

Fabrizio looks irritated. "I don't have any—"

"Let it be, Hanna. Fabrizio didn't mean it that way."

I glance at Lucia in surprise. She's defending him? I draw a sharp breath. "I think he meant exactly what he said. And I think he owes you an apology."

"Considering that you've only been here for two hours," Fabrizio says, "you're walking on pretty thin ice. But there's more Italian in you than one would suspect at first glance." The corners of his mouth twitch, which makes me even angrier.

"Stop being so condescending," I say, and then bid my job good-bye. It would have been so nice—but I guess I don't have to worry anymore how I'll survive two weeks of kitchen duty.

Instead of firing me, though, Fabrizio starts to laugh as if I've told a good joke.

Rosa-Maria rumbles. "Peace and quiet at the table! Nonna would be ashamed if she saw how you're attacking each other." Embarrassed, I study my hands. Maybe I was a little too aggressive.

"Nonna is dead," Fabrizio says coldly. "She's not going to slap our wrists."

Now everyone's eyes are on the plates while Fabrizio's anger rolls through the deadly silent kitchen like an oversized soap bubble.

Alberto claps his hands and I start. "Rosa-Maria, put the rabbit on the table before it runs away from these quarreling children. I'm hungry."

Now I'm more than confused. This family personifies every single Italian cliché, but it's strange, too. While I plan the best way to escape into the toilet and from there to the rainy nowhere outside, Rosa-Maria clears the pasta plates from the table and with them all the arguments. Suddenly everyone's chatting and gesturing wildly. Fabrizio and Lucia are nudging each other and smiling as if they hadn't bickered at all. Used to hour-long reconciliation talks, I almost feel betrayed. I'd never have dared end a discussion with Professor Günther Philipp with a curt "I'm hungry."

A new plate appears in front of me, this one the main course, and Rosa-Maria puts the roasting pan on the table. The aromas of meat, wine, and apricots overwhelm me. Tre Camini must have a special relationship with the fruit—and if I disappear now, I won't find out what it is. I peek at the clock on the wall and then at the window. It's pitch-black outside. And I've definitely had one too many.

I reach for my fork. The meat practically falls off the bone when I lightly poke it. I try to resist, but my mouth starts to water. This dish is miles away from what I ate at the trattoria. Was Fabrizio really telling me the truth about this Carlo?

"I hope you like rabbit," Fabrizio says.

"Of course. I mean, I love it," I add when I see Fabrizio's forehead wrinkle. My god, this man is like a powder keg with four fuses. Looking at him defiantly, I bring the fork to my mouth . . . and my eyes widen in surprise.

"Not bad, is it?" Fabrizio says innocently. His eyes bore into me while I take a second bite, and then a third, just to let him hang. The food journalist in me notes that the sweetness harmonizes exactly with the rabbit, as it would with chicken, and that the method of braising the meat with spices on minimal heat for hours perfectly marries the flavors. It's incredibly delicious. I have to fight the desire to imitate Alberto, who's sucking the marrow from a rabbit bone with abandon. I set my fork and knife next to my plate very properly.

"Do you slaughter them yourself?" I ask to win time. Alberto stops with his bone, and Paolo almost chokes on his drink. He quickly puts the wineglass back on the table. They exchange a glance.

"Why else would we breed rabbits?" Alberto says to Paolo, who nods.

"Well, it's outstanding." I'm smiling at everyone, including Fabrizio, slightly defiantly. He's rocking in his chair, his legs apart, obviously satisfied.

"It's one of Nonna's old family recipes," Lucia says quietly and pats Rosa-Maria's back. Fabrizio's chair legs crash down on the tiles.

"As always, nothing but the best for our guests." The word "guests" rolls over his tongue like the bitter pit of a cherry. It's obvious that he enjoys my presence here about as much as I do.

"Hanna?"

I stop, one hand on the railing for support. Shortly after the espresso, Paolo and Rosa-Maria said good-bye and left for the village. Fabrizio took advantage of the bustle of their departure to beat it out, too, and Alberto followed him like a shadow. Then I sneaked out of the kitchen after two huge, exaggerated yawns and a stammered "I'm dead tired . . . Thank you so much for dinner." But now the whisper in the dim staircase destroys my hope of an elegant escape. I turn around slowly. Lucia stands at the foot of the stairs, looking at me with sparkling eyes.

"Yes?"

She flies upstairs and grabs my hand. I fight the urge to withdraw it. Lucia has been very nice to me, and I've been impolite enough for one evening.

"Please promise me something."

I look into her rosy face. This doesn't bode well. "I'm sorry if I was impolite to Fabrizio . . ."

"No, you were absolutely wonderful!" Lucia's voice trembles. "It was great how you defended me. You know—in this house . . . well, the Caminis are a little old fashioned."

As if I hadn't noticed that. The word "pigheaded" would be more fitting for Fabrizio.

"I just wanted to thank you and . . ." Lucia stops and hugs me. Her cheeks are damp, as if she'd been crying. "We're going through a hard time right now. Our Nonna died recently, and she . . . we . . . we're all out of balance. Not quite ourselves."

Out of balance—an understatement. Luckily, since she's still hugging me, Lucia doesn't see my eye roll. I gently disentangle myself.

"That's all right," I say. Now she's actually crying. "What do you want me to promise?"

"That you'll stay."

Shoot! "I—"

"No, don't say anything. Tonight wasn't normal. Usually we treat each other very lovingly. Give us another chance."

Now what am I supposed to say?

"I just have this feeling about you," Lucia says. "I think you'd be good for us. And right now, we really could use someone who's good for us."

Damn. This isn't fair. I'm drunk, about to start my period, and unable to keep a thought in my head longer than a nanosecond.

In my head, I hear Claire whisper, *"Of course you'll stay."*

"Hanna?" Lucia says.

"Did you practice that look in front of a mirror?" The words escape my mouth—I can't help it.

"Each and every day," she says with a smile. It's strange how it feels as if I'd known her forever, not just for a few hours.

So, fine. Two weeks of kitchen duty.

With any luck, I'll then be able to get rid of the miserable urn and save my job at the same time. After that, I'm out of here. I take a deep breath and cross my fingers behind my back.

"Of course I'll stay. As long as it's . . . necessary."

In my opinion, life's a bitch.

Chapter Five

Fabrizio

When the sun rises over Montesimo, it stands for a moment above the hill like an overripe apricot and casts a lilac hue on the morning mist. The sun hangs there for minutes on end, as if contemplating whether or not to actually rise that day. This daily spectacle would blow away nature lovers, but I ignore it out of habit. Instead, I survey the young trees, which, after their May bloom, are carrying their first fruits: reddish-yellow apricots, deliciously sweet smelling, that give when you lightly press them with your thumb. They're ready for harvest.

Straightening, I squint. Paolo is already out here with the tractor. If I had to describe our foreman in one sentence, I would say he lives to take care of the fields. He's not interested in what income they generate. It's the view of arrow-straight rows of trees and furrows that makes him happy.

In the outer orchard, I see men carrying huge baskets on their backs. They are Polish fruit pickers, super punctual and as sturdy as our mules. There's no better harvest help available in all of Italy, and for sure not in Montesimo.

I was eight years old when my father first sent for Polish helpers—despite strong resistance from his family and the villagers. But Frederico Camini's stubbornness, equal to his father Eduardo's, paid off. The workers were decent and hardworking, and they loved Italian food. So even Nonna buried her prejudices and asked them to stay for espresso after they devoured Rosa-Maria's pasta. Ever since then, the foreign language and coarse laughter have filled our orchards every early summer until the fruit is harvested and the days are hot and dry.

Today the earth is spongy under my feet when I enter the orchard. Crouching, I pick up a clump of soil. It smells peaty and feels soft and damp, exactly as it should. *"Like a rotund woman, ready for love"*—that's what Carlo would say. What an idiot. I smile, but it doesn't reach my heart. Everything points to a good harvest, but then again, you never know.

A figure in a jogging suit, head lowered, approaches fast. He puffs like an ambitious locomotive. I have no idea why he's running through the hills rather than helping Paolo or using his energy for other estate work. I see him long before he notices me, and when Marco finally lifts his head, it's too late to change direction.

"Good morning, Fabrizio," he gasps, jumping up and down. Sweat glistens along his receding hairline. I can't hide my annoyance, even though I promised myself only a few days ago to be more tolerant toward my little brother. I search for something friendly to say.

"You look like your mother-in-law is chasing you. Is there something you're trying to prove with your constant running around?" Honestly, I meant it to sound nicer than it came out. Marco scowls. He's never had a sense of humor and definitely could never laugh at himself, which made him an easy target during recess, no matter how often I defended him with my fists.

He hops up and down again, higher this time. "It's called exercise. People do it to become fit and relaxed. And so it's not obvious how much they like to eat." He checks out my belly.

"Harvesting apricots accomplishes the same thing—with additional results," I say, pulling in my stomach. Marco frowns but at least slows his jumping.

"Did you read the midyear report I wrote?" Typical Marco—he changes the subject as soon as he feels threatened.

"What midyear report?"

"So you did read it?"

There is strength in silence. Marco raises an eyebrow.

"That's all you have to say?" he says.

I have a lot to say. But most of all, I want to wring his neck like I did with the soup chicken the day before yesterday, so he'll stop pushing his calculator down my throat.

"There's nothing to say," I reply.

"So you want to continue supporting the unprofitable farm with the meager profits from our hotel and restaurant business? It's not a viable solution."

"What are you talking about? We rent out a few rooms—it's definitely not a hotel."

"No, Fabrizio. You're the one who's clueless. Economically, the only decision—"

"You're not the one making decisions here," I say. "Father would never have allowed us to get rid of the apricot orchards—and neither would your grandmother, by the way."

"You conveniently forget that father saw your beloved apricots for the last time twenty years ago—just before he abandoned us," Marco snaps. "And Nonna is dead."

"We are not selling any land, not to the golf club and not to your real-estate shark—not even if they triple the offer. Tre Camini is an agricultural enterprise, and I have no plans to turn it into a tourist trap."

"You'd rather dream about making an international killing with your wrinkly organic apricots. Oh yeah, brother, it's clear who wants to prove what to who," Marco says with suppressed anger in his voice.

"Just continue with business as usual and drag your family into the abyss with you because you can't abandon the ideas of our crazy father who never got over the death of his wife. But thanks to Nonna, if we're lucky, things will change soon. In twelve months, to be exact, when I'll be making the decisions around here."

"Watch what you say," I whisper. A smile plays around Marco's lips while I clench my fists in my pants pockets and fight the temptation to beat him black and blue. No one else can make my blood boil as he does.

Marco starts to jog in place again. He turns his back to me, but then dances a few steps toward me. "Mother, Father, Nonna—I keep the dead out of it. That's why I'm so good at what I do. That reminds me: Isn't it time you looked for a wife?"

I'm not sure if it's what Marco said or what he didn't say, but my last string of restraint snaps with a zing, and I pounce on him, snarling like a wild animal.

Hanna

I can't remember ever seeing a more beautiful lilac-colored sunrise. Honestly, I don't remember ever seeing the sun rise at all. I'm not a morning person—not a night owl, either. I need ten hours of sleep—preferably from ten at night until eight in the morning. I stuck to this schedule even while I was a student, in sharp contrast to the trend of tipsily emerging at dawn from one Berlin bar or another and then consuming gallons of coffee during lectures. I didn't make many friends with my attitude, but my final grades were superb. Friends are overrated, anyway. If you want to advance in life, rely on yourself.

I rub my eyes, which are struggling with the unusual hour as much as the rest of my body is. I see people outside, but it wasn't their voices or the tractor that woke me.

The window latch is stuck and takes some work before it opens with a squeak. Cool, dewy air blows into my face when I lean out, searching for the ugly noise that woke me and is still destroying the morning symphony of birds like an out-of-tune instrument.

I can't detect a rattling motorbike or a squealing pulley in the yard, but I do see a white rooster standing on the stone trough in front of the barn and trumpeting loudly at his image in the water.

"Life in the countryside," I mumble. I see no reason to imitate the villagers, so I grab my cell phone and then dive under the covers again. Two missed calls from Claire. She'll be happy that I fixed the situation. I call her back with a grim smile.

"Buon giorno, signora!"

Startled, I almost drop the phone as the door bangs open and Rosa-Maria's chubby face appears above a tray of coffee. She manages to shut the door with a kick hidden by her dress and not spill a drop.

"Morning," I stammer. I sit up and kill the phone call with shaky fingers. Rosa-Maria puts the tray on the bed and puts her hands on her hips.

"You're up. Bravo!" She sounds friendly but so energetic that I say good-bye to the outrageous idea of sleeping in.

"How couldn't I be up?" I grin and hope I don't sound tense. "I had no choice with the rooster down there."

"A rooster?" Rosa-Maria looks at the window.

"Yes, the white rooster—down in the yard," I say, since I'm suddenly not sure if my Italian isn't a bit rusty. Rosa-Maria snorts and waves a hand.

"Oh. Vittoria. She isn't a rooster. She's a hen."

"But he—she crows. I didn't know hens do that."

"Believe me, you don't have to be a rooster to behave like one," Rosa-Maria says, tapping her forehead and smiling mysteriously. I have no idea what she's talking about, but I smile back. I catch a whiff of the coffee and glance at the porcelain mug—then immediately feel uncomfortable. The pattern matches the ashtray I swiped the last time I was here.

"That's very pretty china."

"The tourists think so, too, and pilfer whatever they get their hands on," Rosa-Maria says. She removes the pillow from behind my back and fluffs it up.

"It's really nice of you to bring me coffee," I say.

"You'll get served coffee in bed as long you're considered a guest. When I stop bringing it, you'll know you've passed your probation period. So don't get used to it." She starts to fold the blanket. Now I'm sitting in front of her in my skimpy nightgown.

"You don't have to do that," I protest, pulling at the few inches of material that barely stretch to my knees. Rosa-Maria eyes my plunging neckline, and then points with pursed lips toward the bathroom.

I jump out of bed, grab my jeans from the back of the chair, and hurry into the tiny bathroom, glancing at my suitcase on the way and hoping Signora Camini forgives me for stashing her with my underwear. But as long as Rosa-Maria waltzes in and out of my room as she pleases, I think it's safer to keep the urn hidden.

The staircase looks much friendlier in the daylight. Morning sun shines through a stained-glass window in the dormer, creating rainbow drops on my hand as I hold on to the railing. My knees are wobbly—the result of either yesterday's alcohol or the unfamiliar time of day. Fortunately, no Italian woman with smoldering eyes waits for me at the bottom to make me agree to things I don't want to do.

Instead, I see a man sitting on the wooden bench next to the wall, huffing and puffing and lacing his jogging shoes. His fingers tremble, and the dark sweat stain on his bent back tells of a strenuous final spurt.

"Buon giorno," I call out, and I startle when the greeting echoes loudly through the annex. The man looks up.

"Buon giorno, Hanna."

So my presence is known around here. That's disconcerting. I hate it when strangers know my name.

He inspects me. "You're up early for a city girl." His narrow mouth turns up into a smile, but it immediately disappears as he dabs his lower lip, which I now see is cut open.

"Did you fall?" As I come down the stairs, the last step reacts with an ugly creak. "Are you hurt?"

"Don't worry about it. Did you sleep well?"

"Before I answer such a question, shouldn't you introduce yourself?" I say politely.

"How inconsiderate of me." He smiles wryly. "Marco Camini, black sheep of the family and husband of the wonderful, though chatty, Lucia. She couldn't stop singing your praises." He offers his hand, and I take it hesitantly. It's cool and sweaty.

"You're Marco? I thought—"

"What did you think?" His square face is wary now.

"Nothing," I say, smiling. "We missed you last night—at dinner, I mean."

With a scornful laugh, Marco presses the sleeve of his jacket to his lip. "You don't know my brother yet. Believe me, he didn't miss me."

"Fabrizio is your brother?"

"You're surprised?"

"You don't resemble each other," I say, embarrassed, and look away. Marco's eyes are light brown, almost like copper, and much warmer than his brother's inscrutable and nearly black eyes.

"Our differences go deeper than that. But let's talk about you. You don't look like kitchen help, either."

Grateful for the change of subject, I match his teasing tone. "You don't think?"

"Your hands are too soft, and besides, you're too pretty," he says with a wink. I really can't see a resemblance to Fabrizio at all. Honestly, I'm relieved that Lucia is married to Marco and not Fabrizio—such a lovely, warm woman would wither by his side. I'm sure of that.

"You got me," I say. Lowering my voice, I add, "Please don't give me away. I actually work for German foreign intelligence and I'm on the run."

Marco nods. "That's what I thought. You look as if you're on the lam, or at least on a secret mission."

"Really?" I force a laugh. "Then I'll have to work on my undercover skills."

"Don't worry. I won't tell." Raising three fingers, he adds, "Scout's honor!"

"I'm relieved, Signor Camini. And as an insider, you can probably tell me where I can dig up a croissant before starting kitchen duty."

With a conspiratorial grin, Marco says, "A clever plan, Signora Secret Agent. You'll need sustenance. Just a bit of advice"—he nods in the direction of the kitchen—"don't ever call our cornetti 'croissants' in there, or Rosa-Maria will bite your head off. It would be a pity."

By now I'm confident of one thing: Marco and Fabrizio have absolutely nothing in common.

My amused smile lasts all the way to the kitchen door, where it collapses in a fraction of a second. Steam floods the room, and, as I go inside, I step on an open cookbook, one of many strewn across the stone tiles. Notebooks and loose leaves of paper, kitchen utensils, dirty dishes, and leftovers pile on the counters. White footprints lead from a spilled bag of flour all the way to the stove, where four pots bubble menacingly. Fabrizio Camini is sitting cross-legged next to an open cupboard, leafing through a leather-covered notebook.

"Look where you're going." He snaps the notebook shut, tosses it into a corner, and opens another. I carefully navigate through the chaos and manage to reach the stove undamaged. There, I push away a loose piece of paper before it can catch fire. I squint at the well-formed handwriting. It's a recipe for a Ligurian eggplant pâté.

"What in the world are you doing? Is this the new way to cook Italian? Where's Rosa-Maria?"

"In the village. Went shopping." Fabrizio looks up but hardly notices me. His three-day-old beard covers a third of his face already, and it looks as if a sleepless night has pressed his espresso-colored eyes even deeper into his skull. One eye is bloodshot and swollen. When I realize I'm staring, I face the stove and turn off all the knobs. I drag away the pot of boiling water, scattering dancing drops across the range.

"If you plan to close your restaurant, you could choose a safer way than torching its kitchen," I mutter and let go of the pot handle before it burns me.

"For example?" is his preoccupied response. He pulls out another notebook from the pile on his right. The pile collapses and spills yet another paper avalanche across the floor.

"Well, you could poison your guests with spinach macaroni. Ribollita with frozen vegetables would also work in a pinch."

"I already explained it was an accident. We don't use frozen products," Fabrizio says calmly—too calmly for my taste.

"You don't?"

"What's your problem, Signora Philipp?"

"No problem at all, Signor Camini. I'm just the kitchen help." I bat my eyelashes, and Fabrizio frowns. If I were artistic, I could sketch that expression with my eyes closed by now. "And it looks like a pigsty in here. I didn't think my first day of work would be filled with sorting papers and scrubbing the kitchen."

Fabrizio studies me. "What exactly did you expect?"

Is it my imagination, or is a smile hiding somewhere in his eyes? I throw my arm to the stove. "I thought this was a trattoria. So how about cooking?"

"Cooking," he says, giving me an almost suggestive once-over, "in *that*?"

"What's wrong with my clothes?"

"You're wearing high heels." He straightens his legs and stands up.

"They're slingback pumps."

"Thanks for clearing that up. Your blouse also looks rather expensive, by the way."

"And what exactly is your problem with it, Signor Camini?"

"I don't have a problem, but you'll have one." Fabrizio shrugs, sweeps the papers from the counter, and heaves a bucket of onions onto it—a damn big bucket. "Since you suggested ribollita, Rosa-Maria will need onions, peeled and quartered."

I stare at the container. It's filled to the brim. "I'm supposed to peel onions? Don't you have some help to do that?"

Fabrizio looks irritated. "The help is right in front of me. Or did you forget what we agreed?"

"There was no mention of slavery," I retort. Fabrizio takes two steps toward me. The wrinkle in his forehead is so pronounced now that his heavy eyebrows are almost touching each other. I instinctively move away until my behind bumps against a cupboard.

"Well, signora: welcome to an Italian kitchen. Despite your erroneous assumption, vegetables are still prepared by hand here—your job. Furthermore, I own this trattoria, and you are my kitchen help for the next two weeks. If I want you to peel onions or scrub the stove, that's what you are going to do—until your fingers bleed, if necessary. If that's below you, well, you know the way out."

"I do indeed!" I snap. Straightening my back, I march in the direction of his pointing finger. Unfortunately, my heels slip on the scattered papers, so I skid less than elegantly toward the door.

"You know where to find me if it starts to rain. And don't forget to take my grandmother along," he shouts after me in that mocking tone of his. I respond with a spontaneous gesture, not even turning around.

"So what if it rains—bite me! And your grandmother can shove it, too."

Only when I'm back in my Cinderella chamber, cheeks still burning, do I realize in horror that I just gave Fabrizio Camini the finger.

Fabrizio

It must be jinxed. There's not a corner in this damn house that I haven't turned upside down, but Nonna's recipe book is nowhere to be found. I did find another secret stash of cigarettes and sweets—thirty years too late. When we were kids, we'd never have guessed that she hid chocolate bars under a loose floorboard in the pantry. I pocketed the foil-wrapped bar but returned the box to its hiding place, as if I'd get in trouble if I didn't.

Lucia looks up from the reservation book when I enter the restaurant. The shutters are still rolled down. One hangs crooked and the sun shines through a broken blade. Lucia has turned the reading lamp on and looks strangely forlorn at the front desk. But the wrinkles around her mouth smooth into a smile as soon as she sees me.

"You look like you've done something wrong," she says.

I touch the bar in my pocket but shake my head. "I'm looking for Nonna's notebook, the green one with the red ribbon. Have you seen it?"

Lucia looks at me over her reading glasses. "Isn't it in the kitchen cupboard with all the others?"

"Hm."

"So that's a no? Why don't you take one of the others? Nonna filled at least a hundred notebooks with recipes. I'm sure you'll find what you want in one of them."

"But I need the green book!" I sound harsher than I intended. Lucia seems irritated but shrugs it off and looks again at the reservations. Names fill the whole page. That's unusual on an off-season weekday.

"I didn't see it," she says. "Were you in the kitchen? How is Hanna coming along?"

"Who?" I ask, and peer at the sideboard behind the bar. Nonna would definitely be capable of hiding the notebook among tablecloths and napkins.

"You're kidding, aren't you? Hanna Philipp, our new kitchen help. Hello?"

"She left." Why does Lucia have to remind me, just when I forgot about that arrogant woman? I only hope she was decent enough to leave Nonna here. Otherwise I'll have another problem.

"She what? What did you do to her, Fabrizio Camini?"

"I didn't do anything to her. I'm not interested in an eccentric city girl's moods. Signora Philipp had a choice, she chose, and that's the end of it." I pull on the uppermost drawer of the sideboard. It's locked. Lucia is shaking her head.

"I don't believe it!"

"Do you have the key for this drawer?"

"How is she eccentric, to use your word? What did you say to her?"

"She was going to work in high heels and a silk blouse."

"What about a friendly suggestion and an apron?"

"Oh, I did make a suggestion. That's when she told me I could kiss her ass. Now, do you have the key or not?"

"You'll apologize," Lucia says. I laugh out loud. That'll be the day. "I know you, Fabrizio, and I know exactly what tone you used with her. You are going to apologize."

"The key."

"First, you'll put things right with Hanna."

"Come on, Lucia. The woman's miles away by now."

She looks at me silently. Then she buries her key chain deep in her apron pocket, quick as a flash, and lifts her chin. "In that case, you'll have to get in the car and bring her back."

Chapter Six
Fabrizio

After two cigarettes, I reach two conclusions. First of all, I should stop smoking. Second, you can't win against a determined woman who has a key in her apron.

I kick an empty cola can across the yard. It clatters against the fountain and scares a few chickens. Vittoria puffs up her chest feathers and flutters toward the can with claws spread, as if she's defending the other hens against a monster. I watch for a while as she battles the innocent can and decide to ask Paolo to finally turn the crazy beast into soup.

I crumple up the empty cigarette pack and pull out Nonna's chocolate from my pants pocket. It's soft, melted by my body temperature, and sweet.

I hear Nonna say, *"Bread for the body; chocolate for the soul. Remember that, Fabrizio."*

I'd rather you gave me a hint—where is that recipe that was supposed to make Tre Camini immortal, Nonna? All right, all right. I'm exaggerating. I'd settle for unforgettable. I squish the rest of the chocolate around in my mouth and put the golden foil and the cigarette pack into the flowerpot on the windowsill—the witness to my sins.

Then I head out to find the second woman who managed to get me off course today.

I didn't expect to find the guest room empty. Not sure what to do next, I peep into the wardrobe, as if Frau Philipp would have the ridiculous idea of hiding in it. Another remnant from my childhood—no wardrobe was ever safe from Marco when he came home from school with a bloody nose. Once, we searched for him for hours before finding him in Nonna's hamper—folded up like a pocketknife, his face tear-streaked and snotty.

The wardrobe is empty except for a few hangers. For a minute I consider just forgetting about this woman *and* the sideboard key, but then I realize that I don't see any trace of Nonna in the room, either. That's when determination replaces my resignation. I slam the wardrobe door shut, fish the car key from my pocket, and hoof it to the truck.

Gravel flies in all directions as I back the pickup truck into the yard and turn it toward the driveway, which I drive down at walking speed. After narrowly escaping a car accident, Nonna hated nothing more than driving too fast. Soon I regret this old habit, since it ruins my chance to run over Vittoria, who's blocking the iron gate. I brake and honk, but Vittoria calmly continues to peck at worms in the middle of the road. How in the world did she get from the yard all the way down here in fifteen minutes? I lower the window.

"Beat it, you stupid chick."

Her comb seems to expand, and she clucks aggressively.

"Shoo, shoo!" I hiss and rev the motor, feeling stupid. Vittoria tilts her little head and eyes me. It's almost eerie. She seems to be considering her next step. I honk—without results.

"Fine, I gave you a choice." I shift into first gear and press down the gas pedal but don't release the clutch. Unbelievable. I seem unable to actually run her over. But Vittoria's bored of the game now. In her chicken universe, a soda can is apparently far more dangerous than a truck. She hops to the side of the road, cackling loudly, and I finally shoot out of the gate. I watch her flutter her wings in the rearview mirror. That's what you get when you name your food. I need another cigarette.

I almost faint when I turn back to the road ahead of me. Slamming on the brakes again, I manage to stop just inches away from the yellow Ford Transit. The breath escaping my lungs sounds like a bike's inner tube after a nail puncture.

"Hey, Fabrizio! Is the devil chasing you, and are you planning to take your truck to hell with you?" a clear voice rings out. Ernesto Zanolla is sitting on a stone marker at the side of the road, with a sandwich bag on his knees and a thermos in his hand.

"Why would you park in the middle of the street to eat breakfast?" I bark through the window. The shock throbs all the way to my toes. Ernesto grins, takes a large bite of salami, and lifts the cup to his thick lips.

"Careful what you say, or I'll tell Carlo that you ignore the speed signs."

"What speed signs, Signor Ma-a-a-yor?" I stretch out his title on purpose—I want my answer to drip with sarcasm. When they repaved Via Capelli, the town coffers were so empty they could hardly pay for the asphalt. Not a cent was left for traffic signs. It was a personal defeat for Ernesto, and his idea to print cardboard signs didn't bring him much glory, either. They vanished in the last rains.

"Don't insult an official, my son. Besides, the mayor's shift doesn't start until this afternoon."

"Well, then I can't insult him, can I?"

"Mail carriers are civil servants, too." Ernesto taps his mailman's cap, looking like a ten-year-old allowed to play with his father's electric trains for the first time. "Do you want a panino? I've one left, with pancetta."

"Thanks, but I'm in a hurry." I glance down the street. No trace of Signora Philipp.

"What's the matter with today's young men? Not one of them has time to chat a little with an old man." Ernesto takes a sip of coffee and swishes it around in his mouth. "Shouldn't you be in the kitchen with *bella* Rosa? The restaurant's open, isn't it? Rita will kill me if she can't prance around in her new dress tonight. The times we live in . . . One click, and a dress from Milan arrives at the door. And who pays for it? Poor Ernesto." He pretends to look worried.

"Did you see a woman with a rolling suitcase, by chance?" I'm sure the Signora Kiss-My-Ass couldn't have walked far in half an hour. Ernesto chews thoughtfully.

"A pretty woman?"

I shrug. "Just a woman. Late twenties."

"That's the best description you can come up with?" Ernesto snorts.

"About five foot seven, slim, short black hair, long nose, and green eyes. Like a mermaid. Happy?"

Ernesto's eyes flash. "Ah, Signora Hanna. Why didn't you say so right away?"

"You know her?" I pretend to be surprised, but I'm actually not. Signora Philipp makes an impression.

"Great girl! She likes to talk, but always seems to be in a hurry as well." Ernesto sighs and scratches his head. "She reminds me of someone, but I can't put my finger on it."

"I didn't ask *how* she is, but where she is."

"Did you lose her?" Ernesto tilts his head. "You don't run into a woman like that too often—especially not at such an appropriate moment." He winks, obviously amused by his sly reference. "What did you do to annoy her, you fool?"

"Ernesto, all I want to know is whether you've seen her. If you plan to bring your wife for dinner tonight, stop giving me rambling explanations."

Now we're finally getting somewhere. If there's one person who can rattle our good mayor, it's his wife. Rita Zanolla. She has a sharp tongue, that woman.

"Well, I certainly saw her yesterday."

"And today?"

Ernesto doesn't answer but thoughtfully starts to pick his teeth with his thumbnail. So I have no choice but to head to the Amalfi bar. Hanna can't have made it past our village innkeeper without being forced to down his infamous espresso. No nonlocal ever does. I wave Ernesto away and put the truck in reverse so I can drive around his dilapidated vehicle. The passenger side scrapes against a juniper bush that almost reaches the road. I need to tell Paolo to trim it. Ernesto finishes his dental hygiene, stretches, and yawns widely, revealing several gold teeth.

"Say hi to Salvatore. And if you find Signora Hanna, bring her to the town hall. I owe her a meal."

Hanna

"You can come out now. He's gone."

I fight my way through the prickly juniper bush, feeling embarrassed. A grinning Ernesto watches me struggle with my suitcase. The truck came so fast down the driveway that my only escape was to push the suitcase and myself into this horrible hedge. I hope nothing happened to Giuseppa.

"I guess you finished your little matter at Tre Camini?" Ernesto asks me when I finally stand next to him, totally out of breath.

"I did," I say, and remove some juniper needles from my hair.

"The little matter doesn't seem to have been pleasant."

I look at him sideways, trying to figure out if he's making fun of me, but he just studies the road ahead with a straight face.

My anger dissolves as quickly as it overcame me.

"Oh, Ernesto." Exhausted, I plunk down onto the grass-covered shoulder of the road.

"Tsk, tsk, tsk," says Ernesto. "That bad?"

"Do you have a job for me?"

"I understand."

For some strange reason his empathy is comforting, even though he has no idea what I'm talking about. I don't know myself why this Fabrizio gets so far under my skin. Not even Daniel could make me mad like that, and we were in a relationship, albeit a brief one. I pull out a blade of grass and chew on it.

"How well do you know Signor Camini, Ernesto?"

"I've known both of them since they were that high." Ernesto holds his hand against his hip. "They were up to no good and always looked out for each other. But that's not what you are interested in, is it?"

"Not only," I mumble.

"Fabrizio is a good guy. His heart's in the right place."

"That's hard to believe."

"Are you sure that he's your problem?"

I look up in surprise. "What makes you think I have a problem?"

"You already looked sad yesterday."

Did I? But I'm not at all—sad. I'm furious. At least I was until five minutes ago.

"You see, Signora Hanna, I have no idea what happened between you and Fabrizio. But I have got eyes, and I see two unhappy people.

The question is"—Ernesto pauses, looking for the right phrase—"whether that makes any sense?"

"Whether it makes sense to be unhappy?"

"You're a fast learner."

But I don't actually understand.

"Today's young people overcomplicate their lives," Ernesto says. "They want to know all, see all, and be all. They turn this way and that because there are opportunities everywhere. It makes them dizzy, and soon they can't see the forest for all the trees. All they need to do is take the path that leads them to their goal. Did your path bring you to your goal, Signora Hanna? If it did, I'll take you to the village. I had your pretty car towed to Stefano Gosetti's garage. But if the answer is no, you should take your suitcase and go back to Tre Camini."

Only after an eternity of listening to the birds twitter and insects buzz does it strike me that my mouth is wide open. I'll be damned—a philosophizing mail carrier.

I slowly get up, taking extra time to beat the dust from my pants. Is it really that simple? I imagine Claire gratefully wringing her hands—and Lucia begging me with her eyes. Besides, I took Giuseppa with me. It seemed logical at the time, since apparently she wasn't welcome there, either. But now, the urn is a good reason to rethink my hasty departure—and not just because I don't have a mantelpiece. Unsure, I look at the cypress-lined driveway leading back to Tre Camini.

"I believe there's some work waiting for me up there," I finally say, sighing loudly.

"That's what I thought." Ernesto empties his thermos, crumples up his sandwich bag, and stands up.

"All right, so I'll go back." I turn around in slow motion. Unfortunately, Ernesto doesn't object, like I'd hoped he would. All I hear is the squeak of his car door as he gets in. I stop.

"Ernesto, Fabrizio addressed you as Signor Mayor. Didn't you tell me that you're the mailman?"

Ernesto sticks his head out the window as the van starts. He has to shout to drown out the rattling of the diesel engine. "I'm whatever is needed most at any given time, Signora Hanna. Mail carrier, mayor, and bank manager. Sometimes even a doctor"—he taps his chest meaningfully—"for this."

Fabrizio

Salvatore Bertani, known as Salvi, used to be an overweight and unhappy boy who was quick on the comeback only with his fists. At the end of *scuola primaria*, he got a below-average evaluation from our village teacher, a grumpy man who suffered from insomnia and acid reflux. The teacher actually thought Salvi was intellectually challenged, though he wasn't allowed to say so. For what he did report, old Bertani paid him a visit and bulldozed the way for his son to move up to the next level. Since the Bertanis also had good connections with the mayor's office, the teacher eventually took old Bertani's advice and retired early rather than face an inquiry for incompetence.

So we children had Salvi to thank for a new teacher, a redheaded gazelle whose name sounded like ice cream, standing at the blackboard at the end of summer vacation. She assigned her snub-nosed daughter a seat in the front row for reasons we figured out only eventually. But everything was clear to Salvatore Bertani from the very beginning. The moment he saw little Concetta Fragoletti, his life changed completely.

Concetta is a Bertani today, like her husband and their five redheaded Bertanis whom nobody can tell apart and who continue the old boyhood battles in the winding little streets of Montesimo. The large and unhappy boy turned into an oversized man, but one who leaves unhappiness to those who drown their sorrows at his bar.

Salvi's upper arms, which are the size of my thighs, fascinate me. He is polishing wineglasses as if he were fastening wheel rims with a screwdriver, and with every circle of the dishcloth the underside of his arm wobbles back and forth.

"Tell me, Salvi, do you go to the tanning salon?" I ask. He's as predictable as a Swiss watch, and I know it will annoy him. He considers men who frequent such establishments gay. In his opinion, that's also true about men who drive at a low RPM, eat vegetarian, and find the culture section of the *Gazzetta* more interesting than the sports section. Salvi stops his triceps exercise and looks at me indignantly.

"Has it been so long since you've been here that you've forgotten how many sons I sired, Camini?" His bass reverberates through the room, off the stained linoleum floor and the photo-covered walls. The previous owner made Salvi promise never to use nails on the ugly but antique tiles on the walls. As I understand it, Concetta glued on the pictures when Salvi was once sick with the flu. His own decoration ideas for the cavernous space were limited to the artificial palms and plastic furniture.

I catch Carlo's smirk out of the corner of my eye. He's playing cards at one of the tables with Father Lorenzo and Stefano Gosetti, our car mechanic.

"You're so fast at making kids that we stopped counting, Bertani," Carlo shouts, using the butt of his service-revolver pistol to drum a rimshot on the table. Stefano giggles, red faced, and the padre crosses himself. I briefly wonder if my friend will ever shoot his own balls by mistake.

Salvi gawks at us, his mouth open. I stir my cappuccino and begin to count silently. When I reach nine, he shuts his mouth; at twelve, he laughs, now feeling flattered, and lifts five fingers into the air—one for each of his brats. I sip my coffee, almost relieved that some things never change.

Unfortunately, Inspector Carlo Fescale now focuses on his next victim. "Hey, Fabrizio! Did you ever find the pretty signora that you lost?"

Of course. I should have guessed. Now that Montesimo has gone modern, everyone—even our mayor—knows how to spread gossip online. I hold it against Ernesto, however, that he chose Carlo as his tabloid. Carlo loves nothing more than making fun of other people—especially those he calls his friends.

"I didn't lose her," I say, trying to look bored. "She probably got lost."

"I bet she ran away from you." Carlo winks at the other players. "A woman who doesn't run away from him has yet to be created."

Stefano joins Carlo's laughter with a bobbing Adam's apple. Padre Lorenzo keeps on crossing himself as if to apologize for the fun his companions are having at my expense.

"Don't insult my friend or I won't let you play here anymore," Salvi says—a courageous attempt, but Carlo just laughs. I hate it when he wears his uniform and transforms into a testosterone-drunk loudmouth. Salvi gives the trio a scolding look and draws his hand across his throat. Suddenly he lowers his bearded walrus face to only inches from mine.

"Honestly, did you really already find a wife? That fast? The will was just read yesterday." His breath reeks of peanuts and cigarettes. My bar stool wobbles and creaks as I try to turn away from him.

"I'm not looking for a wife, Salvi," I say patiently. "My new kitchen help wanted to go to the village, and she's been gone for a while. I thought I'd check to see if she came by here."

Salvi wets his lips. He looks around as if just realizing that there might be guests needing his service. A lone couple—tourists, around fifty—sits near the corner window, next to the blinking pinball machine. While the woman tries to translate the menu with a dictionary, the man attempts to stabilize the table with some coasters. Salvi ignores them. "But you need to find a wife . . . because of the estate," he whispers, and pauses to ponder. "Is your kitchen help pretty? Does she have good-looking . . . ?" He covertly spreads his hands in front of his chest.

"Who'd want to know something like that?" I snap. "Have I ever asked you your cleaning woman's bra size?"

"Of course not! She's over seventy."

"Can't you just answer a simple question? Did you run across an unknown woman today? And yes, she has boobs. Besides that, she's an unbearable bitch."

Salvi stares at me, mouth ajar. "You like her!"

I roll my eyes, but Salvi has swallowed the bait. His bulbous nose comes dangerously close when he leans over the counter. "Did you quarrel? If you had a fight, that's good. She has fire in her . . ." He points to his behind.

"I barely know her. And unless you're hiding her in your broom closet, that's the way it'll be. She probably split." With my grandmother. That's something I'll have to get used to. I slide off the stool with a sigh and slap some coins on the counter.

"Don't be sad. We'll find you a pretty wife who'll take good care of you," Salvi says, and glances at Carlo and his pals. Carlo is staring at his cards, but I know from the way he tilts his head that he's listening.

"Don't you dare do anything you might regret later," I threaten him. Not a muscle in his face moving, my friend pushes his pile of coins into the middle of the table.

"All in. The winner gets all."

Something tells me that Carlo is not talking about the card game.

My suspicion is confirmed when I cross the Piazza del Teatro ten minutes later to get my truck, which I parked in a no-parking zone. At first, nothing seems out of the ordinary.

It's market day in Montesimo, and as usual the town square reverberates with a shrill urgency that reaches even into the otherwise-quiet side streets of yellow-stone houses. Marketeers sort their wares and gossip with each other, loud enough to drown out the honking horns.

Women with shopping baskets haggle for oranges, beans, and melons while men play dice on overturned fruit crates, chatting and drinking espresso. Tourists wander around searching for regional souvenirs, but they bypass Bruno's homemade limoncello and reach for the cheap lemon liqueur from up north. I make my way through groups of children, barefoot and grimy, who play catch among the stalls, and I nod to Lucrezia Gosetti, who's sitting in the sun in front of her newspaper stand and staring my way like a vigilant crow.

By the time I reach the middle of the square, I realize that I'm being watched attentively. A few women stop, nudging each other and putting their heads together, as I pass. A few steps later I'm confronted by a flirtatious smile from the baker's daughter, who has ignored me for the last fifteen years. The fat owner of Fonte di Tufi, the bed-and-breakfast, abruptly changes her course and hurries after me.

Suddenly I'm greeted left and right.

"Ciao, Fabrizio!"

"Fabrizio, how are you?"

"*Buon giorno*, Signor Camini. Lovely day, isn't it?"

"We're coming to the trattoria today, Signor Camini."

I hurry to my truck. A traffic ticket is wedged between the windshield and wiper. Typical Carlo! Pretends to go take a leak and sneaks outside to put one over on his best friend. I climb in, add the ticket to the stack on the center console, and turn the key in the ignition. But I haven't reckoned with Signora Gosetti.

A pair of jet-black eyes appears at my window. I can't see much more of the old woman besides her countless hairpins, which glitter in the sun. She always reminds me of a burned matchstick because of her stoop and her black apron dresses and stockings. Cursing Nonna for my good manners, I roll down the window.

"*Buon giorno,* Signora Gosetti."

Signora Gosetti furls her thick black brows, takes a drag of her cigarette, and blows smoke through her hairy nostrils. I hold my breath as the stench of unfiltered Gitanes fills my car.

"Have you found a woman to marry yet?" she rasps without greeting me. One of the advantages of getting old seems to be that you can get right to the crux of the matter.

"Do you plan to be one of the candidates, Signora Gosetti?" I say, and instantly regret the joke. The old woman puckers her lips, actually seeming to consider my offer.

"No, thank you," she answers finally, not very nicely, and inhales through her discolored cigarette holder again. She doesn't take her eyes off the noisy bunch of children that now circles the pickup. Oh, to be a kid. Nobody pesters them with questions like these. "So do you have a bride or not?"

"I'm working on it," I lie, glancing at the bakery. I see Alberto's old bike leaning against its wall. He rides there every morning for an espresso and a few secret biscotti. If Lucia found out . . .

A yellowed finger drills into my arm. "Hurry up with your search. I want to have a feast. A huge celebration."

"You want a feast?"

"A wedding, you dumbbell. What else? It might be the last wedding I attend." She coughs, her eyes bulging with the effort as if her last hour has actually arrived.

"I'll do my best, Signora Gosetti." I beat back a laugh. Despite her forty-a-day habit, Signora Gosetti is as healthy as a horse and determined to outlive her son Stefano, so he doesn't get the idea that he can have a life of his own. Someone bumps against the back of the truck, and a kid yelps. It seems the gang caught their victim. Something scrapes along the side of the truck. Oh, to be a kid again . . .

"And don't forget about the panini, Fabrizio!" Lucrezia says. I stare; she clicks her tongue. "The little ones, the ones with sesame. I want to see them at your wedding buffet. And Rosa-Maria's ribollita, too, lots of it." She raises her bony finger in warning. I wonder how in the world Stefano can stand it—he still lives at home.

"All right," I say obediently. I learned long ago not to contradict Signora Gosetti. "But now you have to let me go. I've got to run a few errands."

"Go, go . . ." She waves her hand and then slaps one of the red-headed Bertani boys who just narrowly avoided running into her. "But don't drive too fast. Don't you dare rob me of my last wedding."

I leave the town square at three miles an hour, wondering if this was all just a bizarre nightmare.

Hanna

Lucia said nothing when I showed up with my suitcase and a guilty face at the back door. She hugged me, led me to my little room—where a flowered apron was spread out on the bed—and quietly asked my shoe size. The slippers she brought me are definitely not hip, but they fit comfortably.

Rosa-Maria isn't back from the market yet—and I'm grateful, because I couldn't take her intensity right now. Lucia and I have been peeling onions at the kitchen table for the past half hour. Even though I don't exactly have the hang of it, and the onion fumes sting my eyes like hell, it's actually not that bad. It's fun watching Lucia work. She deftly peels and quarters the red bulbs with the expression of a lab worker handling highly explosive devices.

So far we haven't talked much. It's not necessary. When I finish an onion, I wipe the tears from my eyes with a kitchen towel and Lucia silently hands me another bulb. Finally the bucket is empty, and I utter, *"There!"* feeling like I've just typed the last word of a difficult article. So what if it was just some stupid onions. Lucia smiles.

"The potatoes are next. After all, we're making ribollita, not onion soup."

I groan.

"Your mother didn't cook with you very often, did she?" Lucia says with a pitying look, and I feel the smile crumble from my mouth.

"Forgive me," she says quickly. "It's none of my business. No need to answer my stupid questions." Her slippers make a shuffling sound as she goes to the sink to wash her hands.

"I don't mind." What am I saying? I have no idea why that just came out of my mouth. Lucia looks out at the yard, meticulously lathering her hands while the water trickles into the stone basin.

"My mother was a very good cook," I hear myself say quietly. "Soups were actually her specialty. But then she stopped. It was easier to pick up some Chinese food on her way home from work."

"But that wasn't the same."

"It got monotonous after a while." My throat constricts. Lucia dries her hands and returns with two bowls and a basket full of potatoes. Her face is soft when she hands me the peeling knife.

"It's never too late to start something that feels like home," she says, and her voice touches me like warm sunshine. She looks out the window again. "Would you do me a favor, Hanna?"

"Of course."

"Fabrizio is back from town. He's probably in the distillery over there, across the yard." She pulls a small item out of her apron pocket. "Would you mind giving him this key? He was looking for it this morning."

I cross the yard with a queasy feeling in my stomach. It's obvious that Lucia wants me to clear things up with Fabrizio. I make a note to myself to never underestimate harmless-looking Italian women. I give a wide berth to a flock of brown chickens, and my heart stops for a moment when I spot the horrible white hen among them. I quickly step under the distillery's overhanging roof and stop in front of the enormous wooden door.

In my head, Claire says, *"Sometimes it's better to confront one's ghosts than run away from them."*

I'm not going to run away anymore, I tell her. I learned my lesson. Besides, this Italian is no ghost. I've written about his kind in hundreds of articles. Claire's laughter mixes with the swooshing of blood in my ears. Fine, laugh! I resolutely turn the doorknob and enter quickly, before I can change my mind.

The barn, nondescript from the outside, consists of one single room that is flooded with light streaming through floor-to-rafters windows. A table in the middle of the room could easily seat twenty, and huge copper vats with attached thermostats and pipes line one wall. The odors of damp soil and fermented fruit are overwhelming. Fabrizio Camini is kneeling in front of ceiling-high shelves filled with glass carboys and bottles. I grip the little key tighter.

"So you're still here," he says without looking up, dousing my conciliatory mood. He sounds like he hadn't expected anything else.

"Certainly not because of your efforts," I say with a thin-lipped smile. I step toward him. "Lucia asked me to give you this."

He reaches out for the key, not bothering to get up. His expression doesn't change as he stows it in the pocket of his overalls. He turns his attention to the jugs again.

"Lucia has always been more skillful at handling employees," he says. "I should have asked her this morning to show you the ropes. I see"—he looks from my slippers to the flowered apron—"that she was more successful."

"Telling someone what's expected of her in a friendly way isn't rocket science," I say.

"It isn't?" His arrogance is infuriating.

"Actually, all you need is a little bit of heart."

His eyes widen when he recognizes his own words. Got him! I feel myself grin. Unfortunately, he seems to think my attack is more amusing than provocative. In the silence, all the other sounds in this high-ceilinged room are excessively loud: the sucking noise from the copper vats, the beeping of something digital, even the creaking of the beams above. With a frown, Fabrizio checks the bottling hoses.

"Is that a distillery machine over there?" I ask when I can't stand the oppressive silence any more.

"You are inside a distillery, Signora Philipp."

"Why do you do that?"

"Why do I make alcohol?

"No, I mean why are you so unpleasant?"

His cheeks twitch. He seems about to answer but then changes his mind. He stands up stiffly, and suddenly his face is only inches from mine.

"You're right," he says slowly. I hold my breath. For a tiny moment, vulnerability replaces the gloom in his eyes. Something stirs in me, something very different from my feelings of only seconds ago. Fabrizio turns away. He pulls a narrow bottle from the middle shelf and another, almost identical, from the shelf below. "Follow me. I'll show you something."

At the huge table, he pulls out a chair for me.

"Are we going to smoke a peace pipe now?" I try to joke as he sets several cordial glasses on the waxed wooden table.

"Sort of." A fleeting smile dimples his cheeks. He has a charming smile. He uncorks the first bottle and fills one of the glasses. He fills another glass from the second bottle. I point to the remaining glasses.

"We need two more to make peace."

"I don't drink high-proof alcohol."

"You make it but don't drink it? That's—"

"Strange?" He tilts his head. "I don't have to drink to make alcohol. I'm interested in your opinion about this liqueur—your expert opinion."

"You can't let it go, can you?" I say.

"I don't understand."

"Your nasty intonation of 'expert.'"

"You know what the problem with women is? They think too much. Forget about my words. Don't analyze what I might have meant. Try them—employer's order."

I take a careful sip from the first glass and allow the sweet flavor to develop on my tongue. "Apricot liqueur—very fruity, with a hint of rosemary. Interesting."

He nods and points to the second glass. I obediently lift it to my lips but look up in surprise when I catch the beguiling aroma.

"Drink," Fabrizio orders.

"Will I wake up naked on the floor if I do?"

Oh my god! I'm flirting with him. Am I?

"I'll make sure you're not on the floor," he says. My cheeks burn and I hear Claire giggling in my head. How embarrassing. I take a long sip, and the taste glues the glass to my lips as a firework of sweetness and fruit shoots to every cell of my body.

"God, this is fantastic. What is it?"

"Apricot liqueur."

"But the taste is totally different. The other liqueur is good, definitely, but this one . . ." I glance at the handwritten label. *Liquore di Albicocche della Nonna.* "This is unique. Are you going to tell me what's in it?"

"I have no idea." He drops into the chair next to mine and looks at his hands—a pianist's hands, long and square, with dirt rimming his short-cut nails. I force myself to look at his face.

"Am I supposed to understand?"

"It's my grandmother's apricot liqueur."

"But then you must know what's in it."

"The ingredients are our apricot schnapps—apricots and sugar—and the rest is top secret. My family passed the recipe to daughters only, and my grandmother, unfortunately, was a stickler for tradition. Since I know you'll ask, yes, it's written down, but the notebook disappeared before I could see what's inside."

"But that means—"

"It means that this bottle is one of the hundred and fifty left. Take it—it's a present. Is that enough of a peace pipe?" The ironic tone again, but I hear the deep frustration below it. I just stare at him.

"I don't think you should do that."

"What? Give you the bottle?"

"You can't just give up. This liqueur could be very successful—and not just in Italy."

"And this is from the woman who slams the door at the tiniest little problem?" His laugh is bitter. "With a product like this, the smallest variation in the ratio of ingredients matters. More or less alcohol, an ounce less of this or half of that—and the flavor changes completely. There's a reason it took decades to develop the recipe. Unfortunately, I don't have that much time. And I can't ask Nonna."

His unintended jab hits its target. I read rage in his eyes—but more than that, pain, which really makes me feel rotten. If I hadn't written the article, maybe Giuseppa could still give Fabrizio the treasured liqueur recipe.

"I didn't mean to offend," I say formally. "I'm sorry, especially about your grandmother. Unfortunately, I can't undo what I did."

"My grandmother was ill, Signora Philipp. I resent what you wrote in the article, but I do not blame you for her death." Fabrizio gets up, and the legs of his chair screech on the stone floor. He recorks the bottles without looking at me and gathers up the glasses. "You should go back. Rosa-Maria needs you in the kitchen. The restaurant will be full tonight."

This man is an enigma. But I'm not angry when I leave the distillery with Fabrizio's reconciliation gift. For the first time since I met him, I'm not so sure that I read him right. I'm not sure that I read his trattoria right, either.

Chapter Seven
Hanna

A few days ago I would have made fun of anyone who claimed I would ever be grateful for a pair of threadbare slippers. Well, today is different.

Groaning, I plop down on the bench. My legs hurt like crazy, and my hands . . . No, let's not talk about my hands. I examine my scrubbed-red fingers and broken nails. My beautician would be appalled. Leafing through one of the dime novels that are always within Rosa-Maria's reach, I watch the cook out the corner of my eye. She's been moving around the little kitchen like a whirling dervish for two hours, stirring pots, draining pasta, turning meat in pans, and plating meals—and she still has energy enough to shoo Lucia and the other servers from one end of the trattoria to the other.

"Fettuccine ai funghi porcini, table three," she barks. An anxious little face appears in the service hatch a moment later.

"Table three? They're still working on the antipasti," the server says timidly.

"Then tell your guests they have to eat faster. The pasta doesn't wait. Just take away their plates. Move it!"

I grin. A serious mistake in hindsight, but how was I supposed to know that Rosa-Maria has eyes in the back of her head? She whirls around, stares at the tattered booklet in my hand, and snaps, "Signorina I'm-Too-Good-for-This! Where are the dessert bowls, eh? We only take breaks with Lady Prudence when all the work's done."

I toss the dime novel on the bench, groan in exaggerated pain, and point to my feet. "But I can't anymore."

Rosa-Maria waddles over and inspects my swollen toes. "They're not bleeding."

They're not bleeding? I look up in disbelief. She scrutinizes me, her hands on her hips.

"As long as they're not bleeding, there's no reason to waste time watching the lemons grow. Get over to the sink. I need little bowls for the panna cotta."

For a second I'm tempted to shoot back a stubborn but truly fitting reply. Fortunately, Lucia slips into the kitchen right then.

"Don't be so strict with Hanna, Rosa-Maria," she shouts. Cheeks red, she balances three artistically plated dishes in the crook of her arm and dashes back out, but not before tossing an "Everything tastes wonderful" to the kitchen commander and a warm smile to me. That woman really is an angel.

Rosa-Maria notices too late that I'm watching her. Sheepishly, she turns the corners of her mouth—which for a moment pointed up—down again. She grumbles as she opens the oven door, and the sauna-like temperature in the kitchen skyrockets with a gust of thyme-infused heat. Her face crimson, she sets an earthen pot on the stove. It could easily accommodate a piglet. An expression of blissful contentment spreads on her chubby cheeks when she removes the lid. I manage to get a glimpse of the roasted lamb's dark-brown crust before her enormous behind blocks my view. Annoyed, I push off to the sink.

"Tomorrow you're going to help me with the cooking, Signora It's-All-Too-Hard-for-Me. That'll teach you what work is."

"I can't wait, Signora Master Sergeant," I say, which makes the dragon gape at me and then laugh hoarsely.

"Master Sergeant? Not bad. I like that. But don't think for a moment that compliments will get you anywhere in my kitchen."

Two hours and a truckload of dirty dishes later, just as I'm contemplating an agonizing suicide in the sudsy water, Lucia comes in with the last dirty plates and removes her serving apron.

"They're all gone. Closing time, my dears!"

Rosa-Maria crosses herself, and I can't hold back an "Amen." By now my hands are so shriveled by the soapy water that they could be a horror-show attraction.

"The nails grow back," Lucia says, and conjures up an emery board from a drawer.

"I hope not," Rosa-Maria mumbles. I shoot her a murderous look and eye the bottle of prosecco Lucia takes out of the fridge. Alcohol is exactly what I need right now.

"Is there something to celebrate?"

"Of course. You're still here, and you survived your fiery baptism."

That is definitely reason to celebrate, although it was actually a more conventional baptism by water. I feel like I've just washed the entire inventory of a giant porcelain factory. From now on, if I ever enter a restaurant through the front door again, I'll leave a generous tip for the dishwasher. I swear.

The cork pops, and a moment later, pale-yellow bubbly flows into long-stemmed glasses.

"Actually, I'd prefer some hard liquor now, served with a tiny umbrella," I sigh after we clink our glasses.

"An umbrella?" Lucia says, amused.

I nod. "I just love those little umbrellas."

Rosa-Maria frowns. "We only have umbrellas outside, on the terrace."

Lucia rubs Rosa-Maria's back. I can't understand her display of affection for that monster. My ears are still ringing with her commands.

"I think Hanna is talking about something else," Lucia says. "I have to say, Rosa-Maria, you were wonderful tonight. Everyone loved the food, and you know how those ladies can be."

"Ladies?" I grin. "You sound as if you served only women tonight." The two exchange a meaningful glance, and my laugh sticks in my throat. "Honestly? Were there really only women in the restaurant?"

Lucia giggles. "And I'm afraid they went home disappointed, despite the great food."

"Why?" I look from Lucia to Rosa-Maria, who studies her untouched glass of prosecco with puckered lips.

"I'm sure they hoped to see Fabrizio."

"Fabrizio?"

"It's a long story. But you know what?" Lucia empties her glass and gets up. "I'll tell you the story on our way to your little umbrellas."

"What? Now?"

"Even Montesimo has a bar that serves cocktails after eleven. Come on, Hanna. Put on your pretty heels. I haven't been out on the town in ages."

Fabrizio

The yard is completely dark except for the porch light outside the trattoria. As I peek out, the last car drives away, and I sigh with relief. I actually planned to go in hours ago and help Lucia serve, but when I noticed the onslaught of femininity, I retreated to the distillery—fast. Now my conscience is giving me trouble, but at least my soul is saved. I sigh. I feel like a stag during hunting season—and every woman carries a rifle.

I'm squinting at the little window next to the kitchen door when I hear steps and whispering. Shit. So that wasn't the last car? A twig snaps. Someone swears.

"Fabrizio." The voice is right next to me. Too late to slip away. Giggles. A very deep voice giggles drunkenly.

"Carlo? What the heck are you doing here? Why are you sneaking around like a burglar?" I snap into the darkness.

"Pssst. Be quiet!" Laughter again, and I see two shadows against the wall.

"Stefano? What's going on?"

"Eh, Fabrizio! *Amico!* My gooood friend."

I turn away in disgust. Carlo's breath alone could make me drunk. Stefano giggles, and his small, skinny body sways dangerously.

"Wan . . . Wanna pick y'up," Stefano slurs. He points at the sky. Carlo punches him.

"Padre Lorenzo's waiting over *there*, you idiot," Carlo says, and Stefano's finger careens in the direction of the driveway.

"Sssure. He's sitting over there."

"You must be crazy," I say. "I'm not going anywhere. Do you have any idea what time it is?"

"Nope."

"No."

"Well, it's late enough for the two of you."

More silly giggling. The trattoria's lights go out.

"Come on, Fabrizio," Carlo says. "For old time's sake."

That's what Carlo always does. When he has no logical argument, he pulls out the old times. I shake my head and eye the main house. I do want to avoid Lucia right now—and our new kitchen help. I'm still embarrassed that I spread out my troubles like a sentimental fool in front of her—especially since she caused some of them.

"In your condition," I say, "you better stagger home. Otherwise you'll hear it from your mamma, Stefano, a whole aria."

"My mamma ca-can't even sing."

"Even worse. I hope the padre is sober enough to drive, regardless."

Carlo beats his chest. "Ha, ha . . . I don't think the *carabinieri* will arrest us. Because I'm it. I'm the only policeman."

What can I do? I laugh.

"So cooome along," Carlo continues. "Let's get a good drop of wine at Salvi's. Just the three—the four of us." He links arms with me and drags me across the yard, whether I'm willing or not. The diesel engine roars to life; the gears grind. The padre never learned how to drive. I bend down to the window, where a fearful, bespectacled face peers out at me.

"Slide over, Lorenzo. I'll drive," I say, and Father Lorenzo climbs into the passenger seat—awkwardly because of his cassock, which he wears even after-hours. Carlo and Stefano hoot loudly and high-five each other—though Stefano misses Carlo's hand by an inch. "One glass, and no more. I'm harvesting tomorrow," I say, trying to curb their exuberance, but Carlo has started to sing Gli Azzurri's hymn. Since Stefano doesn't remember the words of the soccer song, he just goes "na-na-na" and Lorenzo quietly beats the time on the dashboard. He has no sense of rhythm. Ohmigod. What have I gotten myself into?

Hanna

"Fabrizio has to get married to inherit the estate?"

I lean back in the plastic chair. I have to let this settle for a while.

The fat man—who gushingly introduced himself as Salvatore and almost dislocated my arm with his handshake—places two flutes full of strawberry-colored liquid on the small table, which is rickety, despite several coasters under its legs. The little umbrella in my glass is torn and obviously reused, but it's an umbrella.

"Thank you, Salvi." Lucia smiles at the fat guy, who seems to be planted at our table and looks me over with curiosity.

"It's my Concetta's secret recipe. There're strawberries in it. That's all I'm allowed to say."

"Thank you," I repeat, hopefully with enough of a hint to make him leave. I'm dying to hear more about the crazy story of Giuseppa Camini's testament. Salvi bites his lips, which are childlike and too small for his large, round face. He can't take his eyes off my chest. Lucia clears her throat—several times.

"Salvatore, the ladies at the corner table would like to order something."

Salvatore nods without taking his watery eyes from my neckline. I start laughing. The bar is packed and he doesn't seem to notice.

"You're Fabrizio's Aaanna, aren't you?" he says.

"Fabrizio's? No. I mean, yes. I am Hanna, but not Fabrizio's Hanna," I answer, confused, and Lucia seems puzzled, too.

"I knew it." Salvi nods seriously and I nod back—equally seriously but clueless.

"Is there something you want to tell us, Salvatore?" Lucia gives me a sidelong glance. I raise my palms and shake my head.

"One hears things." Salvi puts on a deliberately harmless expression, looks left and right, and bends down to me. "You shouldn't be so strict with him, Signora Aaanna." He whispers so loudly that the ladies at the next table can understand each word. "Fabrizio is a great guy. I know it. I've known him my entire life—maybe two lifetimes, but don't tell Concetta. She's very Catholic and doesn't believe in reincarnation."

I smile. "Thanks for the advice, Salvi. I'll think about it next time Signor Camini annoys me again."

Lucia chuckles and quickly puts her nose into her cocktail.

"Maybe the opportunity will come faster than you think. Please try. I really like you." Salvi pats my shoulder and leaves.

I follow him with my eyes. "What was that all about?"

"That's Salvi for you." Lucia guffaws. "He's in a category of his own." She wipes tears of laughter from her cheeks and rocks in her chair so violently that I'm afraid she might tip over. Her laughter is infectious.

"You Italians are completely crazy," I pant, which makes Lucia squeal again. She rummages in her handbag for a tissue. Two young women passing our table exchange glances, and one of them taps her forehead. When I look over at the bar where Salvi is pouring drinks below a mounted boar's head, it suddenly hits me. I can name the funny feeling I had when we entered the Amalfi bar. "Lucia?"

"*Oh dio!* I can't stop laughing."

"Lucia, where are the men?"

"What men?"

"There are only women in this bar, not counting Salvi and the boys at the pinball machine."

Lucia stops laughing. Her pretty eyes widen and she slowly turns around. Someone has turned on the disco system and cranked up the music. Rainbow-colored lights dance to the beat of a schmaltzy Italian pop tune, up and down skirts and stocking-covered legs.

"It can't be," she whispers.

"It's eerie," I whisper back.

"I'll find out." Lucia gets up and goes over to a tiny woman three tables away. Air kisses, hand gestures, head shakes, and shrugs. Lucia returns and plops down in her chair with a satisfied smile. She takes a large sip of her cocktail.

"*Mamma mia*, that's delicious. I've got to get the recipe from Concetta."

"Strawberries, sugar, Aperol, and possibly prosecco," I say without thinking. Lucia looks at me in surprise.

"Well, you seem to know your cocktails."

I want to bite my tongue. "I just have sharp taste buds," I say quickly. New topic. I point to the other table. "Did you find out what this gathering of women is all about?"

My diversion tactic works. Lucia grins and leans toward me, her breath tickling my ear. "Genova says that her cousin heard from a girlfriend in the next village that Fabrizio is going to select a wife here tonight."

I laugh. Where are we? In Cinderella land?

"You mean—Genova means—he'll be looking for a bride publicly? Is that how it's done around here?"

"Of course not!" Lucia frowns, eyebrows touching comically. "Genova has no idea who started the rumor, but I bet it's that stupid Carlo. It would never be Fabrizio—he'll be furious when he hears about it. But he isn't here, so it'll all come to nothing anyway."

I hear loud welcomes at the entrance and crane my neck. I see a black-haired, bearded man, who bears an uncanny resemblance to Robin Hood's Sheriff of Nottingham, enter the bar with a thin little man sporting a blond goatee. Both of them seem quite drunk. Next, a priest in a black cassock and a man who bears some resemblance to—I sink deeper into my chair, even though I doubt Fabrizio will spot us in this crowded bar.

"You might be wrong about nothing coming of it, Lucia," I say. My mouth is dry. But Lucia is staring at the pinball machine.

"*She's* all we need!"

Taken aback by the hostility in her voice, I look over, too, and stop breathing for a moment. "Who's that?"

Lucia snorts, "That's Sofiiiia." She draws out the name as if she wants to tear it apart. "The nightmare of all women who plan to hold on to their men."

I believe her. Sofia isn't just beautiful, but a new-and-improved version of a young Sophia Loren. I look enviously at her waist-long hair, which reminds me of raven wings. She leans casually against the pinball machine, seemingly detached somehow, even as she chats with the players—like she's standing on an imaginary pedestal. "Wow."

"Wow, all right. But don't be deceived by her pretty facade," Lucia says. She groans when the woman snaps out of her Madonna pose and heads toward our table with swaying hips. Sofia isn't slim—her cherry-red dress accentuates her curves almost obscenely.

"Ciao, Lucia!"

Lucia stares straight ahead and doesn't reply to the smoky greeting.

"It's been a long time. How are you?" Sofia purrs, and sizes me up. I smile back. Eyelashes like hers should be illegal.

"Since when do you care how I am?" Lucia reaches for her cocktail.

Sofia laughs. "So you're still mad at me?"

"Since that would imply that you matter to me, the answer is no, I'm not." Lucia's voice trembles with suppressed fury. I hold my breath. Sofia raises a plucked eyebrow, and her pitch-black eyes seem to eat me up. I'm still smiling, but it's turning into a forced smile.

"Are you the new kitchen help?" she asks me.

I open my mouth, but Lucia is faster. "Hanna is a friend, and she isn't interested in you. Why don't you stagger back to Milan and your rich playmates and leave us alone?"

Sofia glares, all friendliness gone.

"I don't think you can tell me who to play with, little Lucia," she says. "But since we're on the subject, do you know where Fabrizio is? I hear he has a little problem, and I'm eager to help out."

Fabrizio

I've never been into bars with too-loud—and in this case also bad—music, where too many people are pretending to have fun. Usually the Amalfi bar is closed at this hour, for lack of customers—except the one time Salvi fell asleep behind the counter and Carlo fined him for violating the business-curfew laws. But today Carlo couldn't care less about laws and fines. Great for Salvi, who's making a killing tonight.

I glance around to find a quiet corner, but Salvi ruins my plan to hide. His shiny face shows true joy when he discovers me.

"There he is, our future groom!"

Everyone turns around, and I see an ocean of black eyelashes and red lips in front of me. Groom? I look to Lorenzo incredulously. He looks back guiltily, but then disappears in the crowd before I can grab his cassock. This . . . can't . . . be . . . happening. Women call out to me from left and right.

"Ciao, Fabrizio. How nice of you to come by."

"*Buona sera,* Signor Camini. I'm Marta and this is my cousin Franca. We came all the way from Sant'Albino to meet you."

"Fabrizio, share a glass of wine with us."

"May I introduce my friend Cilia?"

The avalanche of fluttering eyelashes and babbling mouths sweeps dangerously closer. Dozens of legs below flowery, striped, and polka-dotted skirts block all escape routes.

"Get me out of here, Gosetti." I grab Stefano's collar as he staggers by, even though I know he's not going to help. He's more afraid of Carlo than of his mother, and that was true even before Carlo declared himself Stefano's protector. They have a strange mutual dependency, and to this day I don't know who profits more. As expected, Stefano just shrugs after escaping my grip and stumbles toward a blonde woman who looks like a bottle in her green dress.

Carlo waves at me from the middle of the crowd, one thumb up. He abandons the padre, who's standing in the middle of the room gaping at a nearby cleavage display. Carlo wades through the crowd, throwing out compliments left and right, and then punches me, proud of himself.

"What a surprise, eh? So many beautiful young ladies, and you have the pick."

"Yeah, what a surprise, you scumbag!" I hiss. Not quietly enough. A young girl, thin as a pencil, gazes at me with big eyes. Carlo grins again and delivers a second punch to my ribs that almost takes my breath away.

"No need to thank me, old pal. It was a pleasure planning it." He looks at the young one, who stares at me with a mixture of fear and admiration. "Who do we have here? What's this lovely signorina's name?"

"I'm Chiara," the girl peeps, and her smile isn't timid at all. God, she's probably underage. That doesn't bother Carlo. He puts his arm around her slight shoulders.

"Chiara, this is my good friend Fabrizio. I'm sure he'll buy you a cocktail if you're nice to him. If not, I will."

What am I supposed to say? Before my friend can put his dirty claws on the kid, I relent and smile at Chiara. It's a forced smile, but a smile it is. Behind it, I'm running terrible scenes of torture through my head, with Carlo in the main role. My feigned interest makes Carlo leave. I just hope he finds a more mature victim for himself.

Chiara climbs on one of the bar stools and checks out Salvi's array of liquor. And then I do what I promised never to do again, after my last hangover about ten years ago: I order a double rum-and-Coke. And a lemonade for Chiara.

Half an hour later, my situation seems much less impossible. Contrary to my expectations, the pencil-thin woman is quite entertaining, even though I don't buy that she's twenty-two. But she at least protects me from the circling hyenas prowling for their chance, blaming occasional bodily contact on the jostling crowd.

I turn my back on the baker's daughter and her two cousins and focus on Chiara. Surely she's the least dangerous of all the women in the room. She's actually quite cute, protruding teeth and all. Although rum-and-Coke number two might be influencing my perception and bathing this entire situation in a softer light. The kid talks nonstop, with wild gestures and dangling legs. I have no idea what she's saying. I just smile and nod—and drink.

Drink number three limits my field of vision to a radius of ten yards. Behind it is the big nothingness, just like in the children's book Nonna used to read to me on Sundays. *La Storia Infinita*. And the girl slouching next to me on a bar stool and drinking lemonade is *The Neverending Story*'s childlike empress.

Salvi puts number four on the counter and I have trouble picking it up. He shouts something, and his triceps wobble left and right. I turn my head with some effort and survey the dimly lit room. I can't see Carlo anywhere, but when the crowd parts for a moment, I see Lucia. My vision clears immediately and I notice two things at Lucia's table. One is confusing and the other more than disturbing. Then the nothingness sweeps back.

"Are you all right, Fabrizio?" Chiara looks up at me hopefully. I reach for her wrist, which disappears in my hand. What the hell is Sofia doing here?

"Know what, Chiara?" I mutter. "You're a nice girl, honest. But whatever you're looking for here—look for it somewhere else. And, mainly, later in life."

Chiara tilts her head. "You're drunk," she says.

"Right." My ass slides off the stool like someone rubbed it with soap. I hang on to the counter for support until my legs adjust to standing up, and I give Chiara my best sage impression. "But as you know, children and drunks always tell the truth." Then I give her a smooch on the forehead and stagger to Lucia's table with unsteady knees.

Hanna

I'm starting to worry. Lucia's face is dark red by now, and her chest rises and falls so fast that I'm afraid she's hyperventilating. Sofia sat down at our table without an invitation, crossed her smooth legs, and is now smoking a cigarette, even though smoking is not allowed in the bar. She uses our almost-empty bowl of peanuts as an ashtray. I've seldom seen someone break rules with such nonchalance before, and I'm upset with myself for grudgingly admiring her. What the hell happened to my insolence? On paper, I checkmate people like Sofia in three effortless moves. In real life, however, I take forever just to line up the players.

So, instead of helping Lucia with a verbal bludgeon, I play with the small pepper shaker—it's shaped like a baseball bat—and slip it unobtrusively into my handbag. That's the moment when I meet Fabrizio's surprised gaze.

Blushing, I remove the mini baseball bat from my bag and return it to the mini baseball salt shaker. I look at Fabrizio as casually as I can. He's now standing behind Lucia and Sofia, but the two don't notice because they're preoccupied with hating each other.

"Why don't you spread your stench at another table, Sofia?"

"Why don't you keep your stupid little nose in your own business? Besides, I'm still waiting for an answer. Is Fabrizio here?" Sofia replies, blowing blue smoke toward Lucia.

I open my mouth and shut it again. Fabrizio crosses his arms as he stares at Sofia's hair. He seems unusually tense. He sways slightly, grabs on to the back of Lucia's chair, but then thinks better of it and puts his hands into his jeans pockets. I almost start to laugh. Signor Camini, the supposed teetotaler, is totally wasted.

"He's right behind you," he says in a surprisingly sober voice. Lucia veers around. Sofia doesn't move. However, something creepy happens to her bored expression: her face relaxes, her eyes become round, and laughter lines appear. She snuffs out her cigarette in one of the remaining peanuts and then turns around with a sparkling smile.

"*Bellissimo!* Where have you been hiding? I've been missing you all evening." She pulls Fabrizio down toward her and kisses both of his cheeks—a touch too slowly to be purely friendly.

"I think I'll throw up," Lucia says, rolling her eyes.

"Your sister-in-law is so witty. Marco must be in stitches half the time." Sofia giggles without taking her arms from Fabrizio's neck. I'm sure the stabbing feeling in my chest is because she's so mean to Lucia. I can't suppress a snort, and Fabrizio disentangles himself from Sofia and moves closer to Lucia.

"I didn't know you were in the area again," he says unemotionally, and tries to catch my eye. "I see you already got to know Hanna."

He used my first name. I'm so stunned that I almost poke out my eye with my sad little umbrella as I sip from my cocktail. "'Got to know' is an overstatement," I mumble into my glass.

"Well, we'll have a chance to do that," Sofia says. "I'll be in Montesimo for a while, since I finished what I had to do in Milan." Her crystal-clear fake laughter drives even me crazy this time. Lucia juts out her chin and grabs Fabrizio's arm.

"Is your ex-girlfriend threatening us?"

It all seems a bit too much for Fabrizio.

Claire, in my head, says, *"Do something, Hanna. Hit the silly cow with something."*

I straighten up.

"Get on with it."

I look at the crucifix on the chain around Sofia's neck. So she's Fabrizio's ex.

"Do it—fast! Otherwise the opportunity goes pffi!"

I feel a smile coming on.

"In that case," I say, "I would be delighted if you came to visit me, Sofia. That is, if you aren't afraid of a steamy kitchen and sweat. And I guess you aren't," I add in a friendly tone, "since you seem quite sturdy." Lucia's mouth drops open and the corners of Fabrizio's twitch. Sofia throws back her hair and glowers at me.

"I am very interested in what's going on at Fabrizio's trattoria. Visiting the kitchen staff would obviously be part of it," is her patronizing reply.

"How nice of you. I'll ask our dear Rosa-Maria if you could work with us for a night. I'm sure she'd develop a soft spot for you right away. A bit of warning, though." I lower my voice and Sofia responds by leaning away from me suspiciously. "Don't use the term 'kitchen staff' in front of Rosa-Maria. I'm afraid she'd cut your pretty little behind into slices if you did."

Everyone is silent, shocked for a moment. Then Fabrizio starts to laugh.

Fabrizio

I underestimated Signora Philipp—very much. I like the new her. What I like more than anything is Sofia's stony face. I gasp for air. I'm obviously in absolute control of the situation, but the room has started to spin, which makes me unable to think clearly. I hold on to Lucia's chair and try not to lose my balance. My sister-in-law watches me through narrow eyes.

"Are you all right, Fabrizio?"

I drop into the chair next to Signora Philipp. She smells good—of oranges. Or is it tangerines?

"Everything A . . . A-OK," I say with a heavy tongue, and I grin. Then Chiara tugs on my sleeve. Unfortunately, my new little friend is more persistent than I anticipated.

"Are you coming back to the bar?" she whispers into my ear, giving me those puppy-dog eyes. After glancing at Signora Philipp, whose expression gives nothing away, I shake my head. To my horror, Chiara's cute eyes fill with tears. "Am I not pretty enough for you?"

"No. I mean, yes, of course. That's not the problem . . ." I look around helplessly. Embarrassed silence everywhere. Even Sofia seems to have lost her voice.

"I'm not pretty enough for you," Chiara repeats.

Suddenly I feel a hand on my shoulder. I look up into the doughy face of the baker's daughter. One of her yellow teeth sticks out. Where did she come from?

"Hello, Fabrizio! When you're done with the lemonade chick, are you going to buy me a real drink?"

"There are two of us, by the way," her friend adds and nudges the baker's daughter with her elbow. I see the owner of Fonte di Tufi making her way through the crowd with her ferret-like daughter in tow. And they aren't alone: an entire scouting unit of women doggedly advances. Help!

"You are definitely pretty, Chiara. I think you're sweet."

My attempt falls flat. Sofia laughs, and a tear rolls down Chiara's cheek. When Lucia almost imperceptibly shakes her head, I feel not just helpless but downright bad. Good lord, I hate this.

"The thing is, though . . ." I go on.

Signora Philipp looks at me with curiosity. Lucia crosses her arms and tilts her head. Sofia sinks her nails into my hand. Several bodies press against my back, and a cloud of cloying perfume mixes with whispers and giggles. I've got to get out of here.

"To tell you the truth, I've"—I cross my fingers behind my back with one hand and, with the other, pull the kid toward me so that my mouth almost touches her ear—"I've already promised to marry another signorina."

Shit! Can I sink any lower?

Chiara stops crying. "Why didn't you say that before?" she says in a huff.

"Yes, how come you didn't tell us?" Carlo's beard tickles my temple. I freeze. Carlo slaps me on the back, swats my hand away from the strawberry-colored glass that I planned to down in my despair, and yanks me up.

"My friend Fabrizio is engaged!" he yells. All chatter stops. The only noise is Eros Ramazzotti crooning "Parla Con Me." Engaged. Engaged?

"You totally misunderstood, Carlo—I only—" But a bloodcurdling scream of joy from the bar drowns my stuttering.

"I knew it!" Salvi trumpets. He dashes around the bar and elbows his way toward us. I can't breathe for several seconds while he presses me against his fat chest. His sweaty shirt muffles my mumbled protest. He then hugs the rather baffled Signora Philipp. "Aren't they wonderful? Aaanna and Fabrizio! Bravo!"

Wonderful. I reach for the strawberry-colored stuff and empty the glass in one gulp. *Madonna*, it burns like fire. Then my chair seems to disintegrate. Something in my head pings, and the ground opens up underneath me—the liberating black nothingness of Nonna's fairy tale. Finally.

Hanna

"Is he dead?"

Sofia contemplates Fabrizio, who is crumpled on the floor, and lights a cigarette. Lucia and I exchange a quick glance and jump up from our chairs at the same time.

"How many times have I told you to buy real chairs, Salvi?" Carlo rumbles, his arms crossed. "I'm going to give you a ticket for severely violating . . . safety rules."

"How is it my fault that he just keels over?" an unhappy Salvi says. "He didn't drink that much."

"Didn't he? How many rum-and-Cokes did you give him, *stronzo*—you jerk? Ten? You were supposed to make him feel good, not knock him out."

"But I . . ."

Neither of the two combatants pays any attention to Fabrizio. Lucia bends over her unconscious brother-in-law and frantically loosens his shirt collar. "Shut up, you idiots!" she hisses and digs her finger into Salvi's overhanging paunch. "Get me something I can put under his head. And you"—she points an accusing finger at Carlo's crown jewels—"you should know he can't tolerate alcohol. What a great friend you are!"

"Don't use that tone with me, Lucia," Carlo says, eyeing the gaping and whispering women gathered around the table. "Remember who you're talking to."

"I will talk to you whatever way I choose, Carlo. If you don't like it, you can park yourself with your new radar gun on the *strada provinciale* and play *carabiniere* there." Lucia is livid. Salvi hands me a jacket, so I scrunch it up and push it under Fabrizio's neck. Anxiously watching his pale face, I feel his pulse while Lucia waves her fist.

"What are you all standing around and gawking at? Go home. And stomp out your filthy cigarette, Sofia."

Sofia gets up and carefully smooths her dress. "He's just drunk, little Lucia. Don't act like he had a stroke," she says, and drops her half-smoked cigarette into Lucia's cocktail. Fabrizio groans and opens his eyes. Relieved, I lean back—accidentally against Sofia's legs.

"I'm sure Fabrizio's fiancée will know what to do. But let me give you a piece of advice," Sofia says, mocking me. "He'll puke his guts out as soon as he's outside. I went through that a few times with him. Enjoy, and *buona notte*."

Having said that, she shows us the plunging back of her dress, which Salvi and Carlo readily admire. The crowd parts for her. Some people get a free pass wherever they go.

"He's all right, Lucia." I take Lucia's arm, but to my surprise she pulls away.

"What's going on?" she asks. "You and Fabrizio?"

I'd like to know that myself. I close my eyes and try to breathe normally. Panicking won't help. "Let's talk about it later, Lucia," I say and stroke her shoulder. "Let's bring Fabrizio outside first."

She nods silently, and I challenge the bigmouthed village policeman with a look, asking him to help. While Salvi quickly kneels down to lift Fabrizio up, Carlo just stands there, pointing his finger to his own chest with a questioning expression.

"Right now," I say quietly. It's obvious that Carlo doesn't like my commanding tone. But because everyone's watching, he grudgingly puts Fabrizio's other arm around his shoulder.

"Go home, signore. The party is over," he says through clenched teeth. Fabrizio hangs between the two men like a sack of wet flour. Lucia and a flock of women follow as they drag the drunk Fabrizio out.

A little later, Fabrizio is propped against the outside of the Amalfi bar and, as the saying goes, puking his guts out. I'm not sure whether I read compassion or disgust in Lucia's expression, but I decide on compassion, since I wouldn't like it if she felt disgust. Salvi beat a pale-faced retreat back to the bar as soon as the retching noises began, mumbling "Gotta clean up," and now Carlo, the blond guy, and the priest are quarreling in the street.

"Sssure I can drive, Carlo," the blond guy slurs. "Nnno problem . . . Where isss Lorenzo's car?"

"You can't see straight, *cretino*," Carlo replies. "Do you think I'd trust a drunken moron with my life?"

"Don't you—don't insult my mother . . ."

"What does anything have to do with your mother?"

"Well then . . . I'll walk . . . that way . . . I think . . ."

"You aren't going anywhere, Stefano. The padre—Lorenzo! Unbelievable! He's asleep standing up." I hear giggling and knee slapping.

"I don't think those three can be left alone," I say, looking at Lucia. She's just standing there motionless, hugging herself. Only her dress moves with the breeze.

"You shouldn't drive, yourself," she whispers. I nod but then realize that she can't see it in the dark.

"I know," I say.

"Do you think you can find the way home on foot? Fabrizio might benefit from some exercise."

"Oh god," we hear from the wall, and then more vomiting sounds.

"I'll find Tre Camini. If I get lost, I'll ask Fabrizio."

Lucia smiles—briefly, but a smile, and I'm surprised at my relief. For some reason I can't stand that she's mad at me.

"Fine. Then I'll drive the boys home and collect you two on my way back," she says. I nod. She strides to the parking lot, yanks the key out of Carlo's hand, and grabs the blond one by the collar.

"Ouch, Lucia. You're hurting me."

"Don't be such a girl, Stefano. Carlo, wake up the Father. We're taking my car—but I dare you to puke on my seat covers."

I almost feel sorry for the three. Grinning, I stroll over to Fabrizio. He seems to have emptied his stomach by now, because he's sitting upright, his back against the wall, staring straight ahead. His face, above his three-day beard, is unnaturally pale in the moonlight.

"Can you get up, Signor Camini?" I ask in a cool voice, trying to ignore the foul-smelling puddle a few feet away. His eyes wander around as if he doesn't know where my voice is coming from. His gaze finally stops at my bare legs. A grin creates the familiar dimple in his cheek. "Ah. Signora Phi . . . Phil . . ." He stops. "Can't pronounce it."

"Kind of embarrassing, since we're supposedly engaged." It slips out. He takes my arm and stands up, groaning, his face only inches from mine. An incredibly potent alcoholic cloud escapes his mouth and makes me turn my head away.

"Uppsala," he mumbles into my hair. Oopsy-daisy.

"Uppsala? Where did you come across that term?" I grab his waist just before he keels over, and my arm becomes the sole support for his entire weight. He's much brawnier than he looks.

"Germany. Studied there . . . That was . . ." He seems to be thinking intensely. "Forgot when."

"Signor Camini, we're going to walk home. Do you think you can manage that?"

"Sssure." He staggers forward a few steps and pulls me along. "Let's go. This way. Just always follow the street."

After a few hundred yards, my shoulder aches and I'm covered in sweat from being his walking stick. "This won't work. You have to walk on your own," I pant. I extricate myself from his tight grip. Fabrizio sways but stays on his feet, resembling a floating buoy.

I look at the sky. The night is completely dark, since clouds hide the moon. I can't see a single star. No house lights, no street lamps, not even the headlights of a distant car. There's no human noise, either, only the rustling of leaves and the chirping of crickets somewhere in the fields out there. An urge to run barefoot suddenly overcomes me, so I strip off my heels—a decision I immediately regret as sharp little stones cut into my feet. Swearing, I pad over to the grassy edge of the path.

"You better put on your shoes again. Dirt paths aren't made for spoiled city girls," an amused voice says behind me. It already sounds slightly more sober. The beneficial effects of fresh air.

"Just like rum isn't made for hardheaded hicks?"

He forces a laugh. A moment later I hear a cry followed by loud rustling and crashing, as if an animal were breaking through the undergrowth. I anxiously hold my breath.

"Signor Camini?" No reply. Except for the clattering of cicadas, there's absolute silence. "Fabrizio?"

"Here." The muffled sound comes from my left, not next to me but below. "Down the slope."

"What are you doing down there?"

"I thought I'd take a shortcut" is the laconic reply, accompanied by a hoarse chuckle. With a sigh, I cautiously make my way down the slope until my foot pushes against something. I stop. Just then the clouds break up and a bright moon lights the meadow. I see Fabrizio lying in the tall grass with his arms outstretched and a blissful smile on his face. It's the first time I've ever seen him totally relaxed. I bend down and awkwardly tap his shoulder.

"We have to go back to the road."

He shakes his head. "The road's too dangerous in the dark. We have to stay here until dawn."

"That's not going to happen." I nudge him, and he grumbles.

"Why not? Do you have an appointment, Frau Journalist?"

"I'm not a—" A car approaches on the road above. Lucia! Straightening, I try to climb up the hill on all fours, but Fabrizio grabs my ankle, and my hands find nothing to hold on to in the dewy grass.

"Where are you running, Signora Phi . . . ?"

"Let go of me! Lucia will drive by if she doesn't see us." I kick—a reflex response. Unfortunately, the alcohol doesn't seem to impede his reaction time. A second hand now grasps my other leg.

"That's what's wrong with you Germans. You're always hurrying somewhere."

"I'm not a German, damn it. Half of one at most, you dumbass," I scream at him. Light sweeps above us, and I struggle to escape his grip. The car's headlights, then taillights, briefly shine over our heads. When the sound of the engine fades away, I stretch out in the wet grass in defeat. I wonder who hands out the shitty cards up above.

"Now that isss much better," Fabrizio mumbles. "Patience bears fruit; that's what my Nonna used to say."

"I am sick and tired of your Nonna! It's her fault that I'm sitting in a ditch with a stinking-drunk Italian," I say, sitting up. "Would you kindly remove your hands from my ankles?"

"I'm not stinking drunk. Slightly tipsy at most."

"Sure, and you can call me Christina Aguilera," I say, rubbing my ankles. They'll probably be black and blue.

"Why do you then insist that your name's Signora Philipp?"

"It was a joke."

"I don't get it."

"You know what? Forget it." Sighing, I stretch out my legs. Why not? I obviously can't talk sense into this guy.

We lie silently in the grass for a while. It's actually not unpleasant. The milky-white moonlight is spectacular. I even see some stars now. Out of habit, I scan the skies for the only constellation I know. There it is: the Big Dipper. The grass is a little scratchy and I don't even want to think about all the insects crawling over me, but . . .

"We can go now," Fabrizio whispers, close to my ear.

I start up. "Why? A minute ago you wanted to spend the night here."

"I thought you needed a break. But now you're ready to walk home. So, signora—after you."

I feel like I've been had.

After a good hour of silent walking, I in my shoes again and he barefoot, Fabrizio stops.

"What is it?" I ask, in less than a good mood. I left my romantic musings about the starry sky and clucking cicadas back in the ditch. A blister on my foot is burning like hell. That's what you get when your half-size feet mean your shoes are always too small or too big. All I want right now is to be far away from here, far from this thing called nature.

"Pssst." Fabrizio puts a finger to his mouth and motions at the darkness in front of us. I recognize the silhouette of a wall and an archway. It's Tre Camini's driveway. Thank god, we're here. I clench my teeth to limp ahead for the next hundred yards, but Fabrizio holds me back.

"We should—"

"Let go," I hiss. "No way are we taking another break."

Fabrizio drops his arm and shrugs. "As you wish. I just thought we—"

A bloodcurdling cry splits the night—shrill, deafening, right out of a horror movie. Something scurries in front of my feet, and an unexpected sharp pain shoots through my leg. Crying out, I jump aside. The thing hops up and down . . . and flaps its wings. The screeching turns into angry clucking.

I don't think I've ever run faster. When I finally collapse on Tre Camini's steps, a cramp is stitching my right side and my heart is pounding. So that's what it's like to bid your life good-bye. That stupid chicken! Fabrizio saunters into the dim circle of porch light a few moments later.

"I tried to warn you." He drops down next to me on the stairs. His sleeve touches my arm. "Everything all right?"

"What do you think?" I grumble and move a few inches away from him. "That beast had it out for me the minute I got here. Don't chickens sleep at night?"

"Usually." Fabrizio smiles. "But Vittoria thinks she's a guard dog."

"Whoop de doo."

"She's just a little chicken."

"Your little chicken bit my leg."

"Let me have a look." Before I can protest, Fabrizio props my leg on his knee and squints at it. I suddenly feel like I'm twelve. Or not. While he strokes my shinbone, I stare at the back of his neck, at all his little black curls of hair, and suddenly I want to touch them. Things are not going the way they're supposed to.

"Hm."

"What?"

"I'm afraid there's not much left to be done." He shakes his head regretfully. I jerk my leg off his knee.

"You're impossible."

"I've heard that before. Do you know that you smell like oranges?"

"Do I?" I say sheepishly.

"I like oranges."

He's drunk and he's flirting with me. He's flirting with me? My throat lumps up and an alarming tingling invades my stomach.

"You like oranges," I say. It's much easier to talk to him when he isn't being nice.

"Yes, I do, signora." He gets up with difficulty and brushes soil and dust from his pants. I don't even want to think how I look after our childish wrestling in the ditch. I touch my hair. "We're home, by the way," he adds. I nod and try to smile.

"Don't you want to go in, Signora Philipp?" He reaches for the door but misses the knob. At least he can fully pronounce my name again. He looks at me so intently that I feel naked.

"I'll be in in a moment. Just go ahead," I whisper, not looking at him. Fabrizio hesitates, but then the alcohol in his system seems to win out over his sense of chivalry. I wonder if he even remembers what happened in the bar. I should confront him about the engagement mess, but his dead-tired face tells me to postpone what will definitely turn out to be a verbal slap in the face—or maybe I should even forget it. It was probably a bad joke that one of his drinking pals started.

"Thanks for bringing me home," he says sluggishly and pushes the door open.

"Glad to do it. *Buona notte.*"

"*Buona notte,* Sofia."

I sit on the steps for almost an hour and watch the clouds turn pink. When I finally go in, I still don't know why it bothers me that he called me by his ex-girlfriend's name.

Chapter Eight
Hanna

There's no coffee in my bedroom when I wake up later that morning. I stare at the ceiling, the blanket pulled up to my chin, and ponder whether that's a good sign or a bad sign. Rosa-Maria did put an installment of a serial novel on my nightstand, under the mistaken assumption that I am interested in pulp fiction. More out of boredom than interest, I pick it up.

La Spinta di Speranza—Propelled by Hope. Who the hell comes up with these titles? I inspect the cover model's impressive abs and then leaf through the booklet. Words and phrases that make me blush jump out from the yellowed pages. So what. For lack of other reading matter, or perhaps just to refresh my Italian, I begin to read.

I toss away the blanket an hour and a half later, flushed, and dash to my tiny bathroom. After a bit, I make my way down the staircase in Lucia's flowered apron dress, carrying the slippers in my hand.

I'm welcomed by the song "Con Me Anche Tu"—"You're with Me, Too"—playing on the portable radio above the kitchen sink. A lone place setting—a cup and a golden-brown cornetto—waits on the table for a late breakfaster. I assume that's me. No sign of the guardian of the kitchen, but the old estate manager is sitting hunched over on the corner bench. He inspects me carefully, and his eyes come to rest on my bare feet. I offer a shy *"Buon giorno"* and pick up the tin espresso maker from the stove. Alberto clicks his tongue a few times, sounding like a gas lighter, and when I look at him, he points to his nose and winks conspiratorially.

"Hanna! There you are." Lucia comes in through the back door. She puts a basket with eggs on the counter and hugs me. A little too tightly for my taste. Hot coffee splashes over my hand. Lucia holds me at arm's length and looks at me intently. I'm immediately on guard.

"Lucia, what happened yesterday—"

"I already know everything. Fabrizio explained it to me this morning. I'm so happy for the two of you." She lets go and claps her hands, as blissful as if she just had a vision of the Virgin Mary. This can't be good.

"Fabrizio did—"

"I admit it, I was mad at first because of your little game—I mean, kitchen help and everything. And you made a real effort to make it seem like you couldn't stand each other. Honestly, though, I knew you liked him. You couldn't hide that."

"Hm . . . yes" is all I can manage in reply.

"But fate has a way of reuniting two people who are meant for each other," she says, giddy with excitement. "For you to meet each other again in Berlin, after all those years—it's so incredibly romantic."

Someone must be playing a huge prank on me right now. I glance over to Alberto, who, taking advantage of the commotion, is spooning real sugar into his coffee.

"Berlin . . . yes, really. An amazing coincidence." I come up for air. "Do you happen to know where Fabrizio is? I need to discuss something with him," I say. Lucia beams.

"He's in the outer apricot field." She points outside and blinks. "I was actually about to bring him and the workers coffee and some tramezzini. They could use some sandwiches right about now. Would you like to do that for me?"

"Absolutely," I say, louder than necessary, and quickly lower my voice. "That way I can talk with Fabrizio."

And wring his neck at the same time.

"By the way, Hanna . . ."

I'm going to draw and quarter him—yes. And then feed him to that nasty chicken.

Lucia's face flushes slightly. "You obviously won't sleep in that little staff room anymore. Rosa-Maria will bring your stuff up to Fabrizio's apartment."

"No!" I shout. Lucia looks confused. "I mean . . ." I search for words, but only come up with expletives for men in general and Italian machos specifically. "I don't think that's a good idea," I say. My fingers twitch, and not just because I'm thinking of the kitchen dragon discovering Giuseppa's sleeping place among my underwear. Just the thought of sharing a bed with that—I clutch my cup and swallow some burning-hot coffee. Lucia watches me with a tilted head, obviously wondering how to interpret my reaction. Suddenly she seems to understand.

"You want to save yourself for marriage! *Dio*, how sweet," she says, enchanted. I nod, relieved, and pick up the brimming tote bag and huge thermos. Claire would be dying of laughter if she were here. It would never cross my mind to take a vow of chastity before marriage. With some effort, I produce a pure and chaste smile.

"Exactly. We're waiting until after the wedding."

That'll never happen, not as long as I breathe.

After a final grin of blissful anticipation, I turn my back on Lucia and rush through the back door.

Fabrizio

I distinctly remember my first apricot. It was hard and tasted horrible. And I got my face slapped for it, one of the many slaps my father used to teach me respect for the fruit of our orchards. The *principale*, as workers and family members alike called him, was convinced that picking an unripe apricot was bad luck.

Today I understand what he meant. Apricots are a difficult business and cost time and nerves. The slender trees are as temperamental as divas, vulnerable to pests, wind, and wetness; a late frost can destroy the entire year's crop. But as soon as the year's first apricot lies in your hand like a velvety little creature, all troubles are forgotten. It breaks apart easily and the pit falls away by itself. Sweet and sour explode in your mouth—and, today, that explosion takes my mind off my throbbing head and heartburn.

I woke up this morning thinking about Sofia's flowing hair, and gradually, more and more frightening scenes filled in the gaps in my memory. The pencil-thin girl. Carlo punching the spot between my ribs, turning me black and blue. The fourth rum-and-Coke, and then the ones that I stopped counting. Sofia's tanned legs. Her lips that I kissed a thousand times in a previous life. Signora Philipp's cool mermaid eyes that did not seem so cold in the moonlight.

Now I think about Lucia's barrage of questions before my first espresso, and my garbled answers, attempts to escape my lovely sister-in-law to whom I can't tell the truth—ever. What shit I'm in.

I morosely toss the apricot pit into a furrow and cover it with soil. Then I pull my straw hat over my face. The midday sun burns my back. I'd rather be in bed in a dark, cool room.

"You seem to have enjoyed yourself last night, judging from how shitty you look this morning," says someone behind me. I turn. Marco is sitting on the bed of the pickup truck, in his running duds, as usual, and covered in sweat. He bites into an apricot with relish. I lift the harvesting basket and lug it to the truck. Unfortunately, Marco jumps aside before I can push him down with it.

"What do you want?" Everything goes black for a second, but I manage to hold on to the truck. A few apricots roll out of the truck bed and land at my feet.

"Hey! What happened to your top physical condition? Or are you still feeling the effects of the alcohol?" Marco grins and spits the pit on the ground.

"Don't you have to count some rolls of toilet paper?" I say and reach for my water bottle. Fighting the temptation to pour it over my head, I drink in gulps.

"Are you in any condition to listen to me, or should I wait until you've had a cold shower?"

"Spit it out and then beat it."

"The golf club sent us another offer. They'll add another fifteen thousand if we make a decision by the end of the year.

"What decision?" I say in a flat voice.

"They're offering twenty percent above market value. The money would solve all our troubles, Fabrizio. We could pay our debts and expand the hotel."

"You had the land appraised without telling me?" My fist itches to land in his smug face; I hold on to my belt buckle to keep it under control.

"Would you have listened if I'd told you about it?" Marco snorts.

"Your snotty friends from the golf club could never offer as much as the land is worth. You still don't get that? It should mean more to you, anyway. But then, your sense of family has always been underdeveloped."

"You're an idiot, Fabrizio. Tell me what a sense of family will do when your dearly beloved fields rob our family of our livelihood any day now. Fortunately, Nonna came to her senses, and I have to say that her insight surprised me. I think she wanted to pass on Tre Camini all along to someone who's reasonable, but she just couldn't bypass her favorite grandson. She knew, though, that you'd rather be rolled over by a tractor than let a girl put a ring on your finger. I, for one, do have a wife—and the sweet grandkids our old lady was so set on are only a matter of time. As for a flourishing business, I'll show it to you as soon as I sign the inheritance transfer naming me as the legitimate heir."

The idea strikes me like a lightning bolt. I listen to Marco's monologue with only half an ear as the solution unfolds in front of me like a signed legal document—with a very special seal.

"I'm getting married," I hear myself say, not very loud, but loud enough to make Marco interrupt his lecture.

"What do you mean?"

"Just what you heard, little brother," I say matter-of-factly, still sorting out my thoughts.

Point one: I need a woman. That can't be changed—but the choice is mine.

"I know you," Marco says with an arrogant smile. "You'd never chain yourself to a village nag just to do what Nonna wanted. And you won't find a woman in Montesimo who'd let a fat fish like you escape again."

Point two: Signora Philipp owes me big-time.

"Who says she's from Montesimo?" I ask.

Point three: she's a foreigner—a pretty foreigner who can't stand me, and therefore will disappear as fast as she appeared. I can marry her, take over the estate, and then get a divorce. No drama in the village, and no danger of an old matron tearing me to pieces because I don't agree till the day I die with everything her daughter, cousin, or whoever says.

Marco stares at me. "Are you thinking about Hanna, the kitchen help? I thought Lucia was joking. Are you still drunk?"

Point four: everyone gets what he or she wants, including Nonna, even though she probably had something else in mind.

I can't suppress a self-satisfied smile. I almost feel sorry for my little brother, who looks as if I've just swiped the last piece of panettone off his plate at Christmas.

"You should know by now that I don't do things halfheartedly. It's been that way since we were kids," I say pleasantly.

"But Nonna wanted—Hanna isn't even a real Italian. And you've only known her since, when—day before yesterday? You're playing games."

"I'm disappointed in you, Marco. You're a true-blue Italian—you should know there are no rules in love." I shrug. "What can I do? Signora Philipp is a beautiful woman, and I'm a man, after all."

"And she shows up just in time. By chance, right?"

Marco's anger makes it easier for me not to feel like a complete fool. *I'm a man, after all.* Did I really just say that? God, I must truly love this estate.

"It's gratifying to see that you're happy for me." I watch the redness on Marco's face spread all the way to his bald spot.

"Your plan won't work, Fabrizio. Maybe you didn't listen closely when the testament was read. Nonna demands a real marriage, not a business deal. I can smell a rat, and the notary will be grateful for any hint that something is wrong with your engagement."

And he won't be able to do anything about it, I think.

I step so close to Marco that I can smell his aftershave and sweat. "My compliments to the *notaio* when you phone him. And since you'll already have him on the line, invite him to the wedding next week," I whisper. I look him straight in the eye. "Anything else?"

My little brother doesn't answer but takes a step away from me.

"Good. Then hop on home in your sneakers and take care of any overdue business on your desk. I'm busy here."

Hanna

Half an hour after my hasty departure, I realize that the term "outer apricot orchard" is a flexible one, distance-wise but also topographically.

I'm struggling down a muddy path—a furrow, really—overgrown with roots. Even though I've been walking in one direction, I've still lost my sense of orientation because of the dense trees lining the way. On top of it, my shoes are completely wrong for this excursion. I've already pulled my right slipper out of the mud twice, and not much is left of its original color, let alone its fluffy white lining. The straps of the bag cut into my shoulders, and the thermos keeps slipping out of my sweaty hands. The helplessness I feel in this jungle fuels my rage. Serene Tuscany. Idyllic fruit orchards. Yeah, great! But only if you stay in your damn convertible on a damn asphalt road and avoid these arrogant, narcissistic Italians.

Huffing, I stop and push aside a tree branch that grabs at my hair. Unfortunately it lashes back like a whip, and I rub my cheek, groaning. I'm about to give up and turn around. How did I end up in this shivering hole of sh—

Suddenly I hear agitated voices through the screen of trees. It takes me a moment to understand the burst of Italian.

"I'm disappointed in you, Marco. You're a true-blue Italian—you should know there are no rules in love. What can I do? Signora Philipp is a beautiful woman, and I'm a man, after all."

My pulse quickens as I remember Fabrizio in the moonlight and feel that same strange tingling sensation as last night. I put down the bag and thermos carefully, take off my slippers, and duck under a low branch. My toes sink into the soil as I sneak closer to the two men.

"Your plan won't work, Fabrizio," Marco says. "Maybe you didn't listen closely when the testament was read. Nonna demands a real marriage, not a business deal. I can smell a rat, and the notary will be grateful for any hint that something is wrong with your engagement."

"My compliments to the *notaio* when you phone him. And since you'll already have him on the line, invite him to the wedding next week—"

I stop suddenly. Did he just say "wedding"?

Something rustles about two yards from me and I automatically hunker down, hand over my mouth. I watch a pair of muscular legs sprint away. The other legs are clothed in dirty jeans and seem stuck to the ground. I beat a crouching retreat through the trees. Back on my marshy trail, I stop and contemplate my mud-encrusted feet.

First the matter of the kitchen job, and now a wedding? There are only two explanations for this absurd soap opera: either the whole thing is a hair-raising but harmless nightmare that will come to an end with the ringing of my alarm clock any moment now—or God is a quarrelsome woman and this is her punishment for sins I committed these past twenty years. Unfortunately that's the more likely explanation.

I might have gotten myself into this unbearable mess because I stole Giuseppa's urn, and I'm willing to face the music for that—but only to a degree.

I seize the lunch bag, stick the thermos under my arm, pick a couple of reddish-yellow apricots from the nearest branch, and then resume my march, head raised high. I'm determined to teach this self-absorbed chauvinist that he can't do whatever he wants, least of all with Hanna Philipp.

But I've underestimated both the soil around here and the apricot trees. Their claw-like branches let me go only after I've lost one shoe (I stumbled somewhere), gotten scratched in the face (it's not always a good idea to walk upright), suffered a blister on my upper arm from the leaky thermos, dropped the lunch bag, and sworn like a fishwife.

Just a few yards down the path, I find him leaning against his olive-green pickup truck. Well, at least part of my plan will work. I drop the bag and thermos and wind up my arm.

I've never been a good thrower—the art of arcing a ball elegantly and landing the damn thing where I want it has remained a mystery to me. Flat pitches that succumb to gravity after two seconds and habitually miss their target are my forte.

But this time I have a hit.

"Lunch, dear!" I shout. "Just a little taste of what awaits you during married life, Signor Camini."

Fabrizio winces, touches the back of his head, and turns around in surprise. I pluck some more apricots from the closest branch and continue to fire. Successful again! I nail his chest.

"Hey! Stop!"

"I don't think so," I scream back. My hand circles another apricot, light yellow and hard. My victim retreats behind the door of his truck.

"This is totally childish, Signora Philipp."

"Is it?" It is, but it's also extremely liberating.

To my irritation, Fabrizio seems amused, not angry, after he recovers from his surprise. "There's more Italian in you than I suspected. But didn't your parents teach you not to play with food? You're wasting my apricots. You'll have to spend an extra day in the kitchen to pay for it."

"Bite me!"

"Not a very proper way to express yourself."

"But it's proper to schedule a wedding without asking the bride if that's what she wants?"

It's quiet behind the car door for a moment, which gives me the opportunity to collect more ammunition. Freed from its load, the branch bobs up and down. I briefly weigh an apricot in my hand, and then throw it against the truck door. Squinting, I follow up with another. I wonder if my insurance will cover the dents. I doubt it.

"I can explain," he shouts.

"I'm listening."

"First you have to stop trying to kill me."

The next apricot whooshes past the door and smashes into a tree trunk. My beginner's luck is running out. Gasping, I drop my hand.

"You have two minutes."

"That's not enough."

"All right, three."

His curly head appears through the car window. "That's unexpected. You're funny." He's grinning, and, even though I'm still mad, I can't help it—I grin back.

"Don't tempt fate," I say.

"I wouldn't dare."

He comes out with hands raised and stops half a yard in front of me, his head tilted. The corners of his mouth twitch when he sees my muddy feet. "Were you on a jungle mission?"

"I was in a hurry and took a shortcut," I say, trying not to let on that I'm embarrassed by my deficient sense of direction.

"Let me guess. You found the pack-animal path, the one the donkeys take along the edge of the orchard. It's narrow and usually muddy. Quite strenuous for two-legged creatures," he says with a smile.

So that's why there were fist-size holes in the mud—hoofprints. I should have guessed. I push my chin forward. "I'm still waiting for your three-minute explanation."

"First I'd like to show you something." He bends down to pick up the lunch bag and motions to the old pickup. "How about breakfast?"

I shake my head, but my stomach growls, contradicting me.

"I take that as a yes." Fabrizio strolls to his truck and opens the passenger door with an inviting bow. "After you, signora."

That's three minutes for you.

Fabrizio

It's unusual to have a woman in my car who isn't related by blood or marriage. Signora Philipp holds the worn armrest stiffly, her knees pressed together, while I rest my elbow on the frame of the open window.

We've barely talked since we took off. The potholed road demands my full attention, and neither of us wants to scream over the Nissan's six-cylinder engine. Signora Philipp looks out the side window with half-closed eyes. She doesn't seem to notice the rocking and jolting.

I make a quick stop at the tractor, where Paolo, Bartek, and two other workers are taking their lunch break, talking and smoking. The Polish workers lift their hats and call out, *"Buon giorno, principale!"* as I hand Lucia's sandwich packages through the window, after having fished out the one marked for me. They crane their necks to get a glimpse of my pretty passenger.

When we reach the gravel path that leads up to Rabbit Hill, I sneak a peek at Signora Philipp's white legs. Her feet are sprinkled with brown, and one is stuck in a dirt-encrusted slipper. I'm astonished that she doesn't seem to mind. Sofia would have demanded I bring her home immediately so she could clean up. I step on the gas, and the truck shoots up the hill with a grinding noise.

I park a few yards away from the covered benches at the top. Signora Philipp gets out before I kill the motor. She stops abruptly, her hand still on the door handle. Her lungs seem to forget their function for a moment—she's holding her breath. I smile. Nobody's unaffected by the view. The arrow-straight lines of trees undulating in all four directions—as if God had tamed the hill with a gigantic comb and liked it so much he couldn't stop—enchant even me.

"Does all this belong to Tre Camini?" she asks quietly when I step up next to her.

"This is Tre Camini," I say proudly.

"It's breathtaking. And now you're going to tell me a story about it, aren't you?"

There is no flippancy in her gaze. Instead, her mermaid eyes look at me with such intensity that I have to turn away. It's been too long since I've had a woman in my bed—that's the only explanation for my attraction to even a cold fish like Signora Philipp.

"You don't like stories?"

"I'm a journalist—did you forget? Stories are my job."

"That doesn't answer my question."

"It does. You might remember that I love my job."

"How could I forget?" I say drily.

She straightens her shoulders. "So?"

I have to laugh. She's curious and doesn't want to admit it. I decide to keep her in suspense. "Right now I'm hungry," I say and turn around to get Lucia's coffee and sandwiches from the pickup. Always considerate, my sister-in-law packed two tramezzini for me and an extra-generous portion of her pâté, which everyone is crazy about. She even added some tiny cherry tomatoes from her sacred kitchen garden. Every meal at Tre Camini is planned carefully.

We eat in silence as we look out over the hills. I gulp it down while she eats like a little bird, seemingly more interested in the view. Lucia's coffee is just the way I like it: black, strong, and sugary. Signora Philipp grimaces when she takes a sip. Her body language is so clear, as clear as her words; she seems to be an open book, until you realize after a few pages that the author's *intentions* are completely unclear. Confusing. When I finish my food, I ask for the rest of hers and she gives it to me.

"Why don't you like your brother?" she suddenly asks.

"What makes you think that I don't?" I reply to buy time. I don't want to let on that I saw her eavesdropping before—or, rather, heard her crashing through the underbrush like a wild boar.

"I just have a feeling. You seem to avoid each other, and you made a remark at dinner on Monday that made me wonder." She lies without blushing.

"Not so, Signora Philipp. Of course I like him. He's my brother. I just don't think highly of him."

She seems amused. "Is that really different?"

"Oh, yes. One concerns the person, the other his attitude, his philosophy of life," I say. "The fact that Marco and I disagree doesn't mean that I don't love him."

"And what exactly is your philosophy of life?"

"Is this an interview? Do you need it for your new article?"

"Maybe." She grins. I begin to relax. She has a way of making you talk. You reveal things you'd rather keep to yourself, without feeling uncomfortable. Besides, she's not sulking anymore. I hate nothing more than a woman who never lets you forget what you did wrong. After a little pause, I look at her, determined not to let her green eyes affect me.

"My grandmother believed that a successful life isn't measured by the amount of money you make. You just have to feel a connection to something to be happy." I gesture from the hills to the sky. "For example, to this land."

"Your grandmother was a wise woman."

"And all her wisdom could really get on your nerves. Tre Camini meant everything in the world to her, even though she didn't know anything about agriculture before she married. Olives or wine would be a more profitable business in this type of soil, but my family has always been obsessed with harvesting the best apricots in the area—the queen of fruits. My grandfather died in these fields. My father was broken here by his unfulfilled dream, to make our apricots known all over Europe.

Nonna passed on this inheritance, and I . . ." I rummage in my jeans pockets until I remember that I smoked the last cigarette last night.

"And you?" Signora Philipp looks at me attentively.

"I can't give it up," I say, and the truth, unspoken until now, almost chokes me. "I can't give it up even if I wanted to."

I swallow hard and clear my throat so this woman doesn't get the impression that I'm about to cry like a girl. "Which leads me to your question about the somewhat unfortunate situation you landed in. My grandmother's last will—"

"Stipulates that you have to get married in order to inherit the estate," she finishes. She looks at me with part amusement and part compassion. "Lucia told me."

I shrug. "What can I say? Nonna was convinced that I need a woman at my side."

She thinks for a moment. "Why don't you ask your ex-girlfriend? She still seems to be into you."

I feel my forehead wrinkle. "Sofia? Are you joking?"

"I'm not."

The mere thought is absurd. Getting involved with Sofia a second time would be like getting back on a motorcycle after breaking both legs—and arms—in a high-speed accident. I might be a fool, but I'm not stupid. "I plan to *get* married but not *stay* married. Divorcing a woman from anywhere around Montesimo is unthinkable—family honor, purgatory, all that stuff."

"I understand. So that's why you thought of me," she says with some heat. "I'm half-German and have no family or any of that other inconvenient stuff."

"Well, you don't seem to be a strict Catholic, and I mean that as a compliment."

The corners of her mouth twitch. "What if I still say no?"

"You wanted to know what I'm going to do about the lawsuit against your magazine." I push aside the feeling that I'm setting something in motion that will turn out badly for everyone involved. No matter how wrong my plan might be, I have no other choice. "I will withdraw the suit in exchange for a short-term marriage—a second business deal. After that, you're free as a bird. An *employed* bird."

"You can't be serious! You have me work as a slave in your kitchen for two weeks, and now you're trying to blackmail me again? Don't you think that's a little over-the-top?"

I'm glad that she's mad as hell—it makes her predictable and lowers my body temperature by ten degrees. Raving women leave me absolutely cold.

"I'm Italian, Signora Philipp. An Italian never goes too far, only as far as it takes. Just look at it this way: I'll pretend that the deal is a request, and we'll forget that you have no choice."

Signora Philipp doesn't barrage me with insults and curses, like an Italian woman would. "I have no choice," she repeats, looking out over the hills. Then she looks straight at me. "We finally seem to agree on something, Signor Camini."

I can't help feeling triumphant. "So we have a deal?" I stretch out my hand.

"Isn't there something you forgot?" she says icily.

I drop my hand. It was too easy.

"It's customary for a man to ask the bride formally."

"Are you kidding? You want a formal marriage proposal?"

She raises her eyebrows. "Just look at it this way: I'll pretend to do it out of my own free will, and we'll forget that you don't have a choice, either."

At first I don't know whether to be impressed or upset. She doesn't look like she's joking. I think of Tre Camini and my apricots; of Alberto, Paolo, and Rosa-Maria; of Nonna and Lucia. Remembering the look on Marco's face does the rest. I'll have to swallow my pride, even if the bitter pill is as big as the giant glass marbles Marco and I used to fight over. I sink down on a knee and take Signora Philipp's hand. It rests limply in mine.

"Dear Signora Philipp, will you marry me?" I say. I just hope that none of the laborers witness this spectacle. She looks down at me silently.

"Not very convincing," she says finally and withdraws her hand. After what seems like an eternity, she adds, "But I'll look the other way."

Relieved, I get up, wishing I could shake myself like a dog—and not because my pants are dusty.

"You're doing me a big favor," I say. It's hard to sound grateful. I'd much rather wring her neck for humiliating me in front of the entire world, even if only a few rabbits saw me on my knees.

"Don't flatter yourself," she says. "I'm doing it for my job, which means at least as much to me as the apricots mean to you. And for Lucia, who liked your stupid idea because she believes in true love. I won't be the one to tell her the truth."

She's right. Disappointing Lucia is like leaving a pizza in the oven too long. You burn your mouth and then do everything you can to never do it again.

"We'll let Lucia believe her fairy tale until I have my fields and your boss has forgiven you. Then you'll be out of here, and I'll take care of everything else," I say, as if everything else will be a breeze. Lucia isn't going to speak to me for the next thirty years.

"And you're sure you're not in the Mafia and 'out of here' means I'll find myself in some lake with my feet in concrete?" She rubs her arms as if she were cold. The gesture makes her seem stubborn and vulnerable at the same time, and I have to fight the urge to step closer to her.

"The Mafia is everywhere around here, Signora Philipp. But you don't have to worry—there's not a single lake."

But she doesn't seem to find me funny.

Her handshake is dry and firm, just like the way she speaks: short and resolute. Then she gathers the sandwich wrappings, neatly folding rather than crumpling the paper, and limps in her one slipper toward the truck. I bite my lip.

"Signora Philipp?"

"What?"

"I think it's time we address each other less formally."

Hanna

I prepared myself for all sorts of responses—anything from a one-minute laughing fit to a sermon. I even prepared myself for a torrent of French expletives. But I didn't expect silence on the other end of the line.

"Claire, are you still there?" I whisper.

"Hm."

"Is that all? You can't come up with anything more than a lame 'hm'?"

Silence again. In the background, I hear the sounds of a metropolis at night. How I'd love to be back in Berlin right now, sitting at my desk in the deserted office, listening to the clicking of my keyboard and the radio on low, while the muted sounds of cars and occasional honking come through the windows. A week ago, silly cow that I am, I had no idea that my life was so together.

"Oooh, I'm still sorting," she finally says. An alarming word. She usually only says "sorting" when she's talking about Jan's socks.

"And how much longer do you need?" I ask.

"Hold on a moment. You don't answer my calls for days. Then you call at one in the morning with a crazy love story and expect a coherent analysis from me? *C'est impossible!*" Claire starts laughing.

"What do you mean, 'love story'?" I say, and she just laughs louder.

"First you have to toil in the kitchen so Fabrizio will take back his poor grandmother, who's languishing in your underwear. Then he wants you to marry him so he'll drop the suit. And now you—both of you—have to play the loving couple for his crazy family even though you aren't in love. And on top of that, this Italian lord of the manor is not an obnoxious country boy, but an educated and extremely sexy man. So if you ask me, it definitely sounds like a love story. Actually, an *amour fou*, if you know what I mean—a tale of passion. Dime-novel writers would kill for that storyline."

"But I don't think Fabrizio is sexy at all."

"Of course not," Claire says. "Your nether regions have always been slower than your brain."

I gasp. This conversation isn't going the way I wanted it to. Whatever her reaction, I didn't expect to be *more* confused after telling her everything.

"Claire, I know it's a disaster. You don't have to rub it in."

"What do you want me to say?" Claire asks, and I can tell that she's smiling. She drives me up the wall sometimes.

"What do you think? I want you to tell me how I can get out of this mess."

"Pas du tout" is her prompt reply.

"What do you mean, 'not at all'?"

"I mean absolutely not. There's a reason you are where you are." I can imagine her nonchalant shrug. "Make the best of it."

Make the best of it? That's easy for her to say. I close my eyes. "So you think I should actually marry him?" I say, even though the answer was obvious even before I called.

"What do you have to lose? Worst-case scenario, you can't show your face in this Monte-whatever again. It seems like Signor Camini will keep his promise. And divorces can be arranged quickly—if you will still want one."

"Of course I'll want a divorce."

"Then it's all crystal clear," Claire says gently, and I can tell she doesn't believe a word I say. "But if you want my two cents' worth: Find things to like at that place. I know you have to sweat it out in the kitchen, and this Rosa-Maria sounds scary, but hey, you're at a romantic manor house in Tuscany with a gorgeously built . . ."

"Shut up, Claire."

"I won't say anything else. Just buckle down and enjoy beautiful Italy. *Savoir vivre*, remember?"

"I'll try. I'm sorry for waking you." I don't want to hang up. I wish Claire could hug me right now. This Italian chaos is wreaking such havoc with me that I even want my mother.

"*Pas de problème*, that's what friends are for. But Hanna?"

"Yes?"

"Just listen to your heart for a change."

Chapter Nine

Hanna

"Hey, Signora Know-It-All! If you want to learn things about Italian food, you've got to watch."

I've been trying—desperately—to see the sunny side of my Italian situation. The last three days, I've gotten up with Vittoria's crowing, worn the apron and slippers, and finished Rosa-Maria's slave labor without complaint. I'm even reading the awful dime novels to soften her up.

Fabrizio's only shown up for meals—which he eats, like his brother, in silence—so my days are an herb-infused blur of Rosa-Maria's commands, Lucia's consolations, and the crushing realization that my article was completely off. Rosa-Maria guards the quality and freshness of her ingredients like a bloodhound.

"*Terribile*, absolutely awful!" Rosa-Maria stares at the content of my pot. I wanted to prove that even Germans can make a delicious Bolognese sauce, but she shakes her head. "The meat is dry and flavorless." She throws the sauce into the sink.

"But you didn't even try it," I protest.

She shrugs. "If the aroma comes out instead of staying in the sauce, the ragù is only good for chickens." The master cook pushes me aside and sets her own tomato sauce on the stove. She opens the freezer and takes out a brick-size package of ground meat.

"You can't sauté the meat first. That destroys the flavor," she tells me. I watch in disbelief as she plops the brick into the sauce. Luckily Lucia rushes into the kitchen right then, drowning out my "Yuck!"

"Does anyone know where I put the guest list?" She glances around the kitchen, lifts a cutting board, checks underneath it, and then drops it back on the counter.

"What guest list? Shouldn't a wedding at city hall be over in half an hour?" I say suspiciously.

Lucia looks at me as if I'd lost my marbles. Rosa-Maria stirs her pot and chuckles quietly.

"Benvenuto in bella Italia," she mumbles and exchanges a glance with Lucia.

"We have to move the ceremony to the community hall," Lucia says.

"Why?"

"Well, there's not enough room at city hall."

"But this family isn't that big." Then I understand—although I'd prefer to not know the answer to my next question. "How many people are coming?"

"According to the mayor, our village has three hundred and fifty-six people, not counting children."

I swallow. Three hundred fifty-six witnesses to the biggest lie of my life. Can it get any worse? I plop down on the bench next to Alberto. He's staring at the television, and I suddenly wonder if he uses the TV as a cover for eavesdropping.

"But do we have to invite everyone? It's not even a church wedding," I say in a tiny voice.

"Fortunately, we don't have to bother to invite *anyone*. Everyone in the village will show up anyway, if only for Rosa-Maria's ribollita,"

Lucia says. "Of course, they'll also come because of you and Fabrizio. They just love your incredibly romantic story."

"How nice." Help!

"We'll obviously have to hold a church wedding later—a grand one, with a wedding dress and a cake and all the works. Otherwise everyone will be insulted. I hope your relatives from Berlin will be able to come then, too. This is just a warm-up celebration." Lucia beams.

Wedding dress and wedding cake. I'm about to throw up.

"All of this really sounds *in-cred-ibly* romantic," says someone behind us. Marco is leaning against the door with arms folded. My cheeks heat up when I notice a crumpled edition of *Genusto* magazine under his arm. Didn't I see Fabrizio stash the article in his desk drawer? I somehow manage to endure Marco's piercing look and paste on a casual smile.

"Ciao, Marco. Would you like an espresso?" I say nonchalantly. It's not that I don't like Marco. I still feel the same way about him as on my first day, when we ran into each other in the hallway. But now I seem to run into him all the time. And he always looks at me as if he knows something is fishy. It makes me very uncomfortable.

He comes into the kitchen, kisses Lucia, and gently touches her nose. "Yes, I'd actually like an espresso. Maybe you could drink one with me, Hanna—in the office. There are a few things that we need to discuss about the wedding."

"Oh, I'd love to, but"—I look at Rosa-Maria for help; she's stirring the frozen ground beef to perfection—"Rosa-Maria needs me."

"Nonsense. It would be nice to not have Hanna under my feet for a while," she says. Well, it was worth a try.

I make a last, desperate attempt. "But we were going to talk about Prudence and Hugh. I'm just at the exciting part where she finds the MacKay coat of arms in her medallion and Hugh's attitude suddenly changes." I have successfully ingratiated myself to the cook through sharing thoughts about *Propelled by Hope*, and I have to admit that I'm now as hooked on each installment as she is. After spending two sleepless nights with the first three, I'm so caught up in this love story—no matter how horrible it is—that I can't wait to read the next part that Rosa-Maria doles out to me. But Rosa-Maria is too stoic for my excuses.

"No, no, Signora Can't-Wait-for-It. I'm not going to tell you what happens next. That'll be the day." She laughs and wiggles her raised finger. At least she has warmed toward me a little, ever since Prudence and the breathtaking Hugh remind me each night that it has been ages since a man was next to me, let alone on me.

Marco gives Lucia another kiss, strokes her belly, and whispers something in her ear that makes her shake a finger in jest. I clear my throat, embarrassed. He turns around with a smirk on his face.

"Well, then, Signora Philipp. Let's leave these experts to their work and have a look at the papers."

"All right," I say and accept two cups of coffee from Lucia.

Her smile comes from the heart. "It isn't right anyway that you still do hard kitchen duty, when you're Fabrizio's fiancée," she says.

Oh, you clueless angel. If you only knew.

"That's exactly why I want to help." I hesitate for a moment—Marco probably notices. "After all, soon I'll be part of the family."

I'm sure the face that Marco makes, as if he just saw a rat scurry across the tiled floor, is not in my imagination.

Fabrizio

"*Dio,* Fabrizio. Why are you sitting here alone in the dark?"

"I'm thinking."

"Can't you do that in the daylight, like a normal person?"

I squint when Lucia pushes the button to open the distillery's blinds, and dust particles shimmer in the morning sun.

"Why are you sitting on the dirty floor?" she asks, both hands on her hips.

"You sound like Nonna," I say, amused, but add, "This is a distillery, dear sister-in-law, not a hotel lobby."

"This is a dirty shed, dear brother-in-law, not a distillery," Lucia replies. She wrinkles her nose and gestures to stacked fruit crates in the middle of the room, broken glass in front of the shelves, and garbage bags piled at the door. Her public-health inspection makes me realize that I've worn the same stained work pants for an entire week.

"That's no way to interact with customers," she says.

"What customers?"

"Exactly. If I were a customer, I wouldn't come here, either—no matter how good the liqueur is. We have to change that."

She grabs a crate, turns it upside down, and sits on it, pressing her knees together. "So?" she says gently and puts her hands in her lap. I eye her suspiciously. Women who suddenly transform from lionesses to kittens have to be approached with caution.

"What do you mean?" Answering a question with a question is a safe approach for a man—most of the time, at least.

"You have to ask?"

"Lucia, help me out here. I'm a man. I have no idea what you women think. Why can't you just ask a straightforward question?"

"Did you find Nonna's recipe notebook?"

"No."

"That's not good, is it?"

"It's a tragedy, at least for me. Marco will be delighted. It gives him one more argument for selling the fields."

"You're wrong about Marco, Fabrizio."

"Maybe, but he hasn't convinced me otherwise," I say. I play with the knob of the thermostat. Maybe the liqueur isn't right because I had it on too high and the water evaporated too quickly.

Without looking at me, Lucia says, "I thought you'd be happy, now that you found Hanna."

"I am."

"So why don't I ever see you together?"

I sidestep her question. "She's here. Isn't that enough?"

"Enough?" She laughs. "You men are strange creatures. Of course it's not enough! You should show her our neighborhood, take her out, introduce her to our friends . . . Show up in the village together. People are already talking."

"Are they? What are they saying?"

"You don't want to know."

"Lucia, if you bring up a subject, you have to make your point. So they're gossiping about me and Hanna in the village," I say, trying not to sound annoyed. I can easily imagine the tongues wagging, led by the old nag Gosetti, and the baker's daughter—who feels cheated out of the title "lady of the manor"—and the lovely mayor's wife.

"A few people claim you're only doing it because of Nonna's inheritance," Lucia blurts out. I feel my cheeks heat up. Some people are actually smarter than I anticipated. "Is that true? Do you only want to marry Hanna because of the estate?"

"Do you think I'm capable of such a thing?"

Lucia hesitates, and then shakes her head. "It doesn't matter what I think. I just don't want to be the target of all this speculation. We're part of a village and have to play by the rules if we want to fit in. Lately Rosa-Maria keeps finding excuses for not going shopping so she can avoid the nasty gossip, and Alberto has been too afraid to go to the bakery for his sweets for the last three days."

"You know about that?"

"You must all think I'm clueless. Obviously Alberto doesn't drive to the village every day to get the mail," she snorts with a tiny smile. "But I don't have to take away all his fun, do I?"

"Have I ever told you that you're a wonderful woman, Lucia?"

"If that's your opinion, you should make sure I don't turn into a cranky nervous wreck. Planning your wedding is all I can handle at the moment."

"And I thought you volunteered for the job," I grin, and duck—Lucia is winding up to hit me. "So you think I don't pay enough attention to Hanna. All right, I can change that. I couldn't care less about the village gossip, but we'll take a few strolls across the town square holding hands, just for you. And we'll go to that stupid dinner at Ernesto's. Are you satisfied?"

"It's not a stupid dinner. I think it's a beautiful tradition that the mayor invites the couple to a dinner at city hall before their marriage," Lucia says. It seems as if she wants to add something, but my warning glance makes her stop. I push aside the ugly thought that I once left Ernesto's private residence slamming the doors and haven't returned since. Today isn't then, and even in small villages the dust eventually settles over scratches and wounds.

"All right, Lucia. We'll have dinner there."

"Good. Now go and shower and put on some clean clothes. If you stink like a donkey, you don't have a chance—even with your fiancée."

I offer an innocent smile. "Believe me, Lucia, Hanna accepts me in practically any condition."

Hanna

It's strange. I'm sitting in the same room, on the same chair that I sat in one week ago across from Fabrizio, and I feel more confused and insecure than ever. I didn't realize that Fabrizio's office is also Marco's, which explains how he got hold of the article that he's now smoothed and placed in the middle of the desk.

I give Marco a sideways glance. He leans back in Fabrizio's chair, arms crossed, and watches a fly climbing along the window. Maybe I feel so uneasy because he doesn't seem to belong in this room. Fabrizio filled it by his mere presence, but Marco looks like a misplaced puzzle piece behind this desk—somehow part of the picture, but trying too hard to fill a gap that he isn't meant for. I'm slowly beginning to understand what Fabrizio said on Rabbit Hill. I startle when Marco suddenly addresses me, still watching the unfortunate fly.

"Did you know that Tre Camini is close to bankruptcy?"

I clear my throat. "No."

He laughs as if my embarrassment delights him. "The advantage numbers have over people is that they can't be misread. They prove where one really is in life."

I fidget in my chair. "What exactly do you want from me, Signor Camini?"

"Call me Marco. After all, we'll be family soon, as you said so beautifully."

My throat constricts. His eyes are too knowing for me to brush away how uneasy I feel. He's guessed that something isn't right with the engagement, and part of the reason lies in front of us. He follows my look and points to the magazine. "Nice article, though somewhat destructive, I'd say," he says. "You didn't tell us that you're a restaurant reviewer."

"And I didn't know that you spoke German," I say.

He just smiles. "There are excellent translators available on the Internet, and they deliver within a few hours."

I exhale. "The article was a mistake, and I'm here to write a retraction—among other things."

"The secret mission, hm?" Marco reaches for a green notebook with a red bookmark and uses it to fan himself. "Drink your espresso. It's getting cold," he says without much interest, deepening my confusion. I follow the dangling bookmark with my eyes. This man is like a slippery eel—if you do manage to catch him, he shocks you. I pick up my cup, but my hand is shaking so much that I have to put it down. That makes me defiant.

"The article is none of your business, and I can't think what we need to discuss about the wedding. So why are we sitting here?"

"I knew you were smart right away."

"Get to the point, Marco. There's work waiting for me," I say coolly, not returning his smile. It promptly collapses. The change in his face is almost eerie, and I wonder how I could have been so wrong about him. His graciousness and good nature evaporate. He slams the notebook down and scrutinizes me like a mongoose stares down a rattlesnake.

"I want to discuss numbers with you—specifically, how much it will cost me for you and your wheeled suitcase to disappear. Whatever Fabrizio offered you to marry him, I'll pay more."

I let his words just sit there. They affect me more than I expected, and my confusion turns into rage within a few beats. The sneaky bastard.

"What makes you think that I can be bought?" I say with ice in my voice, noticing only then that I'm standing, not sitting, both of my hands on the desk. I lean forward, close to Marco's smug grin. "Maybe you're so grief-stricken over your grandmother's death that you don't know what you're talking about." I lower my voice, even though I feel like screaming at him. "But don't you dare ever treat me like a floozy again. I am your brother's fiancée, and you will show me that respect. There's only one reason I'm marrying Fabrizio: I love him. I've loved him from the first moment I met him, and nothing is going to change that, not a bankrupt estate and not a bag of bribe money. So shove your numbers and your Mafioso attitude where the sun don't shine, *brother-in-law*."

The silence lasts forever and my heart throbs hard. *"Mon dieu,"* Claire whispers in my head. *"That was good enough for a movie—you sounded like you meant everything you said."*

But Marco's face shows no emotion at all, not awe or anything else. Finally he shakes his head and bends down. He turns on the shredder under the desk.

"How very tragic. Such true love! And so one sided." He picks up the notebook and holds it in his palm for a while. When I don't answer—partly because of the enormity of what I just said and partly because his own damning words are just starting to make sense—he opens his eyes wide in mock horror: "Don't tell me you didn't know." In one smooth movement, without looking down, he shoves the notebook into the shredder.

"I have no idea what you're talking about," I say, voice raised to compete with the shredder, my arms crossed in front of my chest. This scene has the feel of a dark comedy—and I'm in the tragic main role. The play is Fabrizio's, however, and I promised to be part of it.

After Marco turns off the shredder, he comes around to my side of the desk. I automatically shrink back. I'm taller than he, but still, alarm bells go off in my head. But Marco stops at an appropriate distance and leans against the desk.

"Our dear Fabrizio gave his heart to someone else long ago, Hanna, and you're out of your league in that competition. Nothing to be ashamed of, but even a supermodel has no chance against Sofia. He's using you, and he'll get rid of you as soon as he has secured the inheritance. Everyone knows that, even the people in town."

"I'm sorry to disappoint you, but you're wrong," I lie, cringing on the inside. Sofia. Actually, the signs have all been there. Marco inspects his fingernails with a smile. They're short and neat, and his hands are probably soft as a baby's.

"I hope for your sake that I am wrong," he says. "Because if this marriage actually isn't just a business deal, you'll soon find out that you bet on the wrong horse. I only mean well."

"Thank you for your concern. But I'm used to taking care of myself."

To my relief, Marco doesn't stop me from walking out. But I pause at the door. Damn my curiosity. "Why do you want to prevent this marriage so badly, Marco?"

He looks at me strangely. His chest rises and falls, and I suddenly realize that his cold and calculating behavior is only a facade. "I protect what I love, starting with my wife, all the way to this estate. Lucia has earned a comfortable life in a place where she feels at home. If my brother takes over Tre Camini and keeps dreaming of international success for his apricots, our business will have to declare bankruptcy within a few years. The restaurant and hotel won't be able to offset the deficits in the long run. I cannot allow that."

"I understand." I can't help feeling sorry for Marco. He's in the same hopeless situation as his brother—both are afraid to lose what they love most. Sad, but none of my business. I straighten up and try to stay on script. "I'm going to marry Fabrizio, though. And you won't be able to prevent it."

"We'll see. No hard feelings," he says condescendingly.

I nod and turn to leave.

"One more thing, sister-in-law. Lucia hates to be lied to, especially by people she loves. If there's any truth in my assumptions, you better tell her soon." Pointing to the magazine, he says, "Before someone else decides to tell her."

I'm too agitated to go back to the kitchen and pretend I had a nice little chat with Marco. So I grab the basket Lucia keeps in the hallway for collecting eggs and go to the chicken coop, a decision I regret the very moment I enter. A dozen eyes stare at me. Like the distillery next door, the shed is larger than it looks from outside. A wire cage takes up half the room, and the space smells strongly of straw and bird droppings. Three hens with fluffed feathers sit on metal roosts on one wall. Little wooden houses—for nesting, I assume—are lined up along the cage like a miniature village. There's clucking and cackling inside. I look at the basket in my hand, not sure what to do. It would be embarrassing to leave without eggs. I put the basket down, drop onto a bale of straw, and bury my chin in my hands. The steady cackling is calming, even though I still feel a little nervous to be near the chickens.

I watch a speckled brown hen scratch in the straw and then I get up slowly, slide back the cage's metal bolt, which feels oily against my fingertips, and push open the little door. The hen pauses and then continues scratching. OK. Let's say that was an invitation. I close my eyes, take a deep breath, and step inside the cage.

For quite a while I'm unable to move, more out of disbelief than fear. Nothing actually happens. The brown hen shows no intention of attacking me, but struts slowly away. The hens on the roost don't seem to notice the intruder. I tiptoe to the nearest nesting house, while an army of fists drums against the inside of my chest. One egg. I'd like to leave with at least one egg. I carefully remove the nearest lid, and a deep, throaty sound greets me—not much different from a growl. I freeze and almost cry out. A familiar face stares at me: Vittoria.

Fabrizio

At first, Rosa-Maria doesn't notice me. Elbows on the counter, she's buried in one of her beloved trashy novels. Her mouth is half open, her face distorted like she's about to sob and laugh all at once. The book looks old and tattered. She's probably read it a hundred times. When I lightly knock on the doorframe, she gives a start and puts aside the booklet immediately.

"I don't mean to disturb you, Rosa-Maria. Have you seen Hanna, by any chance?"

"The signora went to the chicken shed," she says. She seems surprised that I don't add one of my usual biting comments about her taste in reading material. She reaches for a wooden spoon and weighs it in her hand as if contemplating what to do with it. Then she starts to stir the large sauce pot energetically.

I cross the yard feeling guilty. It's wrong to make Rosa-Maria feel bad about doing something she likes. I decide to keep my opinion about her books to myself from now on—she's her own person, after all. I have no idea what makes me change my mind about this.

Hanna isn't in the chicken coop or the distillery. Strong cigarette smoke wafts toward me from the woodshed, and I see Alberto and Paolo sitting on the wooden bench in front of it, deep in a conversation that mostly consists of expansive gestures and laughter. They stop immediately when they see me.

"Signora Philipp?" I say curtly, ignoring the bag of cookies that Alberto hides behind his back. He smiles and points right, while Paolo points left. Then they look at each other and laugh that hoarse, old-man laughter that sounds like the decrepit starter of a two-cycle engine. I keep walking.

I find Hanna where I least expected to—behind the shed in Lucia's herb garden. It belonged to Nonna until she had to admit she had no green thumb. Then Nonna tried her luck with Alberto's bees, and, luckily for everyone, that was a success. Lucia has grown everything a cook's heart desires in that garden ever since: wild thyme, garlic, rosemary, and edible wildflowers that Rosa-Maria uses to decorate dessert plates.

I stop in front of the crumbling stone wall that shows signs of losing its battle against the roots of a huge lavender bush. Hanna is huddled against the shed, her hands wrapped around her knees. She is looking at the horizon, where cypresses reach toward the sky like the tips of spears. She sits perfectly still, her graceful posture contrasting strangely with Lucia's washed-out apron dress, which has slid up almost to her thighs.

I suddenly remember something Salvi said: "I always thought that my Concetta's legs were pretty, but now I adore them." There's much to adore about Signora Philipp's legs.

A bee interrupts Hanna's stillness. She gently brushes the pesky insect from her arm. Suddenly I feel like an intruder and quietly step back—not silently enough.

"It's all right, Fabrizio. You can sit down."

I'm unsure. "I didn't want to disturb you."

"You didn't?" She mocks me without turning her head.

"Whatever Lucia might say, I actually can sense when people want to be left alone," I say. My voice betrays my hurt feelings, which upsets me even more. Hanna just smiles and motions with her chin for me to sit down next to her.

We sit silently for a while, but, unlike the last few times we've been alone, it's not an uncomfortable silence. I look at the little basket at her feet and the single brown egg inside.

"Is that today's entire yield? I'll have to ask Alberto to feed the chickens more."

"It's actually a pretty good harvest for someone who's scared stiff of chickens," Hanna says. She sighs, and I sense exhaustion in it but also something else that I can't quite explain. She reminds me of Marco when he's reached the end of his daily run, or of Paolo when he's picked the first apricot of the year.

"Was there a reason you were looking for me?"

My first impulse is to deny it. But then I remember my promise to Lucia and decide to risk annoying Hanna. I am almost certain that she will not like our game's new rules.

"I was going to ask you if you'd go out with me tonight," I say. She gives me a surprised look. "Well, it's actually not a real date, but . . . we are invited to dinner at the mayor's. It's sort of a tradition before—"

"Sure. That's fine."

Now I'm the one to be surprised, but her expression gives nothing away.

"Honestly? You wouldn't mind?"

"We made a business deal, didn't we? If this is part of it, I'm going to play my part." She shrugs.

"There's something else."

"I thought so," she says dryly.

"They're talking about us in the village. Maybe we should—" I can't force the words out.

"Anything but kissing," she says.

"Excuse me?"

"I'm not stupid, Fabrizio. It's obvious that we have to do more than just announce our engagement if we want to succeed," she says and straightens her back. I'm not sure I like her matter-of-fact tone. It sounds too much like the Signora Philipp I didn't like. "So we can whisper sweet nothings, hold hands, and even hug—but no kissing."

"Okay. No kissing." I stare at her mouth and suddenly want to do exactly that—even if she'd slap me. The silence between us stretches again, and this time it's unbearable. Hanna seems to think so, too.

"May I ask *you* something?"

I nod.

"What are you going to do once you inherit the estate?"

"What do you mean, 'do'?"

"I know it's none of my business," she goes on, "but I just wonder if your grandmother might have had a good reason to make a will like that."

"You talked with Marco." I purposefully don't frame it as a question, and her lowered head is answer enough. Anger rises in me. "Did you ever dream you could do something, Hanna?"

She looks at me silently. Then she answers haltingly, "I always wanted to become a writer, to write novels."

"But you didn't—and now you're going to prove to me that you were right to sell your soul instead." Even before I finish, I realize how brutal it sounds.

"I did not sell my soul," Hanna says. "Becoming a journalist was a compromise, one that has paid my rent."

"I'm sure you could have done that by writing novels. I bet you didn't even try."

"I—"

"Just stuff it!" I cut her short. "I know what you're getting at, but I'm not the compromising type—not in any way. My brother wants to cover my fields with a damn golf course, so some fools can hit little white balls around. But I will preserve the estate the way it has been for generations. And if apricots will help me achieve my dream, so much the better."

"I understand. I hope for your sake that you're betting on the right horse," she says in a flat voice. I feel bad that she's hurt, but I have no idea how to fix it.

"Don't worry about my horse. It's none of your business."

"You're right. But whether you want to be or not, you're responsible for everyone else who's affected by your dream."

"It's possible to achieve personal goals and still accept responsibility for others," I say in a tone that allows no contradiction—though I don't sound as self-assured as I intended. Hanna's expression freezes, and she moves away a little.

"For Lucia's sake, I hope you succeed," she says in a cold voice and gets up. She only now notices that her dress is riding up and hastily pulls it to her knees. A few safety pins in the back are pinning the dress tighter, and the belt winds around her waist twice. She bends down to get her slippers. "I'll see you tonight."

I jump up and follow her. She strides across the yard with her chin raised high and her fingers bunched into fists. When I catch up with her, I grab her arm and spin her around. Startled, she stares at me, and I feel her breath on my face. Something happens in my brain.

"Watch out. Lucia's at the window," I lie, and I press my lips against hers.

Never in my life has a slap in the face satisfied me more. I swear.

Chapter Ten
Hanna

She sighed quietly as Hugh bent over her naked shoulders and nuzzled the sensitive skin in the crook of her neck. It made no sense to resist any longer. Hugh's masculinity overwhelmed Prudence like a passionate hurricane, sweeping away her restraint. Her knees went weak and she collapsed into an embrace that . . .

Ohmigod! Snorting, I toss the book onto my pillow, only to pick it up again a minute later. I'm pacing in my Cinderella room, continuing to read and trying to suppress the unpleasant tingling of my skin. For the past few hours, I've also been trying to ignore the imprint of Fabrizio's face on my memory.

With a throaty sigh Hugh lowered Prudence onto the deerskin in front of the fireplace and . . .

What was the matter with him? Hadn't I made it absolutely clear what I wouldn't allow?

. . . possessively . . .

At the window, I spin on my heel and head toward the door for what feels like the three-hundredth time. Lucia at the window—as if!

. . . pushed his hands between the folds of her dress . . .

There wasn't a sign of Lucia anywhere when that guy finally removed his lips from mine and grinned at me.

"I want you," he whispered hoarsely. The lust in Hugh's voice almost made her faint.

I wiped that grin off his face, though I think he somehow expected the slap.

Prudence closed her eyes and murmured, "Take me!" And her fingers dug into his muscular back as his burning lips came closer and closer to her most sensitive spot.

My lips are burning, too—still are. Of course, I'm just imagining it, and it's probably no match for the pain my hand left on his cheek. So there.

Hugh wasted no more words. Skillfully, he undid the lace of her corset.

Fabrizio hadn't wasted any words, either. He simply disappeared for the rest of the afternoon. Not that I looked for him. But to leave me just standing there in the middle of the yard after that outrageous kiss, as if I were a—

I stop abruptly.

What am I saying? I'm complaining about Fabrizio's glaring indifference toward me. As if I cared. I look at my suitcase, propped next to the wardrobe and revealing nothing of its volatile contents.

I continue pacing: door, turn, bed, table, window, turn, bed, door. I'm obviously in a confused state of mind, because then I start talking to the urn. "My life was perfect until I stumbled on you," I say. "But since then I barely know who I am anymore."

What's worse is it's not Giuseppa's fault alone. It's this place. It seems to breathe and suck me in—as if every chest of drawers, every wardrobe, and even the harmless picture of Holy Mary above my bed wants me to become part of it.

What kind of nonsense am I coming up with? A look at my watch makes me even more annoyed. Fabrizio is ten minutes late. Why am I not surprised? Italian punctuality doesn't care about urgent repairs or schedules of any kind. So why should it be different for an appointment with the mayor?

For a second, I consider calling Claire to unload my irritation. But I decide against it. While I appreciate her strong opinions, I'm in no mood to hear "Ooh! Don't make yourself so complicated, *chérie*." So I drop the groaning Hugh and swooning Prudence on my sheets and retreat to the bathroom to kill time.

I've powdered my nose for the third time when I hear a knock on the door. Sulking, I reapply mascara—and do a thorough job of it. Then I count to twenty. Only then do I totter to the door on my way-too-high stilettos, wondering if they've always been this uncomfortable.

The famous mystery writer Donna Leon once said that Italian men have an innate elegance. I look at Fabrizio in disbelief. He's wearing a T-shirt stained with obvious remnants of Rosa-Maria's pasta sauce, and the faded shorts he wore this morning. His knees are as dirty as his feet, which are in his ubiquitous leather sandals. Well, Leon lives in Venice and her comments must have applied to Venetians only. This Italian obviously has his own ideas about what to wear to a formal dinner.

"What's the matter?" Fabrizio says.

"What's supposed to be the matter?" I say, tugging at my dark-blue sheath dress. I feel quite overdressed. Fabrizio frowns.

"You German women are strange."

"That so?" I bite back the retort that half of me is Italian. It doesn't matter anyway; he has permanently labeled me a black-red-and-gold German.

"Any self-respecting Italian woman wouldn't even talk to me before I showered and put on a fine suit. You're forcing a smile and seething silently. Why?"

"First of all, Fabrizio, I couldn't care less what clothes you run around in. And second, I don't teach a grown man how to dress. I'm not your mamma."

Fabrizio laughs. "You're right, there's nothing of an Italian mamma in you."

"And thank goodness for that!" I snort, and dig through my handbag without looking for anything in particular.

"Actually, I came here to let you know I'll be half an hour late. Carlo had a spark-plug problem—well, not he, his car. The old lady's up and running again, though, and Carlo's moved to tears. To say thank you, he's going to drive us to town." Fabrizio turns to leave, but seems to reconsider. I clench my fists behind my back, anticipating his next verbal attack.

"You look very pretty, by the way."

I slam the door shut in his face.

Fabrizio

I'm glad Carlo offered to drive us to city hall. What man would volunteer to spend time alone with an angry woman? Carlo doesn't seem to notice Hanna's grumpy expression or the icy silence in the little car. He turns on the radio full blast and screams to drown out the screeching announcer, as if we're sitting in a soccer stadium. Wildly gesticulating, he explains to Hanna how he jacked up his scooter, while I look out the window and think.

I don't regret kissing Hanna. If I had regrets about all the kisses I've planted on more-or-less willing women, I wouldn't be able to leave Lorenzo's confessional. Fifty daily Hail Marys till the end of my life would not wipe out my transgressions in Göttingen alone, while I studied agricultural economics. And I don't believe the man upstairs would accept a broken heart or too much alcohol as an excuse.

What does it matter? It was just a kiss provoked by the attitude of a beautiful, cool woman—and I paid the expected price for it. Quid pro quo. End of story. So why do I feel that I'm missing something?

I glance in the rearview mirror. I'm happy to see that Hanna is wearing almost no makeup, just a pinkish shimmer on her lips. She immediately evades my glance, and I'm upset that I didn't beat her to it with a pointed turn of my own head. I'm the one who should feel insulted.

She acknowledged my tailor-made suit and white starched shirt with a raised eyebrow, then ignored my offered arm and climbed into the backseat without saying anything. Lucia gave me a surprised look—I'll have to explain it to her, since she's become Signora Philipp's guardian of late. What childish drama, all because of a silly kiss that was more of a battle than surrender.

I loosen my tie and tell Carlo—who's crawling along, using both hands to tell his story—to step on the gas.

"Eh, calm down, my friend. They won't start with the soup until you're there. You're the guests of honor, after all." Carlo winks at Hanna, who, as expected, does not respond. This doesn't faze Carlo, who begins to sing "Ti Amo"—completely off beat and two registers too low. I give up and just stare straight ahead until I finally see the red tiles of Montesimo.

Holy Anthony, make this evening go by fast.

At the piazza, a loud, hungry multitude greets us. Carlo, honking and waving, steers the car through the mass of craning necks. Hanna tries to shrink into the backseat. Nonna always claimed that the nosiest Italians south of Verona live in Montesimo, and tonight's mob would have impressed even her. Some tourists, cameras ready, are recording the native spectacle for their friends at home.

Carlo parks his Fiat. Before he kills the motor, a realization shoots through me like an electric shock. It has nothing to do with the mob outside or the imminent examination disguised as a dinner.

She kissed me back.

Hanna

Fear presses me against the car seat. Even if my mother hadn't taught me as a teenager that neither a future as a superstar nor a future as an international top model awaited me, it would be no less true today that I don't like to be the center of attention. I nod shyly to an elderly woman who knocks on my window, and I smile into the camera of a red-faced man who is unceremoniously pushed aside before he can press the button. Bodies float around the car as if they want to sink it in a sea of enthusiasm. These people act as if there hasn't been a wedding in Montesimo for ages.

Just a moment.

Maybe that's it.

I squint. Try not to panic. Fabrizio is obviously very popular in this village, so his engagement definitely is something special. They're not interested in me.

When the door opens, a wave of warm, whispering air rushes in. Carlo braves the masses first, calling out and joking, and I'm so nervous that I don't understand what he says.

I remember hearing Mamma's calm voice behind the assembly-hall curtain when I was supposed to go out and accept an award at my high-school graduation: "Toss your heart and just follow it, *carissima*."

"Eh, signore." Now Carlo uses an authoritative voice that's a perfect fit for the black-bearded Sheriff of Nottingham. "You're going to see the happy couple often enough in the future. Go home now and let them get out of the car."

In high school, when I crouched behind the heavy brocade curtain, engulfed in its musty odor and my too-sweet perfume, I did throw my heart on the stage—as far as I could. And then I stumbled after it and messed up my big moment by turning my acceptance speech into a flaming plea for the elimination of tuition fees. My parents were proud of me, but I suppressed the memory of it. Only Mamma's words stayed with me.

I will do it again now. I throw my heart into the town square and hope to find it again later.

When I open my eyes, I'm looking right into Fabrizio's face. He props his hands against the roof, creating a space between us, so I can get out of the car without being pushed. The faces out there suddenly fade into a blurry background, and all I see are fine lines, maybe laughter lines, around Fabrizio's mouth.

"Are you all right?" he asks. I nod.

"I'm sorry they're behaving like paparazzi," he whispers and looks intently at my face for a moment, as if he wanted to read my thoughts. "Let's bury the hatchet for tonight?"

"You're not going to apologize, are you?" I whisper back.

"No."

"All right. Neither will I." I take his hand and disentangle myself as gracefully from the little car as is possible in a tight dress. Then I put on a smile that, in my opinion, could be the smile of a bride—a happy soon-to-be bride.

"Ciao, Hanna! Ciao, Fabrizio!"

"What a beautiful couple."

"All the best! God bless you!"

Fabrizio, holding my arm against his ribs, guides me through the throng behind Carlo. I smile until my cheeks hurt and shake slender, calloused, and quite a few tiny, sticky hands. An old woman with a face like a walnut holds back a redheaded boy by the straps of his overalls. A little girl gapes at me as if I'm Cinderella emerging from a pumpkin carriage. Two more young girls, dresses flapping in the breeze, whisper and take my measure less kindly than the rest of the crowd.

Then we ascend a few stone steps, and my window into the life of Princess Kate ends with the thud of the ironclad city-hall door closing behind us.

It takes me a minute in the dimly lit foyer to notice that I'm still clutching Fabrizio's arm. We let go at the same time, and I bump into Carlo. *"Scusi,"* I mumble and step back, but Carlo pushes me toward the elegantly curved flight of stairs.

"The wolves are waiting on the third floor. After you," he says and bows, ignoring both my irritated look and Fabrizio's frown. Actually, my fiancé has looked as if he had a bellyache ever since we entered the building. I thought that was my job today.

"Is city hall the mayor's residence?" I ask.

I swear that Fabrizio pales even more. Carlo laughs out loud, as if I asked a really stupid question.

"Let's say his residence serves special purposes."

"Which are?"

But Carlo just grins and hurries up the steps. Fabrizio seems to steel himself, because he doesn't move until Carlo is nearly halfway up the staircase. Then he follows, acting like he's walking barefoot over shards of broken glass.

Carlo turns left when we reach the second floor instead of following the aroma of roasted meat up to the third. He stops next to a white door and points to its sign, which says "Post Office." I look to Fabrizio for an explanation, but he just leans against the railing and rolls his eyes.

"Wait, Hanna. Look." Carlo sprints to the next door, also white. Its sign reads "Bank Manager." Then Carlo steps in front of the third door, hiding the sign with his broad shoulders. "What do you think it will say?"

"Beauty Salon?" I say, quick like a shot, and hear suppressed laughter from behind me. So Fabrizio hasn't left his sense of humor in the car.

"Office of the Mayor, of course," Carlo says, miffed, and he looks at me expectantly.

"And?" I ask the question he wants to hear. "What's so special about these three doors?"

"There is one single room behind it," Carlo says in a hushed voice.

All right. I am surprised.

"Ernesto uses a spatial illusion to hold his three offices," Fabrizio explains impatiently. "One office, three doors, three opening times. They remodeled the third floor to serve as his apartment since he changes clothes three times a day."

"So Ernesto really is the mail carrier, mayor, and bank manager, all in one? How crazy is that?"

"As crazy as the rest of this town. I can't take a backseat to them," says an amused voice behind us.

And there he is, the cheery mailman with his smile that makes him look like a little kid, even if he now weighs close to two hundred pounds and hides his baldness under a toupee. Skipping the formal greeting, Ernesto hugs me and presses his sweaty cheek against my face. He smells of bacon and garlic and some sweetish cologne I would hate on any other man. But it fits Ernesto perfectly, just as his Panama hat matches his red-dotted tie. Carlo and Fabrizio are caught off guard by our greeting, which shows that we know each other quite well.

"So the pretty Signora Hanna is here after all, and I can keep my promise." Ernesto gives me a friendly once-over from head to toe, his gaze resting a little longer on my legs.

"It looks like it," I say with a grin, and then I cast a defiant look back at my two companions, until Fabrizio looks away.

"Ernesto Zanolla!" a smoky voice calls from upstairs. "What's taking you so long down there? Adriana says the pasta needs to get in the water, unless we want it crunchy as grissini."

"We're on our way, dear!" Ernesto screams back and stands on tiptoe to whisper in my ear, "The command center. Let's hurry or Signora Mayor will start throwing plates." He waves at us to follow him.

My relaxed attitude lasts all of fifteen ruby-carpeted steps. A bulky woman in her midfifties is waiting for us at the apartment door. She has white teeth and tinkling bracelets and looks like a lampshade in her mauve dress. I can't take my eyes off the other woman, however, who stands in the shadow of the hallway, a spitting image of her mother, only younger and less shrill. Blood rushes to my ears when the older woman takes my hand. Ernesto's voice seems to be coming from far away.

"May I introduce my wonderful wife Rita, and my daughter Sofia."

Fabrizio

The Zanolla apartment has changed in the last twelve years. Other than the dining-room table and Ernesto's mother's antique chest of drawers, I don't recognize any of the furniture. Since Rita always falls for fads, it shouldn't surprise me that a leather monstrosity on chrome legs has replaced the comfortable flowered sofa. The bookshelves are gone. Strange steel sculptures and abstract lithographs decorate the walls instead of the previous watercolors by our local artist. It's all very modern, right out of a contemporary-living magazine, and the furnishings fit the soul of this old building like cheap liquor belongs in a hand-blown decanter.

Besides the church, the city hall is the tallest building in town and looks out over Val d'Orcia. I lean against the window, sipping on my aperitivo, and pretend to enjoy the view while I cast sideways glances at the people around the table in the center of the room.

As I feared, the mayor's wife followed protocol to a *T*. She assigned Hanna and me to sit on either end of the table, offering us up like two hazelnuts to the high and mighty village nutcrackers.

My fiancée sits between Lorenzo and Signora Donatelli, who always reminds me of a wrinkled date—a tiny date, since, despite a second pillow on her chair, the village's oldest resident just barely reaches her plate. Hanna is trying not to show how uneasy she feels, but the way she constantly rubs her index finger against her middle finger tells me enough. She valiantly listens to the padre's overly loud conversation with Signora Donatelli, who is hard of hearing. When she thinks no one is watching, Hanna quickly pushes the soup spoon closer to the old woman's gout-ridden hands. The simple gesture surprises and moves me.

Carlo obviously relishes being in the presence of the town elite, his equals since he's chief of police. He rocks on his chair, thumb hooked in his belt, and retells the story of his junior team's spectacular goal that showed the losers from Monticchiello how it's done. That happened last October, and it was the only goal his center forward ever scored in an out-of-town game, but it's been Carlo's favorite topic ever since. When Adriana offers second rounds of aperitivo, he declines with an indignant motion as if the thought alone of a second glass of alcohol were a mortal sin. Adriana responds by filling his glass to the brim.

How the old crow Gosetti, just a newsstand owner, made it to this esteemed table is a mystery to me, but I am sure she spent some money for her spot in the only armchair. She wears the ever-present black apron dress and something on her head that resembles a dead rooster. The bird sways to and fro while Gosetti tries to listen in on every conversation at the same time. I avert my gaze before she can make eye contact—a mistake, since now I'm looking into Sofia's chocolate-brown eyes.

She still has it, that look that drives men crazy. I was too drunk at the Amalfi bar to be affected, but today I am unfortunately sober.

So I drink deeply from my glass. Should I go over to Hanna and ask Lorenzo to switch seats with me? It would be a great move, if only to see the mayor's wife's face when I upset her seating plan. Because Hanna doesn't look all that happy, sitting with a frozen smile as Lorenzo and Signora Donatelli quarrel about the song selection for the wedding—so loud that I can hear every word.

I take all this in while Sofia touches my skin with her eyes, gentle and demanding at the same time. I don't know what's worse: that my body still responds or that Sofia knows it does. So I do what I always do when I can't cope—I escape. I take the last sip of my negroni, chew what's left of the ice cube, and, with a quick "Need more ice," disappear into the kitchen.

Hanna

I have learned two things at this table during the last half hour. First, at an Italian bridal dinner, the temperature of the soup is more important than the bride. And second, I've reached the limits of my knowledge of my mother tongue—the people at this table talk incessantly, very loudly, and all at once.

"I swear, the BMW was fantastic, but this car . . . a rocket."

"But we only sing the Ave Maria at Christmas. Is it Christmas? Well, there you are."

"Rosa-Maria's ribollita has to be part of the buffet. Those panini, too. You know . . . the ones with sesame . . ."

". . . an exhaust pipe large enough to hide a melon . . ."

"Definitely not the Ave Maria!"

"At my age, you never know when your last hour will arrive. It could be the next second—pfft, that's it! And you shouldn't meet your maker hungry."

". . . as clean and clear as *La Traviata* when you step on the gas."

". . . postponing the wedding till Christmas . . . then, if you want, we can sing the Ave Maria . . ."

"Is there any soup left?"

Snippets of conversation swirl through the air like confetti, and I grasp only pieces of them. Other bits evade me like I'm a beginner Italian student. A beginner, by the way, on whom nobody wastes any time, not even her future husband. I'm not surprised, but I expected at least some support from Fabrizio. But since we arrived, he's only been interested in the view outside. And I would rather hang myself from the flashy chandelier than admit that I feel completely out of place in this room, like Cinderella in the ballroom. But this isn't a ballroom, just a dining room trying too hard to be designer chic, and I'm not Cinderella.

And the stupid prince can kiss my—

Leaning back, I put on my poker face. I can tackle any situation with that face. I look around without lingering on anyone in particular, and I grin until I'm dizzy. Then I listen in on the one conversation that's close enough to be understandable, even though it's all about hymns and drags on endlessly because Signora Donatelli nixes every single song the padre suggests: "Too sad . . . not festive enough . . . Do you want us all to fall asleep, Lorenzo? . . . Wrong beat . . . I never liked that one . . ."

Soon poor Lorenzo is as exhausted as his repertoire. Gathering my courage, I offer a suggestion. "What would you say to something modern? There's a beautiful piano sonata by Ludovico Einaudi that . . ." I stop. Signora Donatelli stares at me as if I said I should walk to the altar in a bikini, and Lorenzo seems to be choking on a piece of bread. Before I can quickly add that "Holy God, We Praise Thy Name" is also a fine choice, some conversational confetti from the other end of the table grabs my attention.

"The same buffet menu as last time? Are you sure? Wouldn't that be—how should I say it—irreverent?"

Last time? How can I not strain my ears? I sneakily glance down the table, trying not to look at Sofia, who, since we arrived, has been visually devouring my fiancé as if he were on the menu. However, I don't have to engage in a stare-down with Fabrizio's ex because her seat is empty. Somewhat relieved, I try to follow the battle between the mayor's wife and the old woman in black whose name I've forgotten.

". . . must break her heart . . . the last bridal dinner . . ."

Maybe it's Ernesto's frown, the way he pats his wife's hand, or the gossipy gleam in the old woman's eyes. Maybe it's just my journalist's curiosity or the vague feeling that this conversation has more to do with me than I'd like.

"What bridal dinner are you talking about?" I say loudly.

All heads turn toward me at once. An eerie silence settles under the chandelier, a silence that makes even Carlo interrupt his car talk to gape at me. I smile, although my discomfort intensifies.

The old woman with the pheasant hat finds her voice again first. "She asked what bridal dinner it was," she giggles. The mayor's wife blushes and Ernesto fidgets.

"What's so strange about my question?" I look to Ernesto for an explanation. He clears his throat several times but seems unable to talk. Well! Now I'm intrigued. What's going on here?

"Well, the bridal dinner was—" Ernesto stutters, but his wife interrupts him.

"Leave it to me, Ernesto." Rita Zanolla gracefully dabs the corners of her mouth with her napkin. Her ample bosom lifts as she takes a breath and looks at me directly for the first time this evening. She really is beautiful; she could have been the better half to an aged Al Pacino in *The Godfather*. "The last bridal dinner was held in this room twelve years ago, Signora Philipp," she says in a voice that manages to be friendly and cool at the same time. "It was my daughter Sofia's engagement dinner."

Pain stabs in my stomach, but I decide to ignore the warning and suppress the urge to swipe my dessert spoon. "I assume that's only part of the story."

Ernesto gives me a sympathetic look.

"Hanna!" Carlo lifts his fork. "Did you hear me when I was explaining how to turn a two-stroke into a four-stroke engine?"

"Nice try, Carlo, but I couldn't care less about motors right now," I say. Carlo puts down the fork. I address Rita, who now looks almost hostile. "What's the second part of the story?"

The pheasant hat is faster. The old woman snickers and points a gnarled finger at Fabrizio's empty spot at the window. "The second part of this sad love story was standing over there a minute ago, dear."

Fabrizio

"I thought you'd last a few more minutes before you bolted." Adriana doesn't turn around when I enter the kitchen.

"I'm just getting some ice," I say, embarrassed, to her backside, which is decorated with a bow. I sigh and open the freezer. They used to keep ice bags in the lowest drawer. They still do. When I shut the door, Adriana comes over to me, hands on her hips.

"Are you a high-and-mighty estate owner now, or can a lowly domestic worker still expect a hug?" she says in the same tone Rosa-Maria uses when I forget to praise her pasta. It's obvious whose blood circulates in her veins.

"Since you're the only person who's happy to see me today, I'm the one who should ask you for a hug."

She pinches my cheek and briefly squeezes me. "It's been a while," she says.

"Rosa-Maria sends regards."

"My cousin hasn't talked to me in twelve years, but thanks for trying." She pinches my cheek again, and under her bony fingers the years melt away. I see myself at the cathedral's altar, watching Sofia's veil disappear faster than I can blink. Her breathless *"I'm sorry"* gets caught in a high-up spiderweb that sways gently, as if the building itself were breathing. I watch it, motionless, my arms pressed to my sides, and try to figure out what to do with my shirt. *I can't go to the banquet with sweat stains in my armpits,* I think, not yet realizing that without a bride there won't be a wedding feast.

"Don't look so remorseful, Fabrizio. It's not your fault that two old women are quarreling because each wants to defend the honor of a child that isn't even hers. But Sofia is for me what you are for Rosa-Maria."

"No need to explain, Adriana. I understand. I'm just sorry that we disappointed so many people."

"You're a good guy, always have been. And you belong to this place. That's why you never had much in common, you and Sofia. That girl was always hungry for somewhere else." She lowers her voice. "I really wish you happiness with the pretty German signorina."

"Hanna is actually half-Italian."

"We all wish him that, Mamma Adriana," someone says behind us. I freeze and see gentleness and sternness battling on Adriana's face—her bond with Sofia, who to her is still the pink-stockinged girl who ties empty cans to cats' tails, is strong. She grabs her serving tray and glances at the woman who leans against the doorframe, one hip cocked. Then she hurries out of the kitchen mumbling, "The pasta will be done in a sec."

Minutes pass. We look at each other silently. My heart pounds like crazy, but not in the way that tells a man he's in love. I suddenly find her dress cheap, her lipstick too red, and the wrinkles around her mouth too deep. The way she leans against the door—like one of the cornflake-box toys Marco used to stick on windows with chewing gum—is fake and silly. That's the woman who's caused my wet dreams all my life?

My body, of course, tells me that I want her—as any man would. But it no longer means that I *actually* want her. Damn it. Why did it take twelve years for me to realize this?

"What's so funny?" Sofia comes toward me, trailing her hand along the kitchen counter, touching the container of wooden spoons and the silver tin in which Adriana keeps her homemade biscotti. That's how she's always been—she has to touch the things she likes.

She's only half a step away from me. Her perfume stings my nose, orange and a sharp tinge of mint. The scent reminds me of another woman. I'm all nerves, but I don't see Sofia's chocolate eyes. Instead, I see the other woman's eyes, an indefinable color, somewhere between the color of dry grass and . . . mud? That woman isn't actually beautiful, but she's the most arousing person I can imagine right now.

"What happened to us, Fabrizio?"

"You tell me."

"Well, I'm back home."

"I noticed," I say, and grab her hand as it fiddles with my buttons.

"And?"

"And what?" I push her away from me, and she grimaces.

"So you aren't glad at all? I was thrilled to see you again." Sofia's next advance is grabbing hold of the back of my neck. My body responds, but my head has never been further from an answer.

"What do you want, Sofia?"

"I want to ask you to forgive me, and tell you . . . that you still mean a lot to me."

"In case you didn't hear, I'm getting married next week."

"Are you telling me you're really serious about that mousy German? Please, Fabrizio! She's not your type at all. Besides, she has an ugly nose.

"But you're my type, of course," I say. But Sofia doesn't want to hear the irony in my voice. She slips behind me and grabs my hips. Her nails dig into my flesh.

"I know what you need . . . what you like."

"That you know, for sure." I turn around and she lifts her chin, offering her lips with a victorious smile. She never did take no for an answer. I gently turn her head away. "You'd be perfect if sex were all that matters," I whisper in her ear. "But those times are over, *bellezza*. I've found something much better. And I love her nose."

She tries to tear away from me, but it's too late. I pull her face toward me with both hands and do what I've waited to do for twelve years. I kiss Sofia good-bye, good and long.

Hanna

So that's the secret. Sofia and Fabrizio were not only a couple. They were bride and groom.

As Sasha would say, *well I'll be.*

Right. Amazing.

Not that it matters to me.

Not at all.

It's just embarrassing.

After gaping at the empty window spot, I managed to warble a casual, "Oh, that. Obviously Fabrizio and I talked about it." I dispelled their doubtful looks by adding, "It's so generous of you, Signora Zanolla, to host this dinner. Fabrizio and I are very grateful," and raising my glass in a death-defying toast to Fabrizio and Sofia's friendship. My eye twitched only slightly when I assured everyone that Sofia and I would surely become the best of friends. And then began the longest ten minutes of my life as I counted the seconds until the table veered back to hymns, brake pads, and soup.

Then I somehow managed to stand up, to escape to the bathroom. Only Carlo noticed my wobbling knees. When he whispered, "Are you going to puke?" I responded with a withering look.

I don't have to vomit.

I am only annoyed.

It seems that the wedding twelve years ago never actually happened.

Why?

God, I need to talk to Claire. But where is the bathroom in this damn labyrinth of hallways and doors?

I find the kitchen, or rather the not-quite-closed kitchen door, and stop dead when I recognize the voice inside.

"Are you telling me you're really serious about that mousy German? Please, Fabrizio! She's not your type at all. Besides, she has an ugly nose."

Without any doubt, it's the lovely Sofia spraying her venom again. I step closer. But the gap is too small to see anything.

"But you're my type, of course."

My eyes widen. Cautiously, I wiggle my foot into the gap and open the door a few inches. I see Fabrizio's back—and then the door swings back. Shoot. Now I can see even less than before. I start to sweat.

"I know what you need . . . what you like."

"That you know, for sure."

I hold my breath and grab at the door handle. It's cold and slippery. Why is my heart throbbing? Because I see exactly what I expected: Fabrizio and Sofia—and a long, passionate kiss.

In the bathroom, I slam the door shut behind me, turn the lock, and drop down onto the lid. The cheesy angels on the shower tiles and the gilded fittings above the sink overwhelm the tiny room. When my breathing returns to normal, I press speed dial on my phone. It rings and rings, and then I almost scream in relief when Claire finally picks up. A torrent of words pours out of me before she can even speak.

"Awful bunch of people . . . total lack of manners . . . all at once . . . *has* to be Ernesto's daughter . . . looks like a crow . . . just because I suggested something modern . . . not just dating, they were engaged! Just imagine, how embarrassing . . . and there they are, making out like there's no tomorrow." The other end of the line is silent. "Claire?" I'm about to check my phone to make sure she's actually there, when I hear a cheerful laugh.

"*Ooh là là!* Tell me . . . do you have a crush on Fabrizio?"

"Are you crazy?"

And I mean it. It's completely out of line for her to say that. I haven't had a steady boyfriend in three years—ever since Daniel, to be precise, who couldn't wait to join the Hall of Fame with all the other liars and cheaters in my relationship lineup. It was always the same. With irresistible confidence, a Sven, Mario, or the aforementioned Daniel would sneak into my life, pretending to love strong and independent women. Soon, though, they would take up with my pretty neighbor and blame me for loving my job too much—or accuse me of cheating on them with Hellwig. Or they'd mutate into clingy little children who were upset when I refused to pack their lunches.

Believe me, I know what falling in love feels like. I know the name of each little stomach butterfly that sooner or later turns into a heavy caterpillar. I call this phenomenon "reverse metamorphosis," and it always happens when I give my heart to someone. That's why I stopped doing it—forever—three years ago. And that's why I most certainly am not going to fall in love with Fabrizio Camini.

I feel Claire dissecting me on the other end of the line and regret calling her in my moment of weakness. And I really have to pee now.

"Do you want me to replay our conversation?" Claire says mockingly and, of course, what follows is exactly what she expected. I am defending myself—panties at my ankles, squatting on the toilet seat. I press the phone to my mouth so Claire can't hear the treacherous tinkling.

"It wouldn't bother me if Fabrizio kissed ten women at the same time. But our deal demands that we play a loving couple, and this traitor is kissing his ex-fiancée at the bridal dinner."

"Good thing that at least *you* are sticking to the deal, *chérie*."

"You . . ." I exhale, speechless at her sarcasm. I'm also relieved. My bladder was definitely one glass too full. I gawk at the toilet paper—covered with angels, too.

"Don't make yourself so complicated. Fabrizio kisses another woman who happens to be his ex. So? He's Italian. They kiss all the time—like French men."

"Claire, it's not the stupid kiss I'm worried about."

"So why are you stuck on their past? You're playing your part in your strange deal, aren't you?"

"Of course," I say. "My job is on the line."

There's another pause. It's my chance. Phone pressed into my palm, I flush the toilet. Suppressed laughter on the other end of the line.

"With all due respect, what else are you doing on the toilet?"

"Waiting for some good advice from a friend who's making fun of me instead."

"I'm not making fun of you at all. Just do what's logical."

"But I don't know what's logical anymore."

"*Bon sang,* Hanna. Gosh! Just go back in and show them who's the bride."

Fabrizio

My lips burn as I follow Sofia into the dining room. My ex immediately whispers something to her mother, who looks at me as if I'm a dangerous criminal. I don't care, but I do feel some sympathy for Ernesto, who today has to be a conscientious mayor and thoughtful father and husband, all at the same time. Ernesto solves the problem in his usual way. He pours himself another glass of vino and digs into Adriana's pasta. I cross the room to ask Lorenzo to move so I can sit next to my future wife. But Hanna's chair is empty.

"Where is Hanna?" I mouth to Carlo. He eyes Sofia, then me. I repeat the question and motion to the empty chair. Shoveling a forkful of linguine into his mouth, Carlo shrugs. Just as I'm about to go look for her, Hanna appears at the door. She is pale and somewhat disheveled, obviously one of those women who come back from the ladies' room less put together than before. I find that sexy and catch myself imagining what she looks like when she wakes up in the morning.

She glances around as if she has to remind herself where she is and why she's here. But the moment our eyes meet, the vulnerable look disappears. Her expression tightens, as if invisible strings pull her skin back. Her face lights up in a smile that does not reach her eyes. Reflexively, I straighten my back when she looks right into my eyes. She comes over to me, bends down, and slides both arms around my neck.

"*Amore mio*—did I already tell you today how happy you make me?" she says.

"I don't think so," I say, bewildered. But I use the opportunity to caress her arms. Her skin is soft as the skin of an apricot.

She laughs. It's a little too loud—too cheerful—too forced. But she presses her lips hard against mine, and I hear a many-voiced sigh sizzle around the table like a rustling of newspaper pages. Someone claps.

"I sometimes can't believe it myself," Hanna whispers, lowering her eyelids as if she just remembered we aren't alone. Now I get it—she's acting. Playing along, I smile, but not as bashfully as she does.

"Bravo!" Everyone is clapping now, Signora Donatelli the loudest—perhaps because she's just emptied her second glass of wine. Hanna glides into her seat like a cat and touches my thighs with her knees. She kisses me again, on the cheek this time, and grimaces.

"You really need to shave every day, Fabrizio. You know how sensitive my skin is," she says to the ceiling, and old Gosetti follows her gaze.

Signora Donatelli squeals. Carlo coughs into his napkin, and I nod like a good schoolboy.

"How sweet," says Sofia from the other end of the table.

"See, *amore mio*, Sofia knows exactly what I'm talking about." Hanna winks at Sofia, and I have to suppress a grin—Sofia is forced to smile back, no matter how painful it might be, if she doesn't want to lose face. Hanna gives me a dreamy smile and then turns to Signora Donatelli. "You know, even though Fabrizio and I have just known each other for a short time, we have so much in common."

"Really." Sofia catches the ball. "What, for instance?"

I watch the veins in Hanna's neck pulsate. I have no idea what gets into me, but it might have something to do with her transformation from an icy keep-your-hands-off-me to a passionate, full-blooded woman.

"Yes, Hanna, tell them," I say. "I'm sure they're all very curious." Nobody more than me.

Hanna's lashes tremble. She takes a deep breath and answers with a self-assured smile. "Hiking, for example."

I almost choke on my wine. Did she really say "hiking"?

"Fabrizio and hiking?" Sofia's laugh is shrill.

"Sure." Hanna nods. "Fabrizio and I are true nature lovers. We could roam through fields and forests for hours. That's why Fabrizio wants to get a dog for me. Oops!" Her eyes widen and she covers her mouth with her hand. "I wasn't supposed to mention it. We wanted to discuss it with the family first . . ."

Carlo's grin couldn't be wider. Everyone knows that I use the Land Rover to pick up the mail at the end of the driveway because I don't like walking—and I can't stand dogs.

"Oh Fabrizio, I can't wait for our hike tomorrow—just you and me and the great outdoors. It'll be so romantic."

I know it's better not to contradict a woman, even if said woman is obviously crazy. But I won't let the signorina get away with this that easily. Putting one hand on Hanna's knee, I squeeze until her leg twitches satisfyingly.

"*Amore mio*, this climbing expedition is a grand idea," I say gently. As I expected, the term "climbing" turns her city skin even more ashen. She quivers a little when I touch her nose. "Dizzying heights and your life in my hands. What could be more romantic?"

Chapter Eleven

Hanna

"A climbing expedition. You couldn't come up with something more stupid?" I hear Claire say in my head.

I kick aside a fist-size stone. The trail we've been winding our way uphill on for the past two hours is nothing more than a slope covered with loose stones and no wider than a bath towel. I really have to watch it so I don't lose my balance. Now I'm paying for refusing to wear Lucia's silly straw hat. The summer sun beats down on my scalp. It's hot and quiet. My mood tumbles closer to negative numbers with each step.

Trying to keep up with Fabrizio, I focus on the back of his head. To keep me safe, he made me put on what looks like a dog harness—which makes breathing difficult. I don't know what's worse: my fear of heights, Lucia's tacky trekking shoes, or the fact that I am tied with a thumb-thick rope to the person I loathe more than anyone else on this planet.

OK, maybe that's a slight exaggeration.

The rope jerks and I stagger forward, almost falling. "Don't dawdle, *amore mio*," Fabrizio says over his shoulder.

Actually it wasn't an exaggeration. Furious, I pull on the rope, bracing my feet against the stony ground. I slide along a few steps. Then Fabrizio stops and turns around.

"What's going on?" He isn't even breathing hard.

"You have to ask?" I'm almost screaming, or would be if I had enough air. Instead, only a warbled *"You've t'ask"* escapes my mouth. He studies me, unmoved.

"I need a break," I wheeze.

"Again? We haven't gone more than four hundred yards." He points uphill. "The hard part is still ahead. That's where we come to the wall."

Come to the wall? Did he mention a wall? Up until now, I've done my best to look neither up nor down. Tilting my head now, I promptly understand why Lucia almost choked on her breakfast cornetto when she found out that Fabrizio and I were going to climb Monte Amiata. How did they transport a Himalayan mountain to Tuscany?

"Forget it," I say and cross my arms in front of my chest. Fabrizio raises an eyebrow and wrinkles his forehead in his usual fashion.

"You're behaving like a stubborn goat." He pulls on the rope. "Come on! It's not that bad. The mountain looks more dangerous than it is."

I shake my head. "To hell with the mountain. To hell with your climbing trip. To hell with you!"

"Just to remind you: this was your suggestion."

"I wanted to hike, not break my neck."

"Not true. You aren't a nature lover and you've never been into hiking."

"What makes you so sure? You don't know me at all."

Fabrizio laughs. "I can put two and two together. The Internet is also quite useful. Besides, your ears get red when you lie, and last night your ears were pretty red."

"You Googled me?"

"Isn't that what everyone does these days? What I loved best about the magazine's website were the comments that called you . . . let me think . . . 'an arrogant big-city gal whose taste buds are covered in concrete.' That's someone with a sense of humor, in my opinion."

"You really are the worst."

"Tell me, Hanna . . ." Fabrizio takes a few steps toward me. I step back. Some chunks of rock come loose under my feet. "What's your problem?"

At his sudden gentleness, I lose the thread of my rage. "I suffer from vertigo. Happy?" I'm almost spitting it out, but I sound like a stubborn little kid.

"That's not what I mean." He comes even closer. I hold my breath; my cheeks are burning, and my pulse is racing. I try to answer, but my thoughts get stuck as if the wheels of my brain just jammed up. I suddenly hear Claire again: *"Ooh là là! Tell me . . . do you have a crush on Fabrizio?"*

No. Nooo!

My stomach flutters.

Yes, I do. Oh god!

Fabrizio

It's not easy for me to be nice. I'd like to shake her, but her wide-open eyes stop me. She's only a step away, right next to the edge, looking like a rabbit ready to flee.

"You're angry with me. Tell me why," I say quietly.

"I'm not angry with you."

"So why do you sound like you are?"

"Heavens, you're a pain in the neck!"

"That's possible," I say. "So?"

"Okay, I'm mad."

When I smile, she rolls her eyes.

"If you really want to know, I felt like a fifth wheel at that bridal dinner because you . . ."

"Because I . . . ?"

"Because you kissed Sofia. I'm not mad because of Sofia, but because I'm the bride . . . I was—yesterday . . ." She gasps for air. "You made me look like a fool in front of all those people."

She's jealous. I don't know whether to laugh or to pump my fist in the air. I decide on the former since it seems less macho.

"I'm glad you find that funny," Hanna says, then turns—and steps into nothing.

The next few seconds happen in slow motion: The surprise on Hanna's face turns to panic. Her pale arms, which have resisted the Tuscan sun, flail. The ground underneath her feet gives with a clatter, and a stone avalanche crashes over the drop-off. But by then I'm already holding on to her.

"Got you," I yell, more for my own sake than hers. Her mouth is open in a silent scream, and both of us stare in near-disbelief at my hand around her arm and her feet dangling over air.

"Pull me up! Oh my god, Fabrizio . . . pull me up."

I freeze. The whole thing lasted no more than a few seconds, and now the mass of loose rocks has stopped a few yards below us. Only a few little stones still roll down the hill.

"Fabrizio! Pull. Me. Up!"

"I heard you."

"And what are you waiting for?"

"A 'please' would be nice."

"What? Are you totally crazy?"

I squat down and adjust my weight to get more comfortable. Hanna hasn't realized yet that she only has to stop her panicky kicking to find solid ground under her feet. Instead, her eyes fill with tears. I tilt my head and force myself to endure her fear. "I would like you to ask for help," I say and bend forward, just enough to make my point. Hanna screams.

"Okay. Please!"

I pull her up a few inches and stop. Disbelief replaces her short-term relief.

"That wasn't very convincing." I grit my teeth when she digs her nails into my arm. That's the second price I've paid to tame this woman, after the face slap a few days ago.

"You're going to pull me up from this abyss immediately, otherwise—"

"You're going to tear the skin off my arm? That wouldn't help you."

She gasps for air but retracts her nails. "I did say 'please.' What else do you want?" Her voice is weepy now, and she pants like her pulse is a hundred and eighty—just like mine.

"Have you ever considered that you have a problem accepting help?" I say calmly. "You don't always have to do everything by yourself. There's no shame in asking for help."

"You sound like my friend Claire. How nice of you to clarify that for me at this truly appropriate moment."

"I take what I can get."

Then, unexpectedly, Hanna gives in. Her body relaxes and her mouth, pressed together a moment ago, softens. "Could we please end this? My arms are hurting and I don't want to hang here till tonight. So please, please, pull me up."

The plea in her eyes arouses me, and it takes all my strength not to pull her against me and kiss all her anger away. I grab her under her armpits. Her face is so close to mine that I feel her breath on my cheek.

"Are you sure you won't slap me again?" I whisper. She shakes her head and hooks her arms around my neck. Then I straighten and pull her up all the way.

We stand locked in an embrace. Hanna's head rests on my chest and my hand presses between her shoulder blades, holding her trembling body against me. A relieved sigh—mine or hers? I don't know. She lifts her head. There's no anger in her eyes, just astonishment.

This time we kiss cautiously, almost awkwardly—a kiss between heaven and earth, tasting of fear and redemption. Random images float through my mind: Dr. Buhlfort's waiting room, the lost urn, the funeral, Lucia in the kitchen, Marco running away, the last will, my apricot orchards, the vanished recipe for apricot liqueur, Nonna's frail voice talking about growing and thriving. But then Hanna opens her lips to mine, and everything that was or will be stops mattering.

Hanna

Without saying anything out loud, we agree to go back. I walk down the gravel path behind Fabrizio in a daze, my hand firm and warm in his. I have no idea how long we stood there lost in that incredible kiss before we reluctantly pulled apart with embarrassed grins. Blood still gushes through my ears, I feel faint, and my lips are stuck in a silly smile.

I'm completely flustered and out of control—and I don't even care. Fabrizio guides me around a rock the size of a soccer ball. I scratched my leg on that one on the way up. Then, and I don't know if it's minutes or an hour later, we reach the unpaved road leading to the car. It's wide enough for us to walk next to each other. We still say nothing, as if we're afraid words would destroy the magic that cocoons us like a shimmering bubble.

Fabrizio stops a few steps away from the truck and lets go of my hand. I look up at him. He's smiling and serious at the same time. I almost regret that he breaks the silence.

"Now that's almost eerie," he says.

"What exactly do you mean?" I ask.

"We've got a flat tire."

"A flat tire," I say, not quite getting it. He points, and I see that the truck is leaning to one side. "Oh, a flat tire," I mumble, quite happy, and in my mind Claire shakes her head with a knowing smile. I don't care at all. Fortunately Fabrizio doesn't notice that I'm behaving like a love-struck teenager. He kneels in front of the truck and inspects the deflated tire—my chance to check out his jeans-clad butt. Unfortunately, the delightful sight lasts only a minute, since he gets up and walks around the truck. It seems that everything else is in order. He wipes his hands on his T-shirt.

"I'm afraid we'll have to be towed. There's a nail in the tire, and we don't have a spare." He pulls me to him and buries his face in my hair, his unshaven chin scratching my temple. His heart beats strong and steady, maybe a little too fast, but it calms me. I give in to temptation and slide my hands under his shirt. His back is sweaty and warm, and the muscles underneath contract when I touch him. "I'm going to call Tre Camini," he whispers. "Do you think you can survive one more hour out here with me until Paolo comes with the tow truck?"

"You really ask stupid questions." Desire shoots through me so suddenly that I gasp. Holy shit. I want Fabrizio more than I've ever wanted a man before.

"Nobody says we have to wait outside," he says throatily. And then he slides his hand under my blouse and guides me gently to the truck.

No. We don't have to wait outside.

I once knew a woman who claimed, as we drank coffee together at the university coffee shop, that the right song during sex is like an elevator carrying you straight to heaven. I laughed so loud you could probably hear me outside, and she never sought my company after that. I desperately try to remember her name. Birgit? Bianca? I was a condescending, stupid cow.

I'm flying—at supersonic speed. The hoarse voice on the radio sings of the simplicity of love, and I believe every single word. Everything is easy. We don't take our eyes away from each other for one second—not when Fabrizio takes off his shirt and unbuttons mine; not when he tenderly strokes my belly, which I forget to pull in; not when I undo his belt; and not when he unzips my shorts and slides his hand between my thighs. His face seems transfigured. God, I want him! I claw into the soft skin above his waist. Fabrizio reacts immediately, grabbing my hips and pulling me in. And then . . . our bodies become one, moving in unison. I'm drowning in him, only to burn in his arms a moment later. And then there's nothing but endless satisfaction.

When the radio announcer returns to his chatter, I grudgingly open my eyes and look straight through the side window at Marco.

Startled, I push Fabrizio off me and scramble for my blouse. I find my panties and one sock and start giggling as Fabrizio slides into the driver's seat. He turns down the radio and calmly zips up.

"Ciao, Marco. What are you doing here?" he asks, as if his brother just walked in on a harmless chat over coffee.

"Who called, me or you?" is the biting reply. "Paolo had to help Alberto with the bees, so Lucia sent me."

I wish the ground would open up and swallow me, but Fabrizio doesn't give me time to be embarrassed. After I put on my blouse backward, he pulls me toward him and gives me a good, long kiss that tastes a little of stubbornness and defiance. I sense that Marco's holding his breath and I can't suppress some gloating, even though I know Fabrizio is using me as a ball to slam into Marco's gut.

"Hi, brother-in-law," I say casually and exchange a glance with Fabrizio. He grins and pushes a strand of hair away from my flushed forehead. Marco whirls around, strides back to his car, and returns with a towrope.

"What are you waiting for? Do you plan to stay here overnight?" he says.

"I'm afraid you wouldn't like the answer," Fabrizio says, stepping out.

It's silent on the hour-and-a-half trip back. After a fierce argument—Marco hadn't brought a spare tire and accused Fabrizio of not making it clear what was wrong with the pickup—we towed the truck to the nearest garage. Since it was Sunday, the garage was, of course, closed, and we had to leave it there.

Sitting between the two brothers on the old Ford's front bench, like a living wall, I realize just how muddy their relationship is. Marco stares at the street, his hands clutching the steering wheel of his vintage Oldtimer so tightly that his knuckles are white. Fabrizio absentmindedly strokes my arm and looks out the side window. The scene is rather uncomfortable, but it gives me time to reflect. I steal a glance at Fabrizio. My heart beats faster.

So I did fall in love . . .

With the man I'm supposed to marry.

An enchanting story so far.

But the rest isn't as movie-perfect. The marriage is a business deal based on lies and ending with divorce.

Claire whispers in my head, *"Who says it has to end that way?"*

Maybe I'm more of a romantic than I let on. I have no idea if Fabrizio is thinking the same thing or if it's all part of the game for him. Besides, what would I do in Italy? My life is in Berlin.

Claire again, *"What life, Hanna?"*

Fabrizio reaches for my hand. I look at his fingers, long with straight-cut nails, and I tremble.

Yes. What life? I think of my empty apartment and all the unopened boxes; of the office, quiet at night; of my desk at the window and the lit windows across the street full of people enjoying themselves instead of working; of spending Sundays on a bench in the company of meerkats and a zookeeper whom I know only by his first name. I grip Fabrizio's hand more tightly.

Fabrizio

She's pretty, the way she sits there with closed eyes—even though her smeared eyeliner makes her look like a panda. I almost regret that I have to wake her.

"We're here," I whisper in her ear. Hanna responds immediately, and my heart leaps when she looks at me. I've known many women in many different ways, and they've all looked at me with different expressions. But even Sofia never looked at me this way. I can't explain it, and I honestly don't care what the explanation is. All I know is that I have to be alone with her as soon as possible.

Marco parks the Ford in the garage and gets out without saying a word, slamming the door. He unloads the tool kit, moving slowly and hanging around the truck longer than necessary.

"Would you go out with me tonight?" I say quickly, voice raised. Hanna's gaze rests on Marco, who's stopped to fidget with the gas cap, expressionless.

"I'd love to go out with you," she says. There's something in her tone that I don't get—but at least she didn't say no.

"That's great," I say, wishing Marco would go to hell so I could kiss her and do exactly what we did just a while ago—for hours.

Hanna helps me along: "What do you have in mind?"

"There's a nice little osteria in Montesimo. Well, it's the only osteria, but . . . it's a good one."

She smiles and kisses my cheek. It smacks too much of friendship for my taste. "Good, let's go out to eat."

Then Lucia saves me from my it's-been-a-decade-since-my-last-date embarrassment. She rushes toward us, her dress waving in the wind, and embraces Hanna.

"What has this horrible man done to you? Were you in an accident? Are you all right? Are you hurt?" She shoots me a vicious look. "This jerk didn't tell us anything. Calls, stutters about needing to be towed, and hangs up as if he's late for the bus."

"Everything is fine, Lucia." Hanna gently removes herself from the hug. If Lucia weren't my sister-in-law, I'd be embarrassed. But Lucia is Lucia, and her "bus" comment isn't far off.

"Don't just stand there and grin, Fabrizio. Tell me. What happened?"

Marco slams the trunk. "Calm down, *stellina*. We're all here and nobody got hurt," he says evenly. "At least not as far as we can see. Excuse me. I have to make a phone call."

Lucia frowns and follows Marco's head-down shuffle with her eyes. Then she examines me and Hanna, who lowers her eyes and blushes. Lucia takes a deep breath to say something, but seems to think better of it and crosses her arms in front of her chest.

"Signora I-Have-Better-Things-to-Do, are you growing roots over there, or do you want to learn how to make real pasta? Then get your bony ass into the kitchen." I never thought Rosa-Maria's voice would make me so happy.

"I believe she's talking about me," Hanna says with a smile, and fishes her handbag out of the truck. She hesitates, nods to me, and then dashes across the yard, giving the chickens plenty of room. Lucia squints.

"Hanna," she shouts. "Your blouse is on backward."

Hanna stops and turns around. She's beaming.

"I know."

Hanna

The kitchen is a haven for me this afternoon. Rosa-Maria's strict regimen allows no time for brooding, and I plunge gratefully into the work. I wash the breakfast dishes without being asked and listen attentively when Rosa-Maria explains in what order to mix the pasta-dough ingredients. I learn how to knead air out and love in, and how to recognize when the dough is smooth enough to be pressed, in portions as large as the palm of your hand, through the pasta machine. Then I clean and quarter two cases of plum tomatoes, slice garlic so thinly that Rosa-Maria nods in satisfaction, and make a tomato sauce—a real pomarola—under her close supervision. It's the first time I haven't been in her way, despite the small size of the room. If Rosa-Maria is astonished that I've mutated into a submissive apprentice, she hides it well. But when I take off my apron in the early evening, she presses the tenth and final installment of *Propelled by Hope* in my hands, which are pruney from dishwater.

I'm still smiling when I dry my hands in my dwarfish bathroom. I've grown so fond of Prudence and Hugh by now that I can hardly wait to witness their decidedly X-rated reunion. I'm contemplating starting to read before my date with Fabrizio, when I notice my phone. I haven't touched it since I called Claire.

I suddenly long for my mother's chatty voice. I'd like to tell her about Fabrizio, and about other things as well. She might have some advice for me.

My heart beats faster as I listen to the phone ring. It clicks, and I take a deep breath. "Mamma, it's me, Hanna. I wanted to tell you—"

". . . not home right now. In case of an emergency, you can reach me at . . ."

Disappointed, I exhale and end the call without leaving a message. I cross to the little desk under the window.

Paolo is pushing a wheelbarrow of manure across the yard—straight through a flock of chickens, to Vittoria's great displeasure. I see Lucia walking to the herb garden with her little basket to pick wildflowers for the dessert plates. Men's voices drift up from the barn, and then I see Fabrizio head toward the distillery. I need to ask him tonight if he's discovered the secret of Nonna's liqueur.

Tonight. Some butterflies flit in my stomach as I sit down in my bathrobe on the wooden chair, my knees pushing against the desk. While I boot up my computer, I stare at the letterhead on the writing pad—a curved *T* framed by a *C*, and an address in cursive. It's simple and elegant at the same time, like Tre Camini itself. I glance at the wardrobe that hides my suitcase. My heart pounds. I imagine that I hear an encouraging whisper from behind the door.

I open a new document as soon as my computer's awake and put my fingers on the keyboard. The sooner I start to set things right, the better. Then I close my eyes, tie an imaginary apron around my waist, and mentally rush back to Rosa-Maria's kitchen in Lucia's slippers. I'm going to write the most unusual restaurant review of my career.

I'm so engrossed in typing that I look up only when I feel a draft on my naked legs. Lucia is standing beside me. I manage to quickly press "Save" and close the laptop.

"Sorry to disturb you . . . but I knocked three times, and when you didn't answer I thought—I want to talk about the flower arrangements for the community hall." Lucia waves a notebook that I recognize—it's her wedding bible. She's been carrying it with her for days, looking very serious, as if planning a wedding were rocket science. *And I'm the explosive particle that will whiz around her ears,* I think and immediately feel guilty.

"You're not disturbing me. I was just . . . working." Shoot. Wrong answer. Lucia looks at the writing pad and the notes I've scribbled on it for the article.

"What exactly are you working on?"

I lean back in my chair and look up at her. Her hair has come loose from under her barrette, and it curls over her shoulders like a waterfall. Her sweet and trusting face is the epitome of innocence. I've suddenly had enough of all the lies. I'm fine with deceiving strangers, but Lucia is the first person, since I met Claire, whom I can call "friend" without hesitation. I get up and lead an astonished Lucia to my narrow bed and ask her to sit down next to me. She looks at me expectantly but also patiently, as if she knew it's not easy for me to say what I'm about to say.

"I'm writing, Lucia. It's my profession," I say slowly.

"How beautiful. Do you write books, novels? Maybe love stories? I love romance novels." She smiles.

Man, this is harder than a final exam. I shake my head. "I'm a restaurant critic, Lucia. I write articles about restaurants, good and bad. To be honest, more about the bad ones."

"I don't understand."

I take a deep breath and take her hand. "Fabrizio and I didn't tell you the truth. We don't know each other from years ago, and we didn't meet again by chance recently. I was here a few weeks ago, as a restaurant reviewer."

"You mean here, at Tre Camini? But I didn't see you."

"I was just here for a quick dinner," I say. "It happened to be the day when Carlo was the ruler of the kitchen."

"Carlo, that . . ." Lucia snorts, but I press her hand.

"I wrote an article—not very complimentary. It was an unhappy coincidence. And then your grandmother died, and I . . . found her urn in an airport restaurant. That's why I came to Montesimo, to return Nonna. But Fabrizio demanded that I stay here to form a second opinion about your restaurant."

"You're making fun of me." Her face is pale. She jumps up and paces back and forth. Then she stops and points to my laptop. "I want to read the article. I mean the bad one."

"It's in German," I say.

"Then translate it for me."

Fifteen minutes later, Lucia is sitting silently in the wooden chair. I shut the computer and wait while she stares at the ceiling, her lips pressed together, for a long time. Then she begins to laugh. "That's Fabrizio for you. He makes a reporter slave away in Rosa-Maria's kitchen because he's mad about a bad review."

"You aren't upset about the article?"

"We're in Europe, Hanna. People aren't stoned for voicing their opinion. Besides, Carlo is an abominable cook."

My relief lasts only a few seconds. Lucia continues, "But before we discuss you and Fabrizio, I'd like to find out more about Nonna."

I explain about my meeting with Hellwig at the airport, and how I ended up with the urn, and how Fabrizio made me agree to kitchen duty. I skip the part about the wedding deal so that my future husband doesn't get into more trouble than necessary. She doesn't interrupt me once. Then I end by liberating Giuseppa from her suitcase prison.

Lucia solemnly accepts the striped urn. She stands very still for a moment before carefully putting the container on the desk and taking a step back. "Hello, Nonna," she says quietly.

I feel like a criminal. I should have returned the urn long ago, never mind Fabrizio's stupid terms. "I'm so sorry. I don't know what came over me. You can take her with you, of course," I say.

"I could." Lucia's still looking at the urn. "But I'm not sure it would be the right thing."

Not again! I almost cry out. Lucia sizes me up and clicks her tongue. "Do you know that Giuseppa and Alberto were in love their entire lives, but they were never together?"

I shake my head. What does Nonna and Alberto's sad love story have to do with the urn? But Lucia doesn't seem to be finished. So I sit down on the bed, happy that she's still my friend.

"When Nonna was young, she had everything a woman can have. She was beautiful, smart, the daughter of a rich businessman who sold cheap olive oil. Giuseppa could have chosen an equally wealthy husband and spent the rest of her life in a palazzo. But *la dolce vita*, as we Italians call it, meant nothing to her. Actually, it bored her. So she started to criticize everything. Her anger was mainly directed against her old-fashioned parents. And since her fight needed more than just words, she married a simple farmer just to spite her father. What she didn't count on was that she would fall in love—only not with her husband, Eduardo Camini, but—"

"With Alberto Donati, his estate manager," I finish, and Lucia nods.

"There's no happy ending, unfortunately. Giuseppa was her father's daughter, after all . . . and he had brought her up strictly Catholic. For her, her vows continued even after Eduardo's death, and so she kept her love for Alberto secret." Lucia smiles dreamily. "But you had to be blind not to see the bond between the two."

"And since Giuseppa was unhappy, you aren't sure if you'll accept the urn? I don't get it, Lucia."

"But it's very simple," Lucia says. "Giuseppa wanted to give to others what she most wanted for herself."

"You're saying—" I laugh. "Giuseppa was a matchmaker?"

"Well, she just made sure that people who belonged together found each other. And she was very successful. She dragged Marco along to the same café in Florence so often until he couldn't help but notice the shy server." Lucia blushes, adding, "That was me." Then she counts off on her fingers: she brought Rosa-Maria and Paolo together, Signora Giancomelli, the Portinaris, the Baglionis . . . She put friends together, too. When Signora Caleppio lost her husband and almost died of sorrow, Giuseppa introduced her to Signora Valuzi, who's also a widow. The two became best friends. She persuaded old Benito to share his garage with Stefano, and the old grouch has been a completely different man ever since. They also say that Giuseppa once adopted a young girl from the village whose mother died. But people talk." Lucia paused meaningfully. "Anyway, I believe it's no accident Giuseppa landed in your suitcase. She decided to end up there."

I gulp for air. "Lucia, Giuseppa is dead. She doesn't make decisions anymore."

"You obviously didn't know her," Lucia says. "How many people are at an airport at any given time, Hanna? Tens of thousands. Do you think it's a coincidence that you, out of all of them, found the urn on a windowsill?"

I open my mouth but can't come up with a counterargument that would shake Lucia's belief in fate and divine providence.

"Giuseppa was obsessed with finding the right woman for Fabrizio," Lucia says. "And she succeeded even though she's no longer with us. She did succeed, didn't she?"

I stare at her in disbelief. However absurd her reasoning, there's some truth in what she's saying. Because of the urn, I came to see Fabrizio in person instead of just writing a letter of apology. And I can't deny that something happened between Fabrizio and me that had little to do with a business relationship.

"Looking at it that way, she was successful," I admit, smiling, though I feel pathetic for only telling Lucia half the truth. But sometimes the whole truth isn't the solution, especially not when it involves the less-than-romantic reasons for my upcoming wedding.

"So everything is as it should be," Lucia says, abruptly getting up as if she's afraid I might change my answer. "I don't care when, how, or why you fell in love with each other. You're getting married, and *basta*. If Giuseppa doesn't want to come home yet, we better let her have her way."

"So you're really not going to take the urn?" I ask, and Lucia just shakes her head with a smile.

"Put her back in your suitcase until she's ready, or Fabrizio is." Lucia's almost out the door when she turns and adds, "I really like you a lot, Hanna. Just trust me."

I swallow and fight back tears, mostly because I can't remember when I last heard such words.

"But if you don't treat Tre Camini better in your new article, you'll be sorry. I'll sic Rosa-Maria on you." She winks and closes the door.

Fabrizio

I can't concentrate. I've been kneeling in front of the distillery equipment for half an hour, staring at the temperature gauge without seeing the numbers. With a sigh, I stand up to stretch my legs. I walk over to the table where I've lined up the bottles from last week's production, each labeled with the distillate's ingredients and process.

I uncork the first bottle and exhale in disappointment. The aroma alone tells me I was not successful. The second, third, and fourth bottles are fruity and balanced, but not Nonna's. Something is missing, maybe only one or two ingredients. The colors of bottles five and six are off. I can't smell a thing anymore when I reach bottle seven. I fill half a shot glass, take a sip, and immediately spit it on the floor. It seeps through the cracks between the wooden boards. Damn it!

Elbows resting on the table, I ruffle my hair. I've taken apart the entire house, the barn, and even the chicken coop, but Nonna's green recipe notebook is nowhere to be found. And since I'm too stupid to figure out the right mix of ingredients, Nonna's liqueur will be ancient history faster than Alberto can gobble down a box of cookies. The worst thing is that Marco is right about everything he says, damn it, even though he's my little brother. I have no idea how I'll be able to hang on to the apricot orchards, never mind making a profit and supporting the family.

Angrily I sweep bottles and glasses off the table. Bang and clang—and the strong smell of alcohol permeates the room. I stand in front of the shards with burning eyes and a cut across the heel of my hand, feeling suddenly as empty as I did the day after Nonna's death, and just as tired. I haven't slept through a single night for two weeks—Nonna won't stop rattling around my bedroom and lecturing me on what she expects and doesn't expect from me. Sometimes I really think she's not dead at all.

As I awkwardly try to stop the bleeding with a dishcloth—Lucia is going to kill me—I see Hanna's face, a face that's full of warmth when she thinks nobody is looking.

Much more than bottles have been broken these past few weeks. Why? Because I'm an egotistic idiot who doesn't realize when a dream is over.

This has got to stop.

I wrap the dishcloth tight around my hand and stride to the broom closet. The sooner I start cleaning up the mess, the better.

Chapter Twelve

Hanna

At seven-thirty I get up from the desk and press "Enter" with a pounding heart. I'm drunk with the words and images that seemed to gush out of me—as if this were my usual writing routine. At the same time, I've never been less sure whether the text actually expresses what I want it to say. Staring at the confirmation on my e-mail display, I use my phone to write a short text message to Claire, asking her to check my article for spelling mistakes and bloopers before bringing it to tomorrow's editorial meeting.

Her reply arrives soon after: *Do you want my opinion, too?* How can she sense my state of mind even from over six hundred miles away?

Absolutely not, I type with a smile and put the phone in my handbag. I have to get ready for my date with Fabrizio in five minutes. When I hear a quiet knock at the door, I almost drop my mascara.

"Just a moment," I shout, tugging on my turquoise dress, which looks as wrinkled as I feel.

Lucia's voice comes through the door. "Fabrizio asked me to tell you that he's waiting in the yard." I glance one last time into the tiny mirror—I've looked better, but whatever. I've never liked makeup, and I have the feeling that Fabrizio doesn't mind.

I force myself not to run down the stairs. Nothing is more pathetic than a woman who shows up for a date with a bright-red face. Before my first date, Mamma told me, "A woman in high heels is never late." But I was—forty-five minutes—because I couldn't fix my hair. The young man was too impatient to wait for me, but I didn't care too much since I didn't really like him anyway. Mamma went to the movies with me instead and treated me to a giant bag of popcorn, which she ate up by herself. It hurts to realize how long ago that was. I skip the infamous creaking step, pass the kitchen door—hearing Rosa-Maria's voice beyond—and walk into the yard. Not a single living thing is visible other than Vittoria and her flock.

Fabrizio

My father's motorcycle has been tarped in the garage for years. An old 1950s Agusta, it was his pride and joy, and I still remember how excited I was when he first let me ride it. I wobbled across a field at fifteen miles an hour and felt like Giacomo Agostini, the Grand Prix road racer, while Father ran behind me screaming that I could just as well drive on the road if I wanted to kill myself.

I gently touch the red lacquer, which he kept well polished. I was convinced for years after Father disappeared that he would come back for the bike. He would never leave his Agusta behind, no matter how much Mother's death tortured him. But the bike remained here, and eventually I stopped waiting for him to come and get it.

The kick-starter is stuck, and I have to try several times before the bike roars to life. It stutters its resentment through the exhaust pipe, coughing smoke. But it runs. The gravel crunches under the wheels as I ride into the yard. I tilt up the visor of my helmet.

"Are you ready, *amore mio*?" I ask with a grin, and play with the gas to make the old Agusta growl. Hanna crosses her arms, attempting to look neutral.

"You're scaring the chickens."

"Not just them, it seems." I hand her the second helmet, and she turns it in her hands as if she doesn't know what to do with it. "The visor goes in the front."

Hanna hesitates. "Don't we have a car?"

"You aren't afraid, are you?" I nod my chin at the kitchen window, sure that Rosa-Maria and Lucia are betting on who'll win this tug-of-war.

"Come on, I'm hungry." I pat the seat behind me. She sighs, then straightens and puts on the helmet. A moment later she's crouched behind me like a little monkey.

"You'll be sorry if you don't bring me back in one piece," she shouts over the engine noise. She snaps down her visor and wraps her arms around my waist. I give her the thumbs up and see Rosa-Maria and Lucia applauding through the kitchen window. Out of the corner of my eye, I see Marco coming from the distillery with the phone at his ear. He stops and looks at us. I give Hanna's hand a brief squeeze, and we're off.

Hanna

At the restaurant, we're welcomed by warm air and muted music. I'm still intoxicated from the ride, even though my legs and butt feel like I just did five hundred squats. Why did nobody ever tell me how much fun it is to ride a motorcycle?

I let Fabrizio guide me through the room, noticing that we seem to be the only guests. At a window table, Fabrizio pulls out a chair and asks for my jacket. Confused by his manners, I sit down. He bends toward me. If I weren't already weak at the knees, I would be now—he smells irresistibly manly, a mix of leather and gasoline.

"Everything all right?" he whispers, and I nod. I hope to find my voice again in the course of the evening; otherwise it'll be a quiet dinner. But my silence doesn't seem to bother Fabrizio. Smiling, he sits down across from me while I look around.

The Osteria Maria has no more than five little tables, all covered with simple white tablecloths. A cupboard with latticed wooden doors stands next to the entrance, seeming strangely out of place since it resembles a confessional. There are only a few items on the small blackboard—all solid, plain fare. I realize that I'm not hungry at all, but excited, and very nervous. Yet I don't feel the usual tingling sensation in my fingertips. I pick up the wine-bottle-shaped pepper mill and listen to my inner self. Nothing. Nothing at all. I feel no urge to swipe it. Amazing.

"So? Do you like it here?" Fabrizio looks at me, his chin resting on his hands. How long has he been doing that? One minute? Ten? I'm gradually losing all sense of time and space in this country—and it's disturbing.

"It's pretty nice." I'm annoyed with myself for sounding so reserved. Fabrizio frowns.

"It's probably different from what you're used to. We can drive to Grosseto, if you like. They have a starred restaurant."

"No, I like this osteria. I do."

"You better," someone grumbles. I look up, startled. None other than Salvi—or at least his doppelgänger—is standing next to us. Yet this man is wearing a shirt and tie, and his neatly parted hair covers some of his bald spots. He whips out his ordering pad and says in a formal voice, "*Buona sera,* signori. Will you start with an aperitivo?"

Fabrizio looks at me, but I'm too baffled to answer. A mayor playing mailman, and the bar owner imitating a pretentious server. There's nothing you can't find in this village.

"Aperol Spritz for the lady, Salvi. I'll just have a Coke."

Salvi scribbles on his notepad and, with just a hint of a bow, rushes to the bar. I look on in amazement. Fabrizio clears his throat and leans toward me.

"The Osteria Maria belongs to Salvi's parents. The old couple is so attached to it that they don't want to close. So Salvi runs both: the osteria from Sundays to Wednesdays and the Amalfi bar from Thursdays to Saturdays."

"Weird."

"By the way, he could use a good review. The osteria isn't doing all that great." Fabrizio winks and smiles. My stomach somersaults.

"Is that why you brought me here, so I would write a good review? You want to slip me another business deal—maybe in return for bailing out my car from Stefano's garage?" I sound edgier than I intended. Fabrizio, who's about to light the little lantern on our table, stops.

"I didn't mean it that way." He seems puzzled. "I just thought, if you like the food, you could make Salvi's day by writing about it. I'm sorry if it came out wrong." His espresso-colored eyes are so honest that I feel cheap. What's the matter with me? One moment I'm on top of the world, and the next I'm as jittery as a racehorse. If that's a sign of being in love, I can do without it.

"I'm the one who should apologize. That was stupid." I pick up the pepper mill again, but I still feel no tingling, despite the stress.

"At the risk of really making you mad . . . may I ask you a question, Hanna?"

I put the pepper mill down and sigh. "I owe you one."

"Why do you swipe stuff?"

"Anything except that," I say.

"But it really interests me. I've been watching you. You've been stealing things: the salt shaker in the Amalfi bar, Rosa-Maria's measuring spoon, Lucia's pincushion. Even Alberto's pipe cleaner disappeared into your apron pocket. And you also walked off with my grandmother."

"The thing with the urn was an accident," I say weakly, but add, "Besides, I only *borrow* stuff. I returned the spoon and pincushion a long time ago, and I would have returned Nonna, too, if you'd taken her back."

"Explain it to me, *bellissima*." His voice is soft, and I shiver. No man has ever used a term of endearment for me.

"I can't explain it myself," I say. "It just happens to me—when I'm under a lot of stress. First, my fingers start to tickle, and then I itch all over. I get into a panic and can't breathe. Then more panic and less air—and it only stops when I steal something."

"Have you always had that problem?" he asks.

"I don't understand your question."

"There's always a first time."

"You mean, like in a crime story? The first victim is the key to nabbing a serial killer?"

"Or the key to understanding a motive. It's a strange comparison, but it actually works."

In the back of my mind, I suddenly see my father's emotionless face and Mamma's disappointed head shake.

"I can't remember," I say and push the image away. Fabrizio nods as if he expected that.

"At some point you will."

"Are you a psychotherapist?" I say crossly. Fabrizio just laughs. I don't know if it's because he's obviously compassionate or maybe because he barely knows me, but I suddenly start to talk, the words pouring out.

"You won't like me after you hear this. It's impossible for you to like me—I'm totally messed up. I live in a tiny apartment and don't own a single piece of furniture with any history. I work sixteen-hour days, have no hobbies, and spend even my vacations on a laptop. I have one single girlfriend and she's even crazier than I. My longest relationship lasted two months, four days, and nine hours. I sometimes think I'm adopted because my own mother forgets my birthday every single year. My birth certificate says I'm not, but she would rather bake muffins for refugee children. And my father, ever since I got caught shoplifting when I was fourteen, he's looked at me like I'm an atom that doesn't belong in his universe. What's worse is that I actually feel like a stray particle that has no place anywhere on earth. I come from nowhere, stay nowhere, go nowhere, and that's exactly the reason—"

"That's exactly the reason you're here."

Fabrizio

Hanna turns white as a sheet. I know I've pushed it too far, but I can't take back what I said—or rephrase it without making it sound like a declaration of love. Salvi appears and sets our drinks on the table. He obviously finds it hard to handle the fine glasses—his huge hands are more used to pouring draft beer.

"Are you ready to order?" he says, his mouth in a circle that reminds me of a donut.

"We're the only guests, Salvi. Stop treating us like celebrities."

Salvi purses his lips. "I'm just being polite. You don't often come here with a pretty signora. And if I'm supposed to take care of only one table this evening, then—"

"What do you recommend?" I interrupt. This dimwit is giving the game away. Hanna isn't supposed to know that I asked Salvi to cancel all the reservations for tonight so I could be alone with her.

"We have sole in sage butter," Salvi says, offended.

"You know I don't eat fish."

"But you were the one who suggested the dishes. I don't understand why you're asking for my recommendation."

"Why don't you shut up, Salvi? Bring the fish for Hanna and the damn filet of beef for me."

"On its way." Salvi stalks away. Hanna clears her throat and tilts her head.

"It's not what it looks like," I say, feeling my face redden. "I just told him that you'd probably like fish since you've had to subsist almost exclusively on Rosa-Maria's pasta for the last week."

"That was very thoughtful of you." I want to kiss the tiny smile that appears on her face. "I love sole." I breathe a sigh of relief, but then I notice the sparkle in her eyes. "And now I'd like you to explain why we're the only guests in this nice little restaurant."

Hanna

He has feelings for me! The shocking realization makes me want to jump up and hug Fabrizio, fat Salvi and—no, I'd like to embrace the entire world. I actually figured out the answer when Salvi carried a sign reading "Private Party" by our table with careful nonchalance and put it outside.

Fabrizio is fidgeting, red faced, in his chair. His embarrassment is so sweet and sexy that I have to stop myself from grabbing his sleeves and dragging him outside to some deserted street, and . . . But a persistent ringtone interrupts my fantasies and gives Fabrizio a temporary reprieve. He leans back and downs half his Coke in one gulp. I rummage in my handbag for the disruption, annoyed that I forgot to put it on mute. At first, I'm not sure if I'm reading the caller ID correctly: it's my mother.

I hesitate while the ringtone goes on and on. Then it stops, only to resume a few seconds later. I get up grudgingly.

"Please excuse me for a moment," I say. Salvi, who's leafing through the local paper at the bar, looks up in alarm. I gesture that everything is fine.

I call her back as I step out into a gentle evening breeze that smells of fried food and exhaust fumes. A few kids kick a soccer ball in the street. I can almost see an upstairs window opening and an Italian mother, right from the TV spaghetti-sauce ad, calling her Federiiii-co to dinner. I need a spot where I can talk quietly. Skipping down the steps, I find a fountain in an alcove in the wall across the street. A sign says: "No Drinking Water—Not a Public Place to Rest."

"Mamma? You called?"

"*Carissima!* How did you know it was me? I didn't leave a message," she says. I climb up on the fountain and lean against the wall, still warm from the sun. I reach out and dip my finger in the water.

"My phone tells me when you call."

"Really? That's practical."

I roll my eyes. "How can I help you? I'm in an important meeting right now."

"But darling! It's almost nine and you're still working?"

"Did you call to lecture or do you need something specific?"

"You have one of those laptops, don't you? The ones you can carry around? We bought one of them for the women's shelter so we can do the bookkeeping stuff at home. And since Isadora is more or less on bed rest, she'll have something to do and won't get depressed, poor dear."

If I hear Isadora's name one more time, I'll explode. "How nice for Isadora. But I assume that your laptop isn't the reason you're keeping me from my work, or is it?" It feels good to lay a guilt trip on her.

"Honestly, it is. The nice young man at the electronics store told me that I needed to set up the computer. I already found a good place for it on Papa's desk. But I have no idea what the next step is, and Papa is at a fusion conference. So I thought I'd ask my clever daughter, who works with these things all day long, if she could come by to help."

"Mamma, I'm in Italy."

"What are you doing in Italy?" she asks.

"I told you about it the last time we talked, about ten days ago," I say with ice in my voice.

"You did? I don't remember that at all."

Mamma's carefree laughter brings tears to my eyes. "Why am I not surprised?"

"Oh, Hanna, don't be so rigid. We all forget things every now and then. Maybe I was distracted. It happens to all of us," Mamma says cheerfully.

"But it happens to you all the time! Do you have any idea how it feels to talk to someone whose thoughts are always a million miles away?" I'm almost screaming. And since that feels good and nobody is around, I don't even try to lower my voice. "Do you know I don't remember the last time you asked how I am? You're always talking about people I don't even know. Why should I care about your stupid Isadora? When did you last hug and kiss me? Or just visit me out of the blue? And you forgot my birthday again. Don't you think it matters to me?"

"*Carissima* . . . I didn't know . . . But I did send you a card. It played music when you opened it. You used to love them." Mamma sounds shocked.

"I never got that card," I say, and then the realization hits me. "I moved a year ago. I sent you the new address and you promised you'd make note of it right away."

"That—" Mamma stops, but I hear her exhale—first a long breath, as if she'd been holding it, and then a series of short ones as she realizes what I just said.

"You could have called," I mumble and dip my hand deeper into the water, all the way to my elbow. Suddenly I feel hot and feverish and want to slide all the way in. "I've got to go now. Somebody is waiting for me. Why don't you have someone come in and set up the computer for you? You don't need me for that. And only call me again when you want to talk with your daughter, not when you have some business to discuss. I've had it with business deals with people who mean something to me."

I end the call before my mother can answer, and turn the cell phone off.

Then I hear slow, provocative clapping. It's Marco. He's sitting next to me on the fountain, his feet dangling, an ice-cream cone in his hand.

"Bravo, Signora Philipp. That was crystal clear."

"It's very impolite to listen to other people's phone conversations," I say. "What are you doing here, anyway? Are you following us?" If my tone annoys Marco, he doesn't show it. Instead, he licks his ice cream, looks toward the Osteria Maria, and grins.

"Let me use your own pretty words. I'm bringing a business deal to its close."

Fabrizio

I fiddle with the pepper mill as I wait for Hanna. She's full of surprises: so uptight and arrogant, but warm and tender; smart and proud, but vulnerable. The image she gives off of a strong, independent woman is just that—a facade. Thank god! And she's beautiful—actually, gorgeous—and I should do what every man would do: just enjoy it. But a strange feeling bothers me, as if something isn't right. This wedding . . . Then I see a pair of pretty legs. Isn't Hanna wearing a light-blue dress? I look up.

"Sofia?"

"Here I am." Sofia slides into Hanna's chair, grinning like a cat. Confused, I look over at Salvi behind the counter; he helplessly raises both hands. Then he disappears into the kitchen, probably to give the order to take my by-now-tough steak off the stove.

"So I see," I stammer and silently say good-bye to dinner. I hope Hanna will be on the phone for a while. I don't understand women, but I'm sure that she won't be happy to find my ex-fiancée here. Understandably.

Sofia looks like she's at the Oscars. She gracefully crosses her legs, the slit skirt revealing her thighs. It's strange to watch her—to see how she shows herself off—without feeling aroused.

"Relax, Fabrizio. You don't need to say anything. I'm glad you are reconsidering the matter."

"I'm doing what?" I probably look like old Benito did when Stefano mowed down his fence with his tuned-up Fiat. Sofia grabs my hand and strokes my wrist with her thumb. I gape at her red nails. What the hell is she doing here?

Before I even finish the thought, I remember Marco coming out of the distillery, the phone at his ear. Of course! His look should have tipped me off. The little shit. I withdraw my hand from Sofia's grip. "I don't want to embarrass you, Sofia. I'm here with Hanna," I say calmly.

Sofia laughs. "Good try."

"She just stepped out to make a call."

Sofia's eyes roam the room and return to me with a coquettish look. "In that case, you have time to talk with me."

"The way you look, you didn't come to talk."

"Do you like what you see?" She sounds uncertain, though, which I've never heard before.

"It doesn't matter." I add, a little more gently, "Whoever asked you to come here, it wasn't me."

Sofia pouts. "I'm here to fight for you, Fabrizio. Marco told me that you still love me."

So I was right. A fine brother Marco is, messing with other people's lives. "He lied to you. Marco is trying to prevent me from marrying

Hanna because he wants to get Tre Camini for himself. But he won't succeed, no matter what ammunition he uses."

Sofia's eyes widen and her mouth opens, but she says nothing, just blinks.

"I'm sorry," I say, leaning back.

"But I could apologize to you." She throws back her hair. "Let's forget what happened and start anew. And you'll get the estate."

I can't help it—all my patience evaporates. I propel myself across the table and grab the back of her neck. "Just a minute. What is it you want to apologize for?"

"Don't be cruel, Fabrizio. And let go. You're hurting me."

But I pull her even closer. Her breath smells of cigarettes and alcohol, as if she had a drink before she came, to boost her courage. "I'm not being cruel, just curious. Where do you want to begin? When you left me standing at the altar? Or when you forgot to leave a good-bye letter before starting a new life in Milan? Or should we go further back? Do you want to apologize for your affair with that guy from the model agency? Oh, but he came after the cigar smoker from Florence, didn't he?"

"I was young and stupid, Fabrizio."

I laugh out loud. "That's one thing I can't accuse you of—stupidity." Then I let go of her. She sits back and looks at me like a wounded deer. "You are beautiful and very smart. You even used to be nice. You were so nice that Lucia was your friend, along with some others whom you so badly insulted that today rather than *say* your name, they *spit* it."

"I've changed."

"I hope so, for your sake."

"You have no idea what I've gone through these past few years," she says.

"It doesn't interest me."

"That's too bad." She purses her lips.

"What did you expect?"

Sofia stares at her fingers, flat on the table, for a long time. "Maybe I really don't deserve your sympathy," she finally sniffles, and I'm fascinated to see tears filling her beautiful eyes. "It would have been easier. I mean, coming back, with you at my side. A new beginning that would heal old wounds."

My hands form fists under the table. I almost believed her. But Sofia never changes and she loves only one person on this planet: herself. I suddenly pity her.

"The easiest way is not always the best," I say. "Maybe you could start by becoming someone people like."

"But nobody here gives me a chance," she sobs, and I try not to roll my eyes. "The way they look at me—the traitor who thought she was too good for village life, now crawling back because she didn't make it in the city. Disgraceful—and the mayor's daughter, too. That's what they whisper behind my back, but loud enough that I can hear it."

"Well, Montesimo is a village, and there's always gossip in villages. They'll forget about you as soon as they find something else to bitch about."

"That's a small comfort."

"But it's all I can offer you."

Her body language tells me that she finally understands. Her tears dry up as quickly as they appeared. She slumps down a little and looks at her folded hands. "Do you remember when you bought that rusty bicycle from old Benito? Using your pocket money?" she whispers. I nod, irritated at the abrupt change of subject. Her smile creates tiny wrinkles around her mouth and sparkles in her eyes. I hold my breath in surprise. I had forgotten that enchanting smile. "It took you two weeks to repair it. Then you painted it red and gave it to me as a birthday present."

"And a week later you sold it to Stefano, and he rode it into a ditch somewhere."

She looks dejected. "I never thanked you . . . I mean, for the bicycle. I shouldn't have sold it. That wasn't . . . nice."

"Well, at least for a week I was the happiest boy in Italy," I say dryly and wave it aside. "That was a long time ago."

"You really are a nice guy, you know."

"Don't tell anyone. I have a reputation to consider." Now I grin, and that's all the encouragement Sofia needs.

"Would you help me? Could you be the first to forget what I did?" she murmurs, and grabs my hand again. I don't pull it away this time. Water under the bridge. Why not? I'm tired of holding a grudge against her.

"I could do that."

"Friends?" She leans forward and offers her cheek. With a sigh, I plant a kiss on her cheek.

"Go home now. I don't want Hanna to see you."

Sofia nods, pushes back the chair, and gets up. I notice guiltily how rumpled her hair is, but I don't apologize for being rough before.

"One more question," she says in a low voice.

"Hm?"

"This Hanna . . . you really care for her, don't you?"

"I just realized how much."

Hanna

I turn around and soundlessly sneak back out the door of the Osteria Maria just when Fabrizio leans toward Sofia and pulls her closer by the back of her neck. I stop at the top of the stairs and hold on to the rusty railing. Trying to breathe, I imagine how he is kissing her—with soft, warm lips that I can still feel on mine. My entire body tenses. So this is lovesickness.

Marco, ice cream gone now, is leaning against the wall with crossed arms. A smug smile wins over his faked compassion. He really thinks that he orchestrated this farce. Have I been blind? Is Marco so sure about what's happening inside because it's just common knowledge? Am I so wrong about Fabrizio? Was this all just an illusion leading me to a future that doesn't exist?

As if it isn't bad enough, Marco shoves me harder into reality.

"Now you've seen it, Hanna, the difference between a business deal and true love. Fabrizio might be holding your hand and screwing you, but his soul is still attached to Sofia. You're just a little distraction. You mean next to nothing to him, and it'll all be over as soon as Fabrizio gets his inheritance and puts you on the next plane back to Germany. His words."

"I don't believe it," I say. But my trembling hands clutching the railing aren't very convincing. Marco's expression softens. He pushes himself off the wall and comes closer.

"You're not doing him any favors with this wedding. You're just keeping him from making the right choice. He belongs to another woman. You must see that, at least. Or do you need more evidence?"

If I answer now, I'll start to cry. I refuse to give Marco that satisfaction—I'd rather die. In a daze, I look down the street. It's as empty as I feel.

"I'll drive you to wherever you want." Marco points to his car, parked a few houses down.

"Thanks. I'd rather walk."

He shrugs and strolls away, kicking a stone. The Ford drives by a few minutes later and Marco honks his horn. Watching him disappear, I consider retrieving my jacket from the wardrobe back at the osteria, but decide not to.

The sun has set by now, and twilight paints gray shadows on the houses. Lights glow in some of the windows, and a TV blares somewhere. I crouch down with a sigh and undo the straps of my sandals.

I didn't anticipate a two-mile march this evening, but things never go like you think they will, do they? I force myself to walk barefoot down the steps, avoiding the seams between the tiles—and continue from cobblestone to cobblestone until the path merges with the paved street.

Soon after the city-limits sign, after the last yellow-brick house, a grassy utility road veers off the main street. A faded sign hangs on a fence: "Footpath to Tre Camini—Approximately 2.1 km." Not very assuring, but all I want is privacy, and on the main road I might be discovered by crazy Carlo, talkative Ernesto, or even Fabrizio.

"Let's see what 'approximately' means in Montesimo," I mumble to myself. I start down the grassy median, walking fast, and soon I'm running. The gathering darkness swallows the road behind me.

By the time the silhouettes of the estate buildings appear in front of me, I've lost all sense of time. I recognize the back of the barn and the distillery. Breathing heavily, I crouch and rest my arms on my thighs. Unbelievable: I actually ran the entire distance. My muscles are trembling from the exertion, my lungs whistling and my chest about to burst, but otherwise I feel fine, strangely detached. But my euphoria lasts only a few moments. When I see the brightly lit manor house, my eyes fill with tears. Not a good sign.

"Ooh là là, *you've got it bad,"* Claire whispers in the darkness.

Nonsense. My period is coming up, and that always makes me cry easily. I straighten up defiantly.

I hear Claire again: *"All right—if it helps you deal with the situation."*

Just leave me alone, Claire. I stand up. Then I realize that people are running around in the yard, shouting to each other. I hear car doors slamming, engines starting. I stop dead, my heart beating wildly against my chest. Then an ambulance zooms down the driveway, sirens blaring and lights flashing.

Lucia. Please don't let it be Lucia! I start to run.

When I reach the main building, the commotion is over. The yard lies deserted, dimly lit by the yard light. I look around in panic.

Something white scurries toward me out of the darkness—Vittoria, with feathers fluffed up and her signature growl. I'm so happy to encounter any kind of living thing that I squat and reach out for her. The hen stops. Defying death, I stretch my arm even farther. That's too much for Vittoria. Fluttering her wings and clucking, she hops away.

"Hanna? What are you doing?"

I squint, not knowing whether to laugh or cry. "Lucia!"

She seems strangely foreign as she stands in front of me with drooping shoulders and a dazed look. We hug and Lucia begins to cry, so I pat her trembling back. I know it's unfair, but I'm filled with gratitude that she wasn't the one taken away by the ambulance.

"What happened?" I hold her away from me.

"He—those damn sweets! I told him he could only have two of Rosa-Maria's biscotti. I had no idea he'd already had some birthday cake at Signora Valuzi's . . . and then went for an espresso at Benito's. Who knows what else he stuffed into himself there. He's totally addicted to everything sweet. Alberto just keeled over." With a sob, Lucia adds, "And it's my fault that he's dying."

"Don't be silly. Alberto is a grown man; he's responsible for himself." I gently shake her shoulders. "Why are you still here? You should go to the hospital."

Lucia holds up a bag. "I was grabbing some of Alberto's stuff . . . I mean, he'll need his pajamas and his slippers. Marco went along with the ambulance, and I'm going to take the Ford.

I take the bag out of her hand and smile what I hope is an encouraging smile. "So what are we waiting for?"

"You're coming along?" She rubs her eyes.

"Don't insult me."

With a tiny smile, Lucia looks around. "Where is Fabrizio? I didn't hear the motorbike."

I've been afraid of that question. "He isn't here."

"But why?" Her eyes narrow. "Did you quarrel again? Don't tell me you walked home."

"That's not important right now, Lucia. Let's talk about it later." I completely fail to hide how much it hurts just to hear Fabrizio's name. Lucia seems about to say something, but then just pushes her chin forward, looking less helpless now.

"You're right." She rummages in her bag until she finds her phone and keys. "I'll call Fabrizio and tell him Alberto is in the hospital and we're on the way there." The keys jingle and I nod silently. Lucia's already striding across the yard.

Chapter Thirteen

Hanna

From the outside, the Ospedale Misericordia looks like an alien control center that dropped from the sky by accident. Why do buildings where people are supposed to get well have to be so ugly?

As soon as we step into the emergency room, I understand why Giuseppa consulted a German cardiologist. The waiting room is packed with people of all ages filling all available chairs, the floor, and the standing room. But people laugh, talk, and drink espresso. Somewhere a baby is crying, children crawl around, and a few teenagers play on their phones. The atmosphere is reminiscent of a fairground, were it not for hospital employees in green smocks wandering around among the patients, sometimes dispensing medical care right then and there.

Lucia drags me through the crowd and pushes forward until she reaches a glass enclosure with a round opening above it that says *"Registrazione."* A nurse sits inside, knitting.

I do a double take, but it's no optical illusion. The woman is knitting without a care in the world while at least fifty people line up in front of the desk. Lucia knocks on the glass.

"Prego?"

The nurse doesn't even look up.

"Are you knitting a bonnet for your little grandson, Gina? It's lovely," Lucia says. The knitting needles stop, and the chubby nurse looks up with a smile. So that's how it works here.

"Lucia," Nurse Gina coos over her gold-rimmed glasses. "It's been a while since last time."

When I glance at Lucia, she shakes her head and bends closer to the hole in the glass. "Well, you know how Alberto is. I can't wean him off the sweet stuff, and I can't be after him day and night."

The nurse nods and purses her lips. "Men! If women and fast cars don't kill them, sugar will."

Lucia smiles. "Can you tell me where they brought him?"

"Of course, dear. Room 543—the same block as last time. Listen, can you bring me a jar of your wonderful apricot-blossom honey next time you come in?"

"With pleasure! *Mille grazie.*" Lucia throws an air kiss, grabs my arm, and pulls me into the elevator.

"You have honey at Tre Camini, too?" I say while watching the floor display over the elevator door. It still indicates the first floor, even though we're moving up. The elevator rattles and squeaks. The way my luck runs, we'll probably get stuck or the cable will break.

"Of course we have honey." Lucia chews her lips. "Eduardo—Marco and Fabrizio's grandfather—built the beehives decades ago in the outer orchard. He saw that the bees were crazy about apricot blossoms. I don't care too much for honey myself, but Nonna loved it. She used it with everything, even added it to pasta sauces." Then her forced cheerfulness gives way again to the nervous tension that made the drive to the hospital so uncomfortable.

I try to hide my own nerves about the elevator. "Are the beehives large? I mean, do you produce lots of honey?"

Lucia studies the floor display, too. "We only use it for the kitchen and our hotel guests."

I sigh in relief when the elevator jerks to a halt and the doors rumble open.

"I always think it's scary in there," Lucia mumbles. She heads to the right, and I follow. I'm not usually so puppylike, but she's my friend, after all.

I smile when I see that the sign on Room 543 is crooked. Once Italians decide to be chaotic, they go about it with attention to even the smallest detail. Lucia turns around. Her eyes are as huge as saucers.

"He's not in Intensive Care," I say. "That means Alberto is conscious and probably won't mind having some of your chocolate cookies."

A tiny smile.

"Now go in. I'll wait at the window over there." I point to a cluster of chairs at the end of the hallway—all the seats are taken—and I see Paolo and Rosa-Maria (pressing a handkerchief to her eyes) among the crowd. Lucia gives me a grateful look and opens the door. I hear a babble of voices from inside and I glimpse a tall, slender man. My stomach tenses. So Fabrizio is already here.

Fabrizio

I was still a child when Nonna talked to me about fear, the kind of fear I bring along to this hospital room today. A huge storm raged through the valley that night. To me, the storm was a hungry monster rattling the shutters and trying to get into the house through the roof. Furious that we shut it out, the storm tore down the power lines in the yard and bombarded Nonna's Mercedes with hailstones the size of tennis balls. Nonna never forgave it that.

Marco had been asleep a long time under Nonna's embroidered bedspread, but I pulled the blanket all the way up to my nose and anxiously watched as Nonna lit some candles. When she was done, she looked at me with her usual mixture of strictness and kindness, a deep wrinkle between her eyes and many tiny ones around them. "You aren't afraid, are you, Fabrizio?" I hurriedly shook my head though my heart was thudding. "Good. Because—listen to me—fear does not exist." She sat down on my bed and stroked my hair with her rough hand. I pushed the blanket down to my chin. Nonna tapped my temple and smiled. "We create fear ourselves. That's why we can also control it—unlike love." Her finger wandered to my chest. "Love is made here, very far away from your head. Always remember that, child."

I have remembered. But as I look at Alberto right now—his head sunken into a pillow, his wrinkled face yellow like faded paper—I definitely feel fear in my chest. And although I try, I can't control it.

I study the IV bag and tube attached to Alberto's arm. They're giving him a mixture of saline and insulin, the doctor told me. He explained all kinds of things in medical speak, and I can only remember words like *high blood sugar*, *dehydration*, and *fainting*—and the calming sentence, "He's asleep, but he'll wake up soon, and he'll be very thirsty."

While I tell myself for the hundredth time that my fear for Alberto is unfounded, I study Marco. He's sitting on a stool next to Alberto's bed and staring at the blanket. It's amazing, actually, that the old man is sleeping so peacefully. Family members of the three other patients fill the room. They are eating dinner and discussing the day's events at high volume, oblivious to those who need sleep and rest. Since there aren't enough chairs, two of them wanted to sit on Alberto's bed with their full pasta plates—I fought them off. I've been constantly pulling children out from under his bed, too. Sometimes Italians really get on my nerves.

I only notice Lucia when she approaches Marco and touches his shoulder. He sighs, wraps his arms around her hips, and buries his face in her sweater. It's strange to see him like that. I always thought he couldn't care less about Alberto—or the rest of mankind. That's probably another injustice to him. Lucia loves him, and she must have a reason. The two whisper with each other and I look toward the door. I'm disappointed that Lucia has come alone.

She sees me look. "She's waiting outside." I don't move, even though in my mind I'm already running down the hallway. Lucia clears her throat. "I'd like an espresso, Fabrizio. Is that reason enough for you?"

I frown at her. Lucia raises an eyebrow and nods her chin at the door. The cheerful group at the window starting to say grace pushes me over the edge. I leave the room with a pounding heart.

It takes me a moment to get used to the dim emergency lighting out here. I'm relieved to find the waiting area empty except for a single person leaning against the window.

I stop and watch Hanna. Forehead pressed against the window, hands resting on the sill, she looks relaxed, almost asleep. A floorboard squeaks under my feet. She stiffens slightly.

"Did Paolo and Rosa-Maria go home?" I ask because I can't think of anything better to say.

"Paolo has to look after the animals and dragged Rosa-Maria along, even though she put up a fight," Hanna says without moving. She's still wearing the blue dress, and now I'm so close that I can see the goose bumps on her arms. I take off my jacket and wrap it around her shoulders.

"Your jacket is on the motorcycle. You forgot it at the osteria." I step next to her and look out the window, too—an ocean of lights under a red moon, partially hidden behind clouds.

"It looks creepy outside," she whispers and pulls the jacket tighter around her body.

"It doesn't even come close to what's going on in Alberto's room—it's *The Rocky Horror Picture Show* in there." My attempt at wit is clumsy; what I really want is to ask her why she ran away. But her cool scrutiny makes me insecure. This isn't the Hanna who, a short time ago, laughed with me in Salvi's osteria and let me in on her little secrets. This is the detached and unapproachable Signora Philipp whom I had completely forgotten about.

"How is Alberto?"

"He's tough as Carlo's schnitzel."

Finally a tiny smile, even though it doesn't seem meant for me. "I'm happy for him."

I look at her sideways and fight the urge to embrace her. Instead, I dig my hands into my pockets and wait—for who knows what. Nonna picks this exact moment to interfere in my life again. *"Boy, haven't you learned anything at all?"* she scolds, digging her finger into my chest. *"Your heart is very far from your head. Stop trying to control it! Do what it tells you to do; don't concern yourself with what you might lose."*

But I don't know what it's telling me, Nonna.

"Yes, you do, Fabrizio. Just listen."

My heart pounds like mad.

"If you want, I'll let you out of our deal." What comes out of my mouth, quickly and way too loud, terrifies me. But surprisingly, it also relieves me. Hanna's eyes show no reaction.

"You mean our wedding?" she says.

"It wouldn't be right to force you to marry me," I say slowly, keeping my eyes on her. "I realize that now. I'll drop the case against your magazine. You're free to do whatever you wish." My voice sounds hollow. Never in my life have I wanted a woman more. And never before have I hoped more that a woman would say yes to me if I left the choice up to her.

Hanna

It's not as if I expected something else. I might have hoped—somewhere in a quiet and deserted chamber of my heart, where reality hasn't yet bulldozed all the furnishings. I study Fabrizio, who looks out into the night, and even though I feel more torn up than I've ever felt before, a wave of tenderness floods me. I'm deeply grateful to this man who showed me, no matter how briefly, that I am capable of loving someone—even if he isn't the one. Swallowing, I clench my hands into fists behind my back. It hurts.

"That's very generous of you." I paste on a smile.

"Does that mean you're going to take me up on the offer?" he says, voice flat, shoulders drawn up. He obviously feels guilty.

"Don't worry about me. I can't wait to return to a country where hospital corridors are lit properly."

"I'm sorry I kept you from that for such a long time."

Fabrizio looks at me strangely. It seems he wants to add something, but I beat him to it. "Well, for me, at least, our business deal paid off. I get off easy." I smile, though my insides churn. I just can't lose it now! I'm close to throwing myself at him and confessing my love in a way that would make dime-novel Prudence green with envy. Fabrizio's eyes narrow.

"Our business?"

"Our business!" I wink, feeling foolish—and proud at the same time, because my flippant remark seems to make him feel good about returning to Sofia. His chest rises and he straightens to his full height. He looks me over as if he were an artist evaluating an unfinished painting—and deciding not to finish it.

"I'll contact my attorney first thing tomorrow. Thank you for going through all the trouble with the kitchen duty, the bridal dinner, and everything. You played your role very convincingly."

"So did you—you had me pretty convinced you were a groom in love."

With a crooked smile, Fabrizio looks down the hallway. "I'll go back in before some caring auntie stuffs Alberto with pasta. Should I ask Lucia or Marco to drive you home—to Tre Camini?"

I'm collapsing inside. He is friendly now, but in a businesslike way. I've never felt so forlorn in all my life. "I'd appreciate that."

About two hours and a silent car ride later—I pretended to sleep, to avoid Lucia's questions—I'm standing in my little Cinderella room. I can't bring myself to go to bed. So I snatch up the last installment of *Propelled by Hope* and sit down at the desk to finish my excursion into the world of pulp fiction.

It's dawn when I leave the bedroom of the happily united—or still uniting—couple, with an aching back and an envious sigh. At least Prudence got what she wanted, and I forgot for a few hours that I won't. I put on some jeans and a thin sweater and head outside for fresh air.

But on the spur of the moment, I turn right at the foot of the stairs and enter the narrow hallway that leads to the old part of the house. The ceiling looms lower overhead after a few yards, and I step on well-worn wooden boards. Since I've never been anywhere in the house except the annex and the kitchen, I look around with interest. The walls here are papered with old-fashioned wallpaper instead of being washed white, and framed family photos are everywhere. Some are faded, as if time had painted over them. I resist the temptation to examine them more closely, since I don't want to be surprised here by Lucia, Marco, or Fabrizio. I heard the motorcycle a little earlier, the slamming of a heavy door, and then I saw the distillery light go on. I push away the thought of Fabrizio and his desperate fight with the right liqueur ingredients. It's none of my business anymore. Not sure what to do next, I continue down the corridor to an open, double-leaved door with heavy brass fittings.

The living room beyond, which smells of leather, charcoal, and old books, is so impressive that I pause in the doorway. The enormous oil painting above the stone fireplace mesmerizes me instantly. The woman in the painting is my mother's age and wears her black hair loosely drawn back at her neck. Slim ankles and milky-white feet peek out from her dark-blue apron dress. She sits at a table, a bowl of apricots in front of her, and holds a fruit knife in her hand. She looks straight out of the frame. My mouth dries up. It seems as if the woman is not only flirting with the painter, but penetrating me with her licorice eyes. I don't need anyone to tell me who this is. Spellbound, I move closer to Giuseppa Camini. I can see her pursed lips and the laughter lines in her strict face—as if both I and the entire world amuse her.

"It does you justice," I say and cautiously touch the uneven, shiny surface. My heart beats faster and I shrink back, laughing at myself at the same time. The pulsing sensation in my fingertips is surely nothing more than my own hysteria. I slowly breathe in and out, tilt my head, and lock eyes with the shimmering oily ones of the woman in the painting.

"Thank you for everything," I whisper. Then I wait, holding my breath. Only the ticking of the grandfather clock interrupts the silence. She doesn't answer. Of course not—everything has been said. I nod good-bye to Giuseppa. It's time to go home.

From the end of the driveway, the bus stop is a few hundred yards in the opposite direction from Montesimo, behind a curve covered in juniper bushes. According to the schedule, the bus stops here twice a day, and finally I have some luck: the next one is due in twenty minutes.

Slightly out of breath, I sink down on the little bench on the side of the road. I panicked after leaving the living room. I couldn't get away fast enough from this place that's made me realize how lonely and pathetic my own life is. Like a scared chicken, I hurried back to my room, bundled together my things, and stuffed them into my suitcase without caring that my muddy shoes will ruin my dresses and blouses. Then I sneaked out of the house and ran the entire way to the road.

And now I'm sitting here feeling guilty because I didn't have the decency to say good-bye to Lucia. But she would have tried to make me stay, would have begged with her huge eyes, and would have asked questions I don't want to answer.

I shield my eyes against the sun and watch Vittoria, who followed me like a puppy and resisted all my attempts to shoo her back. Now she stalks around on the grassy roadside, clucking, and I'm worried that some speed freak might run her over. How strange that this chick gave me the jitters only a little while ago. She's actually cute, even pretty, with her snow-white feathers and spotted brown chest.

I sigh and check my watch. The twenty minutes are taking an eternity. Finally I hear the welcome sound of a motor. But what clatters around the curve isn't a bus. Ernesto's dirty yellow postal vehicle comes to a halt next to me with squeaking wheels. This is all I need.

"*Buon giorno*, beautiful signora," Ernesto shouts. "Did you get lost again? If you're looking for Tre Camini, it's in the opposite direction."

"I'm waiting for the bus." Maybe he'll leave me alone if I'm gruff enough. Ernesto scratches underneath his cap.

"That might be a problem."

"Why would there be a problem?" I cross my arms in front of my chest. Ernesto points his thumb behind him.

"The bus is in the garage. Broken axle. Happened last week."

"You're kidding! Don't you have a replacement bus?"

Ernesto shrugs. "Well, yes."

"Yes, and? Where is it?"

"Near Perugia by now, probably. It left here about two hours ago."

"But the schedule says it's due now." I stare at him in disbelief. True, I've heard a lot about the unreliability of public transportation in Italy, but this—it leaves me speechless. Meanwhile Ernesto turns off his engine and smiles at me.

"Pietro isn't much for schedules. To be honest, I don't think he can even read them. But he's a good driver, hasn't had an accident in more than twenty years. That means something in Italy."

"How nice for Pietro, but it doesn't get me to the airport," I say, and immediately regret it because now Ernesto no longer looks at me cheerfully, but eyes my suitcase suspiciously.

"Does Fabrizio know you're leaving?"

"It's none of his business," I say.

Ernesto slowly shakes his head, but his expression actually lightens. "You really make a great couple, you and my ex-future-son-in-law."

"What do you mean?"

"I had to keep my Rita from running away six times. Once, she made it all the way onto the plane to Milan. But the air traffic controller is my cousin's brother-in-law, and he wouldn't let the plane leave. *Mamma mia*, Rita was furious. I had to sing twice to make her get off the plane."

"You sang?"

Ernesto nods. "Twice. Fausto Leali's 'A Chi.' Do you know it?"

"No." I raise my hand. "And I don't want to hear it."

"Pity. It's a nice one." He hums and taps a beat on his steering wheel. I cover my ears.

"Ernesto, could you please just drive me to Stefano's garage so I can pick up my rental car? And would you please do it without saying anything? I beg you."

Maybe because of my intensity, or because of the tears that suddenly roll down my cheeks, Ernesto is immediately serious. He unbuckles his seatbelt, gets out, and picks up my suitcase. Then he waits silently next to the passenger door until I'm settled among the packages and piles of letters. When he's behind the steering wheel again, he nods to me and starts up the engine. Half-blinded by tears, I look in the rearview mirror and catch sight of Vittoria shrinking into a small white spot and then disappearing around the bend.

Fabrizio

I actually just wanted to sit down and rest for a while. But when I reluctantly open my eyes, I find that my head is on the table and throbbing like I have a hangover. On top of it, the sun beats down through the window, bent on burning me.

Groaning, I straighten up, scoot my chair out of the sun, and wait for the carousel to stop turning. Then I see the empty liqueur bottle on the table and the half-full glass next to it, and I'm suddenly wide awake, overtaken by the memory of yesterday. I somehow manage to get up, stagger into the container of corks on my way to the door, and stumble over the dustpan that I forgot to put away yesterday. My wrinkled trousers and dirty fingernails disgust me. I feel filthy and taste something nauseating in my mouth, but there is no time for a shower. I have to talk with Hanna—now.

I cross the yard and head for the back door. Marco is sitting on the bench in front of the kitchen window, his face to the sun. He opens his eyes, destroying my hope of sneaking by him.

"Well, well, well . . . The lord of the manor slept off his hangover. Make sure it doesn't become a habit, brother." He makes a show of stretching and yawning. I reach for the door handle with a snort. Ignoring Marco is the best punishment, and has been ever since we were little.

"By the way, you don't have to rush. She's gone." Another hearty yawn. I stop midstride. "She must have smelled a rat." He clicks his tongue. "I thought she was tougher. But . . . maybe I was right from the start. It's a pity nothing came of your little deal."

I slowly push down the handle without looking at him, because otherwise I might lose control. One thing is certain, I'm going to kill him. I just don't know if it will be now or later. Marco's laughter follows me into the hallway, where I run into Rosa-Maria. She brushes by me with an annoyed "Signora I-Do-Whatever-I-Want."

Without knocking, I rush into Hanna's room. Lucia is sitting at the edge of the bed, her hands in her lap. She gives me a startled look. In one glance I take in the made-up bed and the empty wardrobe, its doors wide open.

"She didn't say good-bye," Lucia says.

I go to the table and touch the apron dress that is neatly folded over the back of the chair. The material is soft and faded, and a safety pin still clips the spot where Hanna took it in. Bending down, I pick up a coat hanger, one of many on the floor. I guess she couldn't leave fast enough.

It's hurtful, but it also proves that I did the right thing. I gave Hanna a choice, and she chose. Actually, it was clear from the beginning. A deal is a deal—and you can't force love. The sex meant nothing. Thing is, a foolish heart is still a foolish heart.

Lucia looks at me questioningly while I pick up the rest of the coat hangers and hang them back up. "It looks like she made a decision," I say and slam the wardrobe door. "Come on, Lucia. We've got work to do."

Hanna

When the plane starts to move, I turn off my phone and lean back in the uncomfortable seat. I'm not sure whether I should laugh at myself or berate myself for hoping until the last moment to be begged over the intercom by a breathless voice, or an off-key love song, to get off the airplane.

But some things happen only in movies—or maybe in Ernesto's world, where anything seems to be possible. In my world, I get on the plane, and that's the end of the story.

I look through the window as we taxi toward the runway and force myself not to check the aisle again. Instead I focus on the flight attendant and her pretty smile. She's a pretty, blue-eyed brunette who doesn't look as if she's ever been lovesick. But what a stupid assumption! Lovesickness is as universal as eating; it affects everyone who doesn't pretend to be an island, as I did for years. My eyes tear up again. All this crying is new to me, too, but I can't help it.

"Is everything all right?" the flight attendant asks me in Italian-accented German. She puts her hand on my arm. In the past, I would have shaken her off and sent her away with an irritated look. Today, I read her name tag, feeling grateful for her concern.

"No, Emilia, nothing is all right, actually." I sniffle. "It would be really nice if you could bring me something alcoholic later."

She nods with a soft expression. "I'll bring you two, signora."

There you have it. Lovesickness is universally understood, no matter how young and pretty you are. I watch her as she asks passengers to turn off electronic devices and bring their seats to an upright position. Then an elderly lady across the aisle in front of me draws my attention. She's looking around with curiosity and keeps grabbing the hand of the younger woman next to her.

"Here we go, Pupetta!" She clasps the golden cross on her necklace.

"Yes, Mamma. We're taking off soon," the daughter says and helps her mother with the seatbelt. The old lady seems to feel my gaze, because she suddenly looks over her shoulder. I am dumbstruck—not because she caught me eavesdropping but because her eyes are just as black and oily as Giuseppa's. Even the smile playing around her wrinkly mouth, friendly and mischievous, could easily belong to the younger woman in the oil painting at Tre Camini.

She winks at me. "My grandson is getting married in Germany."

"That's wonderful," I say lamely, because what I remember all of a sudden makes my pulse jump sky high. Giuseppa.

No.

It can't be.

Did I really . . . ?

I look around nervously, but it's way too late. The engine is already racing at full speed; the stripes on the runway merge into a single line and the plane accelerates, shaking and rocking. The old lady shouts with glee, and I feel the familiar tingling in my belly as the upward lurch presses me against my seat. Then it's over.

I'm still numb half an hour later. The seatbelt sign above me has been off for a while, and two strong-smelling drinks sit in front of me. I toss the first down in one gulp and grimace, and then I do the same with the second. Then I tilt back my seat and try to breathe as I relive my hasty departure from Tre Camini.

In slow motion, I watch myself grabbing blouses and slacks from the wardrobe, dropping coat hangers, and stuffing everything randomly into my suitcase—on top of Giuseppa's urn. And then I run out of the little room as if someone were chasing me.

How stupid can you get?

At that point I burst into loud laughter, to the astonishment of everyone sitting near me.

Chapter Fourteen

Hanna

"Anything to declare?" The uniformed official at the counter seems to find my passport boring.

"Just a grandmother. In here," I say truthfully—and with a somewhat floppy tongue. Emilia, the flight attendant, meant well by giving me three more consoling drinks during the flight, but that's why I twisted my ankle twice on the gangway (I swear I will never wear these pumps again), bumped into an elderly gentleman at baggage claim (I really didn't see him), and almost grabbed the wrong suitcase from the conveyor belt (why are they all black?). Now I'm standing in front of the glassed-in customs counter. Suddenly I want to breathe on the glass and draw a heart in the condensation. Giggling, I brace myself against the window.

"In here," I repeat and point to my suitcase. The customs official frowns without looking up.

"So you have nothing to declare."

He thinks I'm joking. I'm about to explain the misunderstanding when someone touches my arm.

"Oh, there you are," says a clear voice. I only recognize it when I see Emilia's gentle eyes. I open my mouth, but close it again since the ground starts to move. I grab on to Emilia's arm for dear life. The customs guy seems to be as happy to see her as I am.

"Emilia! Done for today?"

Emilia's laughter bubbles like prosecco. I wouldn't mind a glass, a tiny one. I giggle.

"Hello, Reiner. How are the kids?"

The customs official's groan is half-proud and half-annoyed. "What can I say? I found my first gray hairs."

"Men like you never get old," Emilia says. She holds my arms tight, since my feet seem to be sliding apart—like two icebergs, and I'm straddling them. Any farther and I'll do the splits. I giggle again and follow it with an unladylike burp. Nobody notices, since Reiner is luxuriating in Emilia's smile.

"Are you done here so I can take my friend along?" Emilia blinks her eyes. "Ride sharing. You know how expensive cabs are."

I look up in surprise. We carpool? Customs Reiner nods and returns my passport without so much as looking at me. While I'm still contemplating whether I should feel insulted or insist on explaining the urn in my suitcase, Emilia maneuvers me toward the exit. She heads for the parking area instead of the taxi line.

"I have to"—I point to the blue Taxi sign—"go there."

Emilia shakes her head. "My car is waiting in the staff lot. It costs an arm and a leg, but it's worth it. I'll drive you home. After all, it's sort of my fault that you're a little tipsy." I want to protest but think better of it. First, I might not find my way to the taxi stand in my current condition, and second, someone as nice as this Emilia shouldn't be snubbed. So I smile politely and try to walk straight and not trip over her cute wedge sandals every fourth step.

Half an hour later, Emilia stops her car at Pfalzburgerstrasse 53 in Wilmersdorf. She helps me out as if I were an old woman—normally I would be embarrassed—and guides me to the staircase. Then she runs back for my suitcase. She smothers my sheepish "Thank you" with a huge hug and hands me her business card.

"Just call me if you feel like talking."

She drives away, honking the horn and waving. Befuddled, I just stand there, staring at her name—Emilia di Luca—and her address and phone number, all in a playful font. So that's how easy it is to make friends.

While fishing for my keys, I glance at the nameplates next to the apartment-building door. It's as if I never read the names before. For some strange reason, it seems I never provided mine.

When I enter the hallway, the usual odors welcome me: vinegary cleaners and kitchen smells, a spice mixture of cardamom, saffron, and cinnamon that permeates the staircase from the Rahmanis' ground-floor apartment all the way to the attic. Did this really once bother me? I close my eyes and suddenly have some idea what it means to have a place called home. Still wobbly, I grab my suitcase with one hand and the railing with the other.

It has never taken me so long to climb three flights of stairs. When I finally arrive in front of my door, I'm covered in perspiration. Dizzy, too, though I'm not sure if that's from the physical exertion.

Claire tells me off, shaking her head. *"Don't be silly, Hanna. You live here, so go in. And take a bath, for crying out loud. You really need it."*

Just you wait, I talk back to her. *Tomorrow I'll see you in person, and that'll be the end of your voice in my head.* Claire laughs. I turn the key, breathe in, and drag the suitcase into my apartment.

Okay, I'm in.

It smells funky.

Of course it does. The place hasn't been aired or dusted in two weeks. Do I even own a dust cloth? Well, I can fix that easily.

Otherwise it's tidy in here.

No wonder. I have just a few pieces of furniture with almost none of what could be considered shelf space, for spreading out holiday souvenirs and other dust-catchers. Modern design isn't meant for tchotchkes. And I like it modern. To be honest, though, it does look a bit sterile.

Do I really not own a single plant?

I drop down on my white leather couch and study the unopened cardboard boxes. Have I really not needed anything in those boxes since I moved here?

And . . . has it always been this quiet around here?

I fumble in my pocket for Emilia's card and put it on the coffee table. Then I contemplate the suitcase standing in the middle of the room.

"We are a funny couple, you and I," I say, and I grin because I'm talking to a dead person yet again. But hey, who cares? I get up.

"It's time we make the best of what've we got, Giuseppa." I kneel down and open the suitcase. I toss the wrinkled clothes on the floor, take out the urn, and carry it to the table. "You're my guest for the time being, until I figure out how to get you back to Italy."

Looking at the box that says "Living Room" in black Sharpie, I suddenly know what I have to do. I need to make sure this apartment feels like a home for the old lady. I owe her that. I owe it to myself.

Fabrizio

It is seldom this quiet in the kitchen. It's so silent that I think everyone can hear my heart beating, and it isn't even beating particularly loud or fast. And the thing I just said out loud isn't all that surprising, either—no more so than a remark like "I think it's going to rain," or "The tractor's stupid fuel pipe is broken again."

But even though the actual words don't touch me—I've rehashed them in my head so often that they don't terrify me anymore—their effect on my family is dramatic. Lucia drops the sauce ladle and then stares at the wall as if frozen. Rosa-Maria scrutinizes her panino as if she doesn't know what to do with it. Alfredo, who has constantly complained about Lucia's bland diet ever since he came home from the hospital, has stopped grousing. Even Marco drops his arrogant mask and gapes at me in disbelief. However, the reaction that really gets to me is Paolo's. My foreman gulps down the rest of his wine and leaves the room without saying a word.

Lucia breaks the silence. "Could you say that again, please?"

"I said that we'll sell the apricot orchards and put the money into the hotel after paying off the debts." I reach for the pasta bowl. The more I say it out loud, the less I care.

"But why?" Lucia's voice is shrill. "For years, you've put all the money into these fields, and now you suddenly want to give it all up? What about the distillery? What about the apricots? Nonna's liqueur . . . your grandmother sacrificed her entire life to—"

"Nonna is dead. And since I can't keep the estate going like before, I won't accept the inheritance. I don't want to be responsible for losing everything in a year." I nod at Marco, whose mouth still hangs open. "If Marco's numbers are correct, we have no other choice."

"Fabrizio is right, Lucia." Alberto dabs his mouth with his napkin and looks at me. "I've seen the books."

Marco clears his throat. "The present situation is that the apricot orchards have been in the red since last summer, and they get in deeper every single month. Best-case scenario, we have two years until our obligations—"

"Oh, shut up, Marco!" Lucia interrupts. "A lot can happen in two years. Nonna's liqueur is worth any risk. If we sell it abroad, we'll be swimming in money. That's what Nonna said."

"We lost the recipe, Lucia." I shrug and robotically pour spinach sauce over my tagliatelle. I haven't had an appetite since Hanna left two days ago.

"What do you mean, it's lost?" Lucia's eyes narrow. "That green notebook you were looking for the other day?"

I say nothing. Marco reaches for Lucia's hand, but she snatches it away as if he had an infectious disease.

"How can it simply disappear? Nothing gets lost in this house. It's somewhere."

"Believe me, it's gone."

"Then . . . we make our own liqueur." Lucia's eyes spark. She reminds me more of Nonna than I can handle.

"What do you think I've been trying to do in the distillery these past few weeks? It's useless, believe me. It's over." The pasta is flavorless, but I force myself to swallow another forkful and wash it down with some wine. Marco tilts his chair and again looks so full of himself that I want to throw him, headfirst, into chicken manure.

"We have to recognize when a dream is over," he says. "The new distillery machine was a bad investment from the start. I said that."

Lucia raises her chin and sizes up her husband. "You did indeed. More than once."

"Exactly. But nobody listened to me." His left eye twitches. I'm not sure if Lucia is having the same premonition as I have.

"Fabrizio, tell me, where did Nonna keep the notebook?" Lucia says. "I'm sure it wasn't with the other cookbooks. Something so valuable—she'd have left it in a safe place."

"Probably," I say, and Lucia nods without taking her eyes off Marco.

"In the office, for example."

"I looked everywhere there, too."

"What does it matter now?" Marco waves his arm. His forehead looks red. Lucia's eyes darken.

"I'd like to talk with you, Marco. In private."

Hanna

"Hanna?"

Panting, I stop but can't turn around, afraid that I will fall down the stairs or simply collapse right here if I make one more move.

That's what I get for ducking into the tiny flower shop on my way to work—I'd never noticed it before. But I was early this morning. All I wanted was to inquire about an easy-care indoor plant that even a novice like me could handle. Who'd have thought the colors and fragrance would overwhelm me? And then there was the salesperson, an incredibly warm-hearted woman in her midforties, who almost talked me into a cactus. I really thought about it for a moment, but then decided it was too prickly for me.

So I arrived at work with a palmlike plant—named Eve, since it's the first plant I've ever had—in my arms. I also bought a bunch each of sunflowers, gerbera daisies, lilies, roses . . . and lilac-colored blossoms whose name I forget. It's definitely too much for one person to carry.

"Hanna," the voice calls again. "Is it really you?"

I peer over the bunched-up wrapping paper. My intern, standing next to me on the staircase, looks at me in astonishment.

"Sasha! Great to see you," I say, pushing aside a meddlesome lily that tries to tickle my nose. Like she is every morning, Sasha is carrying coffee. That's sweet of her.

"Are you all right?"

The lily persists. I sneeze and have to laugh. Sasha looks at me with even more suspicion. "Could we continue the conversation in my office? My arms are almost falling off," I say. I just barely catch the pink gerbera before it drops to the floor. Pink! I must be crazy.

Sasha doesn't seem to know what to do or say. "Should I . . . can I help you carry . . . ?" She looks like she's expecting me to reprimand her for daring to ask such an impertinent question.

"That would be great!"

Sasha takes Eve from me just before my left arm gives out. I rub the muscles with a groan. At that moment, the door to our offices flies open and Claire appears in front of us with crossed arms.

"We aren't buying anything."

I hand her the sunflowers. "Good—since I only give things away." But Claire just tilts her head and stares at me as skeptically as Sasha did a moment ago.

"What are you doing here? Why aren't you in Italy?" she asks sternly and straightens herself up in the doorway—ridiculous, for someone less than five feet tall. I smile—an indulgent smile, I hope. Claire measures me from top to bottom. She must notice the state of my eyelids. Lovesickness is strenuous—you sob all the time and can't sleep, and it affects your skin, no doubt. Finally her gaze lands on the sunflowers. "Those are pretty."

"Pretty enough that you'll let me come in?"

"You crazy girl! But before I start dancing with joy, I have to tell you," she whispers. "Hellwig is beside himself."

"He is?" I swallow. I've been afraid of that. There are only two reasons the boss could be mad at me, and each qualifies as a midsize catastrophe. Either Fabrizio didn't drop the suit, in which case I'll have to clear out my desk today, or Hellwig hates my article and wants me to change it. But I won't do that—I made a promise. In either situation, my career as a food journalist will be over. I follow Claire somewhat sheepishly into the office and put the flowers on my desk.

Claire snaps her fingers. "Sasha, bring vases." With a look at the desk, she adds, "Many vases."

Sasha rolls her eyes and stalks toward the staff kitchenette, mumbling something about Girl Friday. Then Claire pushes me down into my swivel chair and perches on my desk, her knees only inches from my chest. I stop her just in time from crushing my peach-colored roses.

"Now then! Who are you and what have you done to Hanna?" A paper smacks on my lap, the new Italy issue. I try not to look at it and focus on a brown spot on Claire's blouse. I bet it's Nutella. I grin, even though fists barrage the inside of my chest.

"Did Hellwig accept my article?"

Claire stares at me. "I already told you, he was beside himself."

"Okay, but did he still include it in the special issue?" I clench my fists and try to breathe evenly. Please say yes. Please! I won't be able to look myself in the mirror until the truth about Tre Camini is in print—I don't care if it's black on white or blue on pink.

"Look at me, Hanna."

I blink. Don't cry now. Then again, why not? I've wept so much these past few days that one more tear won't make a difference.

"He was beside himself—with enthusiasm! As we all were. Your article is *formidable,* absolutely brilliant. It's the title story."

My thoughts tumble like dice, and I have no idea what number comes up. Claire picks up the paper from my lap and holds it in front of my nose. When I recognize the picture on the cover—a winding, cypress-lined road leading up to a yellow-stone house—I almost start to bawl. I'm relieved, but my broken heart is acting up again, too.

"But just between the two of us, Hanna, what made you write such a damn sentimental declaration of love?"

And finally tears flood my eyes.

Fabrizio

It's a hot midday under a perfect summer sky, and the burning disk of the sun chases everyone into the shade. Vittoria is the only exception.

Completely unruffled by humans, she scratches doggedly for worms among the fruit trees. She probably senses that nobody will do her any harm, as the throat of every animal at Tre Camini, including the rabbits, is safe.

I puff on the cigarette I'm smoking instead of eating dessert and grin. Everyone knows that Paolo buys all chickens and rabbits needed in the kitchen in the neighboring village because it would break Alberto's heart if one of his beasts were killed. If the two of them continue with this practice, we'll have to enlarge the stables and run a chicken farm. Maybe that's not a bad idea, since I'll have to find another job for our loyal Paolo when our orchards are bulldozed.

I wait for this thought to cause pain in my chest, but I feel only emptiness. I look toward the house and Hanna's window—no different from the other windows now. After stomping out the stub, I light another cigarette. When I inhale, I welcome the pain in my lungs. It's the only pain I feel right now.

Alberto settles himself heavily next to me on the bench and lifts his cup. "You have no idea how awful espresso tastes with artificial sweetener." He spits out a mouthful after swirling it around. I force myself to stop staring at Hanna's window. "You made a wise decision, son," Alberto mutters and awkwardly pats my arm.

"I made a logical decision."

"Not everyone can do that."

"Maybe." I shrug. "It wasn't something I wanted. If I had my choice, I'd keep the fields."

Alberto laughs hoarsely. "Does that go for the pretty German signora, too?"

"I don't know what you mean."

"Yes, you do. Yes, you do, son."

"She left. That's all I have to say about her," I snap—gruffly enough, I hope, to make the old guy shut up. But Alberto is a stubborn old devil who will have his say, no matter what.

"And you did nothing about it."

"Why should I have?"

"Do I really have to answer that, you dumbbell?" Alberto gets up and shuffles toward the house. At the door, he turns around. "Your grandmother made a wrong decision with the girl's mother—and didn't forgive herself to her dying day. Don't make the same mistake."

"What are you talking about, old man?" I stare at him. He waves away my question with an indignant gesture.

"Your little signora was part of this place before you ever lost your simple heart to her. So you better go and get her back!"

Hanna

"Then I unpacked all the boxes, even the ones full of stuff I was going to donate. Now it actually looks like someone lives here. Well, there are no plants, and maybe the balcony could use some furniture . . . and some more things inside, maybe a few decorative items. Maybe you should come shopping with me one of these days. Where did you buy your colorful pillows? Wasn't it that store in Steglitz, the one you always talk about?"

I lean forward. Claire laughs, shakes her head, and raises her hands.

"Hanna, you've really changed."

"Have I?" I say slowly.

"Don't tell me you haven't noticed it yourself."

I shrug. Claire lifts her hand and counts on her fingers. "First of all, you're in jeans and ballerina flats. I didn't even know until now that you owned any flats. Second, you've furnished your apartment and bought flowers. You hate flowers."

"That's not true at all."

"Don't interrupt me." She frowns and lifts a third finger—the middle one, ironically. "You've struck up a friendship with a complete stranger, and the eeriest thing of all—"

"Now I'm really curious."

Claire looks at me expectantly. "Where are your souvenirs?"

I feel myself blush. "I don't have any."

"Are you sure?"

I roll my eyes.

A tiny smile appears on her red mouth. "There you go. No mementoes!" Claire jumps off the desk and does a silly dance around it. It slowly dawns on me what my words mean. After telling Fabrizio about it in the Osteria Maria, I didn't steal anything, didn't feel the tingling in my fingertips, no panic that I would die unless . . . I beam. I didn't bring home anything.

We hear a mocking voice from the kitchen—"Good god, she's cured!"—and, a few moments later, a desperate one—"What in the world am I going to do with all the shoe boxes I collected for returning Hanna's stuff?"

"Shut up, Sasha," we shout at the same time, and start to laugh. But Claire turns serious again fast.

"Are you sure you did the right thing?" she asks in a low voice, pointing to the yellow house on the magazine cover. A lump fills my throat, but I nod. "And what are you going to do with the grandmother? You know you have to return her."

"Could I think about it later?" I whisper. This constant pain of lovesickness in my chest is really wearing me out.

Claire sighs. "Let me tell you, Hanna, there's only one medicine for lovesickness. It's sweet and chocolaty, and you'll find it in a large screw-top jar.

Fabrizio

It takes my brother the whole afternoon to finally talk to me. He's always found it difficult to admit that he did something wrong. And that he's done something wrong is as clear as Rosa-Maria's chicken broth after she's strained it twice through cheesecloth. Lucia must have wrung the truth out of him by whatever means she has at her disposal—in other words, many. Honestly, I don't even want to hear the truth, and so I escaped to the outer apricot field to help Paolo and his men. But at last Marco catches up with me.

I hit the brake when Marco appears out of nowhere in front of the tractor. He's wearing work pants, to my surprise.

"Is there a hole in your running tights?" I shout. But Marco ignores me and looks to Paolo, who has put down his basket to listen to our conversation.

"Could I talk to you for a minute, Fabrizio? Alone?"

I exchange a glance with Paolo and climb down from the tractor. Paolo heaves his basket onto the trailer and takes my seat. Tapping the brim of his hat, he slowly putters away.

"Let's walk," I say curtly, indulging in the spontaneous hostility of turning off the main path.

As I anticipated, Marco soon falls behind on the donkey path. It's muddy, despite the heat. The memory of Hanna striding ahead of me with dirty legs and just one slipper, but her head raised high, weighs heavily on me. Huffing and puffing, I walk even faster to chase away the vision. But my brother's sneakered feet can't keep up with me.

"Man, Fabrizio, don't run like that!" he shouts, and he mumbles to himself. I don't even turn around.

"Don't tell me you're already out of steam, superstar." I hear swearing, cracking sounds, and more swearing. "Step on the roots. That makes it easier." I shake my head and wait with arms crossed until Marco catches up.

"Why do you always do that?" His fists are so tight that his knuckles are white. His eyes glitter with anger.

"What am I doing?"

"You . . . You . . ."

Marco's stutter and the expression that accompanies it have changed little since he was four. His lower lip trembles, and an A-shaped wrinkle appears on his forehead. Nonna called it "the anger barometer" and assigned levels to Marco's temper tantrums—from one to ten. Today it's definitely a nine, even though I'm the one who should be furious.

"You always make me feel like I'm the loser," he gasps.

"Is that why you want to talk with me?"

"No . . . Yes! I—Lucia told me to start at the beginning."

"She did?" I roll my eyes. Women.

"She also told me not to make myself small in front of you."

"But you are smaller than I am."

"She wasn't talking about our heights," Marco says stiffly. He still can't tell when I'm joking, and suddenly I feel sorry for him—and guilty, because once again it's my fault that he's feeling bad. The only difference is that now he's not sobbing in Nonna's armoire. I pat his shoulder and turn right.

"Let's go back to the main path. And then, with all due respect to Lucia, forget her brainwashing, and let's talk like men."

Fifteen minutes later, Marco is still searching for words while we walk the main path toward the manor house.

Finally I lie to get him to spit it out. "Whatever it is, Marco, just assume that I already know it." He hesitates but then looks straight at me for the first time in months.

"I put Nonna's recipe book through the shredder."

I look at the house in silence for a while. I actually imagined it would be something like this, and I've even contemplated how I should react—unsuccessfully. I couldn't decide whether I would beat the living daylights out of Marco or drown him in the well. But now that I know, I feel just as empty as before—and it's because that damn woman stuffed my heart into her suitcase two days ago and took off with it. She also took my grandmother. That's another problem I need to deal with.

"Why?" I ask, not because I'm interested, really, but because I don't want to think about how to get Nonna back to Italy.

"Are you aware that it's hell to be your brother?" Marco blurts out. He tries to clean his shoes in the grass on the shoulder of the road. I blink. I knew Marco had a problem, but I thought it had more to do with him.

"That comes as a surprise to you, doesn't it? I understand. If you get a halo as a child, it's not likely you'll take it off. Why should you? I can still hear her today"—he taps his forehead and rolls his eyes—"'No, not like that, Marco. Look how Fabrizio does it.' 'Marco, leave that to your older brother.' 'Why can't you be just a little like Fabrizio?' 'We'll only let you play with us because Fabrizio is the leader of the gang.' 'Stop bothering me, Marco.' 'Watch your brother—he can drive a tractor already.' 'Fabrizio is stronger, funnier, faster, bolder.' What good are good grades against such competition? I was just the Camini who'd rather sit in the library than help in the fields—a deal breaker for our father. And Nonna, she beamed whenever your name was mentioned." He kicks a stone. "Whatever I did, it was never as cool as what you came up with. I was never good enough."

"Marco, you're four years younger. Obviously there were things you weren't allowed to do, but not because people thought you couldn't do them. Everybody was protecting you. I was, too."

"But I didn't want to be protected. I wanted to . . ." He gasps in a breath and then looks at me defiantly. "I wanted to be like you. There, I said it."

"Believe me, you shouldn't have wished for that," I say, thinking of Father's motorcycle. I wish *I* hadn't convinced myself Father would come back if I just kept slaving away in the fields. I might have read some books, too.

"I realized that eventually—fortunately," Marco says. "I doubt Lucia would have fallen for me otherwise."

"How witty. But I still don't know what all this has to do with Nonna's liqueur recipe."

"It was wrong to destroy the notebook, but I thought I had no other choice," Marco says. "When Nonna gave me the estate's books to keep, I could finally prove that I was good at what I do. No bookkeeping in all of Italy is as clean as ours."

"We all know that, Marco."

"But not one of you ever said so. I could live with that—I can still live with it today. But that nobody listened to me—that was unbearable. Our business has gone downhill constantly these past few years, but nobody wanted to hear the truth, and I didn't want to trouble Lucia with it. Instead, you and Nonna and Alberto became obsessed with this apricot pipe dream. And I was supposed to find the money to fund it, siphoning from the hotel and the restaurant. We haven't been able to pay our suppliers for months. And when Nonna's will was read . . . I just didn't know what to do anymore."

"And so you—"

"So I made sure that this apricot dream would come to an end, once and for all. I did it for the family—so Tre Camini will continue to exist, for my kids and yours. I realize now that I chose the wrong way to do it. Lucia came down hard on me today until I told her everything. Then she slapped my face, and she was right to do so. All I can do now is apologize to you."

"No, I'm the one who should apologize. I was a selfish idiot."

We look at each other. Marco scratches his head.

"We messed that up, didn't we?" he says.

"We definitely did."

"I'm afraid it's also my fault that your little German ran away."

"Her name is Hanna," I say. "And that has nothing to do with you."

"But I talked her into believing that she means nothing to you. I even tried to bribe her. And I sent Sofia to the osteria."

I shake my head. "I meant nothing to Hanna from the start. That's all that matters."

"So your marriage was really only a business deal?"

"You were right as always, you old pessimist."

"For some strange reason that gives me little satisfaction now," Marco says. "She's a tough cookie, but I sort of liked her. And I wouldn't be so certain about her feelings for you, if I were you."

"She's gone, Marco. That's proof enough for me. It's all history now."

"Meaning?"

"We look forward and do what your numbers tell us to do. Our apricot orchards go to your golfing friends, even though I might puke on the contract when I sign it. We pay our debts and work on the new plan—to make Tre Camini the most famous hotel and restaurant in the region. And since I'm definitely not getting married, everything will be in your able bookkeeping hands starting next year. You've earned it, even if you are a real son of a bitch sometimes. But maybe that's the kind of boss we need here."

"Do you really mean it?"

"You should know by now that I always mean what I say. Let's shake on it, little brother." I lift five fingers. Marco tilts his head, and then does what I would do when we were kids: instead of shaking my hand, he punches it.

At the house, we sit in the sun in front of the woodshed for a long time, enjoying being silent together. A smiling Lucia brings us two bottles of beer and then leaves us alone. Amazing how things work out. I hope the same rule will apply to the emptiness I feel inside. We open the bottles with our teeth, a trick that cost Marco a piece of incisor when he was sixteen. We grin at each other and clink our bottles.

Mine is almost empty when Alberto strides by in his beekeeping gear. He reaches the other side of the yard, but then turns and comes back. Marco smirks and I have to suppress a grin, too. Alberto's gear makes him look like an astronaut.

"This is the last time I will say this, Fabrizio." His words sound hollow from under the beekeeper's hat, which Alberto made himself out of an old motorbike helmet and mosquito netting. "Bring Isabella's daughter home!" Then he shuffles off looking at the ground. Marco looks at me.

"Who is Isabella?"

I shake my head. Somewhere, in the back of my mind, the name rings a bell, but I can't make the connection. "I'd like to know that, too."

Hanna

When I put the key in the lock that evening, I get a jolt—the door to my apartment door is slightly open. I remember for sure that I locked it when I left—twice, as is my habit. My heart pounds as I stare from the eerie opening—wondering if I should escape at once—to my new doormat, which shouts a bright-yellow "Welcome."

My unwillingness to haul the armful of foliage back down the stairs again finally defeats my fear. Cautiously, I tap the door, listen with bated breath, and take one step inside. The aroma I thought I smelled outside intensifies, and within seconds I recognize it. My fear evaporates. Annoyed, I squat down, put Eve on the floor, and storm into the kitchen.

"Ah, *carissima*! There you are!" My mother is standing barefoot on my expensive leather stool, rummaging in a cupboard. "Don't tell me you have no dried beans in this house." She sniffs at an open bag of nacho chips in disgust. "You shouldn't eat this junk," she scolds, and throws the bag into the sink. "Salt, pepper, and olive oil—that's all you need on potato chips."

"They're corn chips," I say, trying hard not to lose it. "What are you doing here? And how did you get in?"

"I'm cooking ribollita for you . . . if you have beans somewhere, that is." Now she turns around for the first time and exclaims, "Oh no, you cut your beautiful hair."

"Mamma! You can't just break into other people's apartments to cook soup."

"It's not 'other people's apartments' I broke into—it's my daughter's. And it's not breaking in if you have a key, is it?" She seems pensive for a moment but then waves the thought away. "Anyway, your new landlord is a nice man. Maybe a little lazy, and I don't like his limp handshake. But he promised to take care of the damaged blinds in the guest bathroom first thing tomorrow—"

"Mamma!"

"You know, you could help me instead of standing around." As she climbs down from the stool it wobbles dangerously, but I stubbornly stay at the door. Fine with me if she falls on her nose.

But she doesn't fall. Instead Mamma lands elegantly on the linoleum with both feet, steps into her killer stiletto heels, and smooths her pleated skirt—for no particular reason. That's the only sign that she's nervous.

"Happy Birthday, *principessa*."

I exhale sharply. "It's not my birthday."

"You were put in my arms on April 12, 1983, at seven nineteen in the morning. Every day since then has been your birthday for me," she says quietly. Then she comes toward me, her arms extended.

She only reaches my chin, and her arms look like a twelve-year-old's, but her embrace feels like an enormous fluffy blanket on a chilly autumn day. I try to stiffen, but my resistance melts away. And then the floodgates open and I sink, sobbing, to the ground—Mamma with me, since she doesn't let go.

"Oh, my darling," she whispers, and caresses my back. I hate myself for collapsing into a sniveling picture of misery, but I can't change it.

"I'm sorry that I was so mean to you," I say.

"I'm sorry that I was such a bad mother."

"You weren't a bad mother."

"Oh yes, I was." She releases me from her embrace and holds me in front of her. "But I'll make it up to you. I'll stay with you as long as you want—today, tomorrow, the day after. And we'll make up for what I missed these past few years." She traces my wet cheeks with her thumb.

"But you've got to go in to—to your people. Isadora will be desperate without you—"

"Who is Isadora?" Mamma says calmly. I just look at her.

"Right. Who in the world is she?"

We start to laugh at the same time. Well, Mamma laughs. Mine is something between a giggle and a sob.

"I could use a drink now," she finally says with a smile. She helps me up. "And then you're going to tell me the name of the guy who broke your heart."

Startled, I stop crying. "How do you know?"

My mother smiles serenely. "Child, there are only two reasons for tears like those: death and love. And since I hope that nobody died, there's only one answer."

"Mamma?"

"Yes?"

"I love you."

She brushes a strand of hair off from my forehead. "Forget about soup. Let's have a drink and talk."

I snap my fingers. "I think I have exactly the right drink for us." In the bathroom, I splash cold water over my puffy face for a few minutes. When I look in the mirror, I still see sadness in my eyes, but also something else. I turn away with a smile and get the small, slender bottle from my suitcase.

Liquore di Albicocche della Nonna. I gently touch the label and Lucia's handwriting. I'll write her a long letter tonight. Then I go back out to the kitchen.

"This is a very special liqueur," I say. "You'll love it. I brought it from Ita—" I stop short. My mother has turned deathly pale, staring at the bottle as if I'm holding a grenade. "Mamma? Are you all right?"

She opens her mouth, but what comes out is eerie—the sound of a hurt little animal.

"Where did you get that?" she asks, barely loudly enough to hear, her eyes wide open. And then something unimaginable happens: she cries.

Chapter Fifteen

Hanna

My mother is still totally flustered. She's been turning the little bottle in her hands for twenty minutes, staring at it as if it were Pandora's box—something to be both revered and feared.

I sit next to her on the couch, waiting for her to be able to speak again. Other than some incoherent stammering—I make out the words *Tre Camini* repeated a few times, like a mantra—she hasn't said anything. So I tell her a cleaned-up version of my Italy trip, leaving out the parts about the urn and the marriage deal, since I still feel ashamed about both.

As I finish recounting my hasty escape from the estate, her tears finally subside. She blows her nose noisily.

"I believe that some things we call coincidences are actually no such thing." She wipes her nose again and crumples the tissue into a little ball in her hand. "Here I've been trying to forget Tre Camini for half my life, and then my daughter falls in love with none other than Giuseppa's grandson."

"I wish it had turned out differently, too." Thinking of Fabrizio, I almost start crying again—and wonder when I'll run out of tears.

Mamma scrutinizes me. "The Caminis were always very likable. If the young man takes just a little after Giuseppa, I can understand how you feel." She clicks her tongue. "But before I bombard you with questions, I owe you a story, too. After all, you asked me more than once about Italy and I never gave you an answer."

"I never understood why I never got an answer," I say, which makes Mamma stare off into space.

"Homesickness is an awful feeling, especially if you know you'll never go home again. So you try everything to avoid reopening old wounds—including silence."

"Go home? Does that mean—"My eyes fly wide open with a sudden suspicion. "Am I—I'm not related to Fabrizio, am I?"

"No, no, Hanna." My mother smiles. "Blood is not the only thing you need to make a home. Giuseppa was . . . I don't know the right word for it. We met when I was nine, a Sunday in church, and I wore a black dress because—it was my mother's funeral. Her name was Matilda Colei, and she was only thirty-nine when she died of lung disease. I was hiding in a corner of the choir loft, and I was only going to come out when Mamma came to fetch me with her angel's wings. She didn't, of course. Instead someone else came up the stairs, a very beautiful woman in a glittering dress and heels. She sat down at the organ and looked up at the sky like she was asking permission. Then she started to play like an angel—and I suddenly knew that Mamma had sent me this woman. I crawled from my hiding place, and she made room on the bench so I could watch her flying fingers. When the song was over, she asked if she should show me how to play. I said yes."

I take a deep breath, suddenly realizing that I've been listening without breathing the whole time. "And then?" I gasp.

"Giuseppa Camini came to our house that very evening and talked with Papa . . ." My mother's voice trembles. "The next day after school,

I ran to the yellow house on the hill to practice scales and chords. Soon two days a week turned into three and then four. In half a year, I could play Beethoven's *Moonlight Sonata* with my eyes closed. You probably don't remember, but I used to play it to you when you couldn't fall asleep.

I nod silently. How could I have forgotten? Mamma played the piano beautifully, and I always loved listening to her.

"Then Giuseppa began to teach me other things: cooking, baking, how to make beds and apricot jam, clean out chicken coops . . . everything that needs to be done on such an estate. I became friends with Giuseppa's son Frederico—he was only a few years older than I. I helped with the garden and the apricot harvest, and I spent every single day with the Caminis. I even had my own tiny room next to the kitchen."

"The Cinderella chamber!" I shake my head. "But what about your father and the rest of your relatives? I'm sure the Coleis weren't too happy that you took up with a new family."

Mamma looks sad. "People assume that every Italian family has countless siblings, cousins, uncles, and aunts. It's nonsense. After my mother died, it was just me and my father, and my father started to drink because he wanted to forget. Eventually he forgot that he had a daughter. The sad thing was that I didn't miss him. After all, I had Giuseppa."

I grab her hand, but she shakes her head. "When I was sixteen, he fell down the stairs—and didn't get up again."

"I'm so sorry for you, Mamma."

"There's a lot of that stubborn know-it-all man in you. You would have liked your grandfather."

I hide a smile. "Well, thanks."

"You didn't get those traits from me, that's for sure." She winks at me but then turns serious. "I have a box of photos at home. When you come to visit Papa and me one of these days, I'll give it to you."

"And I thought that I'd turned the entire house upside down."

"Did you think I hadn't noticed?"

We smile at each other.

"But it doesn't sound like it ended happily. Why did you leave Italy, Mamma? Did you have a fight with Giuseppa?"

Mamma's face hardens. "I fell in love with the wrong man."

I lift an eyebrow.

"Giuseppa Camini was a wonderful woman," my mother continues. "She was kind, warm, and compassionate. But I got to know her other side the summer I met your father. Back then, it was all the rage to take hiking tours through Europe, especially for students who financed their trips by taking on odd jobs—such as harvesting apricots. What can I say . . . Günther was different from the men I had met before. He knew so much and expressed himself in a way I wasn't used to from Italian men. For him it was love at first sight, and I fell in love with him, too. It soon went beyond innocent kissing . . . and since Giuseppa watched us like a hawk . . ." She pushes a strand of hair behind her ear and lowers her eyes.

"She found out," I say. "Ouch. I'm sure she didn't like that." The image of arch-Catholic Giuseppa's indignation makes me giggle.

"She was beside herself! After all, I was only seventeen, unmarried, and sleeping with a penniless student. She saw me burning in purgatory."

"What did she do?"

"The obvious, of course. She threw Günther out."

"No!"

"We had a violent argument and said many ugly and hurtful things. Ultimately, I packed my bags and followed Günther to Germany. My own family was dead, and there was no reason to look back. Besides, your father had asked me to marry him. When I got over my rage, I wrote to Giuseppa—and tore up every single letter. Then I got pregnant with you, and there was no more reason to look back—until two months ago, when the postcard arrived."

I can't breathe. "Giuseppa wrote to you?"

"She wanted to meet me on June eleventh, at a pastry shop two streets away from our apartment. Who knows how she found me after all those years."

I groan. June eleventh was the day she died.

Mamma continues. "I contemplated not going there, but then I sat in that café for more than two hours and jumped every time the doorbell jingled. But Giuseppa never came. She probably didn't have the heart to do it after all."

"Mamma . . ." My heart races as I get up and cross to the windowsill, where Giuseppa's urn sits. I pick it up and close my eyes. "What you said before about tears—that one sheds them for love or death"—I set the urn on the table—"I'm afraid someone did die—and on the exact day you were supposed to meet her."

For a long time my mother gazes at the urn, which now looks like a harmless—and quite ugly—vase.

"It would have been a miracle if our story had really ended with reconciliation." My mother touches the urn with her fingertips. "I have no idea how she ended up in your apartment, but I like to imagine that she did plan to come to the pastry shop."

"I'll tell you the entire story another time, Mamma. As to your meeting"—I wrap my arms around her and hug her tight—"if Giuseppa was just a little bit like Fabrizio, she must have been looking forward to it."

Mamma looks at me. "You really love him."

I can't return her gaze. "I just think he's someone who fixes his mistakes."

"He'd be stupid if he didn't," my mother says, a strange undertone in her voice.

"Mamma, I'm not talking about me."

"But I am." She sits up straight. "When are we going to drink that liqueur? I think now's a good moment to find out whether she made it the way she used to."

I get two water glasses from the kitchen, making a note in my head to buy a set of liqueur glasses. When I return, Mamma is sitting in front of Giuseppa with her elbows on her knees and her head in her hands, mumbling. So I'm not the only one who talks to the dead. She carefully pours a glass of the orange-colored liquid and sniffs.

"The aroma is perfect," she says with obvious appreciation, and takes a tiny sip. I watch her closely as she swirls the liqueur in her mouth.

"You seem to know a lot about it."

My mother takes a second sip and smiles. "You can say that again. Giuseppa and I created the recipe together."

"You did?" Something clicks in my mind and I shiver. Does fate actually exist? "Does that mean you know how to make this liqueur?"

My mother looks up. "Of course I do."

Dear Lucia,

I am so sorry that I'm only contacting you now, and in this way. I really wanted to hug you one more time and thank you for making my time at Tre Camini a very special experience. You were the one who made me feel not only at home but also like part of your family. For that I can't thank you enough. You are a wonderful person, and getting to know you meant more to me than you can imagine. I miss all of you very much—yes, even Rosa-Maria and her barking orders. It is very quiet in my small apartment in Berlin. I do hope you forgive me and I beg you to believe me when I say that leaving was the only thing I could do, and that my hasty departure had nothing at all to do with you.

You'll be happy to hear that I had a long conversation with my mother today. Obviously past wounds can't be cured in one evening, but I think that now we'll cook with each other often. I'll call you one of these days and tell you an amazing story. Here is just the gist of it: apparently there was a connection between your Nonna and my mother, Isabella Colei. And this leads me to ask you a very important favor—the main reason I send this letter via courier.

Enclosed is a sealed envelope addressed to Fabrizio. Something very valuable is inside. I know that it will mean a lot to him. Could you please give the envelope to him without telling anyone about it, not even Marco? It's really important.

Considerer yourself hugged and kissed.

Your friend,
Hanna

Fabrizio

While I stare for at least ten minutes at the piece of paper, Lucia focuses on my forehead as if she wants to burn a hole into it. The energetic handwriting, slanted to the right, flows across a piece of paper that—ironically—is apricot colored. My eyes return to the heading again and again: *Il liquore di albicocche della Nonna. Ricetta originale.*

"So? What does it say?" Lucia asks, biting her nails. That's when I regret having told her she could stay while I opened Hanna's envelope.

"Stop biting your nails. It makes your hands ugly." I put the note facedown on the desk. Strangely, I have only one thought, and that thought has nothing to do with the incredible content of the letter. I'm annoyed that there's not one personal remark. And it annoys me that I am annoyed.

"Can I look at the letter Hanna wrote you again?" I ask. Lucia purses her lips, thinks, and then shakes her head.

"Only if you tell me what your letter says." She reaches out quickly, but I'm faster.

"Ouch! Really, Fabrizio." Lucia grimaces and rubs her wrist. Then she reluctantly pushes Hanna's letter across the desk.

I read it again, and then again.

So Isabella Colei is her mother. Now I remember where I heard the name before—she was the unfriendly woman on the phone, the one Nonna had wanted to meet in Berlin. But what does this Isabella have to do with . . . I lower the piece of paper and study my sister-in-law, who sulks in the visitor's chair. Sighing, I nod and Lucia picks up the letter. Her eyes grow bigger—big as espresso cups—as she reads. "But this is . . . it's Nonna's liqueur recipe!"

"Possibly."

"What do you mean, 'possibly'? Of course it is."

"So what?"

"So what?" Lucia jumps up and her chair scratches across the wooden floor.

"Watch the floor," I say coldly. Lucia throws the paper at me, and it flutters to land next to me on the floor.

"Is that all you have to say?" she hisses.

"The parquet was expensive."

Arms akimbo, she shakes her head. I pick up the paper, hold it for a while, and then put it in the lowest desk drawer, the one for items marked "Done," for filing later. Some things lose their meaning when circumstances change. That was one of Nonna's sayings, too. Lucia raises a brow.

"What are you doing?"

"Putting the past where it belongs."

Lucia collapses like a pricked balloon. "Did Hanna hurt you that much?"

Without planning to, I pound my fist on the table. "Hanna has nothing to do with this."

Lucia jumps so high that I regret my outburst immediately. I try a mellower approach. "In case you forgot, I made an agreement with your husband. Even if this is Nonna's original recipe, which I doubt, what are we going to do with it? There's no guarantee that the liqueur would be a success. Even under the best of circumstances, it would take years to be able to live off it, and until then we'd have to invest in the fields and the distillery with money we don't have." It hurts to see how the sparkle goes out of Lucia's eyes. But I take a deep breath and point to the file cabinet. "That piece of paper cannot change the fact that we'd lose the estate. And so it'll stay in the drawer."

"Now you're talking exactly like Marco." Lucia's voice trembles. "The Fabrizio I once knew would have done everything to make his dream a reality, because he believed in it—because he believed in Tre Camini and in himself. Because of that, it would have worked." She carefully folds Hanna's letter three times. Then she gets up and looks at me with a mixture of contempt and compassion. "To be honest, I liked that Fabrizio more."

Hanna

"You managed to surprise us—in a very good way," Hellwig says with his toothpaste-ad smile. He folds his arms behind his neck and rocks back and forth on his ergonomic chair.

I feel myself blushing. The boss has ordered me to his attic office several times during the last few months, but mostly to give me a piece of his mind. I haven't heard such praise from him since the day I showed him my master's thesis.

Fortunately he doesn't seem to expect a reaction, but gets up and goes to his electric kettle and the collection of colorful cups on the sideboard.

"Will you join me for a cup of tea?" he asks in a tone that makes it clear that he wouldn't accept a no. So I answer yes and watch him go to the roof terrace, where he picks some green stems from various pots with great care.

"I had no idea that you grew your own tea," I say, just to say something.

"There's a lot you don't know about me." Hellwig laughs quietly, and I suddenly remember that he's quite attractive. He has some other good traits, too—he left the large, airy rooms for his staff and volunteered to take the attic office, even though it's so small that his desk fills a third of the room. On the other hand, the roof terrace definitely adds to the attraction of this Cinderella cubbyhole . . . My chest spasms familiarly. The prince takes home the wrong bride, no matter how much blood there is in the shoe. But Cinderella is just a story, anyway.

"I assume that's mutual, Frau Philipp. Or may I call you Hanna?"

I look up, startled, since my thoughts have been completely elsewhere, and look directly into Hellwig's ice-gray eyes. The rose-patterned cup he puts in front of me gives off the scent of mint chewing gum. Then he returns to his chair, walking around his desk slightly bent over to avoid hitting the slanted roof.

"Sorry? . . . Um . . . yes. Of course you may call me that . . . Sebastian . . ." I stutter. After the evening with my mother, I thought I wouldn't be baffled by anything ever again. He is still smiling—definitely a record, since I've been in his office for half an hour.

"We—I mean the board and I—really didn't think you could settle the Camini matter. But the fact that Herr Camini not only withdrew the suit but also agreed to pay our attorney fees shows how convincing you were."

"He did . . . what?" I whisper, and my pulse hits the roof. Hellwig's smile widens.

"They didn't even care about your scathing review anymore. Camini's attorney said his client wanted to have the matter over with as soon as possible. So you actually could have toned down your rave review quite a bit."

I don't feel any tears, but I do feel as if Fabrizio just threw a brick at me—and hit me all the way from Italy. He wants to forget the matter as soon as possible. And I had still hoped on the plane that he would sing.

Hellwig studies me, and suddenly understanding flashes across his face. "I guess you didn't want to write the article any other way, did you?"

I nod with a lump in my throat. Hellwig looks at the ceiling beams. For a tiny moment he seems disappointed, but then he leans across his desk and pushes a piece of paper toward me. "The board needs to fill an editor-in-chief position. I think you're the right person for the job."

I'm speechless. "But you—"

"We're talking about the Vienna office. The mess there needs to be cleaned up by a capable person. You have three years to turn the pigsty around. Otherwise there won't be an Austrian edition of *Genusto* anymore. Think you can do it?"

"But why me?" I shake my head and count on my fingers: "I'm the black sheep that causes trouble all the time. My harsh critiques have cost five-digit lawyers' fees. Restaurateurs hate me so much that some write me threatening letters. I'm up here once a month to confess my latest transgression, and besides"—my hands form fists and I take a deep breath—"I don't want to write restaurant reviews any more. I want to report."

There, I finally said it.

"That's exactly why you're the right person for Vienna, Hanna." Hellwig starts to laugh. "You're a fighter. You don't care what others think about you, and if you screw up, you have the courage to face the consequences. You say what you want and what you don't want, and stop at nothing to achieve your goals. That's exactly the kind of editor in chief the board wants for Vienna. Besides, in such a position you can write poetry on the side, if that's what you want."

I want to argue that I'm not sure I'm still the woman he describes, but Hellwig doesn't let me interrupt. "As for the consequences of your reviews, it's a pure cost-benefit calculation for the publisher. Your critical reviews have won us thirty thousand new readers and fifteen thousand new subscribers—most of them restaurateurs. They might not love you, but they value your judgment as much as they fear it. So believe me, the income you generated for *Genusto* offset lawyers' fees—and more."

"I didn't know that," I say, silently annoyed about all of Hellwig's past dressing-downs. But somehow I also understand him. Too much praise makes you complacent, and I might have grown bored and tired of my job. I breathe in and out deeply while he scrutinizes me with his usual emotionless gaze that makes me feel like a nobody.

"You can take three days to decide. After that, I'll offer the job to Frau Durant."

Claire. I swallow. Of course, she started at *Genusto* only two months after me and is as qualified as I am. Whatever I decide, I'll lose my only friend. I get up slowly, and then Sasha's face flashes through my mind, and the article that I put in my drawer without reading. "Could I ask you a favor . . . Sebastian?"

"If it's a raise, you can forget it. That only happens if you accept the Vienna job."

"Sasha Senge. She's our intern—very sassy, very involved, and very reliable. She's almost done with the internship."

"What about her?"

"She wrote an article on a topic you're interested in."

"Is she any good?"

"She's very good," I say, even though I've never read a word she's written. But I've learned by now to listen to my feelings, and something tells me Sasha needs to be given the same chance that I was given, not so long ago, by a benevolent editor named Sebastian Hellwig. And if she writes the way she talks, she might turn out to be the new face for my column.

"Then why is her article not on my desk yet? Send the girl up to me now."

"I'll do it right away . . . and boss?

"What else?"

"Don't scare her off."

Fabrizio

The door is just closing behind Lucia when I reach for the apricot-colored piece of paper. I study the list of ingredients, which I only scanned earlier and stop at the next-to-last item. My stomach feels funny. Can it be that simple? Damn it. Why didn't I figure it out myself?

The butterflies in my stomach multiply, and I drum on the desk with my fingers. For a moment I consider shredding the page right now. But my hand won't do it. I cross the room in four steps and fling open the door, almost running over Lucia, who is leaning against the railing, grinning at me triumphantly.

"Not one word," I grumble and am off, running down the staircase.

I only stop after the door of the distillery building slams shut behind me. I turn the key twice and lean my head against the rough wooden door.

Then I turn around and head for the storage room, where we keep Nonna's canned jam and preserved apricots, bottles of Rosa-Maria's tomato puree, and Lucia's much-loved tomato juice. There's also a shelf of square jars exclusively reserved for Alberto's apricot-blossom honey. When Nonna was alive, the shelf was usually half-empty. But since her death, the square glasses have accumulated, and Alberto has even had to pack them into cardboard boxes and store them in the barn. How strange that I never questioned where all the honey ended up when Nonna was alive.

I grab three jars of honey and line them up on the desk. I should have guessed from just looking at Nonna's hand-drawn bee on the labels. She always insisted that the farm's products have handwritten labels, but she added her drawings to only two of them: Alberto's apricot-blossom honey and the apricot liqueur.

I unscrew one of the lids. The honey doesn't smell like conventional honey—there's no waxy, unpleasant aftertaste. Instead it is fragrant with vanilla and the faint reminiscence of apricots. My senses react immediately—I don't even have to experiment to know that this is the missing ingredient. I laugh out loud when I realize what it all means: Alberto's honey and Nonna's apricots, joined in a lifetime achievement. Hell, Nonna created a monument of her love for Alberto with this liqueur.

Hanna

I watch Sasha start up to the attic. White as a ghost, she presses her portfolio to her chest. I finally allow myself a satisfied smile. Claire hands me a cup of coffee and looks at me, her head tilted.

"You put in a good word for her with the boss," she says in a flat voice.

"That's possible." I grin.

"And you're reading dime novels."

"I . . . what?"

"You . . . read . . . pulp fiction. Do you want me to spell it?"

"First, you should stop snooping through other people's handbags," I shoot back. Claire's not impressed; she plucks at her lower lip.

"Are you all right?" she says at last, hesitantly.

"It's not a crime to read romance novels. Besides, I got it for the special price of ninety-nine cents and just couldn't resist the hero's rippling abs," I joke, but Claire will have none of it.

"You know that I'm always here for you if you want to talk."

A wave of fondness overcomes me when I look at her crinkled, freckled nose and her furrowed forehead—Claire's typical I'm-worried-about-you expression. What a pity that I'm just now realizing how valuable she is. Once I'm in Vienna, I won't have a chance to get to know her better.

"I'm fine," I say, taking her hand. "And I'll take you up on your offer soon. But first I have to take care of one last important thing."

Claire snaps her fingers. "In that case, Madame Philipp, chop chop! And when you're done with the dirty dime novel, put it into my mailbox, OK?"

Chop chop. I'm still grinning when I pick up the receiver and dial the number I dug out from an old file this morning. Volker Saalfranck—a terrible cook with a penchant for alcoholic ingredients, who probably wishes I were dead. But he has the connections in the liquor industry—so he's the only one who can help with the apricot liqueur. My pulse races when the phone starts to ring, and I force myself to breathe calmly. *"Give it your best shot,* carissima,*"* Mamma would say.

"Saalfranck."

"Good morning, Herr Saalfranck. This is Hanna Philipp from *Genusto* magazine. We met two years ago when—"

"You actually have the guts to call me? And on my private cell phone. Who gave you this number?"

"You gave it to me."

"Was I drunk?"

"Listen, Herr Saalfranck—"

"To the left, I said! Not that one, the one on the left. Damn it!"

"Excuse me?"

"Women shouldn't be behind the wheel. They shouldn't do anything they know nothing about—like writing restaurant reviews, if you know what I mean, haha."

"I'm sorry if I—"

"You do realize that I had to close the bistro two years ago because of you. No. Don't say anything. I still tear up when I think about how much time I wasted tossing frozen schnitzels into the deep fryer. Now I'm at least doing what I should have done all along. I hope you aren't calling because you want me to pay you a commission, are you?"

"I don't understand—"

"The alcoholic-beverage business, young woman! I'm talking about the little shop with shelves full of colorful bottles. You liked that, as opposed to the bistro. We're a hit all over Germany now, if I may say so myself. I have two huge warehouses and a chain of fifteen shops, and I'm opening four more this month."

"Hold on—so you're telling me you're grateful, in hindsight, for my bad review?"

"Grateful? I kiss the floor you walk on! What can I do for you? From what I know about you, you wouldn't call for no reason. Are you writing an article about Germany's most successful spirits distributor? I'm at your service."

"I actually only wanted your expert opinion, Herr Saalfranck, but since you ask . . . I think I might have something that could turn into the deal of a lifetime."

"Are you talking about moonshine? Did you slam another poor hobby chef, and he bequeathed you his copper kettle in return? Haha."

"It's something much better than that, and if you want—would you mind having a drink with me . . . now?"

"It sounds like you really hit the jackpot."

"You won't regret it."

"Oh, I've had no regrets these past two years. Can you be in my office in an hour? Schadowstrasse 6. By then my wife will have found the gas pedal, I hope."

"I'm on my way."

Fabrizio

I find our estate manager in the chicken coop, repairing an incubator. Even though he notices me, Alberto keeps working, hitting nail after nail into the wooden frame. With fluffed-up feathers, Vittoria watches his every move from a roost above. When I see how difficult it is for him to bend down, I pick up the cardboard box and hand him the next nail. I stare at his back for a while, wondering how to begin.

"What did Nonna have to do with that Isabella?"

The hammer hangs in midair for a second before slamming down on the nail. I put another in Alberto's hand. When he finishes, he straightens up.

"I told you already that I have nothing more to say on the matter. Find out for yourself."

"And how am I supposed to do that? Nonna is dead and Hanna is gone."

His reply is hoarse laughter. "Sometimes you have to go on a trip to get answers. Besides, it's high time you brought Giuseppa home."

"You know about . . . the urn?" I'm stunned.

"I spent my entire life at your grandmother's side, Fabrizio. It might sound funny, but I can feel that she isn't here," he says quietly. "Just as

I can tell when things aren't complete. Giuseppa, Isabella, Hanna, even Marco, Lucia, Tre Camini, and you—it's all one whole. And since your grandmother can't do it anymore, it's now your job to bring together what belongs together."

I realize that my mouth is hanging open. Obviously one of us is crazy, and it might be me. Alberto clicks his tongue and pats me on the back with such force that I start to cough. Damn cigarettes. "And now go and board a plane, son, before I get all upset and have to steal some cookies from the kitchen to calm down."

Hanna

When I get back to my apartment in the evening, I'm very tired but also immensely satisfied. While I guessed it wouldn't be difficult to interest Saalfranck in Nonna's apricot liqueur, the liquor trader's reaction far exceeded my expectations.

After his first sip, the usually talkative man just sat in his leather chair for a while, staring at the bottle on his desk. After another taste, he jumped up and paced back and forth in his chic office before planting himself in front of me with gleaming eyes.

"You are a crafty little beast."

The rest was all formalities. I gave him Tre Camini's address, named Lucia as contact person, and left after assuring him several times that I wanted nothing for the tip—other than his promise to give the Caminis a fair offer.

I kick off my new ballerina flats and traipse barefoot to the kitchen, where I find, to my surprise, a pot of lukewarm ribollita on the stove. At first I'm annoyed that my mother kept the spare key instead of returning it to the landlord. But I'm hungry, so I shelve the boundaries conversation and warm up the soup.

Half an hour later, after stuffing myself with the thick soup of beans, potatoes, and vegetables, I'm luxuriating on my tiny balcony—as much as I can without patio furniture. Leaning against a large pillow, a glass of wine in my hand, I try to relax.

I actually manage not to think about anything for a moment. But then my stomach tingles again, and the rooftops of Berlin turn into the red bricks of Montesimo. I see the gate and the cypress-lined driveway leading up the hill, and on the way a white chicken scratching for worms.

What the heck, Hanna. It can't be that difficult to get over it. The tingling surges. Now I see Fabrizio's face, his espresso-colored eyes, the laughter lines around his mouth . . . and tears run down my cheeks again. I can't help it.

This lovesickness is as persistent as a chronic cold—and if I could, I'd gladly put up with such a cold for the rest of my life instead of the terrible loneliness that overcomes me whenever I'm alone.

I wipe my face and sit up straight. But it's over. Fabrizio chose Sofia, and I have to accept that. Italy is far away, I'm in Berlin now, and I even have a significant career opportunity in a new, exciting city. I set things right and atoned for my mistakes. Except—my eyes open wide—except for the urn on my windowsill. Shit! I completely forgot Giuseppa.

"You can't just send the grandmother to Italy by mail, Hanna. *Absolutement pas.* It's impossible." Claire looks at me sternly over her glass of wine. I couldn't help but smile, amid all my tears, when she arrived, half an hour after my call, in running clothes and with a forgotten dab of facial cream on her forehead.

"But why not? I'll send the urn by courier and pay extra so that it's guarded like the British crown jewels. All kinds of things are mailed these days, so why not an urn?"

Claire takes my measure. "Because we're not talking about any old urn. This is Giuseppa."

"Your argument is completely irrational." I don't want to get mad, but the mere thought of facing Lucia or Fabrizio—let alone Sofia—squeezes the breath out of me. I clench my fists and shake my head. "I can't go back." The finality of my words brings me close to tears.

Claire moves closer to me on the couch. "I believe you're making a mistake, Hanna."

"Believe me, I'm doing the right thing." I back away from her as far as the arm of the couch allows. Claire shakes her head with a smile.

"Yes, if you follow your brain. But your heart says something completely different."

"What makes you the expert?" The heart she's talking about beats like crazy against my ribs.

Claire smiles. "Because I've been your friend for longer than you realize. You love that man—very much. I can see that."

"So what?" I blow away a strand of hair from my forehead.

"Did you tell him?"

"What would've changed if I had? He belongs to someone else." My voice trembles, and tears push closer to the surface again.

"It could change a whole lot. But first you have to do it. What can you lose? Then it's up to him to decide."

"But—"

"Don't be a silly goose, Hanna—or a chicken. If you love Fabrizio, then fight for him. Otherwise you'll always ask yourself what could have been. And the little thing in there"—she gently taps on my chest—"will break into so many pieces that you'll need a lifetime to pick them up." Claire gets up and goes to her purse. When she comes back, she has an envelope in her hand.

"What's that?" I ask suspiciously.

"I won't just stand by while you head for disaster. I was going to give you this yesterday, but then I wasn't sure if it was the right idea.

Today I'm sure." She puts the envelope in my lap. "Your flight leaves at one twenty tomorrow. So you have one night to decide whether you want to be a mouse or a grown woman ready to fight for her happiness."

Chapter Sixteen

Hanna

I stare at the ceiling above my bed. Last night, my ghosts argued with each other nonstop without reaching a conclusion about what's best for me. So I still don't know what I'm going to do.

My brain tells me to tear up the ticket and concentrate on my career. After all, there are other handsome men in the world, and the men in Vienna are known to be gentlemanly. So then why am I stuck on this loutish farmer, when I'll probably meet a more charming, cosmopolitan man soon?

Yet my heart knows neither reason nor logic. The thought of Fabrizio's espresso eyes is enough to make it turn somersaults. I sit up.

And on top of that dilemma, Claire shows up with her stupid what-if scenario.

Honestly, what if I flew to Italy? Lucia is probably mad at me, and Marco never liked me anyway. Old Alberto is probably still in the hospital—although I hope he isn't. Most likely Rosa-Maria hasn't even noticed that I've been gone, and if she has, she'll be in a huff over how

I've treated Lucia. I'd probably run into Fabrizio and Sofia holding hands, smooching or, even worse, in the act—

Ohmigod! Perspiring, I throw off the blanket. Coffee. I need coffee, lots of it.

Ten minutes later, I'm standing with my second cup at the half-open window, next to Giuseppa. Fog curls down the street below, but the sun's already shining on the rooftops. I soak up the morning air with closed eyes. It feels so good. I gulped down my first cup, but I drink this one more slowly.

"It looks like it'll be a lovely day," I tell Giuseppa, and I imagine that the old woman nods in agreement.

"Couldn't you tell me what to do? A bird in my hand . . . or are two in the bush better after all? What do you think?" I say, laughing at myself. The tired old adage is truer than I like. Farmer or not.

Now I even imagine that I hear the beating of wings, a rustling, as if—then I feel a swoosh of air at my head and I scream. My hands fly up to protect myself, coffee splatters on the windowpane and frame—and I see a plump gray pigeon flutter off the outside sill in search of a better landing strip. Then my elbow pushes against something hard and cold. I reach out, but my fingers touch only air.

"Holy shit!" I watch the urn fall in a daze. It lands on the carpet with a hollow clunk. I squat with wobbling knees and check the container. I breathe a sigh of relief. Thanks to the fluffy rug, the urn is fine.

But then it hits me—what just happened. My pulse accelerates and goose bumps rise on my arms. Is it really possible that Giuseppa just answered my question? I jump up only seconds later and dash into the bathroom.

Fabrizio

"Pronto?"

"Fabrizio, what's that noise in the background? Where in the world are you?"

"That's what I've been asking myself for hours, Lucia."

"It's seven in the morning!" Lucia's voice crackles through my cell phone. "Don't tell me you ended up with Carlo at Salvi's."

"Cold. Try again."

"What?"

I yawn. "No, I'm not at Salvi's."

"Listen, I have no time for games. I have to talk with you—well, Marco has to talk with you, but he went to Grosseto."

"Grosseto?" I'm suddenly wide awake. "Is something wrong with Alberto?"

"No, no . . . Marco went to . . . the bank."

I frown. "Why?"

"I'll tell you in person. So hurry up, wherever you are."

"Lucia, I'm in Florence. At the airport."

The other end is silent for a moment, but I hear Lucia breathing. Panting might be the better word. But I move faster than she can formulate the undoubtedly annoying question she's dying to ask.

"Why is Marco driving to the bank at this ungodly hour?" I snap. Her puffing gets louder.

"This morning we got—well, actually last night, but I was too busy to check e-mail, and you know how we've been finishing in the kitchen later and later—"

"Get to the point, Lucia!" I click the clasp of my bag open and shut.

"Marco wants to apply for a loan—for the distillery."

The clasp breaks off the suitcase. "Say that again?"

I can barely hear Lucia's whisper. "A German distributor wants Nonna's liqueur."

"What exactly are you saying?" I ask tensely, trying to repair the clasp with trembling hands. Questions fill my head, but I can't formulate a single one.

"Last night we got an e-mail from a Herr Saalfranck. I Googled him. He supplies stores and restaurants with fine spirits and liquors, and owns a chain of stores himself. The e-mail said that someone from a leading gourmet magazine told him about our liqueur. Saalfranck had a chance to taste it, and now"—Lucia's voice trembles—"now he wants exclusive distribution rights, internationally, and . . . he wants everything."

"Everything?" The clasp slips from my fingers and clinks to the floor.

"Every drop we produce! And he's willing to pay whatever price we set. Marco didn't hesitate for one second, and you know what that means. So don't you dare tell me that you already destroyed the recipe because I'll have to kill you, unfortunately, if you did."

"Hanna." I get up from the bench I've been waiting on for an hour and a half.

"What did you say? The connection's bad."

"Hanna did that." I start to pace up and down and catch the glance of the elegant woman on the other end of the bench, who's been giving me furtive looks for the past hour and a half. When I raise my eyebrows, she blushes and hides behind her business journal again. My back hurts from sitting, and my forehead throbs. I press two fingers against my temples as the last call for the flight to Berlin mixes with the roaring in my ears. That's my plane. The boarding line gets thinner; the woman folds her paper and uncrosses her legs. The flight attendant at the counter waves me forward, pointing to her wristwatch. "Listen, I have to get on the plane now, and I won't be back before tomorrow evening. Tell Marco—"

"I won't stop him!" She shouts so shrilly that I jerk the phone away from my ear. "This is the chance Nonna waited for all her life, and you, too. If you're not getting involved now, Marco and I will do it ourselves, and for all I care, you can—"

"Shut up, Lucia, and listen carefully," I interrupt. I need to keep my cool now. "Tell Marco that we need fifty thousand to get the distillery ready for mass production. If he can get one hundred, even better. Paolo needs to stop delivering apricots to the juice factory and the supermarket right away. I don't want a single apricot to leave Tre Camini from now on." I grab my carry-on bag and hurry to the counter, squeezing the phone under my chin and rummaging for my boarding pass and ID with my free hand. "Also, tell Marco the banker, Giovanni, has a wife named Rosalia and three children, all girls. Giovanni likes soccer and loves Scottish whiskey. Marco should play all the angles and try to get as much money as he can."

Silence on the line, while I hand the flight attendant my boarding pass with the most charming smile I can muster. "Are you still there, Lucia?"

"Still . . . on the line."

"Hey, are you crying?"

"No—yes—I'm just so glad."

"Don't get your hopes up too high. It's just an offer, but maybe it'll really turn out to be the chance we've been waiting for." I hurry down the gangway. When I glance back over my shoulder, I see the flight attendant watching me curiously as she closes the door to the waiting area.

"Fabrizio? May I ask you something else?" Lucia's voice softens.

"I have to hang up, Lucia." I almost run the last few yards to the door of the plane, past the waiting crew. Despite my determination, I feel somewhat queasy.

"Are you going to bring Hanna home?"

I'm about to scold her, but something holds me back. I'm thinking of Nonna's good-bye letter, of Alberto's words, and of Hanna's soft lips that I want to kiss again. It took me a while to be certain, and maybe it's too late—but maybe not. "I hope so, Lucia."

Hanna

I have never in my life packed a suitcase so fast and disorganized. I'll pay for it in Italy—unless Lucia slams the door in my face right away. I did pack a lot of tops and dresses, but only one pair of jeans and neither socks nor underwear. I even forgot my makeup bag. But if I turn around now, I might change my mind and allow the ticket to go to waste.

It seems that my cab driver thinks I'm going to give birth in his cab if he doesn't drive like a racecar driver. When the horrible ride ends in front of Terminal A, I clutch Giuseppa's urn to my chest and give him way too much of a tip—I'm too nervous to wait for him to count the change. I climb out, grab my suitcase from the backseat, and slam the door shut with my hip.

"Hey—this isn't a tractor," he yells before taking off at full speed.

Just then it starts to rain—of course—so I run into the terminal. My flight isn't listed on the display board—no wonder, since I'm over three hours early. I glance around, not sure what to do. People are running past, clutching their phones, pulling their suitcases to the check-in counters, and dashing into duty-free shops. I see a poster advertising the airport restaurant's breakfast special.

Why not? I can't check my bag yet, and I have nothing in my stomach besides coffee. And I haven't eaten properly in days, so a breakfast croissant will hit the spot—although it'll hardly be as delicious as Rosa-Maria's cornetti. Suddenly I'm looking forward to the trip. At a magazine stand, I buy a women's magazine that's full of calming trivialities like new styles, moisturizers, and recipes. With Giuseppa under my arm, I stroll toward the airport restaurant.

Fabrizio

I'm almost surprised how smoothly everything goes. My plane arrives on time, I don't have to wait for my luggage since I only have a carry-on, and the customs official waves me through without checking my ID. A mere two hours after leaving Florence, I'm in the arrivals terminal in Berlin. I stop in the crowd of people laughing, hugging, and kissing. Fragments of German sentences drift through the air, and it takes a moment for me to adjust to the unfamiliar language again. Then I remember that I don't have Hanna's phone number or address.

Retreating to a quieter corner, I take out my phone. But the battery is dead, and I didn't bring the charger. I curse loudly, scaring an elderly lady pushing a luggage cart. I'm about to apologize when two little girls greet her with hugs and screeches. A magazine falls from her purse to the floor, and I stare in disbelief at the yellow house on the cover. I reach for it quickly.

"You've lost . . . something," I say lamely and hand the overwhelmed lady her magazine, still staring at it. The mother rushes up and calls the girls, Pia and Pippa, to order. The Germans have a sense of humor, after all.

"Very kind." The woman takes the magazine, but I don't let go. I suddenly have an idea.

"Forgive me . . . this magazine . . . Where can I buy one?" Now I let go, and the woman looks startled.

"You can get it at any newspaper stand." She speaks slowly as if I were half-witted.

"A newspaper stand, of course." I nod, feeling embarrassed. Bowing a little, I turn and hurry away.

I run almost to the other end of the airport before finding a stand that isn't sold out of *Genusto Gourmet*. But in the departure terminal, I manage to get my hands on the next-to-last copy, and, still in line, search for the masthead. I'm dying to read the lead article, but I have to find Hanna first.

The text blurs—the sleepless night is catching up with me—and I do a double take, imagining that I saw Hanna in the crowd. I need to take something for this headache, get a bite to eat, and wash it all down with a double espresso.

While pocketing the change, I almost crash into a display for the airport restaurant that some genius put right outside the door. Ouch. I rub my elbow and eye the poster, a smiling blonde woman holding out a breakfast cornetto.

And even though I feel strange about returning to the place where all the trouble started, I follow the pretty blonde's pointing finger.

Hanna

Nothing has changed in the airport restaurant. The place smells of roast pork, coffee, and broken air conditioning. Servers hoisting trays squeeze by people, suitcases, and strollers. There's even a tour group at the bar again, although its members are wearing matching T-shirts instead of green baseball caps. I make my way through the crowd to the back of the restaurant, half expecting to see my boss somewhere near the window—or a dark-haired man with a three-day beard and sad eyes. That doesn't happen, of course—a relief but also, however irrationally, disappointing at the same time.

I head to a table for two next to the window and put Giuseppa on the empty chair, and then on the windowsill, despite the déjà vu. I have no time to ponder—the server's already waiting for my order. She doesn't recognize me, which is understandable, considering the hundreds of guests she sees every day. I return her impersonal smile with a warm, friendly one and order a corne—*croissant* and a coffee with milk.

Then I delve into an article about potted plants for balconies. I'd like to have a garden—of course, not one as big as Lucia's at Tre Camini. Maybe I'll get lucky and snatch a first-floor apartment in Vienna. I could grow strawberries or cherry tomatoes. I start to smile when I think of Sasha and how she flung her arms around my neck last night because Hellwig decided to run her article on urban vegetable gardening in the next issue.

"You know, I'm a little proud of myself," I tell Giuseppa, and my heart beats faster. The old lady is going home, and so am I—even though I don't yet know where that might be. The idea of a new beginning in Vienna is definitely exciting. But my life seems suddenly full of opportunities and maybe . . . maybe Fabrizio is one of them.

When the waitress brings my breakfast, I remember that I wanted to stop at the restroom when I bought the magazine. I lean toward the next table, where a couple in their thirties is studying a Thailand travel guide.

"Excuse me."

The ginger-haired woman looks up.

"Could you please watch my stuff for a moment while I run to the restroom?" I ask. She looks confused for a moment, but then nods. I hurry off after mouthing thanks.

Fabrizio

My blood sugar has definitely zeroed out. I saw three Hannas on the short walk to the restaurant and even followed the last one, only to see her embrace a blond giant of a man.

A sobering thought.

Until now I've assumed that there is no other man in Hanna's life. What if that's not true? What if he was the reason she left? I briefly close my eyes and realize that it's harder every day to imagine Nonna's face. *"If you don't ask, the answer is no, kiddo,"* she says. *You're right. I will find out if her heart is taken.*

The airport restaurant is so crammed that I contemplate just grabbing a bratwurst at a stand. But then I see an empty table at the window, and a moment later look down in confusion at the untouched breakfast awaiting me. Did I black out and order already?

"That table is taken," a woman with red curls says next to me. "The lady will be back any moment."

Disappointed, I nod and look around. My stomach growls so loudly that the redhead starts to laugh. "She just asked us to watch her luggage. I'm sure she wouldn't mind if you take the other seat," she says.

Needing no more encouragement, I drop my bag and sit down. Even if this lady does mind, I'm so hungry by now that I don't care—and I have to curb my impulse to eat her crispy cornetto.

Then the curvy waitress comes over. God forbid! It's the same as last time.

"Don't tell me you came back because of our excellent pork roast," she beams. I grin back at her with what I hope is not too forced a smile.

"Obviously I only came back to see you again."

She blushes, not hearing the sarcasm in my voice. Damn. Now I'll have to wait forever to get something to eat.

"You're unfortunately too late. I have a new boyfriend," she giggles. The ginger woman at the next table rolls her eyes. I raise an eyebrow and try not to look too relieved.

"What a pity."

She shrugs and winks. "I could put you on the waiting list. Just in case."

"That's a generous offer. But before you do that, could you bring me . . . the same order as this one, a coffee and a cornetto?"

"I'll be right back."

I feel the redhead measure me from top to bottom and almost sense the darkness around me as she files me in a drawer labeled "typical Southern European," slams it shut, and turns the key twice. Sighing, I take the magazine out of my bag and flip to Hanna's article. My stomach contracts when I see her photo. She's laughing—a beautiful woman. I breathe in and out deeply and begin to read.

Dear Reader,

I am turning to you today about a partly personal matter. First of all, thank you for your loyalty, encouragement, and expressions of gratitude, and also for your criticism, which has helped me improve my work.

What follows is not the type of restaurant critique you're used to reading. It starts with two apologies—to you, dear reader, for misinforming you, and to the owners of a small Italian trattoria whom my critique in the May 2014 issue—though it was written in good faith—unjustly wronged.

Had I known then that the truth about Tre Camini is more than frozen vegetables and mushy spinach sauce, my review would not have been better, but might have sounded milder. For sometimes, good taste is a matter of not only the stomach but the heart. The gustatory catastrophe that ended up on my plate that day was the result of a well-meaning act of friendship, the work of the local policeman who wanted to make sure his best friend's restaurant wouldn't be closed because the cook was ill. I hope Carlo Fescale will forgive me for saying so, but I strongly advise you to avoid brushes with the law in the vicinity of Montesimo—the food in prison is abominable.

But let's talk about Tre Camini itself. Much more than a trattoria, the Camini family's agricultural estate has been dedicated to the perpetuation of *cucina bella Italiana* for generations, not just in its kitchen, but also in its apricot fields. After the owner, Fabrizio Camini, pointed out why my original critique was incorrect, the family graciously gave me the opportunity to reconsider my opinion during a two-week stay at Tre Camini.

What I discovered during those weeks far exceeded my expectations, not just in regard to the kitchen. Even though my own roots are Italian, I had no idea that the true taste of Italy is not only founded on fresh and first-class ingredients, carefully selected herbs, and a knowledgeable local cook—all of that goes without saying at Tre Camini. No, an Italian meal is perfect only if it's been brought to the table by a family's efforts.

It is Rosa-Maria's patience as she stirs the pasta sauce for hours; the tune Lucia Camini hums as she collects wildflower blossoms to decorate the desserts; old estate manager Alberto's words that encourage the bees to exchange honey for sugar water. It is the passion in Fabrizio Camini's espresso-colored eyes when he talks about his grandmother's apricot liqueur, and the willpower and persistence needed to face the ups and downs of agriculture and business to produce a unique product. It is the contentment on everyone's face when the lid of the roasting dish lifts and the aromas of wine and apricots mingle with cheerful chatter and harmless quarrels around the table; the laughter when thyme-infused panini slide out of the oven or handmade pasta tumbles into boiling salted water. It is the wine that tastes twice as good because one has someone to clink glasses with.

Simply said, Tre Camini enchanted me. It offers far more than authentic Tuscan ribollita, spicy pasta Zanolla with speck and fava beans, or soft-as-butter roast rabbit prepared with apricots from the estate orchard. The venerable stone building radiates a living tradition and carries the spirit of an old woman who taught me what is important: the meaning of feeling at home—and of giving your heart to someone special.

Today I can say with conviction that there is no place in all of Italy that is more Italian than this dot on the map, hardly visible to the naked eye. You should not miss it, whether you're traveling through or decide to make a special trip there. You won't regret it. I promise.

Your Hanna Philipp

Hanna

At first I'm sure that I'm the victim of an optical illusion. I see Fabrizio. Not in passing, like spotting a familiar face in a crowd, there one moment and then gone. Not like the figure that disappears around the corner at the exact moment you glance back, and not like the back of a head in line in front of you that turns out to be a stranger. No. This hallucination is sitting at *my* table, and no matter how often I blink, he doesn't disappear.

I stop dead, and the chubby waitress almost runs into me. She veers to the side, and the only victims are the croissant and coffee on her tray.

"Excuse me," I mumble. I suddenly feel . . . as if there's no substance to me . . . as if I'd dissolved into countless particles that now hover, cloudlike, where I stood before. The woman's pink lips move, but the sound seems to be off. In a daze, I stare at the spilled coffee and soaked cornetto on her tray.

Fabrizio is sitting at my table.

It's not a mirage.

Someone touches my arm. "Are you all right?"

Good. The audio is back on. I smile at the worried server, and then my body reacts. I'm suddenly cold and sweating at the same time. I want to run to Fabrizio, take him in my arms, and whisper all the words that have circulated in my head for days. Instead, I turn around and run back to the restroom.

Fabrizio

I lower the magazine. I've read the article three times and still don't have a clue. Good heavens. I could really use Lucia's help, and what do I have? A dead battery. I study Hanna's photo as if the answer were in her eyes. The next-to-last paragraph—does it say what I think it does, *bellissima*? Is she talking about me? Was I so blind?

My gaze wanders to the window, but then catches between two potted palms, where—

I gasp.

It can't be true.

It's Nonna.

I bend forward to inspect my absent tablemate's suitcase more thoroughly. It's simple and black, streaked with dirt, and the wheels are caked with mud. I grab the handle and move the suitcase back and forth. One of the wheels is stuck. Bingo!

"Hey, what are you doing?" The redhead looks at me suspiciously.

"The woman who's sitting here"—I clear my froggy throat—"where exactly did she go?"

"The toilet," her companion says, and gets a nudge in the ribs.

"I don't think it's any of his business," she hisses.

"Could you please . . ." I motion to my bag and jump up, and my elbow knocks into something. A woman cries out; I hear a clink and a clatter.

"Oh no! Not again," the waitress whines.

"Sure, man. No problem." The redhead's friend gestures in the direction of the restrooms. "She just now turned on her heels and ran back in the direction she came from. Was quite green in the face."

"Thank you," I yell, but then rush back and take the urn from the windowsill. Better safe than sorry.

"Hold on. That belongs—" the redheaded woman shouts, but her friend silences her with a kiss. I slow down to protect Nonna and follow the signs to the restrooms.

Hanna

I've been staring at the white stall door for about five minutes. I know, of course, that I can't sit here indefinitely—that's not only childish but stupid, since the man I love is right outside. He might disappear if I can't get this panic attack under control. I take a deep breath and exhale while counting to two. At least I didn't throw up. Right now I just feel a little queasy, but my heart throbs as if it's pumping goo through my veins instead of blood.

I need some more time—to think about what I should tell him. Out of all the things I want to lay out, what should I say? Five more minutes. Then I'll leave this stall, splash some cold water on my face, and return to the restaurant to tell Fabrizio with a radiant smile . . . Why is he in Germany?

I hear Claire again. *"Ooh, Hanna! What do you think he's doing here?"*

He wants to get his grandmother. What else?

Or is he really here because of me? I tremble, groan, and bury my head in my hands. I'm exactly where I wanted to be, and now I don't have the courage to face him.

"Hanna?" says a deep, gentle voice that I am very familiar with. OK, no cold water. I bite my lips and cautiously lift my legs. If I stay completely silent, I might get lucky and he'll leave.

"Hanna, I know you're there. So put your legs back on the floor and stop holding your breath."

"I'm not holding my breath!" I clap my hand against my mouth, but it's too late. A pair of polished men's shoes appears under the stall door.

"Hello, *bellissima*."

"Hi." Giving up, I put my feet on the floor.

"What are you doing in there?"

"What kind of question is that? This is a toilet."

"I realize that. But you aren't in there to do the normal things. So?" I can hear that he is grinning.

"Beat it, Fabrizio," I snap.

"In your dreams."

"But I've got to think."

He's silent for a while.

"How about coming out and sharing your thoughts with me?" Fabrizio asks softly. I gasp for air.

"That's . . . not possible."

"Oh. Why not?"

"Because—*hic!*—I'm thinking about you." Wonderful. Now I have the hiccups. I hear quiet laughter outside.

"That's good."

"It's not good at all—*hic!*—because . . ." I hear a shuffling noise and the shoes disappear. "What are you doing?"

"Sitting down. Since you're not coming out, I'll just have to listen to you from here. By the way, I brought Nonna along so nobody would swipe her by mistake from the windowsill. You can take your time."

"You brought your grandmother to the restroom?" I'm in such shock that I forget about the hiccups.

"I think Nonna is used to quite a few things by now. But why isn't it good that you're thinking about me, *bellissima*?

"Stop calling me that. I'm sure Sofia wouldn't like it."

"Why does it matter what Sofia likes or doesn't like?" He sounds genuinely surprised, which annoys me. Men can be so ignorant.

"My god! Don't play dumb. Because Sofia is your . . . whatever it is she is."

Silence on the other side of the door.

"Sofia is my ex-girlfriend, Hanna. Nothing more, nothing less."

"Ex-fiancée," I say stubbornly.

"If you insist."

"Nothing else?"

"Absolutely nothing else."

"But . . . really?"

"Was that why you left? You thought Sofia and I—"

"I didn't want to stand in the way of your happiness," I say.

"Oh Hanna, you silly goose."

"Go ahead. Insult me."

"It's not very romantic in here . . . but I'll take my chances." Fabrizio sounds so serious now that a chill goes down my spine. "I'm in love with only one woman—so in love that I can't think of anything else. And this woman happens to be on the other side of this toilet door and refuses to come out."

Now it's my turn to be silent, embarrassed. Did he really just say "in love"? He's in love—and I think he's talking about me.

"That's pretty stupid of that woman, isn't it?" I whisper.

"She's probably as afraid of her feelings as I am of mine. It took me way too long to understand what my heart was telling me. I'm really sorry about that."

I take a deep breath. I'm so nervous that I start biting my fingernails. What if I'm just imagining all this? What if—but I can hear him breathing. I straighten up.

"Fabrizio?"

"Hanna?"

I get up and lean my forehead against the door. "What . . . are we going to do now?"

"Opening this door would be a good start, since I can't kiss you otherwise. And who's ever heard of a declaration of love without a kiss?"

I smile as I reach for the handle. Then a strange thought pops into my head. "But I have one more question."

"Ask whatever you want, *bellissima*."

I slide back the lock and open the door with a little push.

He's sitting cross-legged on the floor, his back against the tiled wall, tie loosened, expensive jacket crumpled on the ground. My eyes focus on the urn in his lap and then wander up to his face. He looks tired, exhausted—exactly the way I feel. A wave of warmth washes over me and my pulse slows.

Fabrizio smiles and tilts his head.

"Tell me," I say, "can you sing?"

Epilogue
Fabrizio

My grandmother, Giuseppa Camini, returned home on a mild summer night. It was a secret ceremony, close family only, conducted by Padre Lorenzo—whom we had to bribe with a case of Nonna's liqueur to enter the cemetery after midnight.

Nobody said much after Lorenzo stopped stammering, because no words were necessary. Marco and I carried the urn together, and Alberto laid her to rest under a perfect starry sky—next to her husband, Eduardo, to whom she remained faithful her entire life even though her heart belonged to another.

I'm not a believer in the supernatural, but it sometimes seems to me that Nonna returned home late on purpose, so that people she cared about could return home as well—Hanna's mother, for one, who quietly stood next to Hanna during the ceremony. She took Alberto's hand when he started to cry silently—out of sorrow, but maybe also for joy, since he knew how much Isabella's presence would have meant to Nonna.

But Marco and I have also found our place because of Nonna, even if it's not quite the way she planned.

I didn't accept the inheritance. It was a good decision, I realized, when I looked more closely at all the paperwork that I'd just tossed into Marco's drawer without ever reading. Now I fully respect the way Marco deals with income and expenditure lists, lawyers and bank directors, and excited creditors.

After we received the German distributor's offer, we never talked about selling the apricot orchards again. Marco insisted, despite my objections, on signing over the agricultural part of the estate to me, since he wants to concentrate fully on administering Tre Camini. He has also started, however, to take some interest in hard physical labor on the estate. Despite being all thumbs out in the fields, which makes the laborers laugh, he really wants to become a good lord of the manor.

My little brother and I still disagree on many things. I doubt that will change. But Lucia's eyes sparkle when Marco shuffles into the kitchen in work pants, like a true Camini, and devours Rosa-Maria's pasta. Her happy face, more than anything, tells me that we are on the way to securing a future for Tre Camini.

Speaking of the future, I'm going to be an uncle—Lucia is finally pregnant. I just hope the baby doesn't turn out like Marco . . . or, god forbid, like me.

For now, Hanna has accepted the position in Vienna. I'm trying hard to persuade her to come to Italy not just on weekends, but for good—even though I'm no longer an estate owner, but just a simple farmer.

I worked like a mule with Alberto all summer so Saalfranck would get what he wanted: at least two thousand five hundred gallons of Nonna's apricot liqueur. He sold out within weeks to top restaurants all over Germany. He has more orders than he can fill.

Everything points to a good harvest—and to a happy end.

That is, if Hanna says yes to the little ring I've been carrying around in my pocket for the past few days. I struggled with myself for a long time—wondering if I should dare. Then I came across Nonna's letter in my desk drawer and read that last sentence again and again.

"Deep down, all Caminis are mothers and fathers, wives and husbands."

How can I not follow suit?

A Note of Thanks

In our digital age, books have become a fast-paced medium—which offers authors many opportunities but also pitfalls on the road to quality rather than quantity.

My novels are close to my heart. They arise out of love for the written word and need time to grow, since I have to feel good about them before sending them out into the world. That's why I first of all want to thank my readers for their patience and loyalty.

Just as much gratitude is due to the wonderful people who made it possible for the novel to appear in its present form:

Christina Schulz, for her encouragement and enthusiasm. Without you, I might have tossed the laptop out the window long ago.

Katrin Koppold, who always has good advice for enhancing the narrative.

Julia Dessalles, who made me realize how dreadful my school-French is.

And Jochen Lang, who still asks only for coffee when it takes hours to repair my computer even though it never seemed like too much of a problem at first.

I want to express special thanks to my literary agents, Michaela and Klaus Gröner, who make me feel that I am in good hands—as an author, but also as a human being.

I also want to thank the entire AmazonCrossing team for this great English edition, especially my editor, Gabriella Page-Fort, and my translator, Maria Poglitsch Bauer.

Last but certainly not least, there is my small family of two legs and eight paws. I could not write this type of book without their love. And: you know who you are!

Recipes

Ribollita
(the way Hanna's mother makes it)

Serves 4

Ingredients

- A mixture of dried beans, peas, lentils, and barley—about two handfuls, but adjust as you wish and based on what is available
- 3 carrots, sliced
- 10 ounces of potatoes, cubed
- 2 stalks of celery, sliced
- 1 medium onion, cubed
- 1 clove of garlic, diced
- 1 cup of vegetable stock
- 1 can of diced tomatoes
- Half a head of Savoy cabbage, cut into strips
- A few sprigs of thyme
- A pinch each of sugar, salt, and pepper
- 4–6 slices of day-old white bread
- 3 tbsp. olive oil

Cooking Instructions

Soak the legumes overnight, and then simmer them for one to two hours until soft. Heat the olive oil in a large pot. Sauté the carrots, potatoes, and celery for about five minutes. Add the onion and garlic and continue to sauté until the onions are translucent but not brown. Stir in the stock and tomatoes and bring to a boil. Then simmer on low heat for ten to twelve minutes. Add the cooked legumes, the Savoy cabbage, the thyme, and a pinch of sugar. Cook on low heat for two hours. At the end of the cooking time, season with salt and pepper, and let the stew cool.

Place alternating layers of bread and stew in an ovenproof dish and bake at 300 degrees F for half an hour.

Hanna's advice: Add a dash of olive oil once the ribollita is served. At home, we make an *S* with the oil on top of the soup—*facciamo una S.*

Nonna's Roast Rabbit with Apricots

Serves 4

Ingredients

- 1 rabbit, cut up
- Salt and pepper
- 1–2 tbsp. olive oil
- 2 tsp. fennel seeds
- 7 ounces of onion, cut into eighths
- 3 tbsp. tomato paste
- 4 tomatoes, stemmed and quartered
- 8 fresh apricots, cut into wedges, pits removed
- 3 sprigs of thyme
- 1 cup of white wine
- Brown sugar to taste

Cooking Instructions

Rub the rabbit parts with salt and pepper. Heat the olive oil and fennel seeds in a Dutch oven. Brown the rabbit parts and then remove from the pot. Sauté onions until translucent, add tomato paste, cover, and cook on low heat for about five minutes. Add tomatoes, apricots, thyme, and rabbit parts. Stir, add the wine, cover, and let braise for forty-five minutes. Remove the lid and cook another fifteen minutes. Adjust seasoning with salt, pepper, and a dash of sugar. Remove the thyme sprigs.

This dish pairs well with pasta or ciabatta.

Nonna's advice: Never use cheap wine for this dish! Choose a sweeter wine to emphasize the flavor of the apricots.

Ragù Tre Camini

Serves 4

Ingredients

- 1–2 tbsp. olive oil
- 1 large onion, chopped fine
- 1–2 cloves of garlic, minced
- 1 carrot, cubed
- 1/2 cup of beef broth
- 1 tube of Italian tomato paste
- 1 can of diced tomatoes
- 1–2 tsp. sugar
- 1–1 1/4 pounds of frozen ground beef
- Salt, pepper, and a mixture of fresh Italian herbs (flat-leaf parsley, thyme, oregano, marjoram, basil, etc.)

Cooking Instructions

Heat olive oil in a large pot and sauté the onions until glassy. Add the garlic and carrot and continue sautéing for two minutes. Deglaze with the beef broth, add tomato paste, diced tomatoes, and sugar, and cook on low heat. Add the frozen beef and simmer, stirring often. Continue stirring until the meat and tomato sauce are completely integrated. Add the herbs, season with salt and pepper, and simmer on the lowest possible heat for an hour. Adjust seasoning and serve with your choice of pasta.

Rosa-Maria's advice: The method of adding frozen beef to the sauce prevents the ground beef from drying out when it is browned. This way, the ragù stays smooth and all ingredients are perfectly combined. (Rosa-Maria refuses to reveal the source of this secret Neapolitan tip.)

Pasta alla Zanolla

Serves 4

Ingredients

- 1/2 pound of fresh or frozen fava beans
- 14 ounces of penne rigate
- 2–3 tsp. olive oil
- 1 onion, finely chopped
- 1/2 pound of speck from Alto Adige, cut in strips
- 2 cloves of garlic, minced
- 2 fresh pepperoncini peppers, chopped
- Fresh rosemary, chopped
- Fresh Parmesan, for serving

Cooking Instructions

Bring a pot of salted water to a boil. Cook the beans and the penne rigate in the same pot until al dente (watch the cooking times). Meanwhile, heat the olive oil in a deep pan. Sauté the onion and the speck, add the garlic, pepperoncini, and rosemary, and cook until the onions are golden brown. Add the dripping-wet pasta and the beans to the onion/speck mixture in the pan. Stir thoroughly and serve at once with freshly shaved Parmesan.

About the Author

Photo © 2011 Alexandra Zoth, Photo-Stage

Claudia Winter has been writing since childhood. She has previously published two romantic comedies, a crime novel, and several short stories. She works as an author, editor, and writer's coach, as well as a certified specialist in social pedagogy at an elementary school. Winter lives with her partner and two dogs in a small town in Germany.

For more information, visit www.c-winter.de.

About the Translator

Maria Poglitsch Bauer grew up in Carinthia, Austria, and fell in love with the English language early in life. Her first translation attempt happened at age twelve, when after little more than two years of high-school English, she stumbled across an abridged version of *The Great Gatsby*, judged it "great," and wanted to share it with those who did not speak the language. Fortunately, the unfinished opus languished in the drawer of a desk which was eventually stolen. The joy of hunting for the right word stayed with her.

She would like to dedicate her translation of *Apricot Kisses* to the memory of Friederike, her mother.